Inside the Grey

Bobbi Groover

To Ken, Pierce and Logan—the heroes I will love for a lifetime~

To M~

And to my darling cousin, Linda, for all the OMGs and LOLs and for whom the character SB Belinda is named.

CHAPTER ONE

Brayden Wakefield sat on the hill watching the horses graze. He felt rather ridiculous glued to that stump, the remnant of the tree he'd chopped to pieces the day after her death. His mouth pulled back into a mirthless grin, and he shook his head. The very spot was right in front of him, the dark depression staring up at him like an accusatory eye. He didn't want to return yet everyday here he sat with his toe digging in the dirt, flicking small pebbles out of the hole. He blew out a deep breath. He'd had his dreams once. Now he could state the exact day, the exact hour when he had gone from being cocky to confused.

An altercation in the pasture caused one of the mares to toss her head with a high-pitched squeal that sounded almost human. The sound ruthlessly took him back to that day, that hour. The muscles in his chest hardened to stone, encasing him in a breathless prison. The mare's screeching reminded him of Lavinia's screams when she had been bitten.

A thump on his back forced the muscles to relax, and Brayden gasped.

"So here you are, Bry. I should have known."

Brayden didn't have to turn to know the speaker behind him. The gravelly voice belonged to his good friend and neighbor, Fletcher Stedman. Fletcher had been savagely knifed years ago. The attack had taken his voice and nearly his life. "It's been two years, Bry. It's time to let go. We've all had our tragedies."

"No censure, Fletcher. Please, not today."

1

Fletcher walked around to face him and slowly pulled off his gloves finger by finger. Brayden averted his gaze as he studied the legs of the two geldings whose reins were slung across Fletcher's arm. Fletcher's tall, black boots were clearly in view but the man casting the huge shadow remained silent.

Brayden finally raised his eyes. "Two years today, Fletcher." Brayden clucked his tongue, yanked off his hat and ran a distracted hand back and forth through his hair.

"I know." Fletcher took two giant steps to his saddle, returned with his crystal flask and handed it to Brayden. When Brayden refused, he flipped the silver top and shoved it back toward him. "Yes, Bry. You've probably been sitting on that stump long enough to blister your backside."

Brayden drew in a quick breath to retort, but Fletcher grabbed his hand and slammed the flask into his palm.

"No, Bry, swill first, then mount. I'll listen to anything you have to say along the way. I'm starving. Perhaps you've forgotten you did invite my family to supper. I could only entertain everyone with my fiddle for so long. I began hunting when your chair remained empty, and I was dispatched to find you."

Brayden nearly choked on his mouthful. "Fletcher, my humblest apologies. I don't know where my mind is these days."

Fletcher smacked his shoulder as they mounted. "These days?"

Brayden dragged another long swig of the flask before handing it to Fletcher who slid it neatly into its cylindrical leather case along the saddle. "Touché." He chirruped to his mount and the two galloped with purpose.

———

A bit later Brayden sighed as his hearty laughter subsided. The laughter felt good. There had been little of it in the years since his wife's tragic death. Every day remorse shrouded him—haunting and profound— waiting for Fate to claim reparation. Still, the day had been salvaged, culminating with a sumptuous meal. This was an intimate gathering, these friends around his table: Fletcher, Kyndee and Trey. He had known Fletcher and his wife, Kyndee, since childhood and had grown to admire the third. Brayden and Fletcher were wealthy landowners, born of privilege but they had both been shattered by tragedy. It was those tragedies which had bonded them together as tightly as brothers. Trey was the spunky, rusty-haired godson of whom Caleb was extremely proud. Caleb, the stately attorney of their friends, had been unable to attend and had sent young Trey to steady any heated discussion.

He put down his fork and noted that the conversation around him had faded, even though he could still see the lips of his guests moving. As he surreptitiously rubbed his ear, he wondered why his hearing had suddenly failed him, why his ear seemed to be listening for a different sound. The hair on the back of his neck bristled and a peculiar sense of dread covered him like a miasmic cocoon.

With a smile pasted on his face, the host of the evening ran his palm along his hair in an effort to appear calm. Though the world around them was in turmoil after the attack on Fort Sumter, though their friends and neighbors were still arguing for or against the Union, whether or not the state had had the right to secede, the four of them were trying to concentrate on the blessings in their lives. Here they could shut out the chaos and celebrate the first birthday of Fletcher's son, Tristan. But outside their properties was bedlam.

Abraham Lincoln had called for troops. The Confederate capital had been moved to Richmond; now all-out war loomed. Dear God, none of them was ready to face another war. They had all just managed to recover from their own private wars—scarred, broken and no one's hero. The man knew, in the marrow of his bones, that a war between the states would prove to be no different. A confrontation wouldn't be won in a few months as his neighbors boasted. Nothing of magnitude was ever achieved in short order; why did no one see that? Brayden needed no crystal ball to see conflagration and bloodshed—nations, states, counties, and families torn asunder, hemorrhaging with wounds that might never heal. Neither he nor the others was ready to be drawn into the world outside of their properties. They didn't hate the Yankees; they just wanted peace.

No one else at the table seemed to be aware that he had suddenly withdrawn from the merriment. He felt the tension in the air before the sound of galloping hoof beats shattered the revelry like splintering glass.

As apprehension slithered down his spine, as he silently prayed he was wrong, Fate arrived at his door.

Sage Jenkins burst through, trembling, disheveled, her face drawn and covered in tears. "They've taken him!"

Already on edge, Brayden was the first to jump from the table. He caught Sage before she fell. "Who? Who have they taken? Who are they?"

"Caleb! Union raiders have taken Caleb!"

"Caleb?" shouted the group as they scattered from the table and huddled around Sage.

Brayden grasped Sage by the shoulders. "How do you know they were with the Union? What would Federal raiders want with Caleb?"

"They—" Sage shook her head as if searching for words. "—they accused him of hiding a rebel convict!"

"But that's absurd. Caleb isn't hiding anyone." Brayden turned toward the door. "I'll ride into town and have Judge Winston straighten this out immediately."

Sage ran after him. "It's too late for that! They dragged him from the house. I followed them out of town until my mare couldn't keep up. They said they intend to hang him!"

Union raiders! Bushwhackers unencumbered by superior orders! Caleb Jenkins, their friend, the quintessential gentleman and the smartest man they knew. Brayden Wakefield couldn't halt the sudden boiling rage erupting inside him. God help him; God help them all. They could no longer remain neutral. The war had found them.

Fletcher and Kyndee Stedman shot across the room. When Sage wobbled, Fletcher pulled her into a chair. Her blonde hair was mussed, half fallen around her shoulders, and her hands were shaking. Kyndee offered her a goblet. Sage refused it but Kyndee insisted. The alcohol seemed to furnish a surge of strength.

"Tell us as much as you know, Sage." The jagged scar stood out along Fletcher's right cheek and neck. It seemed to darken with his obvious concern.

"Yes, Aunt Sage. We need to know everything…and fast," agreed Trey.

Brayden drilled Caleb's wife with his eyes, hoping to steady and calm her. "What do you mean they intend to hang him? Why? Sage, slow down and try to remember every detail. I need you to tell us everything."

"There's no more to tell and no time! Caleb heard the raiders shouting and breaking down the door. He had scarcely shoved me into the tunnel when they broke through the front."

"How many were there?"

"I don't know. I heard five, maybe six different voices in the room." Sage pulled her hair from her face. "They beat him, Brayden!" She uttered a pitiful wail. "I heard them pounding on him. They were shouting that he was a traitor, that they would make him pay for what he did. I heard him groaning. It went on and on until I thought I would scream. The voices finally faded and then there was silence. When I was sure they'd left, I opened the tunnel door and saw the broken furniture with blood all over it." Sage covered her eyes and rocked back and forth. "A bloody trail was smeared across the floor where they must have dragged him out. Oh, God...Caleb...Caleb!"

"Sweet mercy," cried Kyndee as she pulled Sage into her arms.

Sage calmed and pulled away. "That's when I took off through the tunnel to the stable and followed them but I lost them a few miles later, and I came straight here. I didn't know what else to do."

"Were there more of them on the road?" queried Fletcher as he stepped closer.

"Yes, maybe ten or fifteen more."

"Was one of the riders astride a large palomino?"

"Yes. How did you know?"

"It sounds like Bickmore's Raiders."

"You know of them?" Sage grabbed Kyndee's arm as if about to fall from the chair.

"Yes, from what I've heard, the band isn't mustered into enlisted Federal service, they're irregulars—"

"A band of guerrillas and marauders—basic outlaws," added Brayden. "Yes, I heard the same about them."

"Do you have any idea where they might be taking Caleb?" begged Sage. "They only need a tall tree to carry out their threat of hanging."

Fletcher shook his head. "I don't think so. If it was Bickmore's Raiders who took him, they won't hang him any time soon. He's worth too much."

"What do you mean?"

Brayden touched Sage's shoulder. "Fletcher means that Caleb is worth more alive in ransom than dead and buried. We can only hope it was Bickmore's handiwork tonight. Bickmore is a whore for money, and he needs a lot of it to support his quest for fame."

"And if it wasn't Bickmore?" Sage asked with tears welling in her eyes.

"Then God help him," Fletcher muttered as he turned. "I heard they're shipping off civilian prisoners to those camps...or worse."

Brayden hoped Sage didn't hear. He tried to warn Fletcher off but the other doggedly continued. "Dear God, I'd beg to be hanged rather than languish in the conditions there. We have to find him first. What's our next move, Bry?"

"We're going to need help to spread out and gather information as to where Bickmore camps and hides. If we can bribe a few local bushwhackers, I'm sure they will have valuable information we can use."

"How do you know all this?" Fletcher queried, shoving his hands into his gloves.

"Just because I don't want to be involved in the war doesn't mean that I'm uninformed as to what's happening around us."

"Right. I'll ride for Rush, Clive and Royce. I'm sure the others will want to join us when they hear that Caleb is in peril."

"Rush, Clive and Royce might join you," said Kyndee. "But Morgan and Dillon have enlisted."

"What?" shouted Fletcher as he spun in the doorway. "When?"

"They left last week."

"Fools." He clucked his tongue and shook his head. "They've marched off to get themselves killed."

"Why do you say that?" asked Trey. "We showed our strength at Manassas."

"Yes, we won but at what cost?" Brayden sighed. "That makes six of us if Rush, Clive, Royce and Gabriel ride with us."

"I'm riding with you, too," Sage interjected. "It's my fault they took Caleb."

"What do you mean?"

"If I hadn't been feeling poorly, Caleb and I would have been here tonight instead of at home."

"No, Sage. If those raiders wanted Caleb, it would have been only a matter of time until they would have captured him someplace else."

"Don't care." Sage's voice rose to a shrill shriek. "I'm still riding out with you."

Trey stomped forward. "So am I."

"Don't be ridiculous."

"I'm not! If Aunt Sage goes, so do I," Trey bellowed with arms akimbo, leaving no doubt as to his determination.

"Absolutely not!" shouted the other two men in unison.

Brayden turned to Sage, hoping to appeal to her rational nature. "Woman, have you no idea of the danger of the thing? We're probably heading behind enemy lines."

Sage approached him and gazed deeply into his eyes. "Brayden, Caleb is my husband and my life. I would ride headfirst into the bowels of the earth to find him."

Brayden drew Sage into an embrace. "That very well may be where we have to go to rescue him." He opened his arms and his eyes locked on hers. "But don't you realize that if we're captured—assuming they don't kill us—the long road to prison will be the very least of your suffering. These are men who've been without the comforts of a woman for a very long time. Fletcher and I would be powerless to protect you."

"I can take care of myself!"

"Oh, dear God," muttered Fletcher as he shoved his hand through his hair. "Most of these renegades have been in the field for nearly a year. This whole idea is preposterous!"

"Yes, it's preposterous," Kyndee interjected. "I've been silent, listening to everyone jabber on while Caleb is out there, somewhere, in God only knows what condition and you're wasting time arguing."

"Nothing is settled!" the men shouted with force.

"It's settled! No more discussion! You men ride for the others while I convince Sage and Trey that their riding with you would be more hardship than help."

"Fletcher," Brayden queried, "how did you and Caleb manage to marry the only two women of the world who are too smart and too brazen for their own good?"

His longtime friend rolled his eyes and pulled at his ear. "Don't you mean for *our* own good?"

———

A short time later, Fletcher, Brayden and Royce burst through the door, flushed and breathing hard.

"Clive, Rush and Gabriel are all outside with fresh horses and supplies." Brayden noticed that Sage and Trey were not in the room. "Did you convince them to stay?"

Kyndee inclined her head toward the stairs. "Sage collapsed, and I put her to bed. Trey gathered his things and stormed out. I think you needled his honor by refusing to allow him to go with you. He and Caleb are very close."

Fletcher threw his arms in the air. "I...I...didn't...I didn't know what else to say."

Brayden shook his head and rolled his eyes. "Neither did I," he muttered. "Trey's barely what? Twelve? Thirteen? We'd probably end up having to rescue him as well."

"Just tell me you'll find Caleb and bring yourselves back to me safely," cried Kyndee as she ran to Fletcher's arms. "I don't want any of you to leave me, but I know you have to go."

"Caleb would do no differently for any of us," Brayden muttered.

The four of them hugged and kissed. Kyndee picked up her son as the others headed toward the door and the waiting horses.

Brayden watched Fletcher turn in the doorway with an agonized mien. The man seemed to savor one last look at Kyndee, his son, and his life. He and Brayden locked eyes. "For ten long years I fought to return to this home, swearing I would never leave again. The war apparently has other plans."

Without malice, Brayden envied Fletcher. He, himself, had no one to leave behind and no love in his heart—the Moirai had seen to that. His young wife's death had caused him to question everything since— from the bonds of marriage, to the sovereignty of the South to secede, to his possibly granting freedom and land rights to his dark-skinned servants now that his father had died. The freedom issue had been a constant, secret discussion shared only with the group seated at his table tonight. Now his time of retribution was at hand and until it tallied with his sin, there would be no other heart to share his own. He mastered, beautified, and preserved an estate for a life he no longer had. Yet he wondered why, like the others, he was reluctant to leave Avalon and the agonizing ghosts it held. With a shudder, the evening's host clenched his fists and cast the bitter, throbbing memories aside. For now all else would have to wait. He and Fletcher were both survivors of needless tragedy. Brayden fervently hoped that this would not be another tragedy to be survived, not with the war just outside their midst. Caleb was the best of them. They had to find him; they had to.

———

Dawn was breaking, and they were preparing to break camp when Brayden heard a twig snap. He slapped Fletcher's shoulder and jerked his head. The two of them drew their guns, and Fletcher darted sideways to circle behind.

"There are six barrels ready to cut you down so you'd best show yourself before we start plugging you full of holes," Brayden yelled.

Trey stepped out from behind a tree. "Then you'd have to do some mighty fine explaining to Uncle Caleb when you find him."

"You have a death wish, son? What were you thinking sneaking up on us like that?" Brayden roared.

Fletcher slapped his thigh. "I thought we settled it that you were to stay home."

"You settled it. I didn't!" Trey's brows were furrowed with his hazel eyes glaring. "I wasn't there to help Uncle Caleb when they captured him but I sure as blazes intend to help bring him home."

"I offered to ride with you, Brayden, but I'm not riding with no whippersnapper," snarled Gabriel. "He'll slow us down and young'uns are just plum bad luck."

"Your choice, Gabe, but Trey has the right to find Caleb," Brayden answered as he stomped out the fire, "and even if I don't agree with his being here, you know Trey can damn well outshoot you any day of the week. So either get back over there or back off because at this point, he's riding with us."

"Then I wish you well, but I just can't go with you," came Gabe's retort as he mounted and turned his horse.

"Clive, Rush, Royce, you feel the same?" Fletcher asked as he approached. He pulled his gloves from his pocket and slapped them in his palm in clear irritation.

The other two wore hangdog faces but nodded.

With hands on his hips, Brayden froze in an imperious stance. "Then what's it to be? We have a lot of ground to cover...and fast."

"But," Rush stated, "something tells me Caleb wouldn't let anything stand in his way if the roles were reversed, so I'll ride with you until we find him."

"Me, too," added Clive. "But as soon as we find him—" He shot a glance directly at Trey. "—one way or the other, I'm heading out."

Brayden tipped his hat. "Appreciate the help." He turned and called to the other one. "Just so you know, Gabe, no hard feelings."

Gabe cast him a terse nod and cantered into the dark.

"Anything else need settling before we ride out?" Brayden asked with an irritated undertone. Receiving no response, he mounted. Though a mite shorter than Fletcher, he looked every bit an impressive force astride his gelding. "Gentlemen, let's ride."

With his charcoal hair streaked in pewter, Brayden Wakefield looked the senior of the group though, with the exception of Trey, he was younger than the other four who rode beside him into the night. During the past years the greedy Fates, Clotho, Lachesis and Atropos, had etched his sin into his face and hair for all to see. An animal in the woods squealed as if captured. Did the same fate await them? Brayden sucked in a deep breath and urged his gelding forward. He and Fletcher were followed by the newest rider of the group, tailed by Rush, Royce and Clive taking up the drag. The six of them were bonded in their cause and their loyalty to their kidnapped comrade, Caleb Jenkins.

CHAPTER TWO

THE GAUNT WOMAN GRABBED HER YOUNG SON, SHELTERED HIM WITHIN her arms and plastered the two of them between the cupboard and the wall. Her eyes were large as saucers and her chest heaved. "We ain't got nothing left," she shrieked. "That other mob took everything." A mongrel dog slipped out from one of the side rooms, its teeth bared. The cur crept slowly forward, threatening the intruders. Clive jumped forward, brandishing his sidearm.

"No! Don't hurt him," screamed the boy, wrenching himself from the woman and throwing his arms around the dog's neck.

Brayden seized Clive's arm and deflected his pistol. "We're not going to hurt him, son. Just put him in the other room so no one gets bitten, all right?" The boy, plainly near to tears, took a deep breath and led the dog away.

"What do you want?" the woman clamored. Her blue dress was well-worn and tattered. She clasped the neck of her bodice in a tight fist. Her other arm was wrapped around the front of her. "I know nothing. I've got nothing. Please just go away and leave us alone." Her voice cracked as she spoke. The boy returned, and she huddled him against her. "What do you want?" The last words were barely above a whisper.

"We're searching for a pack who has taken our friend prisoner. We had reason to believe that they were holed up at your farm."

"If they are a loud, rowdy, disgusting mob, they were. I 'spect your friends were with them."

"Friends?"

Plainly more at ease, the woman inched from her perch and slid into a nearby chair. What appeared to be years of hardship were etched into her face. "It was mighty clear to me that two of them were getting the worst of it. Looked like brothers, they did. Both of them were tied up and had black eyes, 'cept one was spittin' blood. They commit a crime or something? Why was that mob threatening them with hanging every minute?"

Trey gasped at the woman's words. "Oh, God, Uncle Caleb."

Fletcher pulled at the back of his neck. "Bry, we've missed them again."

"By at least half a day," the woman added.

Brayden heaved a deep, breath and blew it out slowly. He pursed his lips and clucked his tongue. "Don't know how they are always one step ahead of us. It's as if someone is tipping them off." He stomped his foot and shoved his hand through his hair.

In the past week, chasing a zigzag trail, they had been so near twice and had been just too late twice. He begrudgingly admitted Trey had been an invaluable help. Posing as an orphan running scared, he had done the impossible. He had extracted food, supplies and information from farms and stations along the way. The supplies filled their bellies and the information kept them on what they hoped was the correct trail. After one scouting trip he even returned with a smug grin and a fat turkey, having never fired a shot.

"It'll be light in two hours, and we can pick up the trail then," said Fletcher. He and the others had started backing to the door. "Sorry for scaring you, ma'am."

"Ain't no need asking for pardon," the woman replied. She heaved a heavy sigh and pulled the messy hair from her face. "My man is out there, God knows where. I know I'd shoot down anyone trying to hurt him. You all can settle in the barn if you like. There's room 'cause that mob chased off whatever they didn't steal."

"If only we had a clue where they were taking Caleb, then possibly we could head them off." Fletcher threw his words to the ceiling as if knowing there was no answer.

"Maybe there's an answer in their sack," offered the little boy.

The woman knelt and took the boy in her arms. "What are you talkin' about? What sack?"

"That mean man had a sack on his shoulder when he came but I found it after they left."

Brayden tried to contain his eagerness so as not to frighten the child. "A sack, you say? May I see it?"

The child nodded and retrieved the sack from the other room. He handed it to Brayden sporting a very serious expression. "Do you think this might help you find your friend? It has lots of pretty pictures in it. I liked the pictures."

As the others gathered around, Brayden sank into a chair. "My God, Fletcher, Royce, it's a Union dispatch." He rummaged through the small bundle and spilled the contents onto the table. There was a letter and, as the boy had said, a sheet with pictures. The message was written in a small, scraggly hand. Several of the characters were smudged.

"What good is that?" said Clive. "Ain't even written in English. Come on, let's get some rest." He headed toward the door.

"It's a cipher!" Brayden exclaimed. "The cipher is the key to the letter."

Fletcher shook his head. "No. Yankee spies would never send the cipher in the same pouch with the message. If it is a cipher, it's most likely the key for future messages."

"Damn." Brayden scanned the message with his hope fading. He slapped the message closed. "But then again—" He reopened the paper and perused the message again. "—perhaps they only changed parts of the cipher." He checked character by character. The letters were sheer gibberish. He slammed the dispatch over. "Useless!" Then he noticed scribbling he'd missed before. "Fletcher, look here."

"Let me see that." Royce scanned the back of the dispatch and spelled out: "Frezer, Tremhalm, C Jenkins."

"Isn't that a cotton broker in Charleston?" asked Fletcher.

"I thought they were based in Liverpool." Brayden locked his fingers atop his head. "Either way it's a might curious. My God, that 'C' could be Caleb or even Cheston. How would Caleb's father be involved with a broker in Liverpool? Why?"

Fletcher shrugged. "Would make sense. Caleb would be worth quite a ransom if Cheston is involved in a deal overseas right now."

"Then we'll pick up the trail at dawn." Clive and Rush left as Brayden turned to Royce. "Fletcher and I can pick through this message again to see if there is anything else here. Why don't you and Trey settle in the barn for a bit?"

The woman stepped out from the shadows. "I don't mean to meddle with your plans none, but don't you think your Mr. Royce there should be taking the boy home rather than on the trail?"

The room fell silent.

"I don't mean to be butting my nose in where it don't belong but I'm still remembering how those men were beating their two prisoners." She pointed to Trey. "This young one would be dead in a day."

Trey raised his hands in blatant protest. "I'm not going home without Uncle Caleb. I can't."

The mantle of responsibility and loss closed around him until Brayden couldn't breathe. The woman was right. He shuddered. "You can, and you will."

"No. Not until we find him!"

Brayden silenced him with a stern grip on his shoulder and whispered in his ear. "Go, Trey. Caleb deserves to know you are safe."

"Can I talk to you private like, sir?"

The two of them moved a few steps. "What is it you needed to tell me?"

Trey glanced around and leaned closer. "No one else knows. I wasn't sneaking around. God's truth."

"No one else knows what, Trey?"

"I would only tell because I thought it might give Uncle Caleb a reason to keep fightin' to live."

"Trey, what are you trying to tell me?"

"I heard Aunt Sage say she was having a baby sometime in the spring."

"Having a—" Brayden's mouth snapped shut. Dear God, what if Sage had come with them?

"You won't tell, will you?"

"No, Trey. It's Sage's surprise when Caleb returns."

Brayden turned and crossed the room. "Royce?"

Royce's face was the picture of resignation. "I know I'm the one to go, and I agree with you. I'll make sure he reaches home and stays put. We'll start at first light."

"Fletcher, you take Clive and Rush and head north toward the abandoned Seneca mission. I'll hang here for half a day in case anyone of that mob trails back for the pouch. I've also had the feeling that we've been dogged, and I'd like to track around just in case. I'll catch up to you near Seneca."

Alone in the room, Brayden sank into a chair with the coded message still clasped in his hand. He yawned and ran his hand over his eyes. He was glad Trey was headed home. The boy had been a tremendous asset but the further the group inched north, the more Brayden worried for his safety. He stared again at the coded dispatch and shook it as if some new secrets might fall from the page. The implications it posed scared him. At least they had renewed hope Caleb was still alive—for the moment. Wracked by 'what ifs' he closed his eyes and drifted.

———

Dawn burst on the horizon a few seconds later or at least it felt that way. Napping in the chair made his muscles ache, and Brayden's head was pounding. The group slid around him and said little, plainly sensing his dark mood. The woman offered them a meager meal—a sacrifice for her to be sure. Fletcher, Rush and Clive rode out through the narrow trail where the woman said the mob had bounded and, though he continued with relentless protests, in the end Trey and Royce headed for home.

"We're beholden to you for your kindness, ma'am," Brayden told the woman as he tightened the girth of his saddle.

"Hush now. Ain't no thanks needed nohow. I'm a southerner just like yourself, don't ya know."

He knelt before the little boy. "You're a hero for finding that pouch, son. It might well be the key to finding our friend. You take good care of that pup. He's a good protector for you and your ma."

Brayden handed the woman a small stack of coins. At first, she squared her shoulders and refused but he insisted. "For the boy," he said. "You'll need supplies until his father comes home."

The woman nodded and took the coins. "Until his pa comes home."

———

Again and again Brayden looked back on all the events of that grim evening that had brought him to this moment and rubbed his chin with his fist. If that mob managed to bury themselves in the mountains, he and Fletcher might never find them. They now had reason to believe Caleb was still alive but for how long? Where were they taking him and why? Questions. Always questions with no answers. He continued scouting the area but when no one returned to retrieve the pouch, he felt confident to leave the farm and continue toward the mission to meet the others. They had to find Caleb; they had to. He was the best of all of them. He glanced skyward and thought perhaps if he saved a life...

He was about to mount when a snake slithered across the dirt, and he jumped out of the way. It didn't matter how or when; Brayden was still surprised how quickly the sighting would transport him back to that day in the meadow with Lavinia years ago. Would he never be free of it? He grunted. Surely not until the greedy Fates, Clotho, Lachesis and Atropos allowed him forgiveness for his part in Lavinia's death. The hair bristled on the back of his neck, and an eerie shudder coursed through him but as he yanked his pistol the words rang out.

"Drop it, mister, and move away real slow like."

Berating himself for being careless, Brayden dropped his pistol, took two steps and turned around. His captor was a small, wiry little fellow, poorly dressed, looking as if he hadn't seen the full side of a square meal in years.

"I didn't say you could turn around."

"You didn't say I couldn't, either. When you pull a gun on someone you should be specific."

"Watch your mouth, big man. I may not have your height, but you don't have my gun. Now move!"

Brayden took another step back. "Exactly where is it that we're going?"

"Quit asking so many fool questions." The man inched forward and extended his hand to retrieve the pistol on the ground, never breaking eye contact.

As the stranger stretched, Brayden kicked out to knock the gun from his captor's hand but misjudged the distance. The other one fired a shot, holing Brayden's vest but luckily not his skin.

"Try that little trick again, and I won't be as generous the next time. Start walking and keep your hands where I can see them."

Brayden turned. "Going to tell me where you're taking me?"

The barrel of the pistol bumped between his shoulder blades. "You'll know when we get there."

Fuming, Brayden scuttled up the narrow trail. Judging by the penurious manner of his dress and the fact that the man never demanded the courier pouch, Brayden surmised this loner was not one of the irregulars holding Caleb. That thought eased Brayden's tension and left his mind racing for an escape plan. They had only gone a short distance when a small fox startled and jumped from the brush. The intruder turned and fired. In a flash Brayden spun, knocked the gun from the man's hand and secured him in a headlock. He yanked the knife from the man's belt and held it against his neck. The slender fellow, who barely reached Brayden's chin, was breathing hard and continued to scramble.

"Stop struggling. I don't want to kill you. I just want answers." Brayden wrestled with the man to hold his head hard without slicing his neck, but the man's hat started to come away and slid across his head. Heavy ropes fell from the cap. Like a shot hitting him, Brayden realized what they were—thick, burgundy braids—and threw the person to the ground in horror. "You're a woman!"

"Quick-witted, aren't you?"

"I could have killed you," Brayden shouted as he slapped his forehead in exasperation.

The woman stood and dusted herself off. She scooped up the cap, coiled her braids and shoved the hat on her head. "You didn't seem so all-fired worried about killing me when you thought I was a man." With arms outstretched her deep, blue eyes glared at him. "Easier to kill me now?" She snorted. "Didn't think so." The fiery wench swiveled and stomped off. "I'm leaving."

"Come back here. I'm not finished with you," Brayden bellowed. He picked up the pistol and cocked the hammer. "I'll shoot."

The brazen female flipped her hand with an apparent wave of dismissal and kept walking.

———

Kawley Chatterton darted into the brush. She knew the man wouldn't shoot. He was still in shock with his mouth hanging open when she turned. Besides, he was too much of a gentleman. She had been studying him as she dogged the group on their trail, and she would again as soon as he left to follow the others. This one and the one they called Fletcher appeared the leaders of the group. She wondered if they might be brothers. Physically the two of them bore a great resemblance, both tall and broad shouldered with thick, dark hair. Even on the trail, those broad shoulders bore the elegant trappings of wealth and self-confidence. Their temperaments, however, could not have appeared more different. Fletcher seemed impetuous and headstrong. He might have fired but not this one—the one they called Brayden. While a mite shorter than Fletcher, Brayden struck her as being moody and withdrawn. Several nights in camp she watched him sit alone and write in a small book. If she didn't have her own urgent plans, she might have taken the time to wonder who or what the imposing, elegant gentleman deemed of such consequence that he would carry such an item on his quest. She was jolted when something snapped behind her.

"I said I wasn't finished with you yet," Brayden barked as he spun her around and trussed her like chattel. He sat her on the ground and backed away. "There."

"How dare you," she spat at him, straining against the rope. "Untie me now!"

"Not until you start talking."

"I don't owe you any explanations."

"On the contrary, you held a pistol on me and did this." He poked his finger through the hole in his vest. "Now I want to know why." Brayden plopped himself on a nearby rock, plucked a weed from the brush and chewed the end as though he had all the time in the world. Kawley knew neither of them did. She had seen Brayden's group split in the morning—two leisurely headed south, three hightailed it north. Kawley knew which three she wanted to be after…and soon.

Brayden flicked the weed away, took a bite of something from his pocket and chewed it. He yanked his hat from his head and parked it on his knee. "Going to be dark soon enough. Be hard to eat with your hands trussed up like they are. You'll starve long before I will."

He acted as if her discomfiture actually amused him. Scattered silver strands in his dark hair gleamed in the late afternoon sun. Could she trust him?

"Well?" His eyes drilled hers. "Start with your name."

Kawley was getting nowhere fast. She blew out a long breath. "Kawley."

Brayden grunted. "Excuse me? That's what you name a cow."

"Wish someone had told that to my father," Kawley muttered. She decided to gamble and threw down a card. "You enjoy being called Brayden?" His reaction startled her. He jumped from the rock, his amusement gone. He yanked her up with fire flashing from his eyes.

"All right. Enough games. Talk, and I mean now! You've been trailing us, haven't you?"

Kawley met his stare with indignant arrogance. "I talk a lot better when I'm not trussed like that cow waiting to be branded."

Brayden raised an eyebrow and cocked his head to the side. "Can I trust you not to run?"

She shook her head and pursed her lips. "Nope. But I'm not saying a word tethered like this."

Plainly annoyed, Brayden ripped the cords, apparently not caring if they scraped her. "Now, talk! You've been trailing us, haven't you?"

Kawley rubbed her skin where the ropes had pinched her. "Yes."

"Why?" When she hesitated Brayden grabbed her by the shoulders. "Why?"

He was so close she could feel his breath on her cheeks. She studied his face. His features were striking and there was something about him, something genuine that pushed her to trust him. "Because that mob has my brother, all right? They were holed up at that farmhouse, and I thought I had a good chance of helping him when a rider shows up, throws something at the sentry and takes off. Next thing I know, they're scrambling, mounted and gone. I would have been gone, too, but my horse came up lame and while I took time to rest her, you all showed up and—"

Brayden released her and held up his hands. "Whoa. Whoa. Hold it right there. Someone tipped them that we were close?" His eyes darted back and forth. "But if you were tailing us, then how did you arrive before we did?"

"Simple. It's a full moon, and I don't sleep."

"The rider who tipped the sentry…what did he look like?"

Kawley shrugged her shoulders. "Actually, he looked a lot like you on a different horse. Took off like a shot though."

Brayden scratched his cheek and glanced around. "Fletcher and the others might be riding into a trap. We should have an hour or so before dark. Mount up. We'll talk on the way."

Kawley pulled back. The change in his tactics baffled her. "On the way where? I'm not going anywhere with you. I don't know you. I was doing just fine on my own."

"All evidence to the contrary. And for the record, you are one exasperating woman but if that mob has your brother and my friend, I can't take any chances that you might spoil any possibility of rescue."

"Me? You're the ones who—"

"Enough, woman! We're losing time. Now keep that cap on your head, start riding and start talking. If you're coming with us, I want to know exactly what you're dragging me into."

"I'm not dragging you into anything. Leave me be." Kawley shouldered past him in a huff.

"No. I'm not leaving you here to be captured—" He spun her around, and she slammed into his chest. "—or worse."

For a moment it seemed he encased all of her within his powerful grasp. Clearly, they were at an impasse, one as pigheaded as the other. His grasp gentled, became more of an embrace, and she was again awestruck by the open concern in his green eyes.

Kawley wanted none of it. She pushed at his chest with her fist. "I'll go wherever I want."

Brayden held her at arm's length. "Have you no idea of the danger you're in? I'm not asking for the Virginia reel. I'm telling you to mount up."

"And I'm telling you to stop ordering me around."

"Arrrgh!" Brayden picked her up, strode to the horses and plopped her into the saddle. "Woman—" He cleared his throat. "—Miss Kawley, will you *please* start riding? We have a lot of ground to cover."

Kawley cast him a triumphant grin and threw her boots in the stirrups. "All right. I'll oblige you—" She picked up the reins. "—for a while." She knew the 'miss' would disappear as soon as they reached the others, but it surely felt nice to hear. The small kindness reminded her of another time long ago when life had made sense. For the moment, why shouldn't she allow the dashing, elegant gentleman to bear the brunt of the hunt for a day or two?

Brayden retrieved his hat and turned to mount his horse. As he swung into the saddle, he glanced over his shoulder at her, and Kawley caught the hint of a crinkle pull at the side of his cheek. She led her horse in behind his on the trail. She would surely watch her back and trust no one but after weeks on the trail, God knows she could use the rest, the food and—Kawley smiled—the view.

─────

They rode at a steady clip for quite a while and Kawley's legs were tiring but she wasn't about to say anything to the handsome yet arrogant gent who demanded the lead. She constantly thought of shooting off, half doubting that he would bother to chase her but argued with herself that if his comrade was being held captive with her brother, he and his friends might be of help to her.

Kawley lengthened her horse's stride and pulled her a little to the left while closing the gap she had left between them. While she considered herself to be an excellent horsewoman, she had to admit that Brayden rode a horse well. He sat tall in the saddle, arms at his sides, hands low, creating soft contact with the horse's mouth. His dark hair snuck out from beneath his hat and hung in waves along the bottom of his collar. The darkness of his beard shrouded the bottom half of his face, making it difficult to discern if he wore a frown or a grimace. Except for a few remnants of what appeared to have been dried mud, he was impeccably dressed, which was surprising considering he had been on the trail.

Plainly tiring, her horse shortened her stride and pulled back behind the other cantering animal. Kawley chided herself that she could be assessing the physical attributes of the man while her brother was in peril. One side of her rationalized that she'd been alone for many weeks, tired and hungry. Fear also played a big part in her decision not to bolt, fear she would never find Riley, fear that she'd be discovered as a woman, fear of what was done to women deprived of protection. The other side of her argued that because she had clothed and fed herself and managed to stay hidden for so long, she had proven she needed no man's protection. She was deep in her thoughts when the man suddenly pulled his horse to a halt. Her mare slammed into the rump in front of them, and Brayden's horse bucked out at the intrusion, nearing unseating his rider.

"Woman, can't you control your animal?" Brayden hissed as he attempted to control his leaping mount. His horse snorted, kicked out and spun. "Easy, Jax. Calm down."

Kawley begrudgingly admired the manner in which Brayden handled the animal. The man never appeared off balance, had one hand on the reins and was soothing the horse with the other.

When the horse settled, Brayden leaped off and inspected Jax's hips and flanks. He ran his hand down each leg. He glared at Kawley. "That's a good way to break a hip, his or even possibly mine. If you cause me to shoot him, I'd be hard pressed not to drop you there next to him."

Kawley dismounted. She was genuinely sorry for having slammed into his mount. "The horse means that much to you?" She knew he most likely had his pick from a stable full of well-bred animals. The magnificent chestnut he rode had a commanding presence, sporting a white blaze and four white socks.

"I'd take this boy over a number of people I know." Brayden ran his hand down the equine's neck. The horse nuzzled him and nickered. "I bred for him. I held him the day he was born. I broke him and trained him. We understand one another."

She had never met a man who seemed to have such empathy for an animal. Or, if they did, they never voiced it. Somehow it touched her.

"Do you think you are capable of holding both of them?"

The warm feeling she'd had moments before immediately disappeared with his obvious sarcasm. "Of course I can," she shot back at him as she grabbed Jax's reins from him.

Brayden snorted. "Well, see that you don't lose them. We're a long way from anywhere. That ridge is a good vantage point. I'll be back in five minutes." He started off and then abruptly turned. "I trust you will be here when I get back, won't you? I don't want to find Ajax tied to a tree and you gone because I don't have time to be chasing after you."

"You'll just have to see when you get back, won't you?"

"Damn it, woman. Then do what you want." He grabbed the reins from her hand and scrambled up the ridge.

Kawley turned to mount, happy to be on her way, when something in the dirt caught her eye. She picked up a small book and mounted. As she took a few steps, preparing to gallop off, she flipped through the pages. Certain words jumped out at her, and she realized that the book must have fallen from Brayden's saddle bag. These must be the pages he penned night after night while she watched his group on the trail. Though she felt like an interloper, Kawley could not help but read a few lines.

"If only we could change the things we say and do. How naive and arrogant I was not to realize that one moment in time could change the course of my life. On days like this one, when everything seems the same, I wish I could live that day over and do it right. But was there any right way to do what I did? Even in the best of circumstances, forgiveness will be a long time in coming."

She halted her horse. This Brayden was certainly an enigma. Despite his brusque demeanor, she felt a tenderness in his words, different from any man she had ever known. This man would help rescue her brother; she felt it. No one who had the sense of morality to feel those emotions and the daring to put them on paper would refuse. She whirled her horse around and trotted back to where she seen the book, dismounted and placed it where she had found it. Then she turned her back and fiddled with her gear. She was adjusting a stirrup and checking the girth when she heard scrambling in the trees. Kawley grabbed her pistol and whirled around to make sure the scrambling was Brayden and his mount coming through.

Brayden harrumphed with his blatant surprise. "So you stayed after all." His eyes widened and his head snapped back at the pistol in her hand. Then he clucked and drew his hands to each side. "We going to start this all over again?"

Kawley holstered the pistol. "You could have been anyone coming through. You see anything from up there?"

"Nothing worth mentioning. Mount up. We've wasted enough time as it is."

She suspected that the 'vantage point' Brayden spoke of was probably more a call of nature, but she said nothing and mounted.

"How did this fall out here?"

Kawley turned her head to watch Brayden pick up the grey book and shove it into his saddle bag. He hesitated a bit with his hand on the bag, patting the bag lightly, as if thankful somehow the book had not been lost.

He mounted and pulled his horse in next to her. "And just to make sure your unruly animal doesn't break something on Jax's back end, you ride next to me from here on out."

She jutted her chin at the insult. "Pickles is not unruly and quit bossing me around."

A quiet yet deep throaty laughter filled the air between them. Brayden's entire face crinkled with a wide smile that she had to admit was warm and inviting. "Pickles? Your mare is named, Pickles?"

"Yes, Pickles. You have problem with that?" The man was not only bossy, he was annoying as well.

He cantered off. A rapid flick of his hand pressured her to canter up next to him. "A horse as salty as her rider. Let's just hope some of that saltiness will serve you in good stead where we're headed."

"Since I seem to be your prisoner, exactly where is it we are headed?"

"An abandoned mission near Seneca."

"Is that where Fletcher and the other two fellows are meeting you?"

Brayden ground his horse to a halt and grabbed Pickles reins. The crinkled grin was gone, replaced by a scowling glare. "How do you know about that?"

Kawley lifted on eyebrow and sucked in a triumphant breath. "I dogged your group for a bit, and I have excellent hearing."

The bossy, annoying gentleman puckered his lips and nodded a few times as if deep in thought. "Well, Miss Pickles, where we're headed a little salt might just come in handy. Come on."

————

Brayden Wakefield was shocked that he could still feel such a myriad of emotions. He feared for Caleb and for the rest of them in their rescue efforts. The war around them was raging as was the war within him. Now it seemed not only were they searching for Caleb, but he would be honor bound to search for the woman's brother as well. Had the Fates decreed him this quest to save a life to make up for the one he took?

He glanced at the rider cantering next to him. Was she also now under his protection? He had to admit the woman with the cow name and a pickled horse had done a very good job of disguising her femininity. She had fooled him. Her deep, slightly raspy voice Brayden assumed was her God given tone because it didn't change even when he had discovered her to be a woman. Still, the idea of taking a woman on this mission was reckless. But sending her off on her own, knowing full well she would carry on alone was madness.

He laughed to himself. Pickles. The name suited her mare because it also suited her. She appeared ready and able to secure herself and her intentions but was not afraid to burn all that might stand in her way. He had to respect that. Her pluck intrigued him. Yet Brayden intuited a fragility under all the salt, and it was that fragility which drew him and, much to his surprise, touched the dark, cold place deep within him. Who was this woman who had ridden into his life? How did she fit into the painful puzzle which had plagued him since his wife's death?

———

The rhythmic thud of the equine canter seemed to lull both Brayden and Kawley into a comfortable silence as the miles slid under the hooves. Brayden reluctantly admitted to himself that Kawley sat a horse as well as he did. She appeared tireless, with a tight seat and gentle hands. The occasional furtive glance captured her determined expression darkened by what he surmised were probably leftover campfire ashes. Scrappy looking to be sure but the double vested waistcoat added bulk in the right places. A thick black belt and holster topped off the loose-fitting trousers and heavy brown boots. With her head held high and her shoulders squared, the 'man' might be short in stature but appeared nonetheless a force with which to be reckoned.

Pickles jutted against Ajax to avoid a hole in the path, and Kawley's leg slammed into Brayden's. The woman gritted her teeth and hissed, falling forward onto the horse's neck. She quickly righted herself without breaking stride. "Sorry," she called through clenched teeth.

"You all right?"

"I'm fine. Just keep riding."

Her face had gone pale despite the disguise. Her back was hunched, and she was gripping the reins with clenched fists.

Brayden used another approach. "Let's walk for a bit and give the horses a rest."

"No! Let's go."

Since she seemed to punch out her words but appeared to have no intention of stopping, Brayden grabbed her reins and ground their horses to a halt. "I said to walk, and I meant it."

"Since when do I have to obey your slightest command?"

"Since I can clearly see that something is wrong, and I want to know what it is."

Kawley yanked her reins back. "Why do you keep asking? There's nothing wrong." She urged her horse forward.

"The hell there isn't." Brayden jumped from his horse and grabbed Kawley's leg.

Kawley yelped and fell forward again. "How dare you use such language in front of a woman."

"You're a man, remember?" He pulled again on her leg. "Now get down here and let me have a look at what's under those trousers."

She sucked in a quick, loud breath and slapped his hand away. "How dare you even suggest such a thing. Leave me be."

Her entire face scrunched into obvious pain—teeth clenched, and eyes shut—giving Brayden the advantage he needed to pull her from the saddle. "I said let me see. I want to know what's under there." With her struggling, he had to fairly throw her to the ground and sit on her to lift the leg of her trousers. He stripped off the bloody wrapping to find an angry red, gory mess. Brayden softened his grip and sat back on one leg. "Dear God, woman, what the devil happened?"

She grabbed the wrapping out of his hand, wadded it and dabbed the wound, wincing with every touch. "Bullet came out of nowhere, but Pickles side-stepped just in time."

Brayden sat straighter. "Until now you hid this quite well. You didn't even limp. I'm also wondering how is it that you have this nasty gash, yet your trousers are not torn or bloodied?"

Kawley avoided his glare.

"Hmmm?"

"I snitched clothes drying on a line."

"So you're a thief!"

"That make you happy?"

He begrudgingly admired her resourcefulness to hide her weak point from view, not sure he would have thought of it. Brayden lifted her leg for a closer look. "There's infection here. Do you have a fever?" He put his hand to her forehead, but she slapped it away. He clucked his tongue in annoyance, grabbed both her wrists, held them captive with one giant hand and used the other to feel for fever. "None yet." He rose, walked to his horse and retrieved his flask and a tin from his pack. She seemed rather stunned when he sat close and faced her. He handed her the flask. "It has a kick like a mule, but you are going to need it." When she hesitated he pushed the flask to her lips. "Now, please."

Kawley lifted the flask to her lips, guzzled a generous swig, swallowed and started coughing.

"Little sips. I told you it kicks like a mule."

She swallowed several more sips and turned her head away. "Enough, enough." She handed back the flask as she wiped her chin with the back of her hand.

"Don't mind if I do." Genuinely impressed and yet puzzled by her tolerance for his mixture, Brayden tipped the flask and allowed a huge draft to slip down his throat, smiling as the burn hit his belly. "Now your turn again."

Kawley shook her head. "I said, enough."

"This time it's down your leg, not your throat."

She attempted to scurry away. "Oh no. You're not pouring that on my leg. That'll burn like hell."

Brayden grabbed her and pulled his head back. "Why Miss Kawley, I'm appalled at your language. I see you are well practiced at cursing like a man. And yes, I am pouring this on your leg. That infection gets out of hand, and you'll be losing this leg. I might be excellent with a pistol, but I haven't had much experience with a saw."

Her eyes widened as if his description became a reality in her mind.

Kawley shook her head. "I'd die first before I'd allow you or anyone else to butcher me like a cow."

He snickered. "Interesting choice of words for the woman with the cow's name."

Kawley slapped the air. "Stop saying that!"

"I'm simply trying to make you understand that if this infection spreads, you will lose the leg...or worse."

"Then get to it."

He took off his stock, laid it across his leg and positioned himself closer. "Grab my arm and squeeze as hard as you want. Bite my coat sleeve to muffle any sounds. We don't need more surprises." He gave her a minute to compose herself. "Ready?"

She nodded and gripped his arm. "Do it now before I lose my nerve."

For a minute Brayden was about to lose his nerve because he knew the pain he was about to inflict on her. He looked deep into her eyes, eyes so deep blue he was lost in their oceans. Then she clamped shut her eyes and furrowed her brows. "Now."

Brayden tipped the flask and the liquid lathered the gash. Kawley's soft howls were muffled by his sleeve but her whole body convulsed. He sloshed the savaged, gaping wound a second time. Again she seized and clawed at him. When the muted wails died to whimpers and her shoulders stopped shaking, Brayden wrapped her leg tightly with his stock and pinned it. "That's enough for now."

"For now?" she whispered, plainly exhausted by the ordeal. She leaned back against a tree, closed her eyes and pulled down her trouser leg. "I don't want to see it." Her eyes opened but her face was still a tight grimace. Kawley reached for the flask. "One more for the pain I suffered?"

"One more for the pain or because it's a tasty brew? We can't be wasting this."

"Give me that." She yanked the flask from his hand and bolted a mouthful. She grinned as she scraped the droplets on her chin and licked them from her finger. The frisky woman seemed to savor the burn in several small gulps.

While he admired her grit, he questioned her actions. He had never known a woman who could match him swallow for swallow. In addition, she had ridden with the wound for hours without uttering a word and suffered his awkward ministrations with not much more than whimpers. "Have any idea where the shot came from?"

She shook her head. "No. But if I find the coward, I'll only need one shot to fix his rooster."

"His? I thought you said you didn't see who it was. How do you know it was a man?"

Kawley lowered her eyes. "I... I don't." She struggled to rise. "Just sayin' is all."

Brayden offered his arm. She refused, hobbled to her horse and scrambled aboard.

CHAPTER THREE

BRAYDEN DIDN'T WANT TO CHANCE GLANCING AT HIS FATHER'S WATCH AS they rode. He wasn't certain how long they had ridden, perhaps an hour or two. But the heavy silence between them was deafening and awkward. He wanted to know more about this woman who had entered his life and added to his mission. Several opening lines drifted through his brain, but he rejected them before they fell over his lips. As they pulled their horses to a restful walk, finally one came to mind.

"I'm curious why you named your mare 'Pickles'."

"Why do you even care?"

"Oh for God's sake, woman, it's a simple question. You're right. I don't care. I just thought a bit of simple conversation might make the miles pass quicker."

Kawley cleared her throat and clucked her tongue. "Well, if you must know, when she was a filly, she escaped from the field one day. She was missing for hours while we searched everywhere. The sun was going down, and we thought possibly she had been prey for a coyote and was lost. It was only by chance I wandered into the summer kitchen and there she was with her muzzle in the giant pickle barrel. She seemed quite innocent as if she belonged there. She was Pickles, PJ for short, ever since." Kawley glared at Brayden, openly daring him to utter a sarcastic retort.

Brayden chuckled softly, "If it's true that's a story for the ages."

"You already called me a thief. You're now calling me a liar, too?"

"They usually go hand in hand."

"You think I made it up?"

He raised his hand to stop the argumentative steamrolling direction of the conversation. "Not at all. I've just never known a horse who liked pickles. As I said, that's a story to tell your grandchildren one day."

Kawley clamped her mouth shut and pursed her lips. Her entire demeanor stated that the discussion was ended.

His attempt at polite conversation was clearly not going well. "I was simply trying to say that I like the name. It suits her—" He hesitated. "—and you."

She waved her hand in marked dismissal. "You're right. I'm a lying thief who's sour and caustic."

Brayden wondered why he even started the conversation. The silence was infinitely more enjoyable. He chirruped Ajax into a canter.

"Well, I'm certainly glad we have that cleared up," he tossed at her as he passed.

———

His annoyance with Kawley diminished as the miles passed. Although she never complained, now that he had seen her leg wound, he felt guilty pushing her to ride hard as he wanted. His mind was a mosaic that swirled and checkered his thoughts. Brayden wanted to be riding alone. Since Lavinia's death he had avoided all social gatherings and situations. Only Fletcher always managed to insinuate himself within the hard-shell Brayden had erected. Now Brayden wanted nothing more than to be rushing headlong to join Fletcher, Rush and Clive to rescue Caleb, not some other person who may or may not be held with him.

On the other hand, it shocked him how much he had savored the sensation of her lithe body against him as he had struggled with her to attend to her wound. They were sensations he had never felt before, not even with Lavinia. But now he was saddled with another mission and as intriguing, alluring and delightfully amusing as Kawley was, he felt the weight of her protection. Considering how he failed to protect Lavinia, Brayden was inwardly fearful of the job. He worried once they reached the mission, the others might not agree to allow Kawley to travel with them, especially if they discovered her secret. Prior to meeting Kawley his mind was filled daily with 'if only.' Since being saddled with her, he was deluged with disturbing 'what ifs.' He wanted none of these added complications, especially when the Yankees were threatening Caleb's life as well as their entire world.

Brayden was deep in his thoughts when he felt Jax's muscles tighten as a whinny filled the air. He shoved out his arm to stop Kawley and Pickles from moving any further forward. He put his finger to his lips to prevent the question he knew was coming. Brayden quickly reached around to give both horses a few treats so they would not answer with whinnies of their own. Kawley pointed in the direction of the noise, and Brayden nodded. Both drew their pistols and slowly urged their horses forward. Deep in the trees they found a riderless horse, fully saddled, grazing but caught by its reins.

"Look at the brand," Kawley whispered. "That boy carried a Yankee for sure."

Brayden stretched tall in the saddle and searched all around them. "I agree, but where is that Yankee now?"

"Can't be far because the horse is still sweaty."

Brayden put up his hand to silence her and tapped his ear. *Listen,* he mouthed. The confused expression on her face told him she didn't hear what he did. She shrugged her shoulders and shook her head. He tapped the air in the direction in front of them with his forefinger. Again he heard a snapping noise and a low growl. Kawley's head snapped up and her eyes opened wide. It was obvious she heard it that time. She started to dismount but Brayden grabbed her arm.

"I think an escape is safer if we stay mounted," he whispered. "Stay behind me."

Kawley opened her mouth as if to argue but Brayden's glare clearly stopped her, and she reined Pickles in behind Ajax.

Within a short time they saw the source of the sounds in the distance. A bloodied man was pinned against a boulder, threatened by a trio of wolves. The man was swinging a board to fend them off, but it didn't take a fortune teller to know that he would soon be losing his battle. Kawley cocked her pistol to fire but Brayden stopped her.

"No! A shot would call attention to us and bring around God knows who." He pulled his whip from the saddle. "If Pickles can handle a growling wolf, snap your whip as we run them off. If not, stay here while I chase them."

Kawley slid out her whip. "Lead on."

While Brayden had no doubt the wolves would have finished the wounded man, he guessed they were young because they scattered without a fight when they caught sight of the two giant horses and crackling whips.

Brayden and Kawley dismounted and approached the wounded man with caution. He was breathing hard, a small trickle of blood dripped from his lips. His face was covered in bruises, and one eye was swollen shut. Brayden wondered why someone had worked him over so badly. The man lay in an odd position with his lower half in an awkward twisted pretzel.

"Damn wolves want me for lunch," he forced out. More blood spouted from his lips.

"Why were you out here riding alone?" Kawley asked. "Where are the others?"

Brayden was stunned, not by her question but by the fact that her southern drawl had completely disappeared. She sounded just like the Yankee. Since the man seemed willing to talk to 'him' Brayden kept his silence.

"Got separated from 'em." He coughed and spit out a mouthful of blood.

"You hit a tree? How did you mess up your face if you were riding alone?"

"Nosy buck, aren't ya? Help me back on my horse. My legs aren't working good." He struggled with one arm but fell back, bleeding profusely from his nose and mouth.

Kawley growled at him. "You didn't get separated, did you? I'm guessing you're a deserter. Who did you kill to get those clothes and a horse?"

The deserter smiled with blatant cynicism. "Rider was headed back from the group for some bag or something. Put up a good fight, he did. Stupid runt. I told him I only wanted the horse, but he wouldn't give it up."

"Bag? What bag?"

"Listen, friend. You gonna help me or what?"

Kawley knelt near the man and pointed her pistol squarely at his head. "First of all, I'm not your friend. I'll help you when you tell me what I want to know. Since you're bleeding like a stuck pig you'd better talk fast." She cocked the hammer. "What bag?"

The man spit blood at Kawley's knee. "Don't rightly know. He wasn't real talkative while he was swinging punches." He coughed again. "It was some message bag for Capitol City. They were taking two traitors to prison."

While his heart was pounding at the mention of the two 'prisoners', Brayden was profoundly impressed that Kawley never showed what she surely was feeling. "What prisoners?" Kawley leaned closer. "Talk or I'll shoot!"

The derelict coughed hard and slouched lower, clearly failing. "Go ahead and shoot. I'm probably dead already."

Brayden had seen enough, and his control fled. He bustled between them and grabbed the fellow by the shoulders. "Don't you die before you tell me about the prisoners." Unlike Kawley, his speech definitely gave him away.

"They were Southern trash, just like you." The man grinned, showing several broken teeth. "They'll be…lucky…if they…they don't get hung before prison." His good eye closed halfway, and his head rolled back. A long gurgling sound escaped, and he was quiet.

Brayden dug his fingers into the man's shoulders. "Where are they taking them?" He shook him. "What prison?" He shook him again. "What prison?"

"The pig's gone." He felt Kawley's hand on his shoulder. "Brayden, he's dead."

In his head Brayden knew she was right, but he couldn't stop himself. "What prison?" He shook the body twice more before he let go and threw his hands in the air in frustration. "Argh!"

Neither of them spoke for a long while. Brayden was desperate to regain his control. The deserter's death snatched away the information they sorely needed. He heaved several deep breaths and rubbed his palms along his breeches.

"Brayden?"

He spun his head to look at her. "What?" The word shot off his lips. He lowered his head and ran his hand over his face. He had not meant to take out his anger and frustration on Kawley. He glanced back at her. "What?" he repeated in a softer tone.

"Would it be indecent to rifle through his pockets? If he stole the clothes, maybe there's a clue we can use?"

He snorted and gave her a quick nod. "Absolutely not. I should have thought of it myself."

Unfortunately, they found nothing to indicate where the group was headed, nor whether the 'prisoners' were actually Caleb and Riley. Brayden sat back on one leg. "Nothing."

Kawley stood. "Not nothing, really."

"What do you mean?"

"If the group was taking the bag to Capitol City, then probably Old Capitol would be where they would house Caleb and Riley, at least at first."

Brayden stood and mounted. "Well, then, we'll meet up with Fletcher and the rest. If they haven't any other clues, we'll head to Capitol City." He turned Ajax in the direction they had come.

"Where are you going? The Seneca mission you talked about is the other way."

"Headed back to search for clues and salvage any supplies from the Yankee's horse."

Kawley mounted. "Now I'm embarrassed I didn't think of it myself."

The horse yielded no further clues but did have abundant supplies. Brayden yanked the saddle and bridle and threw them to the ground. "Go on, boy. Now you'll be fine." He saw the baffled expression on Kawley's face. "I'll not leave a horse caught and fully tacked. Loose and free, he'll be able to run and protect himself."

"You'll see to the horse's safety—" She raised an eyebrow. "—yet we left a man's body to be fodder for the wolves."

Brayden shook his head. "That man was a deserter and, most likely, a murderer. He knew exactly what he was doing. The horse is innocent; he deserves my protection." He mounted. "Why are you grinning?"

"Because there's finally something we can agree on."

He clucked to his horse and legged him forward. "Well, that's something." The nagging thought which continued to bother him forced him to ask, "As long as we are in agreement, would you agree to disclose where you pulled that Yankee speech from? It really loosened his tongue."

"I knew it would. He might have kept talking if—"

"Yes, I know," Brayden interjected. "He shut up the minute I opened my mouth." He shook his head at his own stupidity, and they rode in silence. Once again, the nagging thought bothered him. "Well?"

"Well what?"

"Are you going to tell me how you became a Yankee so easily back there?" The muscles of his chest tightened. He pulled Ajax to a halt. "Or have I been traveling with a Yankee all along and your southern drawl is just an act to get me to help rescue someone?"

Kawley leered at him but didn't speak, most likely being deliberate in what she was about to say. Her hesitation alone made Brayden suspicious that the answer might be less than truthful.

"Have you forgotten that I never wanted to ride with you in the first place?"

Kawley's southern drawl had returned quite heavily. *Was it purposeful? A pretense to throw him off the track?*

"Have you forgotten this duet we've got going here was your idea, not mine? I was doing just fine on my own."

Brayden was still not convinced. "Then explain how you can sound southern one minute and northern the next."

Kawley batted her eyelashes and smirked. *"Ce qui si je te parlais en francais? Est-ce que ce serait meilleur? Or...Si tibi placet Latine?"*

Her sapphire eyes captivated him. Brayden smacked his forehead. "My God, woman, you're a veritable chameleon." He snorted and shook his head. "I don't understand what you're saying or how you're able to say it."

"There's a simple explanation."

"That I am still waiting to hear."

"My father wanted a son."

"That's your explanation? Every man wants a son."

Kawley continued, clearly ignoring the interruption. "My father wanted a son. He wanted to name him after Lord Kawlon of Westfordshire. But he ended up with me. Kawlon became Kawley but that's not where it stopped. He showered me with everything money could buy. Everything except…"

"Except?"

"Hmm?" She shook her head. "Nothing." Kawley pulled in a deep breath. "I was exceedingly well educated and raised as a son. He also taught me to swagger, shoot, smoke, drink, spit—"

"Spit?"

"Yes, spit as well as any man out there. My mother was horrified."

Brayden whistled. "I can imagine she would be."

"My poor mother tried to erase it all but without success. So she simply added the womanly discipline and attributes to my pocketful of talents. They've come in handy on several occasions, today being one of them."

He stared at her with utter incredulity. He had no idea whether to believe her or not. With such a talent, how could he ever be sure who she really was? Or what her real purpose was, for that matter. She could be a Yankee spy, and he would have no way of discerning it. He could be leading a fox straight to the roosters.

"You do realize your expression is ridiculously transparent, don't you?"

"What do you mean?"

"I mean your thoughts are an open book."

"You think you know so much? Tell me what I'm thinking."

"You're wondering how you can ever be sure who I really am. You're wondering if I'm a spy. You're wondering if that's why someone took a shot at me. You're worried you are leading Reynard to the quarry."

While Brayden was annoyed that he was so barefaced, he was begrudgingly impressed that Kawley was so perceptive.

"Well?"

Now it was his turn. "Well what?"

"Did my 'X' mark the spot or did I miss the target?"

Brayden hesitated. "Apparently your father taught you to shoot quite well."

Kawley leaned from her horse and brought her face closer to Brayden. "Look into my eyes, sir, and know that except for posing as a man, everything I've told you has been the truth. I give you my word—" She winked. "—as a gentleman."

With the horses in perfect step, Brayden rolled his upper body into her. "As a gentleman? Madam, I..." Their faces were close enough to touch. He could see the rise and fall of her chest, could feel her breath. The blue of her eyes held him captive. Something changed in that moment; the feeling was palpable. Both of them seemed to step out of their respective identities. She lowered her eyes to his lips and back again. He tilted his head ever slightly, wanting to feel the softness of her lips on his. The other didn't pull away. It was shocking to actually feel alive again. He closed his eyes, Ajax stomped his hoof and reality came crashing down. He cleared his throat and quickly sat back in his saddle as if the moment had never happened. "Woman, except that you're hunting for your brother, you've told me virtually nothing."

Kawley reseated herself and fussed with her cap. "Then I haven't lied, have I?"

"Haven't you?"

"What do you mean?"

"If you haven't lied, then please explain how you are searching for your—" Brayden lowered his head and glared. "—brother when you just finished telling me you were an only child." He lifted one eyebrow. "Hmmm?"

Kawley visibly paled, then seemed to recover her composure. "I guess that would appear a trifle odd."

"A trifle? Shall we say impossible?"

"Before branding a giant 'L' for liar on my cheek, would you give me a chance to explain?"

Brayden leaned back in his saddle and rested his palms on the horse's rump. "I'm on tenterhooks. Please do elucidate."

"I will if you wipe that skeptical sneer off your face."

Brayden averted his face. "I'm listening."

She heaved a deep breath. "Riley is not really my brother."

"Undoubtedly."

"Do you want to hear this or not?"

"Sorry. Do go on."

"My father found Riley—"

Brayden sat back up and swiveled his head. "Found? Like an old horseshoe?"

Kawley jutted her chin. "Actually, yes. Like an old discarded horseshoe."

"And?"

"And nothing. He found him, raised and educated him, and that's all you need to know."

"Whoa there. That's hardly all I need to know. Especially since you asked me to help rescue him. I think I have a right to know who he really is."

Kawley grabbed up her reins. "When are you going to get it through your thick head that I never asked to ride with you. I don't want your help. I don't need your help." She drove her legs into Pickle's sides and the horse half reared. "And I am done with this perlustration, if you can shut your mouth long enough to figure out what that means." Pickles lurched forward and she cantered away.

Perlustration? What the devil did that mean? He galloped after her, genuinely surprised that the liver chestnut mare could cover that much ground. A few miles later, when he finally caught up to them, Brayden snatched her reins and ground the two equines to a halt. "I'm not done with you, yet."

"Well I'm done with you." Kawley succeeded in slipping the reins back from his hand and took off into the woods.

"Damn it." Brayden kicked Ajax and flew into the woods after her. He galloped through the trees, careful to protect his knees as he rounded the tree trunks. As he glanced down to secure their footing, he rounded a cluster of trunks, and Ajax slammed into Pickle's rump. They careened sideways, and the crash nearly unseated Brayden. He was about the say something very uncharitable when he realized Kawley was glued to the saddle as though she were made of stone. Both hands covered her mouth, plainly stifling a scream. Tears glistened on her cheeks. "Oh God! Oh God! Oh God!"

Brayden turned his head in the direction of her wide-eyed stare. In the distance he saw two hanging bodies in dirty, frayed clothes, not uniforms. They were bound hand and foot with hoods covering their heads. His heart thudded in his chest, and bile rose in his throat.

"The deserter said they might hang them," Kawley whimpered. She clutched her belly. "Oh, dear Lord. I think I'm going to be sick."

Brayden quickly dismounted and pulled Kawley from the saddle. He carried her a short distance, gently set her down and urged her to the bushes. "Come over here."

"I'm all right." Her breaths were shallow and quick as though holding in a frightful emotion that belied her words. "The worst is passing."

She was still within his arms when she lifted her face to his. The sorrow he saw there ripped him to pieces. Her cheeks were suddenly sunken and drawn, her striking eyes dull and welled with tears. The anguish was genuine, soulful and deep. Whoever Riley was to her—brother, beau, or friend—it was obvious the loss cut Kawley to her core as much as Caleb's loss would cut through him. He pulled her to his chest and rocked her gently.

"We were too late. We failed them," she whispered into his shoulder.

He held her close a moment longer. "Only if the two of them are actually Riley and Caleb." He slid her from him. "Stay here."

"Where are you going?"

"To cut them down."

In the dirt below the bodies someone had scratched the words 'southern traitors' with a stick. He kicked the branch away with a vengeance and scratched out the words with his boot. His knife hacked through the stretched length of rope but the thud of the bodies hitting the ground was a gruesome sound. They fell on the dirt in grotesque positions like puppets without their strings. The stench of death stung his nostrils. It actually felt as if someone kicked him in the gut. "Turn your head or you might really be sick this time." He hoped Kawley didn't notice the quiver in his voice.

Kawley leaned against a tree and faced away. Brayden hoped he, himself, wouldn't spill his guts at the sight of their macabre, suffocated faces, especially if one of them turned out to be Caleb. He steeled himself and slowly lifted back one of the hoods. Not Caleb. If the other body was Caleb's, then this would be Riley.

"Is it—?"

"Stay where you are. I need a minute." His guts lurched, and his eyes watered. He wasn't prepared for the sight to hit him so hard. Brayden swallowed several times, bit the inside of his cheek and whispered a silent prayer. Slowly he raised the other hood. Not Caleb! But that didn't mean one of them was not Riley. "Kawley, describe Riley."

"B-blond hair." Her voice quaked.

Brayden replaced the hoods, sat back on the ground and put his head in his hands. "Oh, thank God. Kawley, it's not them. Both of these men have dark hair." He jumped up and neared her in three giant strides. "I've covered their faces. You can come out now." He reached for her and squeezed her hard against him, finally allowing himself to release the terror within him. He didn't know which of them was shaking more. Somehow it didn't matter. The world of death and war didn't exist for him beyond this moment. The feeling of her snug in his arms enraptured him, suffused his dark places with a startling contentment and calm he hadn't experienced in a very long time. It was hard to believe he could be so moved by her touch. He was loath to release her, but she pulled away. Brayden swiveled, blinked several times and remembered where they were, what they needed to do.

"We have to bury them," she whispered, wiping her cheeks.

"I know but with what? I don't have a shovel hidden in my saddle bag. Do you?"

Kawley looked around. "We'll have to improvise. There must be something around here we can use."

"You know we have to be riding out soon."

"They have to be in the ground before we leave, even if it's not deep." Kawley's voice rose, and she stomped her foot. "They deserve to be in the ground, not discarded on it."

Brayden acknowledged her glaring reprimand quietly. "Yes. Yes, they do." He silently chided himself for his disrespect as he trudged around and searched for implements. His search yielded nothing more than a lone, dirty brick and an old, half eaten boot. At the base of a trunk under a pile of leaves his hand touched a coil of rope, probably part of what they used to hang the two men. He threw it as far as he could and then wiped his hands on his breeches, feeling tainted for having touched it. He kept overturning debris, certain that something would appear. Kawley rounded the tree behind him.

"I found this old bucket. The ground is soft enough from the last rain for us to drag it along." Kawley banged the sides and dumped the contents.

"Shhhh." Brayden waved his hand. "You want to end up hanging from a tree like them?"

She found an open area, knelt, filled the bucket and moved the dirt to the side. A small trench emerged after several swipes. "Hard going but it's working. Did you find anything yet?"

"Just a brick and half a boot." He spied something sticking up out of a pile of brush and wrestled it from the pile. It was a wooden stake from what must have been a former fence. "I could point the end of this and loosen the dirt for your bucket."

Kawley was breathing hard from her labors. "Then get to it."

Brayden used his knife to sharpen the end of the stake. He knelt and sliced through the dirt with his tiny plow. Left hand on the top of the stake, right hand on the bottom, he pulled from front to back again and again. Kawley then filled her bucket with the loosened dirt and deposited it in a mound near them. After a bit his knees ached so he searched for a taller stake, sharpened the point, planted one foot out in front of him and plowed. Again and again he reached forward and pulled back. After countless plow swipes, he heard a soft giggle behind him. He turned. Kawley was grinning and shaking her head.

"I realize that you are plowing and not rowing, and I haven't the slightest idea why, but right now you remind me of a drawing of George Washington crossing the Delaware."

He stood tall and hooked his thumbs in his lapels. "I don't mind being Mr. President but if I'm rowing then we must be sinking because you are taking the bilge water out with every bucketful." He resumed plowing the stake through the dirt.

Kawley surprised him by whispering the tune of a child's rowing song, yet Brayden joined her softly. For both of them it seemed a release of tension as well as a distraction from their grisly task.

Suddenly Kawley clamped her mouth shut. "We are being so inappropriate. It's downright disrespectful."

"On the contrary, this is the most respectful, appropriate thing we can do for these men. They were southern comrades and rather than just leaving them to the coyotes, we are placing them in the ground with song. I realize it's a child's rhyme but each of these men was a mother's child somewhere, sometime and her heart will mourn forever. I can only hope some stranger would do the same for us if the roles were reversed."

Kawley stopped wielding her bucket and stared at him. Her

befuddled expression surprised him, and he wondered what he had said that would have caused such a reaction from her.

"I've never heard a man speak with such gentleness and kindness before. The men I've known would have viewed it as weakness to entertain such thoughts, let alone express them." Before he could answer, he watched the moment pass as quickly as it had started. She abruptly went back to her labors with a vengeance as though sorry and surprised she had spoken her thoughts out loud.

When the graves were as deep as they could manage, they arranged the bodies within them reverently, considering the circumstances. They used the bucket to drag the dirt and padded the mounds firmly.

"Kawley—"

"Don't," she interjected.

"I was about to ask if you wanted to say something over the graves."

"You do it."

Brayden nodded but as he recited the scripture, Kawley stunned him again by humming a chorus of *Amazing Grace*. He inwardly hoped the mothers of these men would have been pleased and believed they would have been grateful for the kindness of strangers. Even after they had finished and he walked away, Kawley continued to stand next to the mounds. She rubbed the inside of her left arm, apparently deep in thought.

He returned to her. "There's nothing more we can do for them, Kawley. It's done. Riley and Caleb need us."

Without a word she spun, yanked her cap tighter on her head, slapped the dirt from her trousers and mounted. Brayden followed suit, and they rode away in silence. He knew he would later write in his journal that her face was unreadable as they rode but when she squared her shoulders and sat taller in the saddle, he intuited that she was putting this incident behind her into some vast chasm overflowing with painful experiences. He didn't know how or why he was sure of that belief, but he knew it in his heart to be true. Perhaps because he, himself, was wading in a dark place, he recognized the same state in others.

In his mind and later in his journal he would be sure to question over and over. Who was this woman? What was her true objective? Why had she been thrown in his path? Always questions. Watching Kawley with the deserter and the burials, why did he now fear the answers?

CHAPTER FOUR

BRAYDEN PULLED OPEN THE DOOR, AND THEY LED THE HORSES INSIDE. He retrieved a match from his inside pocket and lit the lantern hanging on the hook.

"Not exactly The Palace Hotel."

"Look here, little miss. Considering I endured a rifle barrel in my face, begging the owner of this broken-down barn to allow us shelter for the night, these are certainly adequate quarters with the storm coming. If you're unhappy with it, you are certainly welcome to find another roof to keep you dry."

Kawley didn't answer, merely started loosening her horse's girth. Brayden assumed it was her intention to stay. There was a partition separating the farmer's animals from them. "Certainly, this side is roomy enough for the four of us," he offered.

"The four of us?"

"Ajax stays with me. If you want your picklepuss on the other side with the farm animals, that's fine with me."

"She stays with me."

Brayden gave a terse nod in acknowledgement. "Like I said, the four of us." He looked around and was pleased that there was a pump in the barn. "We have water for the horses and our supplies." He motioned with his forefinger. "There's a workbench here. Set yourself down and let's get a closer look at the leg."

44

"It's fine. Barely hurts at all. Just leave me be," Kawley replied as she turned her back and pumped water into a bucket.

In one swift motion, Brayden grabbed her around the waist and plopped her on the workbench. "Sit. Don't you ever do what you are told?"

"Not since I uttered my first word." She slapped at his hand and struggled with his grip. "Let me go. How dare you!"

"How dare I what? Keep you alive? I've seen too many leg wounds. If you want to die, remember I don't have a shovel. We left the bucket and stakes back where we found them."

Kawley's hand flew to her lips, and her shoulders shook. "Oh my. No, no, no." She extended her leg, raised her trouser leg and squinted her eyes.

Brayden unwrapped the bloody stock tie and examined the wound. "The salve is doing its job. It looks much better." He looked at the stock tie and shook his head. "Need to find another bandage." He looked around for towels. Seeing none, he pulled his shirt from his breeches and ripped off the bottom. "This will have to do. We can rinse out the stock tie and hopefully it will dry by morning. This wound had better heal fast or I shall soon be unclothed, having been ripped apart bit by bit."

After Brayden cleansed and bandaged Kawley's wound, they untacked the horses. While Brayden was brushing Ajax, he noticed Kawley rearranging the extra planks from the side of the barn.

"May I ask what you are doing?"

"Creating a partition. You didn't think we were all sleeping together, did you?"

"Not in the way you mean. I am a gentleman, after all. Although, I did literally just give you the shirt off my back."

Kawley snorted. "Gentleman or not, I prefer something of substance between us." She secured another plank. "And by the way, you are sleeping on the side nearest the door."

Brayden folded his arms and planted his feet. "And why might that be?"

"Because, as a gentleman, it's your job to protect a lady by sleeping nearest any possible intruders."

"Now you're a lady? You've been working awfully hard to convince the world otherwise."

"But you know the truth. Therefore, as the gentleman you say you are, I expect to be treated properly."

"In other words, I get to die first?"

"Well, someone has to survive to rescue your friend and my brother. The decision is yours—sleep over there with the horses or in the *stall* I've built next to the door."

"Hmmm. Let me be sure I understand the choices. I can risk being trampled, or risk being shot? That's a tough choice." He whistled softly. "I think the chances are slimmer that there will be an intruder so I will sleep in the *stall* next to the door. I fear the greater risk is that your swiftly built partition will collapse on me during the night." He grabbed a pitchfork and jammed it into a pile of straw. "Kindly move aside, my lady whilst I, as a gentleman, prepare your chamber." Brayden layered the straw deeply in each opening. Next, he placed their saddle blankets and finally their bedrolls. "There. I trust this meets with your approval?"

"Passable."

"Passable?" He plopped down on his bedroll. "There is just no pleasing a woman."

Kawley placed another plank across the front of her *stall*.

Brayden folded his arms under his head. "You locking your door? You do realize that I see through the planks?"

"Just putting up a reminder for you to stay on your own side."

Brayden sat up and rested an elbow on his raised knee. "You have my word, as a gentleman, that I will not trespass on your property nor will I invite you to trespass on mine." He heaved a heavy breath. "Now can we call a truce?"

"Truce. Good night." Kawley lowered the lamp, laid down and covered herself with the blanket.

The storm found them, and rain pelted the roof and sides of the barn. Slivers of brightness from the lightning shot through every inconspicuous break in the wood sides. The slivers shot like shards of glass, and Brayden half expected the shards to rain down on them. It lit up the barn with a ghastly light. The thunder boomed and shook the ground although the horses seemed unaffected and continued munching on their hay. The woman on the other side of the partition, however, was tossing and turning.

"You afraid of storms?"

There was a long silence. "Yes," Kawley finally answered. "Ever since my uncle died during one."

"Sorry for your loss." He hesitated. "Would it help to talk?"

"Talk about what?"

Brayden laid back down and stared at the ceiling, counting the knots in the wood as the crackling light and thunder continued. "Well, considering we are riding into danger together, perhaps you'd tell me a bit more about yourself. So far all I know is that you ride well, shoot straight, are book-learned, apparently can spit a great distance and seem to have a high tolerance for pain."

"Well then, big man, considering the war is all around us and we may not survive, I think you know all you need to know."

Brayden shot up and clucked his tongue. "Now see here, missy. If your brother is being held by the same mercenaries as Caleb, then I think you should at least provide any information that might help. Even the smallest detail might be a significant key."

His companion growled. "Drop the 'missy' and tell me exactly what you would like to know."

"Since we are stuck here for the night, why not try being civil and start at the beginning? Where do you hail from? Why are you following your brother? Why not your parents? Why do you suspect they targeted your plantation to raid? All of that information might provide clues."

Kawley hiked herself up and balanced on one arm. "Far western part of the state, parents are dead, and the Confiscation Act took care of the farm. Satisfied? I'm alone and penniless with nothing and no one to go back to."

"How long ago did your parents die?"

"Not long. They were killed by a lady."

"Killed, you say? Was there a trial? Was she convicted?"

Kawley shook her head before she plopped back down and turned away from him. "She drowned before there was a trial. It's done and over with, and I don't want to talk about it anymore."

The determination in her voice told Brayden that Kawley would not be volunteering any further information. He was desperate to ask her what she meant by the Confiscation Act having anything to do with her brother's kidnapping. The Act was only utilized under serious accusations. Somehow, some way he would have to pry more information out of her.

He laid his arm along one of the planks and stared at the woman lying near him. The even rise and fall of her back told him she might have drifted off. Even in the dim light he could see Kawley had unbraided her hair and wondered exactly when she had done so. The deep burgundy strands surrounded her shoulders. Without her hat and darkened face she was definitely all woman. He had to resist the urge to run his palm along her shoulder. What love she must have for her brother to have attempted this perilous journey alone. She was so much like two other women he knew and admired, Sage and Kyndee—beautiful, strong and determined. God willing they would succeed in finding Caleb and her brother, and Kawley might one day wish to meet them. Brayden sighed. If there was one thing they needed in their quest it was Divine Intervention. Yes, God willing.

———

Brayden was jolted from a sound sleep by a jut into his foot. He grabbed his pistol and hiked himself up on one elbow. Kawley was standing at his feet. "Good Lord, woman. I could have killed you. What's wrong?"

"You have to switch stalls with me."

"Wha…What?" He uncocked his pistol and sat up.

"You have to switch areas with me."

Brayden ran his hand through his hair. He was tired and not in the mood for riddles. "Woman did you or did you not order me to bed down on this side?"

"Yes, but I've changed my mind."

He closed his eyes and shook his head. "Indulge me. The reason for that change of heart would be…?"

"My side leaks."

Brayden squinted and, for the first time, noticed Kawley's clothes clung provocatively to her slender frame. The picture was anything but unattractive and a jolt shot through him, surprising and annoying him at the same time.

"Well?"

The words erupted from her through chattering teeth, and he realized that she was shivering. He jumped up, grabbed his coat and slipped it around her. "Dear God, Kawley. You are determined to die, aren't you?"

"N-no. I j-just woke up sopping w-wet." She pulled the coat tightly around her.

Brayden motioned to his bed roll. "You can settle yourself in my blanket until you dry." He knelt down to position himself near her.

Kawley scooted away from him. "What do you think you're doing?"

"Going back to sleep, I hope. You have a problem with that?"

"You sleep on the other side. You did say you were a gentleman."

"I'm a gentleman, not an idiot. I have no intention of voluntarily sleeping under a waterfall."

"But I can't have you next to me."

Brayden stood up. "I'm already next to you. Your leg is wrapped in a quarter of my shirt. And if the stock tie isn't dry in the morning, you'll be wearing another quarter of it. I'm sincerely hoping I have another shirt in my saddle bag, or I'll be sneaking into Capitol City clothed only in my vest. Not exactly helpful in remaining inconspicuous. You're also wearing my coat and are hunched in my bedroll. I hardly think dozing ten feet from me is scandalous." Having punched out his thoughts on a single breath, Brayden kicked a tuft of hay, fisted a hip and grunted in frustration.

It was becoming increasingly hard to argue his point with the lovely picture this woman presented. He was shocked at the length of her thick hair. She seemed enveloped in the lush dark, redness of it. He shook his head to rid himself of the thoughts. "And, to be perfectly clear, I am not in the habit of ravaging unwilling and vulnerable women."

Kawley jumped up, stomped her foot with arms spread wide. "I am not vulnerable!"

The coat swung open, leaving her wet, clingy clothes in full view for Brayden to peruse a shapely female frame. He savored the view in all its glory from the tip of her toes upwards.

Kawley realized the change in his demeanor, squeaked and yanked the coat around her. Her face reddened to match the roots of her hair. "You are crude, coarse and I've had enough of this conversation. Watch yourself, sir, because I could take you down if I cared to."

This fiery redhead was quickly becoming an itch in his side. "Need I remind you again that no matter which of us dies, neither of us possesses a shovel?"

"You are wrong again, sir." She pointed to the other side of the barn. "I saw two of them near the workbench last night."

In an unguarded moment, Brayden glanced where she pointed. Within the blink of an eye, he felt a blade at his throat. Her face came around until she was nose to nose with him, blue eyes blazing. He should have protected himself but instead of fear, his confused brain was concentrating on her features—her heart-shaped face, her flawless skin, one tiny freckle on her right cheek, her petite nose and full lips. How could he ever have mistaken her for a man? Again a jolt shot through him like fire. A month ago his insides were coal black ashes. This burgundy blast had sparked a red-hot flame, and the fire was spreading. This was the second time her body had been full length against his. Brayden feared a third. It had been years since he had felt anything, and his lagging spirit thirsted for more.

For what seemed an eternity, they stared into one another's eyes, but Brayden couldn't fathom what was behind her stare. His mind finally returned to the blade at his throat.

"Perhaps I should rephrase the word 'vulnerable'?"

"Me thinks you should." Kawley smiled with scarcely veiled triumph, stepped back and clamped her knife.

"Spouting Shakespeare now? We are plainly not *Romeo and Juliet.* No... definitely more like *Taming of the Shrew*."

"Watch what you say, sir. There's more where that came from."

Brayden chuckled softly, and the mood eased. "That's quite a little weapon you have there. May I see it?"

Kawley hesitated. "Why?" Plainly wary, she handed it to him. "Haven't you ever seen a knife before?"

"I've seen plenty of knives. This is an Ames, isn't it? Think you could actually do damage with this small a blade?"

She jutted her chin at him. "You seemed to think so when it was pressed in your neck. It's sharp enough to reshape your uneven beard without you even feeling the pull."

Not quite believing her boast, Brayden ran his thumb along the blade. It sliced his skin before he could even stop his other hand from moving. A trickle of blood appeared, and he put his thumb to his lips. "I see what you mean." He absently placed his hand at his throat where the blade had pressed against him. "I'm grateful now for your steady hand." He closed the knife and turned it over and over. "Actually, I was more interested in the unique leg shape and the etching. "What does 'KiKi' mean?"

She snatched it from his hand. "Nosy, aren't you?"

"In the interest of peace can we just call it 'interested'?" He sat down against the boards, leaned back his head and closed his eyes. "We can still catch two hours or so of sleep if you'd just think of it as 'interested' or 'intrigued'." When she didn't answer him, he threw a hand in the air in resignation. "Fine. Nosy. I'm a nosy son of a buck."

"Thank you."

He never opened his eyes, but he knew she was smiling just by the tone of her voice and the fact that he heard her sit across from him. They were like two prize fighters, acknowledging one another's strengths and retreating to their separate corners. He found it odd that the very raspiness in her tone which had irritated him when he had thought her a man, was now a delightful sensual huskiness. Yes, the woman across the space from him was a fiery, red enigma.

"Kiki was my family's name for me. But don't you dare ever use it."

Brayden folded his arms and shifted to a more comfortable reclining position. "Wouldn't think of it, Miss Kawley. No ma'am. Wouldn't think of it. Just wanted to know. Good night."

———

Not fully trusting the man sleeping less than ten feet from her, Kawley sat quietly, wrapped in the man's belongings. Was he lying in wait for her to drop her guard? But then again, he hadn't before as she slept. Why would he now? Kawley argued with herself back and forth for nearly an hour while she took the chance to study Brayden's still form. She was surprised that such a tall man could fold himself into such a small package. The tender side of her wondered if he did it purposely as an attempt to put more space between them. The suspicious side wondered if it was his way of giving her a false sense of security. Either way, she was not closing her eyes. She wanted to be on the move toward Capitol

City but traveling in the dark and the rain would be suicide. Kawley yawned and settled herself with a better view and a faster escape path.

Brayden was quite handsome, she decided. That is, if she could get him to allow her to even out the left side of his beard. The stragglers bothered her sense of shape the way a crooked picture sometimes did. Kawley giggled to herself. The beard looked as if he had tried to trim it and failed miserably. How well she knew that being on the trail did nothing for anyone's appearance.

She cocked her head to one side to align her face with Brayden's. Strands of his hair lay across his forehead. Their color was shockingly black against his skin. Had it not been for their silky shine, they could have been drips of tar. She had never known anyone with hair so black. Kawley remembered his eyes behind those closed lids. They were the color of the grass in the pastures of a previous life, a life she sorely missed. He wore a peaceful expression, so incongruous to their situation. She ran her finger along her lips as she stared at his and remembered something her mother had whispered to her years ago. "Why, Kawley, that man has such kissable lips." They had laughed and giggled in their private scandalous conversation. With her mother gone, Kawley hadn't thought of that occasion in years but here it was again. The man sleeping across from her definitely had kissable lips.

A movement with his hand caused her to straighten. Kawley settled back as she realized he was deep asleep when his hand slipped from his crossed arm and lay open and quiet. His hands were large with long, lean fingers. For a fleeting moment she wondered how that hand would feel caressing her cheek, how his lips would feel against hers. She chided herself and shook her head to rid her mind of the ridiculous thoughts. The wall of defense she had erected around herself was crumbling and there didn't seem to be anything she could do about it. She had been on her own for so long that riding with Brayden had taken away her edge. For the first time she gave in to the tension and allowed a single tear to overflow. She squared her shoulders. A moment was all she allowed.

Although her clothes were quickly drying, she pulled his coat tighter around her. With the storm still raging, it gave her an odd sense of security with its pleasing masculine scents. Brandy? Peppermint? Kawley decided either one would rid her mouth of its sour taste. The flask was still attached to Brayden's saddle too far away. Perhaps one of his pockets held a delicious peppermint? Surreptitiously she checked his pockets—no peppermints, only chunks of sweet potatoes. She smiled. To her, it spoke volumes that a man would carry sweet potatoes because his horse was so fond of them.

Patting more pockets she felt the outline of a book. Kawley glanced at Brayden but he was still. She lifted out the book and realized that it was the grey leather journal which had originally fallen from his saddlebag. While keeping sentry on Brayden as he slept, she violated his thoughts and leafed through the pages. The handwriting was even, firm and neat. In a sea of words, he poured out his regrets and hopes. Guilt finally overcame her, and she was just closing the journal when something caught her eye. It was her own name between the lines.

"I know nothing of the woman and yet...And yet what? I don't even know why I insist she ride with me. She has told me parts, yet I feel there is much more to her story. But all of us have a hidden story. God knows I have my own past. I've had trouble glancing at my own reflection in the mirror, fearing my dark secret might be visible for all to see. Some might actually run from me if they knew. The woman's name, Kawley, seems much too coarse a name for her. She is kind and fine and braver than most men I know. I'm ashamed to say that today she actually had me at knifepoint. She is knowledgeable on topics of the day —something I find rare, intriguing and, frankly, refreshing. This red headed woman and I are on a journey together, the end of which I cannot envision. I pray we can find and rescue her brother and Caleb. If there is a way, I have no doubt that Kawley will ride through the portals of fire with me..."

Kawley closed the book; her cheeks burned for her trespass. A sudden movement from the man startled her, and she almost dropped the journal. She was caught red handed but any attempt to slide it back into the pocket might attract too much attention. With a frightened shudder she surreptitiously lowered the book within the folds of her lap, sat stone still, held her breath and waited. The gamble paid off. Brayden never opened his eyes. He shifted his position, cleared his throat and licked his lips. After a moment he appeared to drift soundly once more.

Suffused with a guilt she had never known, she circled her lips and blew out a long, protracted breath. While she deeply regretted her transgression, she had to admit how very much his admiration of her intelligence pleased her. So many men had derided her for it. She appreciated his obvious intention to rescue her brother as well as his friend though he didn't even know him. Yes, this Brayden was unique. She yawned deeply. Perhaps tomorrow she should discover more about the man who had touched her spirit in so many ways. Feeling safer than she had in a long time, she braided her hair, leaned back her head and closed her eyes. She chuckled softly. Perhaps tomorrow she should first discover his family name.

———

The storm had finally abated when the morning haze was rent. Kawley was stiff from the odd cramped position. Brayden was stretched out on his side, his head nestled in his folded arm. The shredded ends of his shirt exposed a peek at his taut belly. Smooth dark hair trailed in a thin line that disappeared beneath his breeches. He had dark circles under his eyes, plainly evident of restless nights of concern for his friend. Still, even asleep on a mattress of straw, he cut a fine figure of a man.

Kawley assumed that her own dark circles would only add to her masculine disguise. She stretched out her injured leg and stifled a cry. Lifting her trouser leg, she removed the makeshift bandage and examined the wound. It was still an angry red and a bit swollen, but at least she could look at it without feeling bile rise in her throat. Unfortunately, the shirttail bandage was wet with the ooze from the wound.

"How does it look today?"

She jumped with the sudden intrusion on her silence. The movement jerked her leg and she hissed. "Don't startle me like that." She dabbed her leg with the bandage to wipe off the fluid.

Brayden rose, stretched and walked—no, glided would be a better word—to the water pump. He sucked in a mouthful of water, sloshed it inside his mouth and spit it out. Then he filled his hands with water, splashed his face and finger combed his hair several times. She wondered his age because his long, silky hair sported several strands of gray, made more prominent with the water. "Good morning to you, too, Miss Kawley."

How she did cherish the 'Miss' before her name. She gave him a quick nod in acknowledgment of her rudeness. "Sorry."

Brayden retrieved the tin and flask from his saddle bag and sat near her. "Apology accepted. Now let's have a look at that leg." He took the wet shirttail from her and made a wry face. "This bandage has done all that it can do." He tossed it to the side.

"Why did you throw it in the dirt. Now what will we use for a bandage?"

He chortled and cast her a sly grin. "Brayden Wakefield is ever the source of fresh bandages." He unbuttoned his cuff and ripped off his sleeve. "Voila, Miss Kawley, ma'am. One fresh bandage." He held up his other arm. "With another staying warm for the next wound change."

She could not help but smile at his obvious attempt to put her at ease. "Do you really need to burn it again?"

"I can burn it with gunpowder or my brew. Your choice but we really need the powder for protection."

Kawley steeled herself for the moments of fire by grabbing Brayden's arm and burying her face. "Do it." She heard the top flip as he unscrewed the flask, but the burn didn't happen. She waited a moment and then looked up. Brayden was leisurely sipping the flask.

"I needed a little courage before I poured."

"Argh!"

"—and, quite frankly, I was enjoying the feeling of you in my arms."

Kawley ripped the flask from him, sucked a draught and tipped the flask on the wound. The fire caused her to choke and cough.

"I would have done that for you. Now you've wasted your generous mouthful." When the gash had finished dripping, he lathered it with the salve and wound the sleeve around it. "We should change it again in a few hours."

"There's something I have to take care of before we mount up."

Brayden nodded. "Don't wander far. Could be Yankee scouts in the woods."

"It's not me I'm talking about. It's you."

"Me?"

"Yes you, Brayden. It's bad enough you are wandering around with half a shirt." She lifted his chin with her forefinger. "You can't ride out with half a beard."

Brayden lowered his face in obvious abashment of his unkempt appearance. Then he met her stare and smiled. "Perhaps you can even it out for me?"

Kawley discerned an obvious double meaning in his gaze. She dug her knife from her pocket. "With pleasure, sir."

"Whoa. Hold on there. Not with that you're not."

"The shears I saw on the workbench are larger than your whole head. Want me to use those instead?" She attempted to rise but he stopped her.

"Alright, use your knife. But please have a steady hand and leave the flesh intact."

Kawley lifted the hairs of his beard and, true to her boast, sliced through them like butter. She smirked triumphantly as she flicked them away and continued cutting. Brayden sat obediently while she turned his face from side to side assuring herself of the evenness and shape. His eyes studied her intently the entire time, from her chin to her hairline, then back to her eyes as if he were attempting to delve deep inside her. His face was so close she could feel his breath on her cheek.

"There. You now look quite the gentleman instead of a renegade." She sat back but Brayden never moved. Her senses reeled as he continued to gaze at her. "Yes. It's perfect except—" She reached for his chin. "—for a strand right here." Kawley leaned into him and gently tugged at his beard until his face was a hairsbreadth away. Then, as lightly as she could, touched his kissable lips with her own.

"Oh my," she whispered, quickly averting her face. "Mama would have said that was very unladylike."

Brayden tugged one of her braids until she looked at him. He coiled the braids on top of her head and secured them with her hat. "But you weren't dressed like a lady when you kissed me so it doesn't count—" He slid his hand behind her neck. "—and neither does this."

Kawley melted into the softness of his touch. His lips touched hers once but didn't demand, rather implored. She waited. When he kissed her again, he didn't rush; he seemed to savor. She didn't know how to react, how to respond. She had never been treated this way.

She reluctantly pulled away. "We should be on our way."

Brayden appeared as awkward as she felt. He cleared his throat as he rose and offered her his hand. "Yes. We have a lot of miles to cover." As she turned to walk away, he pulled her back.

"You neatened my beard. Now allow me to neaten yours. Come to the pump."

Brayden ripped off the cuff of his remaining sleeve. He shrugged his shoulders. "We need what's left of the sleeve for another bandage." He wet the cuff and wiped her face, especially under her eyes. "I know your leg hurts, but tear tracks would be a dead giveaway."

Kawley tried to turn away. "I wasn't crying."

He held fast by her arm. "I know you weren't. Just saying is all. If you are going to keep up this cover, then you have to do it right. Now cover your eyes."

She closed her eyes, and he blew dirt on her face. It felt disgusting but probably looked better than what she could have done herself.

They saddled the horses and were about to leave when Kawley remembered the stock tie. "Wait." She retrieved it and attempted to put it around his neck, but he stopped her.

"It's still wet."

"Stop whining. It will dry." She smiled. "And besides, with your coat on and the tie in place, no one will realize you have not much of a shirt." She knotted the stock and pinned it. "If you are going to keep up this cover, then you have to do it right."

Brayden's face crinkled just short of a grin. "You know, Miss Kawley, you are quickly becoming the most intriguing comrade I've ever ridden with."

———

Brayden and Kawley rode slowly, giving the horses a rest.

"How's your leg feeling?"

"Throbbing a little."

"I'm glad we changed the bandage a second time. I don't see any fresh blood stains."

Kawley smirked and shook her head. "But now we have no more bandages. You're out of sleeves."

Brayden patted his chest. "Never fear, my lady. I still have the rest of the chest and back if necessary."

"A regular field hospital you are but—"

"But no shovel," they said in unison and laughed, easy, open and comfortable.

When their laughter eased, Kawley realized how good it felt and savored the moment. "Thank you."

Brayden cocked his head to the side. "For what?"

"For your kindness, your flask, your salve—" She chuckled and shrugged her shoulders. "—your sleeves, your help, your company. It's been like a miracle."

"No, Kawley, when we find and rescue Caleb and your brother, that will be a miracle. The rest of it was just lucky I guess."

"Lucky?"

"Yes, ma'am. You lucky that coward's shot wasn't higher and me lucky that you didn't shoot me before you could find out what a perfect gentleman I am." Brayden flashed her a quick nod and winked. He gathered his reins. "Ready?"

Before Kawley could chirrup to her mount, she stiffened. "Hear that?"

"Yes. That's somebody making some fast tracks." He stood in his stirrups and strained to see clearly behind them. He spun back and kicked into his horse's sides. "Into the woods. Now!"

Pickles had already sensed the excitement and reared. Kawley urged her forward to no avail. Brayden flew alongside, grabbed her reins and pulled the two of them into the woods. He reached into his pocket and handed her a fistful of sweet potato bits.

"Keep feeding them to Pickles so hopefully she won't nicker and give away our position."

Brayden offered the same to Ajax as the two of them waited to see who was in such a hurry. They didn't have to wait long. A rider galloped past their hiding spot.

Kawley stood in her stirrups and leaned forward. "Wasn't that—" A group of five, maybe six riders galloped in the same direction as the rider they were plainly chasing. "Brayden, wasn't that first rider your friend, Fletcher?"

Brayden shook his head. "Couldn't be. Fletcher is supposed to be with Rush and Clive at the old Seneca Mission."

"Then Fletcher has a twin because he looked just like the man you were traveling with when I was trailing you. And one of the horses in the group hounding him had a Union brand."

"How did you notice all that in the two seconds they flew by?"

Kawley shrugged her shoulders. "I'm a woman, remember? My father said we notice everything so we have plenty to gossip about."

"Then let's do some hounding of our own. If they are Union, then maybe they have more information of Caleb and Riley. Ever play fox and hounds?"

"Sure did." Kawley gathered her reins. She apparently legged Pickles too hard because the mare shot out of the woods like a bullet and bucked.

"Stay on there since we're nearly out of bandages." He legged Ajax to catch her and the two galloped after the group. Once they had the riders in sight they fired into the air, turned, doubled back and circled around. The riders did as expected, stopped and turned, clearly confused. The lone rider had put some distance between them but he, too, stopped and then circled around and doubled back.

"They don't know, but that rider clearly understands what we did." Brayden smacked Kawley's shoulder. "Come on. It's our turn."

The game for survival continued for nearly an hour until the group was finally chasing their tails and had ridden off in the wrong direction at a frantic gallop.

"I think that lone rider is safely on his own by now. Let's give the horses a rest." Brayden dismounted and arched his back. He held the mare while Kawley threw her leg over and sprung to the ground. Leaning over, he rested a hand on each knee and heaved a heavy sigh. "For a while there, it seemed more like cat and mouse than fox and hounds. Things got a bit out of hand, and I wasn't quite sure we'd lose them." When Kawley didn't answer, he glanced up at her. Her eyes were wide as saucers.

"Ah, apparently we didn't," she whispered.

Brayden turned to face a blue coated rider with a pistol aimed straight at them.

"Some of us play fox and hounds up North, too." He flashed them a quick nod fairly dripping with sarcasm. "You may have sent the others on your goose chase, but I knew I was right." He pointed the pistol first at Brayden, then at Kawley and back again. "I'm tired and hungry, and I'm not heading back without a trophy to prove I was right. Which one of you wants it first?"

"Look friend." Brayden put his hands in the air. "We can give you whatever you want to take back. You don't have to kill anyone."

"I'm not your friend, and I can tell by your accent that you're one of them dirty rebels. Because of you, I'm down here sleeping on the ground and eating dust and biscuits with maggots. Two less vermin is still two less vermin." He pointed the pistol at Brayden. "You first?"

"Listen—"

In a flash the intruder shifted his aim. "All right…him." He fired.

"No!" Brayden screamed and lunged in front of Kawley. He went down into her and the shocking force twisted him backwards. Shots seemed to ring out from nowhere, and he rolled to protect her. As they rolled, he grabbed his pistol and fired until it was empty. The barrage of death finally stopped.

Brayden lifted his head and panicked when he saw Kawley's closed eyes beneath him. "Are you all right? Are you hit?" When she didn't answer, he shook her shoulders and arched his neck at the surprising pain it cost him. "Talk to me. Are you hit?"

"N-no. I don't think so." Kawley opened her eyes. "Oh God, but you are."

With Kawley safe, his mind exploded with the pain. He managed to slither off Kawley to view the rider motionless on the ground and his horse a few yards away. With a raging fire in his shoulder growing by the second, Brayden feared his ability to fend off any new threats.

"Bry, thank God you're not dead. When I saw you fall, I feared the worst."

He knew that voice! Brayden scrambled awkwardly to shove Kawley's hat back on her head. He attempted to rise only to fall back down, fighting a wicked dizziness. An odd warmth flooded his chest. "You sure took your sweet time getting here," he fired through clenched teeth. He shook his head to clear it and grasped his shoulder. "What are you doing here anyway?"

Fletcher jumped from his horse, dragged Brayden to a nearby tree and lowered him to the ground. "When you didn't show up at the mission, I left Rush and Clive to scout there, and I doubled back. I was worried something had happened." His face was flushed, and he was breathing hard. "Apparently I was right." He knelt on one side of Brayden as Kawley knelt on the other.

Brayden saw the quizzical expression of Fletcher's face. He whizzed his forefinger back and forth. "Fletcher, Kawley. Kawley, Fletcher." When Fletcher's expression did not change, Brayden gritted his teeth, heaved his hips to a less painful position and waved his hand in dismissal. "Long story...don't ask."

"Wasn't going to, Bry. First let's get a look at that shoulder." He gingerly helped remove Brayden's coat. "Good Lord, man. Where's the rest of your shirt?"

Brayden frantically flipped his hand, in too much pain to answer.

"Another long story?"

With his eyes clamped shut Brayden nodded, hissed and grabbed again at his shoulder. "Shot or not, I s-surely do appreciate your showing up when you did. If you hadn't t-taken him out, we'd be two dead trophies." He couldn't control his shaking.

Fletcher shook his head and made a wry face. "I didn't shoot him."

With the hair on the back of his neck bristling on alert, Brayden looked at Kawley and back at Fletcher. "If you didn't, then I hit him?" He willed himself to not pass out.

"No, I did." A voice from behind the trees startled them. A lean long-limbed fellow appeared with a rifle held to his side.

Oh dear God, what now? Bloodied or not, Brayden's primal instincts kicked in. Was the stranger friend or foe? The intruder's brown hair hung around the shoulders of his striped shirt, and a feather was tucked into the brim of his hat. "Fletcher, be ready," he whispered.

The other man took a step forward. "I saw you all playing fox and hounds. At first it was amusing to watch even if I didn't like the odds. I would have killed the lot of them if I thought I could have taken them." He kicked at the motionless body. "Then I saw this brute sneaking back, and I had a feeling the bastard was up to no good." Seeming satisfied with the deed, he turned to them but did not approach further. "Name's Oscar Weston." He flipped a finger in Brayden's direction. "How bad did he get him?"

"Bad enough."

"He just winged me," Brayden forced out, trying to believe his own words.

"I'll be the judge of that." Fletcher poked and prodded at the gaping bleeding holes. Brayden moaned loudly despite his best efforts to keep silent. The pain was increasing with every passing moment.

"Best I can tell, Bry, the shot went clean through but probably ricocheted off a bone because it tore a hell of a lot on its way out." He ripped off more cloth from Brayden's shirt and twisted it around the wounds.

"Keep pressure on this," he told Kawley. Then he took off Brayden's stock and bound the shoulder. "That will have to do for now until we find a doctor."

Oscar took two steps toward them. "I'm afraid there hasn't been a doctor around these parts for more than a year. From the amount of blood, looks like that shoulder needs major tending and right soon. If you think you can get him on his horse, you can come home with me. It's not too far." He jerked his chin toward the body on the ground. "Hell, since I had a good day hunting, I'll even give the big guy another shirt. My wife would probably take it kindly if you'd stay for a meal. The little spud with you looks like he could use a square meal." He turned to his horse and mounted.

"Aren't we going to bury the body?" Kawley asked.

Oscar walked his horse over to the dead body and spit on it. "I wouldn't do him the courtesy. The damn, dirty blue coats shot my boy for trying to protect his dog. Rotting is too good for the son of a bitch." As if he noticed that no one spoke, he threw his hand in the air. "Besides, I don't have a shovel." He turned his horse and started walking.

Weakened by the loss of blood, Brayden coughed to keep from chuckling and glanced at Kawley. She appeared to be busying herself folding Brayden's coat. Their eyes met, and she pursed her lips.

Fletcher rose. "Let's try to get you mounted."

Much as he wanted the help, Brayden shook off his offer. Despite the pain, it somehow bothered him that Kawley should see him as weak. "I'm fine…leave me be."

"You've got gaping holes in your shoulder, and your face is as gray as Nana Hazel's shawl. You're not fine." Fletcher glanced at his bloodied hands, looked around, then yanked out his shirttail and wiped the stains from his hands. "Stop being so damn stubborn. That stock is not likely to hold it together for long. Those wounds need threading." He leaned down and offered his hand.

Again Brayden slapped his hand away. "I said, I'm fine." It was an awkward, painful struggle but when Ajax cooperated and knelt, Brayden growled and managed to pull himself into the saddle with his good arm. Kawley tied his coat to the back of his saddle.

When they were all mounted, Oscar turned back. "Long as I'm bringing all of you along, I think names might be in order."

"Sorry. I'm Fletcher Stedman and this is my good friend, Brayden Wakefield."

"And the quiet spud with you?"

Kawley urged her horse forward. "I'm neither quiet nor a little spud. I'm a gentleman like yourself, and my name is Kawley Chatterton."

Oscar stared at Kawley for a few seconds and then grunted. "Kawley, you say, huh?" He turned his horse and kicked him forward. "Once had a cow named Kawley," he yelled over his shoulder. He nodded a few times. "I really liked that cow."

Even bloodied, nauseated and dizzy, if it wouldn't have hurt too much to remount, Brayden knew he would have fallen off his horse with laughter. By the way she tossed her shoulders, he assumed Kawley didn't see the humor.

CHAPTER FIVE

KAWLEY WAS STILL SHAKING WHEN SHE ENTERED THE SEMI-DARKENED room. The ride to Oscar's had seemed interminable. She watched Brayden suffer through the first few miles and noticed he was slumping lower with each stride. She reined her horse closer to Fletcher.

"Fletcher, I don't think Brayden is going to make it to Oscar's under his own power."

"I was thinking the same thing. Oscar, pull up." Fletcher dismounted and stared at Kawley. "Little man, take my reins." He took two strides away and turned back. "And make sure you don't lose him! You can lose yourself, I don't care." He shook an authoritative finger at his horse. "But don't you dare lose this horse."

When Fletcher leaned alongside of Ajax, Brayden didn't protest. He was teetering precariously offside, as if he could no longer balance himself. The reason was painfully obvious. The bandage was not holding, and he was bleeding profusely. Fletcher put his foot in the stirrup and threw his leg over Ajax. He grasped Brayden around the waist, took the reins in one hand and pushed the cloth harder into Brayden's shoulder with the other. "Lean back into me, Bry. I've got you. Let's get there as fast as we can."

They galloped to Oscar's and fairly dragged a mumbling, stumbling Brayden to a back room. Kawley remembered meeting Ada, Oscar's wife, but all of the scurrying after that was mostly a blur of pouring whiskey, ripping bandages and emptying bowls of bloody water. Yet, certain moments of Fletcher's panic stood out vividly in her mind. It was the quiver in his voice that shot fear through her. How much blood could Brayden lose and still live? The scene replayed over and over in her head, each time more vivid that the first...

———

"Damn. It's worse than I thought. We can't stitch these wounds until we dig out all the dirt and debris," Fletcher muttered. "We don't have the right instruments to reach in there, and I don't have the skills. I'm not a doctor with his bag of tricks."

Oscar flicked his hand. "Well, today you have to be. Think of him as that big gelding out there you seem to love so much. It will steady your hand."

"But he's not my horse. He's my friend."

"That he is. All the more reason for you to get to it." Oscar glanced around. "Ada, bring me your sewing box. Hurry. Maybe there's something in there that we can use."

Ada dropped her sewing tools as well as a variety of cooking utensils on a plate and poured whiskey over them. Oscar and Fletcher chose several pieces and dug in the holes, retrieving bits of bloodied cloth and pebbles while Brayden groaned and writhed beneath their ministrations.

"Too much blood, Fletcher," Oscar warned. "Stitch now or we might lose him."

"I know! I know! Don't you think I know that?" He growled and shifted positions. "For God's sake, little man, hold the lamp closer. I can barely see what I'm doing."

Kawley held the lamp closer. She did not envy Fletcher's position. He held his friend's very life in his hands, hands that lacked the knowledge and skill to save him.

She watched Fletcher's quivering hand twist and turn in the wounds over and over again. His eyebrows were scrunched together and beads of sweat dripped down his temple. He shook his head, wiped his brow on his sleeve and threw the pinchers in the bowl.

"I can't do this!"

"You can."

"No, I can't. Shoving my fingers in there is probably doing more damage than good."

Oscar grabbed Fletcher's wrist and forced him forward. "My gut tells me that if it were you bleeding out, your friend there would punch his whole fist in your shoulder to save you."

Fletcher stared at Brayden for a full minute as though terrified his friend might die beneath his touch. He sucked in a deep breath and grabbed the tools from the alcohol. "All right. Hold him." Every time Brayden cried out, and Fletcher flinched. "I'm sorry, Bry," he repeated over and over, seemingly a litany to calm himself as he dug again and again. Finally and delicately he lifted a small bloody piece. He tossed it in the pile. "There, I have it. Best I can do."

Finally satisfied the wounds were clean, the two men had then worked frantically to stitch the jagged edges, but the flesh refused to hold. They had had no choice left but to cauterize.

———

Through the entire inept doctoring, Kawley hadn't uttered a word, had been struggling to not heave her insides. In the woods she had witnessed blood and guts from every direction, some of which had saturated her clothes. She rubbed the inside of her left arm. Brayden's blood was still damp on her sleeve and the front of her vest. Later she intended to attempt rinsing it but for the moment, Kawley just wanted peace and quiet and the reassurance that Brayden would survive. His blood was literally on her hands; she didn't want it there figuratively, too.

Brayden now lay shirtless, draped across the chaise. His left shoulder was tightly bound with another band around his chest, forming a sling for his arm. His right leg hung down with his stockinged foot on the floor as if he had attempted to rise and failed. His left knee jerked every few seconds. Eyes closed, his breathing was shallow. His face held a grimace, and he emitted an odd clucking noise, most likely his body trying to deal with the pain but clearly showing the torture of his wounds.

She waited several minutes and watched him. The hand encased in the band was fisted, periodically stretched open, shook and then dragged closed again into a tight fist. She could hear his fingernails scrape across the linen bandage.

Kawley savored the length of him. How was it possible that even wounded he was devastatingly dashing? She chided herself that she could have puerile thoughts at such an inappropriate time. Still, she remembered the feel of his body full length against hers as he shielded her from the gunfire. He had wrapped himself around her and held her so tightly that it was difficult to breathe. She had never experienced those sensations in her life. Staring at his half naked body now, she wasn't sure whether it was the fear of death or the feel of him that had taken her breath away. The memory made her weak in the knees. Why had he shielded her? Why had he sacrificed himself? If he hadn't done so, the shot would have hit her in the head. It would have been her rotting corpse out there. Instead, she was fine, and he was profoundly suffering.

She had seen the hole in his shoulder where the shot had ripped through him and the torn, jagged holes in his back where it raged out. The cloths in the bowl next to him were saturated with his blood. Everyone was too exhausted to have even carried them away. Vile mucus gushed in her throat when she recalled how the cloths were thrown there as they worked on him. She had wanted to cover her ears to block out the wretched sounds he spewed, but they made her help hold Brayden down as they cleansed the bloody holes and pressed the red-hot metal to his lesions.

With his head thrown back, the vessels had bulged in his neck as he gurgled remnants of the whiskey forced on him. She nearly fainted from relief when he had finally passed out. When they were finished, Fletcher had buried his face in a towel and sat hunched over for a long while. His shoulders had visibly shaken.

He had risen abruptly and thrown the towel on the floor. "I need a drink and some air."

When he passed her, he had stopped and cast Kawley a glare as scorching as the sizzling blade he had just used. Oscar was on Fletcher's heels when the two of them shot out the door.

Kawley remembered the welcomed silence as she now sat riddled with guilt and the images that would haunt her forever. Brayden was enduring all this because he had insisted she ride with him, had offered his help. Again, she asked herself why. Always questions with no answers.

She finally gathered the courage to step closer and check on him. She approached him on tiptoe, but the floorboard squeaked on the fourth step. She stopped. Brayden's eyes opened and closed several times, then closed again. Hopefully the whiskey was holding the worst of the pain at bay. She continued closer and eased a hip next to him. Feelings new to her were bombarding her mind.

His skin was bronzed, not pale as she would have assumed it to be. It somehow added to the enigmatic allure of the man. His chest was covered with smooth, dark hair, well-muscled and beautifully proportioned. He made her feel so safe that she wanted to crawl inside his skin. Instead she reached out her hand to touch him but lost her nerve and yanked it back. She drank in the sight and sound of this man who had risked his life to save hers. Again she reached out a hand and touched the backs of her fingers to his taut skin.

He flinched as his right hand took her wrist and lifted her hand from him. "Don't. D-don't touch me. Not now."

Thinking him asleep his voice shocked her, and she tried to pull away, but he held her fast. "I'm sorry, Brayden. Did I hurt you?"

"Everything...hurts but I'm also very d-drunk and this is very d-dangerous." His eyes opened and stared at her. "Because I h-hurt women."

Kawley's voice failed her. She felt her composure slipping but she tried to sound casual. "Ada is in the summer kitchen. Fletcher and Oscar said they arranged for you to stay abed here to regain your strength. They went to the stable to bed the horses and see Oscar's stallion. Fletcher told me to keep an eye on you."

Brayden still held her wrist prisoner. "An eye, not a h-hand." He finally released her, but he did so one finger at a time. "Kawley, I've h-hurt every w-woman who has ever cared for me." He pushed his knuckles into his temple as if trying to block out a savage pain. Whether it was the present or a painful past she didn't know. "The last one I k-killed."

Her hand flew to her mouth. Was a murder the secret he had referred to in his grey journal? Is that why he wrote people would run from him if they knew the truth? Her heart pounded in her ears as if she had run the journey to Oscar's on foot. She shivered more every passing minute. Had she spent days and miles with a murderer? Her mind was racing, and she stepped back from him. She shuddered thinking she might have spent the night in a barn sleeping across from a cold-blooded killer. Her trembling finger touched her lips. Had she kissed a murderer?

Brayden closed his eyes and lay quiet. Was he gauging her reaction?

While she watched him, she remembered how tenderly he had dressed her leg wound, how softly his lips had touched her own. Could his gentlemanly behavior have been merely a veneer to conceal something dark and sinister? She had known another and felt the consequences when the veneer crumbled. Could Brayden be the same? Could his hands that had been so gentle with her, be the same hands that could have snuffed out the life of another? Could she really have been that wrong in her assessment of him? Part of her wanted to saddle Pickles and hightail it out of there before the others returned but memories of Brayden's kindness pushed her to press on. Apparently, the loss of blood and the whiskey had loosened his tongue and his guard.

"Killed?" Her voice sounded more of a croak. She cleared her throat. "Did you say killed?"

"Yes. I...I k-killed her."

The word lingered in the air for several moments. The silence was so heavy and frightening that Kawley was physically unable to find her feet and flee. The fingers that covered her lips trembled so hard that she raised her other hand to stop it.

"I d-didn't know...I s-should have known when she...when she...and then it h-happened. So fast. Dear God, so f-fast. She w-withered and d-died because of me. I caused her death because—" He coughed and swallowed. "—because I couldn't—" He frowned. "—because I'm not cap...not capable of love. It's j-just not in me." He seemed to force out the last part, and his words were slurred, but she finally realized what he meant.

Though she didn't know the circumstances, she sensed his inner torment and desolation. She nearly collapsed with relief as her defenses subsided.

"No. You're wrong. You're so wrong, Brayden. How could you even think such a thing, especially after what just happened? What you did today was the ultimate act, the ultimate coin. You sacrificed yourself for me. The man you describe would never have done so. You barely know me and yet your protection was the greatest act of concern and devotion. Please, I want to know why."

Brayden didn't answer. He heaved a deep sigh and, as his chest lifted and fell, his face contorted with the stab of torture the movement must have cost him. "I don't...know." His whole body stiffened. "I don't...know. Maybe I couldn't b-bear another life on my conscience."

She covered the space between them in three strides and brushed the backs of her fingers across his forehead and down his cheek. "Shhh. Be still. Everything's all right." The tips of her fingers touched his chest, then her whole hand, trying to soothe his agitation. His skin was smooth and warm. "Your conscience is clear, Brayden. I'm a bit bruised and bloodied but otherwise fine." She took his hand and laid it over her heart. "Can you feel my heart beating? It's whole and beating strong because of you."

With his eyes clamped shut, he shook his head and tried to pull his hand away. "I h-hurt women, Kawley." The crack in his voice evidenced his misery.

She knew it was unfair to take advantage of his vulnerability, but she feared he might never offer another unguarded moment. Unless she trespassed again in his journal, his thoughts were forever hidden from her. Kawley kissed his hand and down his arm. She entwined her arm around his, leaned down and kissed his shoulder, his chest, his neck. "But you said while I'm dressed as a man, none of this counts, remember? Mama could not chide me that I was acting unladylike. Look at me, Brayden." When he didn't respond, she pressed him again. "Brayden, look at me."

His green eyes opened and delved hers. They captivated her, but even as he lay wounded, she could sense the power coiled within him. Slowly his right hand slid behind her neck. He pulled her to him, and his whole body shuddered. His arm trembled as though attempting to quiet a groan.

"Brayden, don't move. You'll break open your wounds."

This time his deep, husky voice was smooth as velvet. "I thought if I c-closed my eyes you would flee. I m-must be d-dreaming because you're still here." Just before his lips touched hers, he murmured, "I know all this is the p-pain and whiskey but, oh God, you f-feel so real,

Kiki." He covered her mouth, robbed her of breath and will, until the back of her mind wondered at his strength and tenacity.

When he pulled back, his head fell into the pillow and his arm flopped to the side. He lay still and limp. Kawley thought he had passed out again but then she saw the corners of his mouth crinkle, giving her the distinct impression a devil's grin lurked just below the surface. "I must be...so...so damn drunk. What is the n-name of that whiskey? I'll t-take a barrel of it." He reached for her again. "The best p-part about dreams, Kiki—" He kissed her again. "—is you can keep begging for more—" His lips grazed hers. "—and more—" The kiss deepened. "—and more."

Kawley trailed her fingers through his thick hair and answered his need. It somehow pleased her that he had whispered her familial name. "The best part about dreams is you won't remember any of this." She kissed, embraced and soothed him until he drifted. Then she set his right arm along his side and raised his leg again on the chaise.

Yes, he was an enigma, a dark-haired green-eyed mystery. The jagged, mangled flesh of his shoulder was presumably a mere scratch when compared to the senseless battle in his mind. What she had just witnessed suggested that tucked under his authoritative, assured mien lay a soul cruelly nailed to a past. It left her with little doubt that many pages of his grey journal were just as raw and tortured. She smoothed the hair from his face and kissed his very kissable lips. His eyes opened. Merely inches apart, the moment seemed to go on forever.

"Rest now, Brayden Wakefield."

His lids fell. His head slowly slid to the side, and he seemed to slip away with deep, even breaths.

"Yes, rest now and heal."

———

Kawley was dozing in a chair outside the back room when Fletcher and Oscar's return from the stable yanked her to full alertness. Fletcher's stare told her that the moment of explanations had arrived.

Fletcher inclined his head toward the door. "How is he?"

"Still sleeping."

"Bleeding stopped?"

Kawley nodded. "As best I can tell. A few stains here and there but nothing major last I checked." She fisted her hands so he wouldn't see her shaking.

"All right, young man. Kawley is it?"

Kawley nodded again and scratched behind her ear.

"First of all, I want to know why Brayden took that shot for you. When I saw him drop, I feared he was dead."

"Truthfully, I've been asking myself that same question over and over because I have not a clue as to what he was thinking."

Fletcher widened his stance and fisted each hip. "Then can you answer me where you met up with Brayden and why he allowed you to ride with him?"

She was about to explain the where and what for, but it seemed all jumbled in her head with this giant man hovering over her with his withering stare. Kawley stood to meet his glare. "I think my brother was kidnapped by the same mob that has your friend, Caleb," she blurted out.

Fletcher's scowl grew more intense, and he grabbed her arm. "How do you know this?"

Her temper flared, and she snatched her arm away. "Keep your hands off me." She rubbed the spot where his fingers had dug into her flesh.

He stepped back, clearly shocked by the rebuff. "Then answer my questions and be quick about it. I have one friend missing and another back there in sore need of a doctor. If you have information about any of this, then spit it out."

"Brayden and I met up when he doubled back after you and your friends left for the Seneca Mission—"

"You know about the mission?"

She cast him a withering stare of her own for his rudeness. "I was trailing my brother's kidnappers and ended up trailing you. I was nearby when I heard you and Brayden talking."

"So Brayden was right. We were being dogged."

"Yes, you were, and by somebody other than me," she said matter-of-factly. She shifted from one foot to the other. "After Brayden and I had gone a spell, we came across a deserter. From what Brayden and I could force out of him, that mob held two men prisoner and were headed east. As he died, he mentioned a name that put the fear of God into me. Don't know who the two prisoners were but if it's them, your friend and my brother might be headed to Old Capitol."

"Old Capitol? The prison in Capitol City?" Oscar asked from across the room.

Kawley leaned around Fletcher. "Don't know for sure but it's the only lead there's been so far."

Oscar whistled softly and scratched his forehead. "Heard bad things about that place. Could just be rumors meant to scare everyone. Can't really say for certain. Tough patrols and weekly hangings." He snapped his mouth shut when it seemed he realized he had spoken his thoughts out loud. He lifted his chin. "Tough to escape but not impossible," he added in a rush. "You just need a plan so insane the guards wouldn't think of it and someone insane enough to pull it off." He cleared his throat. "Like I said, tough but not impossible."

"Anyhow, that's all I know." Kawley turned to Fletcher. "Brayden and I were headed to the mission to meet you when all of this—" She made a circle with her forefinger. "—started. You found us and you know the rest." She hitched a thumb toward the back room. "He going to be all right?"

Fletcher shrugged his shoulders. "You mean if my awkward ministrations didn't kill him? I think we cleaned that shoulder pretty well and the bleeding seems to have stopped although he did lose one hell of a lot of blood. That'll take down even a strong man like Bry."

"I've seen wounds as bad before," Oscar added. "If he's lucky and there's no infection, I expect he'll heal."

Fletcher grunted and turned as if to move away but then swiveled back toward Kawley with an expression that spit barbs. "Leastwise you, little man, had sure as hell better pray he heals." There was a palpable threat in his words that caused Kawley to shudder. If Brayden died, the consequences would be dire. Her hide would be on the block; Fletcher would see to that. As much as she wanted to be certain Brayden would be up and about, it was definitely time to be back on her own.

Ada entered and crossed the room. She turned and smiled.

"You may be too young to know better, but a gentleman takes his hat off in front of a lady."

Fletcher reached for her hat but Kawley saw him out of the corner of her eye, and she jumped out of the way before he could touch her.

"Leave the boy be," Ada said in a soft voice.

Fletcher seemed intent on removing her hat but Kawley ducked out of the way again.

"I said to leave the boy be," Ada shouted. "Micah always wore his hat in the house." Her hand flew to her mouth, and she ran from the room sniffling.

"Ada's having a really hard time without Micah," Oscar muttered. "I can't seem to find a way to comfort her." He made a pistol with his hand, aimed, fired and blew away the imaginary smoke from his pistol finger. "Maybe if she killed a Yankee or two, she'd feel better."

Kawley rolled her eyes, slammed her hat tighter on her head and stammered, "Maybe I'll go and, ah, apologize." She was still shaken by the close encounter with Fletcher and wanted an excuse to move. "Maybe I can do something for her."

"You're welcome to try," Oscar said as she passed him to leave the room.

"Make it a proper apology," Fletcher called. "And take off that hat."

After a short awkward search, Kawley found Ada two rooms away. She wasn't quite sure what to say but felt the need to say something. "You and your husband have been so very kind. I apologize if I did anything to upset you."

Ada smiled and appeared perfectly composed, a composure that seemed out of place considering her outburst moments before. One hand was across her waist and the other was hidden in the fold of her dress. "Come in, young man. I wanted to talk to you alone and that outburst was a gamble to see if you would follow me."

Kawley stiffened and pulled at her collar with her fingers. "I don't understand. What do you mean it was a gamble? If you wanted to talk to me all you need do was ask."

The older woman shook her head. "The others would have become suspicious and this opportunity now would never have presented itself."

Kawley's senses bristled, and she stepped back. "Please talk plainly, Mrs. Weston. If you have something to say to me, then say it. Otherwise, I'm leaving."

Oscar's wife stood, walked to the door and locked it. As she turned, her dress folds opened. She lifted her arm and her hand held a derringer aimed directly at Kawley. "I want you to move over here and do exactly as I say." Her foot scooted the rug back. She tapped her foot and a floorboard flipped up. "In that hole is a handle. I want you to turn it and lift the door."

Kawley wanted to call out, but the crazed woman might pull the trigger, so her senses told her to remain silent.

"I see from your expression that you are thinking of yelling for help, thinking I'm an unhinged grieving mother." She smiled a confusing, cryptic smile. "While part of that might be true, if you are who you say you are, you have nothing to fear from me."

The trap door opened with stairs leading into a darkened hole. Ada motioned with the pistol. "Down, please."

With nothing to do but oblige, Kawley lowered herself to the floor. Ada followed with amazing speed and agility. The light from above cast eerie shadows. Kawley's heart made a pounding thud in her ears. It grew nearly deafening. "What do you want from me?"

"I want nothing from you." Again she smiled. "I want every chance *for* you."

"I don't understand." Kawley backed a few steps.

"Those men upstairs may be totally blind, but I know a woman when I see one."

Kawley wrung her hands and frantically searched for an answer. "I...I don't know what you mean."

"Only a woman's tenderness and empathy would have followed me to apologize."

"Stop it," Kawley protested. "I'm as good as the next man."

"No, you're not." Ada lowered the gun. "You're better."

Kawley was powerless to object as Ada approached and reached for her hat. When the long braids fell around her, Kawley's shoulders shook. "Why are you doing this?"

"Because I heard you talking about heading into the gates of hell, and I want you to have a chance of coming back."

Kawley was now more intrigued than scared. "What do you know about Old Capitol?"

Ada snorted. The woman who moments ago appeared frail and broken, suddenly stood tall and confident. "More than I care to."

"I don't understand. How do you know?" Kawley's thumping heart was now racing for a different reason. "Mrs. Weston, if you can give us any information that would help...I mean...we're not even sure that's where they are."

Ada took Kawley's arm. "Settle down, stop rambling and please, call me Ada." She struck a match and lit a lamp. There was a bench nearby as well as shelving filled with put up fruits and vegetables. As if she read Kawley's mind again, she smiled. "Yes, Kawley, I brought you to the root cellar."

Kawley lowered her eyes. "Sorry. But when you locked the door, and pulled out the derringer, I didn't know what else to think."

"I didn't lock the door. I just clicked it so you would think it was locked. I had to be sure of you, and I know that down here you would not be discovered."

Kawley allowed herself a soft giggle. "You were very convincing."

Ada seemed to preen under the praise. "Thank you. I have to be to survive."

"To survive? Mrs. Weston—"

"Ada, please."

Kawley swallowed hard in frustration. "Ada, you are being very mysterious."

"What I'm about to tell you must be just between us." Ada moved closer. "Even Oscar does not know because he would never allow it."

"Allow what?"

"Since Micah was murdered, I have been a courier. I have moved messages behind enemy lines as well as brought morphine and quinine for our brave men."

Kawley sat down with a thud. "I would never have thought it of you."

"No one does, and that's why it works." She smacked her lips. "Unfortunately right now I have no laudanum to offer you for your friend because my supplies are empty."

"You two all right down there?" Oscar's voice boomed down the steps.

"Yes, husband. Kawley was helping me move some items down here. We will be there directly."

Ada turned back to Kawley. "We don't have much time. Oscar will

advise that if you make it to Capitol City glean information in the pubs."
She shook her head. "Don't do it. Your voices will give you away.
Instead, furtively seek out a woman named Belinda Dunigan. She is well
known and will be easy to find. No one will question you if you are
careful and wear what I give you. Belinda will give you much needed
weekly information about Old Capitol. She will also lend you all the
clothes and disguises you need. I'm certain she will help in any plan you
devise. But speak to Belinda and only Belinda. Be wary of a woman
named Brooke. I don't remember her last name. I've just heard that
grisly woman is the eyes and ears of Ben Crawford, head of Old
Capitol."

"Ada, you comin' up here soon?" Oscar's voice carried a tone of
impatience.

"How do you slip out, Ada? Seems Oscar keeps a close eye on you."

The other woman smiled. "Every good root cellar has its secrets."

Kawley moved toward the stairs but Ada stopped her. The smile had
disappeared.

"One more thing." Ada handed her the derringer.

Kawley refused. "I already have a pistol."

"Yes, I know and so does everyone else who sees it. But this—"
She touched the derringer."—can be concealed in many places." She
folded Kawley's hand around the tiny weapon. "You are a player in a
very dangerous game. Being a woman makes it twice so. If you are
caught, use this weapon on him or on yourself because what your
captor has planned for you would be worse than death." Ada stared into
Kawley's eyes until she seemed satisfied that Kawley understood her
meaning.

The older woman then reached into a small opening in the wall,
pulled out a satchel, retrieved several rosettes and handed them to
Kawley. They were a colorful red, white and blue with a gilt button in
the center sporting an eagle and stars.

Kawley held one to her chest. "If we wear these, won't we be calling
attention to ourselves?"

"On the contrary, the lack of one would call you out. As you
approach the line, attach one to your lapel. It says you are one of them,
not one of us. But do not speak. A southern purr will be your undoing."

Kawley stood tall and hooked a thumb in her lapel. "Whatever do you mean, madam?" she answered in a perfect northern voice. "Why, my family has called Philadelphia home for generations."

Ada squinted her eyes and snatched the derringer from Kawley's hand. "You'd best tell me exactly where your loyalties lie, missy, and be right quick about it. At this very moment, I'm worried that I have sorely misjudged you and my mind is scrambling to find a solution. I'm not sure you would like the solution Oscar might devise."

Kawley quickly pushed both hands in front of herself with her palms open. "I'm so sorry, Ada. Please forgive me. It's not what it looks like."

"Then please enlighten me."

"I was schooled in the north and found myself less than welcome as soon as I opened my mouth. I was determined to beat them at their own game. I learned to imitate them—their words, their mannerisms and their voices. Playing the part of a Yankee has served me well on several occasions." She crossed her palms across her chest in desperate supplication. "I may have been schooled in the north, but I am a southerner through and through."

Ada's eyes darted back and forth, plainly suspicious but then she grinned, as if positively gleeful. "Splendid! That talent and rasp might just save your life. I was so hoping my first impression of you was correct." She took a deep breath, her smile disappeared yet again, and Kawley's heart sank.

"Ada, don't you believe me?"

"I believe you, Kawley. It's just that what I'm about to do will be hard for me."

"Ada, I—"

The older woman cut her off. "Shhh. Lastly, I want you to have these." Ada opened a trunk and brought out a hat, vest and shirt. "They were Micah's. I want you to wear them. If you kill any blue coats—" She slammed one fist into the other palm. "—I want Micah there to see it and guide your hand."

Though her chest was bound, in a moment of modesty Kawley turned her back to Ada as she slipped out of her shirt.

"Lord have mercy, woman. What in the name of Heaven—"

Kawley scrambled away, holding her shirt to her chest. "It's...it's nothing."

Ada pulled her back and spun her around. "You've been flogged. I don't care what the reason. What monster did this and why?"

"I made the mistake of defying a monster well-moneyed, and well-connected." She plopped on the bench and yanked the hair from her face.

The other woman sucked in a quick breath. "I take it he did that, too?"

Kawley glanced at brand scorched into the underside of her forearm. "He bragged I would be forever his."

"I assume you had the gall to refuse such a man, and he took the refusal poorly?" Ada sat and encircled her with a comforting arm. "My brave, brave girl. I am so proud of you."

It was the first time anyone had ever told her they were proud of her. Her mother had been kind and gentle but submissive. Her father, though very generous with her, had always been aloof and distant. He had always appeared just a bit disappointed she was not his male heir. Kawley savored the moment.

"As you seem not wanting to talk about it, I won't press you further. Just please tell me he suffered horribly for this heinous act of cruelty."

"No, ma'am." She turned and stared deep into the other's eyes. "But he will." She lifted one eyebrow and nodded. "Someway...someday, he will."

"Despite knowing you only this brief time, I have no doubt of it. Come, let's get you covered." She helped Kawley into the shirt and vest, then tucked Kawley's braids under the hat and snugged it down. Clearly happy with her work, she stepped back. "There. Blood stains all gone. You are one fine looking little gentleman." Ada handed back the derringer, and Kawley slipped the weapon into her inner pocket.

A gentleman, Kawley thought to herself as she took the stairs. How she wanted to be free of the binding on her chest, to unplait her hair and wear it in curls, to kick off her clunky boots and dance in pretty blue slippers. But that was another time and place. Not now. Perhaps not ever again. For the moment she had to be satisfied with being a fine looking little gentleman.

When they reached the others, Ada's appearance had returned to the soft, frail persona it had been before. "I want to thank you, young man, for all your help. Husband, I hope you don't mind but I gave the young one a few of Micah's things. I couldn't let him ride out covered in blood as he was. Mr. Stedman?"

"Fletcher, please."

"As you wish. Fletcher, you told him he couldn't wear his hat in the house so I gave him the hat my Micah always wore in the house."

Kawley had to fiddle with her hands to keep from laughing. Fletcher cast her a disgruntled stare. She wondered how she could steer the focus from herself when the door opened, and Brayden staggered into the room. Silence descended like a dense fog.

———

He had dressed himself in the clean shirt and vest that Oscar had left in the room. He had even managed to tuck in the shirttail. It was quite clear to him from the gaggle of stunned faces that they all had the same thoughts. Fletcher voiced them.

"Good Lord, man. What the devil are you doing up and about? Oscar and I barely managed to stop the bleeding and here you are daring another red deluge. And appropriately dressed, I might add. How did you ever manage to pull on that shirt and vest? Don't you realize that any pulling might open those wounds?"

Brayden held up his hand and gently shook his head, silently begging for the barrage of questions to stop. His head was pounding, his shoulder was on fire and felt as if Ajax had trampled it. Every turn of his head angered all the wrenched neck muscles. Moreover, his guts threatened to upchuck on the clean shirt and vest that he had just spent what seemed like an hour to pull on.

"To answer your questions: slowly, in the dark, with no one badgering me. I'm up and walking because I have to be. We have to meet Clive and Rush at the mission. There will be plenty of time for resting when we've found Caleb."

Fletcher waved his hand back and forth in the air. "You are half right. Yes, I have to meet Clive and Rush but you, my friend, are not going anywhere until that shoulder is fit to travel. With the amount of blood you lost, you'd be lucky if you could even stay upright in the saddle. You don't have enough blood left to lose if that shoulder breaks open again." He pointed at Kawley. "The little manling there can stay here, too."

"I'm not a little manling, and I'll go wherever I please. You're not my master, and I'm not your servant."

"I'd watch my mouth if I were you, little man. I don't know you and I don't know why you're here. All I know is that you almost got my friend here killed. So I don't need you tagging along and getting in my way."

"Why you…"

Kawley jumped out at Fletcher but Brayden instinctively grabbed her midstride and fairly shoved her out of the way. He spun, screamed, grabbed his shoulder and fell to one knee. The remnants of the whiskey left in his gut filled his throat. The vile taste threatened to spill all over the floor. He gagged it back and swallowed. "Stop it!" He gasped a few times to get himself under control. Grasping the back of a nearby chair, he struggled to pull himself upright. Fletcher stepped toward him, but Brayden cast him a withering stare to ward off the help. After several tries, he stood. "We have the whole northern forces to fight without quibbling amongst ourselves." He flicked his hand. "Now go to your separate corners and cool off." He leaned against the wall to balance himself. "We are all going and that's that."

"Bry, you'll never make it."

"The hell I won't." Brayden knew his bravado was a bluff that even he, himself, barely believed. Despite the pain, he jerked upright to bolster his swaggering words.

His friend jammed his hands through his hair and paced the floor."Bry, listen—"

"No. You listen. Fletcher, I'm going with you. I have to go."

"And just why is it, Mr. Wakefield sir, that you have to ride out with me?"

"Stop the caustic remarks. You, of all people, should know why."

"Well I don't. Oscar and I just did our best to keep you from bleeding to death. I'm not willing to sit by while you stubbornly attempt to undo it all."

Brayden shuddered and took two deep breaths. He had to throw his right arm against the wall again to steady himself.

"There, you see? You are practically passing out already, and we haven't even mounted up. Your bluff is not working."

"Fletcher, do you remember that giant flood we all lived through when we were children?"

Fletcher rolled his eyes. "Why yes, I do and I'm so glad you're bringing up that unpleasant memory at this important moment."

"For once would you button your lips and listen? Caleb and I were caught up in the river. He somehow managed to catch a branch and save himself. I was drowning, and he could have run. Instead, he ran downstream and dove in to catch me as I came by. He ripped the skin off his arm and broke it in three places, but he saved my life. Caleb hung on to me as he struggled toward shore. 'Swim, Brayden, swim. I can't do it alone,' he kept yelling. He never gave up until he saved us both." Brayden hesitated as he watched his friend look up at the ceiling as though trying to recall the details of the incident. "Remember he was always going to be a doctor but suddenly changed to study law?"

"Yes, so what?"

"Why do you think he changed?"

"I have no idea. Maybe because he decided he didn't much care for the sight of blood? I must admit I've seen enough of yours lately to last me a lifetime."

"No. It was because his arm was broken so badly he didn't think he could perform surgery, so he gave up his dream and went into law."

Fletcher's eyes widened. "Is that the reason? All these years, and he never told me."

"My life cost him his dream. Now do you see why I will find him at all costs?"

Fletcher fisted his hips and continued to pace, nodding. "Caleb, Caleb, what else haven't you told me?"

Brayden slumped into the chair. The irony that Caleb had saved him with one arm and now he would attempt to save Caleb with one arm was not lost on him. Secretly, he hoped he had enough blood and balance left to back up his bold words. He kept swallowing to control a wave of nausea so the others wouldn't notice he was about to spill his guts.

"Well now," Oscar interjected. "If all of you are done doing what you've been doing—" He pointed around the room at each of them. "—you dying in that chair, and you wearing a path across Ada's fine carpet, and you skulking in the corner—" He sucked in a quick breath. "—why don't you put your differences aside and work on a plan to save this Caleb fella?" He turned to his wife. "Ada darlin', why don't we fill their flasks and saddle bags with what we can spare and send these gents on their way."

Brayden glanced at Kawley, who was indeed skulking in the corner. She was sitting with her hip on the windowsill, staring out the window. As she turned her head and their eyes met, he was bombarded with bits and pieces of a salacious dream. It stunned him, and his mind immediately began searching for answers, struggling to wring more from his weary, whiskey drenched memories. If he had not been so worried about Caleb, he would have dragged himself back to the chaise in an effort to recapture the moments that were now out of his reach.

Ada pulled a cloth from the cupboard. She ripped lengths of it and rolled them. "This old linen will have to do for bandages on your trip. I do wish I had medicine to go with it. From the look of you, a bit of laudanum would be more welcome, I'm sure." She lifted Brayden's coat from the chair. "Please don't be offended but I took the liberty of repairing your coat. I had a fine soft hide that I was saving for..." Ada stopped and lowered her eyes. Within a moment she looked up and stood tall. "I covered the repair and matched it on the other shoulder to make the patch inconspicuous unless one is looking for it."

"Your kindness is much appreciated, Miss Ada," said Fletcher. "I don't think there's a lick of sewing skills among the lot of us."

Ada gave a quick nod and started toward the door. "Now I'll see to the other supplies."

For a moment Brayden thought he caught a secretive exchange between Kawley and Ada as the older woman passed her. He shook it off as his shoulder and neck throbbed tediously. "I have a few tins of salve in my saddle bag that should suffice."

"Good Lord! Not that disgusting concoction you mix up for your horse?" Fletcher asked incredulously. "I wouldn't use that on a cow."

"Yes, my disgusting concoction as you call it. What's good enough for Ajax is good enough for me."

Brayden shot a peek at Kawley. She had turned her face back to the window, but he thought he saw an almost imperceptible shake in her shoulders. He hoped it was nothing more than a girlish giggle and not a tearful annoyance. He lowered his eyes to her legs. Since he had not seen her limping while he had been up, he assumed at least her leg was healing nicely.

Oscar poured several glasses of whiskey and handed one to each of them. "To good hunting, my newfound friends." He tapped his glass to each of theirs. "Whether it be your way—" He winked. "—or my way, may we both succeed."

Brayden wasn't entirely certain the drink wouldn't come back up faster than it went down but he hurt too much to care. As the hot burn slithered to his belly, Brayden relished the entire descent. He felt the throbbing ease a bit but the fire in his shoulder continued to rage out of control. Kawley swilled hers down in one gulp without coughing, which Brayden found quite impressive. His gulp stayed down and since he needed a jolt of confidence, he extended his hand with the glass. "For medicinal purposes?"

Oscar smiled and refilled the glass. "For any purpose. I say, why not?" He refilled his own glass and put the bottle on the sideboard. "Now to business. From the rumors I have heard out of Richmond it seems, mind you I don't know for sure, but I've heard that the damn politicians have hired themselves someone with a balloon to spy on our southern brethren. Someone named LaMountain demonstrated for the president a balloon that can send messages over the telegraph to him."

"A balloon, you say?" Brayden pushed himself to a more comfortable position in the chair. Surprisingly, for the moment, he felt a bit better. "That could certainly tip the scales in their favor, couldn't it?"

Fletcher clucked his tongue. "Hell, they could know what we were doing before we did."

"So as you're watching your backs, you'd sure as shootin' better be watching your skies. If they send any rangers after you, I think those partisans would hang you for sure. They wouldn't bother taking you to any camp."

"We saw two examples of their idea of justice on the way here," Kawley offered.

Oscar nodded. "I've seen more than my share, too. But I've been doin' my damn best to give as much back in kind." He formed a pistol with his hand and 'fired' several shots.

Ada returned. "Your packs are filled with as much as I could fit. Not fancy, mind you, but filling."

Brayden sucked in a deep breath, grimaced against the pain and threw himself from the chair. He sincerely hoped the gifts from these gentle souls had not depleted their seemingly already diminished means and offered his hand to the woman. "Miss Ada, you and your husband have been more than generous. I only hope I can repay your kindness one day."

"I heartily agree, Miss Ada," Fletcher added. He crossed the room to the door. "I'll bring the horses around."

Kawley took Ada's hand in hers. "I pray the Heavens keep you safe, Miss Ada."

When he watched Kawley keep Ada's hand longer than he thought proper, Brayden had the same strange thought he'd had earlier that some secretive connection passed between the two women. But, as before, he pushed the thought to the back of his mind because he was too overcome with the surprising struggle of ordinary movement. The same movements he had always performed without a thought were now monumental tasks.

"Need help?" Kawley muttered as she came alongside of him. Her stance lent an air of sarcasm to her words.

Her remark was like an arrow rammed up his spine. Brayden stood insouciantly. "I'm fine. Go mount up." He did not intend to let Kawley or Fletcher know that all he wanted to do was collapse and drink himself into a stupor to escape his misery. Guilt suddenly washed over him. Caleb had saved him despite his pain. Brayden knew he could do no less.

Oscar held their horses while they mounted. "When you get close to Capitol City, listen to the gossip in the pubs. Liquor loosens tongues. Before you go barging in, you might want to know if those two prisoners are really the fellas you're looking for. You might also hear which regiment is on guard when. Some can be bribed, others can't. You'll have to know the difference, or you will be a resident of Old Capitol instead of a visitor. If your friends are there, I hope you find them safe and unharmed." He extended his hand to Brayden as well as a cylindrical leather case which he buckled to Brayden's saddle. "Made it myself...the case and the brew." Oscar winked. "I figure that shoulder is going to require more than what you are packing. God speed, and I wish you safe home."

CHAPTER SIX

After they left Oscar's, the three of them rode in single file silence. Brayden wondered if Fletcher was still miffed that Kawley was with them. Fletcher led the group with Kawley in the middle, and Brayden bringing up the rear. Even riding one handed, the miles were grueling for him. Ajax's long, lanky stride, usually a joy to ride, shoved his shoulder forward and back, over and over until Brayden questioned whether the shot had splintered a bone on its journey through him. Along with the fire, it felt as if something was crackling to and fro under the skin. When they stopped to rest the horses, he intended to ask Fletcher to redo the wrapping tighter.

In the meantime, Brayden tried desperately to distract his mind from the constant torture. He daydreamed about the rider in front of him. Kawley sat Pickles beautifully. He tried to imagine her lithe frame riding sidesaddle. She would be wearing a fawn colored habit. No, a blue riding habit to match the sapphire blue of her eyes. Her hat would be draped in pale blue tulle with a lovely bow at the back. The ends of the bow would trail down her back and flutter with the breeze. Her black boots would peek out from under her skirt, their shine reflecting the sunlight.

Without warning Ajax tripped, nearly unseating Brayden and wrenching his shoulder. He bit the inside of his cheek to keep from crying out what he really felt. Instead he growled, "Pay attention, Jax!"

"You all right back there?" Fletcher muttered, presumably trying not to call any unwanted attention to their group. "Do you need us to stop?"

Brayden gathered all his strength to answer. "No. Just tripped is all. I'm good for a bit." *A very little bit*, he wanted to say but didn't.

Kawley stood in her stirrups and turned back to look at him. Her eyes studied him from the top of his head to the tip of his boots and back again. Without saying a word, she sat back down and rode on.

He remembered the shot that tore through him. He remembered laying atop her while the volley of death ricocheted around them. He remembered wrapping his body around hers as if he truly belonged there, wondering how he could have those thoughts in the midst of a hail of fire.

Once again Brayden was bombarded with visions of a dream. They flipped through his head like paintings at a picture show. His mind saw them; his body felt them; his heart savored them. Risking another Ajax trip, he closed his eyes and reviewed the visions again and again. The feelings took him further away from the present—the rocking, the pulling, the stabbing fire which tore at the left side of his body.

Lovely as it was, dreams can only help so much.

Brayden reached for his flask and swallowed a large gulp, followed by another. Why was he so drawn to Kawley? He had never truly loved a woman and had foolishly married Lavinia. After Lavinia died he had sealed off his heart, directed all his energies to the plantation and accepted the fact that love would never happen for him. It was his punishment for having selfishly caused the death of another. Yet here he was daydreaming about a woman who was a total enigma. He had allowed her to travel with them. He had offered his help in rescuing her brother. He had almost given his life for hers, not even knowing if the life story she had imparted was true or not. Brayden lifted the flask to his lips again. At this point he wasn't sure whether it was the searing blaze in his shoulder, the confusion in his head or the surprising ache in his heart that was driving his need for the rotgut in his flask.

Fletcher raised a hand, indicating a halt. "Hear that?"

"Yes," Kawley replied. "Sounds distant but definitely something big moving this way."

Brayden was too exhausted to hear anything but nodded agreement to fend off any further questions. He slid the flask back into its case.

"You two stay in the trees. I'm going to scout over the hill and see if I can figure out where it's coming from."

Kawley turned her horse and halted next to Brayden. "Guess Fletcher figures I'm safer protecting your back instead of his."

Brayden snorted. "Hardly. I think he's annoyed I brought you along because he can't figure out why."

"Frankly, Brayden, neither can I." She patted the horse's neck. "You don't know me. You don't owe me. In fact, you don't know whether one word of what I've told you is the truth or not."

"I've said those same words to myself over and over since we've been together." Brayden gazed up into the trees in search of answers that he knew were not forthcoming.

Kawley touched his arm. "Yet you threw yourself in front of a slug for me. Why?"

For some unknown reason that surprised himself, Brayden grinned and stroked his beard. "You're a good little barber?"

"Are you serious? You'd die for someone who can even out your beard?" She whistled softly. "Don't you know an undertaker can do that too?"

"Well, I got to thinkin' that if you got shot it'd be very messy and remember—"

"I know, I know. You didn't have a shovel."

"Exactly."

"But if you had died, I didn't have a shovel either."

The humor left him. "If I had died, the lack of a shovel would have been the least of your problems. I hesitate to think what he would have done to you."

"But my disguise—"

"Having probably been without a woman for a long time, I don't think he would have cared."

Kawley reddened and looked away. "And once he realized I was a woman—"

"You would have prayed for death to take you quickly."

Brayden watched as she turned back to him and truly felt the warmth in her eyes as she studied his face for a while before she spoke. "And all of this went through your mind in the span of a heartbeat?" she whispered.

"I remembered your gentleness as you trimmed my beard that morning in the barn. I remembered your soft touch when you stroked my cheek. I remembered the feel of your lips when you kissed me, that kiss that your mother would say was unladylike. Yes, in the span of a heartbeat, I knew I would never allow that crude, coarse piece of dirt to sully a hair on your head."

"But I'm still confused as to why."

Before Brayden opened his mouth to answer, Fletcher bounded down the hill. "We have to hide. It's a whole regiment, and they are headed this way. Let's head for the bridge down the way."

"Why are we leaving the woods?" The idea of galloping anywhere was an abhorrent idea to Brayden in his current condition.

"It's not enough cover, Bry. Their sharp shooters would pick us off like ducks at a traveling sideshow."

Brayden looked around. "I see your point. But we'll be in the wide open if they see us cross it," he called as they took off.

"Not if we're under the bridge before they get there."

"What does he mean by *under* it?" Kawley mouthed to Brayden.

"We have to make it under the bridge before that regiment comes over the hill. I crossed this bridge on my journey to find you." Fletcher punched out the words as he galloped alongside of them. "There's about a four to five foot jump down into the river. From there we can canter upstream and hide under the bridge."

"Isn't there a lower bank to the water?" Brayden was thinking about Kawley and wondering if her mare would take the jump.

"That *is* the lowest point. Come on, man. We have to move fast."

The three of them galloped the distance to the riverbank. Fletcher kicked his gelding. Man and beast flew through the air without hesitation and splashed into the river below. Pickles skidded to the edge with such force Kawley flew up her neck with the horse's ears ending up between her legs.

Kawley quickly scurried back into the saddle. "She's never jumped before."

"Hurry," Fletcher yelled from below.

"Listen, Kawley, she will do it. You just have to give her the confidence. That means you have to believe in her. Now put her nose in

Jax's rump, leg her hard and hang on." Brayden whirled Ajax around, cantered back a few strides and turned. "Now, Kawley, now!"

Brayden launched Ajax into a frenzy and took off. He glanced behind, and Kawley was right on his heels. One stride from the bank he yelled back, "Leg her! Leg her!"

"Jump or we die," Fletcher's voice echoed their panic.

Apparently, the flying tail in her face was the incentive Pickles needed because the mare splashed into the water and bounded down river ahead of the other two. With his reins doubled in one hand, Brayden held a death grip on the pommel of the saddle to steady himself. First the galloping and then the jump from the bank had been almost more than he could bear.

It was a tight fit for the three of them and their horses, but they were all safely off their mounts and under the bridge when they heard thundering hooves in the distance. Ajax's frenzy didn't end when they were under the bridge. He kept dancing around, throwing his rump out from under the shadow of the bridge. While Brayden offered the chunks of sweet potatoes to their bewhiskered lips, Kawley dove under Jax's belly, came up on the other side and grabbed her hat just before it was washed downstream. She jammed the hat on her head and poked the horse's rump back under to safety. Brayden was thankful Jax's huge rump had hidden her braids from Fletcher.

Soon enough dirt and stones rained down on them through the cracks in the boards. They shielded their eyes and those of the horses. The boom of the hooves on the wood was deafening. It felt as if they might be crushed to death at any given moment. The pounding dirt and noise continued for what seemed like hours. Eventually the thunder stopped, and the hoof beats became faint. None of them spoke for several minutes, watching, waiting, straining to hear. The sound of the swirling water was welcome and comforting.

"Bry, I promise I will never make fun of your sweet potato treats again," Fletcher uttered. He turned to Kawley. "And while that dip under the belly was an exceedingly dangerous move and I hope I never see you do that again, it was quick thinking and helped to save us."

Kawley nodded, seeming to appreciate the praise. Brayden hoped that a bit of the animosity between the two had eased. He watched her pull her vest away from her water-soaked shirt and was thankful the dark color had not washed off her cheeks. He cupped his hand and splashed water on his face to combat his dizziness.

"You still with us, old man? You're looking a bit out of sorts."

"Barely." He kept his fingers woven in Jax's mane, hoping the threatening dizziness would pass before he fell in the river and drowned.

"Let me take a look at that shoulder before we leap out of here." Fletcher sloshed toward him and opened Brayden's coat. "Looks like you bled out a bit but, thank heaven, nothing is gushing."

"Good to hear." He was slowly regaining control of his head again. "Comforting to know I'm bleeding to death slowly instead of all at once."

"Quit your grousing." Fletcher peeked around Brayden's shoulder to Kawley. "Bry is never happy with any situation."

"Yes, I have noticed that about him since we've been riding together."

"It's quite rude of the two of you to gang up on a dying man."

"Dying, are you? Hmmm. Come on then. We'd better find somewhere to camp for the night so I can tend to this *dying* man's shoulder." Fletcher gave Brayden a leg up and then mounted himself. "Oscar told me if we ride down river, there are one or two large caves we can use for cover."

"Let's just hope something or someone else didn't have the same idea." Kawley said as she mounted. "They'll hear us coming a mile away. I'm so wet I squeak."

"I am, too, but if we strip down, a small fire should dry things right quick," Fletcher retorted.

Brayden tried to imagine Kawley sitting naked by the fire waiting for her garments to dry. While the thought was delightfully delicious, his mind scrambled to consider a reason for Kawley not to change in front of them. Her pursed lips and wide-eyed expression told him she was thinking the exact same thing. As Fletcher cantered along ahead of them, seemingly oblivious to the situation, Brayden offered Kawley a quick nod of assurance that he would help figure out a way.

"What possessed you to dive under Jax?"

"My father taught me to swim, too."

Brayden snorted and grinned. "Remind me never to underestimate you again."

It was nearly dark, but they had still not seen the opening that Oscar had suggested. While Kawley was tired and sore, the extra time nearly dried her clothes. Then in the trees they spied what looked like a small cabin.

Fletcher dismounted to explore and seemed pleased when he returned. "Looks like no one has been there for a very long time, something much to our advantage. There's no furniture save a table and a fire might be too risky but it's shelter for the night. There's also a lean-to in the back for the horses. Feels as if a storm is on the way so let's get settled."

Brayden was quiet and sullen. Considering what he been through in the last twenty-four hours, Kawley was surprised that he was still able to sit the saddle at all. Even in the semi-darkness, she could discern how pale he was. He had his shoulders hunched. His right hand held the buckle of the reins and had a claw-like grip on his left arm as though it might just drop to the ground if he released his hold. When they neared the cabin, he swung his leg over Ajax's head and dropped to the ground. His legs buckled a bit, and he grimaced with his eyes clamped shut. Kawley counted several seconds before he straightened.

Kawley reached for Jax's reins, wondering if Brayden might object. He didn't. She led both horses into the lean-to and as she came back around with the saddle bags, she watched Brayden trudge into the cabin and plop to the floor.

"Let's get a clean bandage on that shoulder, Bry."

Brayden didn't answer at first. His head fell back against the wall. "Just secure it tighter this time. I think something might be busted in there. Jax's stride makes it feel like the bones are rubbing against one another. Kawley, get the tin from my saddle bag."

"Oh no," Fletcher protested. "I refuse to rub that concoction into the wound. Hell, at best you might start to whinny or moo or something. At worst you might lose your arm."

"It's my bloody arm, damn it." He grabbed the tin from Kawley's hand. "Then I'll rub, and you bandage. That way your conscience is clear."

When the bandages fell away, Kawley wanted to vomit but swallowed hard to prevent it. The burns were an ugly, gory, red and she truly hoped the shoulder didn't hurt as bad as it looked. She offered more of the clean bandages that Ada had provided, lathered the lesions with the salve and supported Brayden's arm while Fletcher wrapped it tightly.

"There. Feel better, Bry?"

"For the moment. I'd probably feel much better if you'd hand me my flask."

"You should eat something first."

Brayden shifted his position and groaned. "I'm not hungry."

Kawley stood. "I'm sure Ada packed something in here that might entice you."

Fletcher nodded. "Sure smelled good when she packed it."

"I said I'm not hungry, damn it!" Brayden growled and flung out his hand.

The back of his hand struck Kawley's leg right across her wound. She jumped back but bit her lip to not cry out lest Fletcher find out that she, too, was injured. She glanced around for a reason to leave. There in the corner she spied an old bucket. "I'll get us some fresh water."

———

The pain in her leg subsided by the time she reached the river's edge, but she sat and checked it. The scab had not broken open. Kawley had just retied the bandage when a twig cracked behind her. She jumped up to find Fletcher coming through the trees.

"He didn't mean it, you know. Bry was just lashing out."

"But he lashed out at me, not you."

Fletcher shook his head. "No, Kawley. Bry lashed out with the only arm he had, and you were on that side. It's only because he's in pain."

His sudden quiet concern disarmed her. "Are you daft? I know he's in pain. Do you not remember that I was there when he was shot? Because I distinctly remember the blood splattering and the shot whizzing past my head as it went through him."

Again Fletcher shook his head. "I'm talking about the pain you don't see."

"Speak the king's English, man. You're talking in riddles, and I'm too dog-tired to play games."

Fletcher raised an eyebrow. "You are a tough little buck, aren't you?"

Kawley turned her back to him and sloshed the bucket in the water. "You were going to explain something about Brayden. Either spit it out or leave me alone."

"The pain I'm talking about is Lavinia."

She stopped moving for a few seconds and swiveled her head. "Lavinia?"

"Lavinia. His wife. He didn't tell you?"

"No." She turned away, oddly disappointed to find Brayden was married.

"She died a few years back, and Bry has not been the same since."

Kawley rinsed the bucket again and poured out the water, relieved that she had not kissed a married man. "What killed her?"

"Snakebite."

She whistled, sat back on her heels and glanced at Fletcher. "I see what you mean. Not exactly a peaceful way to go." Kawley hesitated then voiced the question anyway. "Did he...did they have young ones?"

"No. They were only married a short time before the accident. Why she was in that spot when she knew rattlers were there, we never knew, and Bry has never spoken about it. I've also never seen him smile or laugh since."

The man with her said Brayden had not smiled or laughed since his wife's death. Kawley remembered several times in their short acquaintance that Brayden had done both. For some odd reason the thought pleased her.

Fletcher looked off into the distance. "We've always been good friends, Bry, Caleb, Royce, Rush and I but I haven't been able to get him to talk about it. He's totally withdrawn from all of us. His best friend seems to be that damn journal he carries everywhere." He heaved a heavy sigh. "Riding after Caleb is the most animated I've seen him in years." He turned to Kawley. "That's why I find his apparent friendship with you to be extraordinary."

Kawley presented her back again, filled the bucket and set it on the bank. "I don't know what you mean. We're not friends. We only ride together for a mutual purpose—to rescue my brother and your friend, Caleb, who we believe are being held together."

Fletcher yanked her up and turned her to face him. He grabbed her two hands with one of his giant ones. "You are not friends, yet he took a shot for you. Now I find that right curious."

Kawley wrenched her hands away and took a few steps backward. Her heart was pounding. When she had originally tailed their group, she thought this Fletcher to be hot-tempered. "I already told you I have no idea why he did that."

"Well, young man, Bry is my good friend so I'm going to trust he must have had a damn good reason for what he did. But just know that if you are a deserter or a spy or do anything to betray his trust, you will have to answer to me."

Brayden appeared out of nowhere. "Answer to you for what, Fletcher?"

Fletcher cleared his throat. "If you lose that arm because Kawley lathered that horse concoction on it after I expressly forbid it."

"If I lose this arm it's because some blue coat ripped holes in it."

Fletcher pointed at Kawley. "Holes meant for his head. Now just why do you suppose someone might want to do that?"

"Enough, Fletcher. You're making my head hurt worse than my shoulder."

The other man threw up his hands and headed back to the cabin. "Then he's your responsibility. It's your job to make certain the little manling doesn't get in the way of our rescuing Caleb," he muttered over his shoulder.

Kawley rolled her eyes and heaved a sigh of relief. "Exactly what's a 'manling'?"

Brayden tilted his head. "Duck, duckling, man, manling?"

"He called me a buck, a bucko and a manling. Well, at least, it wasn't anything female. When he put his face right into mine, I was afraid my disguise was finished."

Brayden came close until they were almost touching. "Kawley, I dragged myself down here to tell you I'm sorry I struck you. I was just flinging my arm through the air, and I misjudged where you were. I know I must have hit your wound and caused you a great deal of pain."

She gently touched his shoulder. "Not nearly as much pain as I have caused you." She glanced back toward the cabin. "And if I knew Fletcher wasn't watching, I would properly thank you."

"I don't think Fletcher is spying on us, but one can't be too careful."

"Why do I think it's not the only reason you came out here?"

"These bandages are making me too hot. I thought dipping my feet in the river might cool me down."

Kawley bustled through Brayden's resistance and touched his forehead. "Good Lord, Brayden, you are burning up. Let me grab Fletcher so we can help you inside."

Brayden stopped her. "No. If Fletcher knows about the fever, he'll never let us continue. He'll feel bound to accompany me back to Oscar's and that will waste valuable time getting to Riley and Caleb. If my legs are in the water, and I keep splashing cold on my head, this might be gone by morning."

"You're planning to stay out here all night?"

"Or until the fever breaks. That salve has always worked before. I'm counting on it working for me now. Lives are depending on it."

"I see your point. What can I do to help?"

"Pull my boots?"

"All right. That's definitely something a manling can do."

With his hand on her shoulder, she yanked off his boots and stockings and then helped him to roll up the legs of his breeches. It was the first time she had ever touched a man's legs. The muscles were hard, the skin smooth and covered with dark hair. Their eyes met for a brief moment when her hand slid from knee to ankle. The moment faded on the breeze, elusive and fleeting.

His hand was warm as he used her for balance so as not to fall over while he found a comfortable position. He threw his feet into the water and then yanked them back out. "Whoa that water is cold!"

"Feet in, Brayden. Remember this was your brilliant idea." She looked around. "I need something for your head so I'll...I'll...oh hell." She pulled out her shirttail and ripped off the bottom.

"Your mama would definitely have said that was very unladylike."

"Fortunately, she's not here to hear it, and I needed a cloth." She dipped the cloth in the bucket. "I'll use this to keep the cold on your forehead."

"Am I delirious or is this shirt ripping becoming a habit?"

"You're delirious. Now lie back. I'm going to let Fletcher know you want to stay out here for a while."

"What?" Brayden jerked upright. "I just finished telling you—"

Kawley pushed him back. "I know what you told me. I have no intention of telling him why you want to stay out here for a bit. Just that you are. No need for him getting his hackles up."

―――――

When Kawley opened the door, Fletcher immediately barked at her. "Where's Bry?"

"By the river. He—"

"You left him out there alone, wounded and unarmed? Damn it, Kawley. Are you that naive?"

Kawley stomped her foot and jammed her fists into her hips. "Stop flapping your jaws, Fletcher. I came back for my pistol." She baited him and sincerely hoped it didn't backfire. She grabbed the weapon and handed it to Fletcher. "Here. You can go sit there with him because he's not coming in until he's damn good and ready."

Fletcher rubbed his forehead with the back of his hand. Then he stared at the ceiling and blew out a deep breath in clear frustration. "He's in that state again I guess, wanting to be left alone. I imagine he's writing in that damn journal?"

"I don't think so. I didn't see a journal."

He drummed his fingers on the table. "He won't want to be seeing me when he's like this. You best go stand guard. Nearby but not too close. He'd just as soon bite you as look at you when he wanders off." He shook his head. "Damn. I knew I should have forced him to stay at Oscar's." He shooed Kawley out the door. "Go. Make yourself useful, little man."

―――――

Kawley found Brayden stretched out on the ground. He was so still she feared he had fainted or worse, bled out and died. She holstered the pistol, ran and knelt beside him. "Brayden? Brayden, talk to me!"

Without opening his eyes or moving a muscle he whispered, "And what do you want me to say?"

She slapped his right shoulder and sat back on the ground. "Argh! You scared the devil out of me."

"Pity. I rather liked the devil in you."

Without thinking, she slapped his shoulder again. "Liar."

"If you keep slamming my shoulder, I'll be a liar and a murderer."

Kawley gasped. "Oh my Goodness. I'm so sorry." She jumped up, refilled the bucket with fresh water and dampened the cloth. Feeling miserable for her thoughtlessness, she dabbed his cheek, his neck, dipped it once more in the bucket and laid it across his forehead. "Do you feel any better?"

"As long as I move absolutely nothing," he muttered through a barely opened mouth, "not even my eyelids or my lips, I can contain the pain." He was quiet for a long time.

Finally she hugged her raised knees and snorted.

"What was that for?"

"I was just laughing at myself for being silly."

"Right now I could use some silliness. It would be a most welcome distraction."

"May I ask you a question first?"

"You may."

"When was the last time you frolicked?"

Brayden clamped his lips together. Kawley wasn't certain if it were a stab of pain that caused it. Then she heard a distinct rumble, almost a snort, as if he were attempting to hide a deep belly laugh.

"Hmmmm. I'm not sure. Do men actually frolic, or at least where anyone can see them do so?"

Kawley harrumphed. "Do you even know what frolic means?"

Brayden jutted his chin. "Certainly I do, and I've heard it is most unladylike. Why do you ask?"

She closed her eyes and leaned back on her arms. "Because I want to frolic again. Someday before I die, I want to experience that glorious innocence—" She leaned closer to him. "—even if it is unladylike."

"Your silliness is rapidly becoming sassy, madam."

"I was also contemplating what might have been if we had met under different circumstances, at a different time, in a different place. At a barbeque perhaps?"

"No. We would have met later, after the barbeque at the ball." Brayden's voice was low, more of a drawl, as if he might be caught up in her reverie. "I would be surprised that I hadn't seen you earlier. I would surreptitiously attempt to discover your name."

"Would I be dancing or sitting?"

"Dancing, of course. Every one of your dances would have been promised." He bent his knees and pulled his feet from the water. "Have to let them warm up for a minute before I crack at the knees." He heaved a heavy breath, glanced at her and closed his eyes again.

Kawley waited a full minute, expecting him to continue. "I'm...still...dancing, sir."

The corners of his lips crinkled. "I know. I'm just enjoying the view in my mind."

She scooted a bit closer, thoroughly savoring the repartee. "And what do you see?"

"I'm leaning against the sideboard, one ear listening to the gentlemen on one side of me discussing the latest news from Capitol City and the women on my other side giggling over frills and furbelows. But I'm watching a blue gown waltz past me over and over. I'm intrigued and intoxicated by a mass of burgundy curls above a wave of burgundy silk cascading down one shoulder. The woman and her partner spin close to me, and she smiles as she passes. I noted that the blue of her eyes matches the cerulean satin waves draped around her diminutive frame. Both are exquisite."

"I'm complimented you noticed me."

"You? I was describing Melinda Sue Bartlett the last time I saw her."

Kawley growled. "You're incorrigible." She turned her back to him.

"Don't you like Melinda Sue?"

"I hate her. She stole my best friend's beau and then she was caught kissing him in the arbor." Kawley turned back. "That Melinda woman has a most terrible reputation. I heard the matrons whispering about her all night at the ball. Personally I'm surprised you would even notice such a girl with the rumors swirling about her."

"My apologies, madam."

Kawley nodded. "Apology accepted." She was relishing the game as a respite from the last few weeks. "You may continue."

"Hmmm. Let me see, where was I?" He took his time as if he enjoyed teasing her. "After my cigar and brandy, Rush told me I had been mistaken. It's wasn't Melinda Sue after all. It was a lovely lass who had been visiting for the last month. She was only to be here three more days. Small wonder every dance had been promised. What a tragedy. It was too late to arrange an introduction. She returns home but I remember her smile for the rest of my life. The end."

"A smile? That's the best you can muster?"

"Do you not remember that I was recently shot, and my mind was deprived of buckets of blood?"

Kawley ignored his excuse. "So you're saying that if we had first met at a ball that's the only connection we would have had? A glance and a smile?" She whistled. "Apparently you fare better meeting women at gunpoint."

"How would you have envisioned it?" Brayden put his legs back into the water. "Whoa. Cold, cold, cold, cold."

"Yes, that's exactly how I would put it."

"Put what? Woman, you are making no sense."

"Hmmmm." Kawley tapped her chin with her finger. "I saw you standing there at the sideboard studying me. You were looking quite dapper I might add. Your striking green eyes intrigued and drew me because your look was far too bold to be proper. I glanced away and then looked back. Your gaze continued with a transparent expression, an expression as if you saw right through my gown. I looked away again because—"

"Your mama would have scolded it was unladylike to do otherwise?"

Kawley giggled. "Yes. But, frankly at the moment, I really didn't care. I was so bored with my dance partners. Not one of them had a stimulating thing to say as if they thought I had not a lick of common sense. Then there you were. I could almost touch you. I wanted to know if you were studying me with your eyes or undressing me with them. My smile was simply an entreaty for you to rescue me, but you coldly turned away, plainly preferring brandy and cigars to securing an introduction." She smacked her lips. "Hmmm. You were right. A tragedy. A romance not to be."

"I must admit you did look as if you'd rather be riding Pickles in the moonlight, or perhaps joining the men discussing Mr. Lincoln's latest moves...anything rather than waltzing. You should have followed me to the library. I'm sure your opinions would have caused quite a stir. I know

I would have been interested to hear them. So interested I might have walked you to the garden to hear more. I might have watched your blue eyes as you stated them, yearned for the feel of your soft lips as you emphasized your points, touched your cheek as I admired your wisdom and wit." Brayden pulled his legs from the water and stretched them along the bank. "I might have risked wrinkling your beautiful gown as I encircled and lifted you to me. Would I have dared a kiss? Depends."

Kawley hugged her knees tighter. Their delightful bantering had chased the tension of their quest to the background for a short while, and she was grateful. "Depends on what?"

"Depends on whether the sapphire of your eyes tells me that kiss would cost me a sore cheek."

"But it would be worth it. Remember, sir, I leave in three days."

"Madam, are you always so forthright?"

Kawley suppressed a titter. "Always."

"Good."

She noted that while Brayden had spoken, he had not moved a muscle toward her, had barely even moved his lips as he whispered, yet she could feel the power that his words held over her. If only she had met someone like Brayden years ago. Perhaps she might never have been in her present situation. She might have been married and settled, might never have lost their land. Dressed in dingy and dirty men's clothes made the silly dream all the more enticing. It had been so long since she had felt like a woman. Once again, she was touched that Brayden acknowledged she had a serious idea in her head and opinions that mattered. Without filtering the thought, the words fell out of her mouth. "Was your wife outspoken." In that instant the spell shattered into slivers.

"My—" Brayden clamped his mouth shut with such force she heard his teeth clatter.

Kawley rushed to explain. "Brayden, Fletcher...". She licked her lips and said no more. There was no way to take back the shock and hurt she sensed in his demeanor. Had she stomped on his wounded shoulder, she could not have created the painful heaviness that suddenly enveloped them and spit them out. She watched his chest rise and fall; she heard his heavy breathing with his mouth pursed. Kawley didn't have to know the full circumstances of his wife's demise to realize that she had mortally trespassed on forbidden territory. There was no way to take back her words or her gaffe. All she could do was wait.

With his eyes still closed, Brayden rubbed his shoulder with such force that he seemed to rock slowly. She wondered if the sudden movement was an effort to contain some deep emotion, to slap shut the door that she had carelessly, if unknowingly, opened.

The gurgling of the water and the wind rustling in the trees did nothing to overcome the silence between them. The awkward heaviness was palpable. Sadness? Anger? Kawley had no way of discerning. She watched the clouds thicken and threaten them as she struggled for the right words to say.

Finally Brayden lay quiet. He cleared his throat. "Before you came back from Fletcher, I was lying here contemplating that tree over there."

She nearly cried with relief that he had changed the subject. The abrupt change was clearly protective. She glanced around. "Which one?"

"The one with the extremely large trunk. I noticed it as I struggled down here. I surmise it would take twelve to fourteen steps to walk around it."

"Looks like a sugar maple or oak or something. A tree with that large a girth must be decades old."

"I imagine it might have been just a sapling during our first fight for freedom eighty-five years ago."

"Now we are fighting for our freedom once again. If only its branches could wrap around us and protect us from harm."

Brayden snorted. "If those branches could reach us, they would probably slap us silly for seeking war once again."

When it seemed a bit of the tension had eased, Kawley stretched out her legs and leaned back on her arms again, mindful of a poem she had once heard.

> *"I asked of the bark and*
> *the boughs up above;*
> *What have you seen o'er the years*
> *Hate or love?*
> *Hearts and initials,*
> *Songs that are sung.*

Ropes o'er the branches,
Men that are hung.
You saw fights for freedom
In seventy-six or so;
We seek freedom again
But they won't let us go."

Kawley didn't even realize she had spoken out loud until Brayden joined her in the recitation.

"Now fathers, sons and
husbands will die;
Now wives and daughters and
Mothers will cry.
Wounds will be opened and
Rivers flow red;
The land will be littered
With North and South dead.
But for now let me sit;
In your shade let me hide.
Let me savor the moments of
Peace you provide."

Kawley was stunned. "You know Dalisco Moore?"

"I heard him speak on many occasions. He's one of the few men who actually realize that this war will not be over in a few months. He speaks out about it and luckily doesn't get pelted with tomatoes for his trouble. I'm not sure many of our neighbors have listened. They are too filled with Southern arrogance."

The words were again out of her mouth before she could stop them. "Do you and Fletcher have slaves?"

Brayden seemed to be hesitating. He licked his lips. He slowly opened his eyes and turned his head. "We both grew up with our families having slaves, as did their fathers and generations before them. It seemed to be just the way things were. We were never taught to question the practice; it just was the way of it. Then when our fathers died, we inherited the land and everything on it, including the people."

103

"And now the war is here. The law makers passed that Crittenden Resolution saying the war is to preserve the union, but we all know the truth of it." She bit her lip. "Brayden, what do you and Fletcher fight for?"

He looked off into the distance as if asking himself the same thing. "Fletcher and I have talked about this in the past years. We fight for the wisdom to make the right choice."

"The right choice about what? Seceding from the Union or freeing your slaves?"

Brayden struggled to a sitting position. "Fletcher and I have never spoken of this outside of our homes, seeing as how it's practically treason to do so. He and I are searching for a way to free our people and keep them safe." Brayden turned his head and stared at her with a raised eyebrow. "In truth, I don't know why I've shared any of this with you but..."

Kawley slid closer to him as if the trees might hear what he was about to share. "But?"

As he opened his mouth to speak, the two of them were pelted with flecks of ice. Brayden winced as the pelting continued and strengthened. Within minutes, hailstones rained down on them with a fury, collecting on the ground like minute snowballs.

With the other's help, Brayden managed to rise. He whirled the hail from his boots and shoved a foot down. "Impossible one handed," he growled. "I'll never get these on." He grabbed Kawley's arm. "Come on. This hail hurts like hell."

Hoofing through the woods barefooted couldn't have been easy, but Brayden kept up a good stride. If she hadn't been dodging the hailstones herself, she might have giggled at the sight of this muscular man tiptoeing across the uneven ground. She had recently buried two men with her bare hands, been shot, been shot at and held down a man as others fried his shoulder. While she knew it to be oddly inappropriate, she savored the humor of watching him attempt to avoid the sharp twigs that surely were digging into his feet.

CHAPTER SEVEN

WITH HIS BOOTS IN HIS RIGHT ARMPIT AND HIS RIGHT HAND STEADYING his left arm to keep his wounded shoulder close to his body, Brayden was unsteady on his feet. The fact that every stick and pebble dug into his bare feet and the ferocious hailstorm slapped every inch of the rest of him did nothing to help. Kawley was running next to him with her hands above her head and a cryptic grin on her face. He really couldn't blame her. Had it been a different place and time he, himself, might have seen the humor in it. But this was war and no laughing matter. Brayden was worried about having the strength to make it back to the cabin, let alone find Caleb and bring him home.

As if she read his mind, Kawley took his boots from him and wrapped his arm around her shoulders. "Lean on me. No sense in you falling and breaking open your wound."

Brayden knew he was fading and welcomed her support. Unfortunately she was much shorter in stature so the support was minimal but at least it kept him upright. The hail was falling so heavily it was difficult to see their way.

"I distinctly remember telling you the storm was coming!" Fletcher's voice boomed from the trees.

Brayden couldn't remember a more welcomed sight. He shifted his arm to Fletcher's shoulders, allowing the other one to drag him along. He knew he had to save his strength so he would be up to riding out in the morning.

Without breaking stride Fletcher called over his shoulder, "Keep up there, little manling. I can't be dragging the both of you."

Kawley scooted around Brayden's other side and slipped her arm around his waist. He was glad of the extra support so that he could tread lightly over the prickly, wooded ground.

"I thought the two of you would have had brains enough to have come back before the storm. While I really didn't want to get pelted to save your sorry backside, I realized little man there wasn't big enough or strong enough to carry you back."

Kawley's scrunched expression told him she was fuming with Fletcher's insults. He was not even certain Fletcher wasn't spouting to see if he could get a rise out of the younger one. Brayden hoped Kawley could keep her silence and her disguise.

Brayden stepped on something sharp. He double stepped and tripped. Fletcher swung his other arm around in front to catch him.

"Bry, why are you barefooted? Where the hell are your boots?"

Brayden yanked Fletcher's shoulder forward as if to hurry him along. "It's—"

"Another long story? My God, Bry, you are going to have an arm's length list of long stories to tell my son if we ever get out of this mess." He glanced around at Kawley. "Something tells me you have something to do with this. I don't remember Bry having a plethora of long stories before you appeared."

Brayden felt Kawley's whole body stiffen as she spewed, "And I suppose this entire hailstorm is my fault, too?"

Fletcher shook the hail from his face. "If your scrawny ass wants to take the blame for this hailstorm, be my guest."

"All right, you two, can we just get back to the cabin and take up this discussion later? The hail is stinging every inch of me."

"The pelting ice might cool down little mister hot head over there. And by the way, I'm still waiting for an explanation of why you are here in the first place, mister."

Kawley bit off his sentence. "For your information I don't even want to be here!"

Brayden had no free arm to tighten around Kawley as a warning. He concentrated his thoughts, hoping to reach her. *Kawley, please don't say any more.*

The hail pelting intensified, and Brayden was grateful for it. Thankfully it quieted the two at his sides, and the cabin came into view. Once inside, the three of them literally fell to the floor. No one spoke for a long time.

"With this storm, I don't think anyone will be noticing a smoke trail so I think it's safe to light a fire," Fletcher muttered. His surly expression made Brayden fear he was not finished with the conversation he had started outside.

Fletcher grabbed Brayden's coat and threw it over his shoulders. "Put this on. I can hear your teeth chattering. If you spike a fever, I'll be leaving you and squirt there by the side of the road, and you can limp back to Oscar's farm."

"In a way I'm glad it was hail and not rain or we would all be drenched," Brayden offered. He was thankful the fever had finally broken. "Anything we can use to boil up a bit of coffee?"

Kawley rose and searched through the dusty cabinets. She found several dented tin cups, a plate and container with a lid. "Here's a pot but it looks like it hasn't been used since John Rolfe stayed here."

Fletcher was down on one knee preparing a fire. He whipped his head around. "Who?"

"John Rolfe? Pocahontas?"

"Not sure Pocahontas drank coffee, Kawley," Brayden interjected, trying to cool the confrontation. "But I'm sure she would have welcomed a cup if she were here."

Kawley jutted her chin. "Actually Captain John Smith was rumored to have shared coffee with Pocahontas."

Fletcher crossed the room in two large strides. "Give me that." He grabbed the pot from Kawley's hand, turned it upside down and slammed its side with the palm of his hand several times. Flecks of dirt and a few pebbles hit the floor. Fletcher kicked at them with a huff, and the pebbles danced across the floor. He wiped it out with his handkerchief. "It's going to have to do. Where's the bucket of water?"

Kawley threw her hand toward the door. "It's back by the river. We'll have to wait until the storm lets up a bit."

"Damn it, Kawley," Fletcher yelled.

"Fletcher!" Brayden admonished him.

Fletcher whirled around to face Brayden. "He took it to bring back fresh water, didn't he?"

Kawley jumped in between them. "Well I brought Brayden back instead!"

"*I* dragged Brayden back. You were supposed to bring fresh water. We need it to drink as well as to change the bandages. Now fetch the water."

"Fletcher, no! Remember it's hailing outside?"

Before Brayden could say another word, Kawley stomped out and slammed the door. "Help me into my boots, Fletcher. I'm going after him."

Fletcher yanked Brayden's arm from the boot. "Like hell you are. I just dragged you back in here. The little manling left the bucket, now he can fetch it."

Brayden snatched his arm away and nearly passed out from the pain the abrupt jerk caused him. "Let go of me. Why are you riding him so hard? Answer me. I've never seen you like this."

"Why? Our best friend was brutally beaten and kidnapped. We were hot on their trail when you didn't show up at the mission. I double back thinking I'd meet up with you and we'd rejoin Clive and Rush in no time. Instead, I watch you nearly die for a complete stranger. I find out we are now saddled with mister manling out there on the chance he is who he says he is. Do I have it straight so far?"

"My God, Fletcher. What's gotten into you?"

"Me? You haven't been yourself since Lavinia died."

"You don't know what happened that day."

"No, I don't. But I know your spirit crept into Lavinia's coffin and never came back out."

"Leave it be, Fletcher," Brayden growled.

"No. I won't leave it be. This has been a long time in coming and needs to be said. We've always been friends, yet since that day you've been nothing more than a shell. Your damn journal has become a bandage on a permanent wound. You've retreated so far into those cursed pages until I want to burn it to get a reaction out of you. Any reaction, good or bad! You put up a wall for me to beat my head against, but you take a shot for someone you just met. Why? Do you have a death wish?"

"Fletcher, don't."

"Couldn't bring yourself to do the deed so better a blue coat do it for you?"

Brayden felt his strength fading and dizziness clouding his thoughts. He rubbed his forehead and took a step backwards.

Clearly, Fletcher interpreted his silence and step as an admission. He jerked forward with an outstretched hand. "My God, Bry. Why didn't you confide in me?"

Brayden slapped away the proffered hand and sidestepped. "If that was my wish, Fletcher, a blue coat would certainly not be my way."

"Then explain it to me, Bry. Who is this little man and why the hell are we saddled with him?"

"If you stop badgering me, I'll explain." He hesitated a moment to conquer and quell the fire raging through his left side.

"Well?"

"Dear God, Fletcher. Have you no mercy?" Brayden shook his head and blinked hard several times. "I met him along the road as I was on my way to the mission. He told me his brother was kidnapped by the same mob as Caleb."

Fletcher pointed his index finger toward the door. "So *he* says. And for that you took him at his word and offered to bring him along?"

"Yes. Do you not remember the farmer's wife had said there were two prisoners? You heard her."

"You only have his word that the second prisoner is his brother. Kawley and his mystery brother could both be deserters for all you know. We don't even know if one of those prisoners is Caleb. I'm telling you, Bry, there's something not right here. I feel it." He marched across the room and slammed the door with his fist. "What if he's not who he says he is?"

Brayden leaned into the wall for support. He was fading fast. "But what if he is? Would you have refused to help him? What if people hadn't believed you when you returned unrecognizable after ten years away? What if no one had helped you when you lost your memory? What if they had doubted your story and turned you away? You might never have reunited with Kyndee. You wouldn't have had little Tristan."

Quite plainly Brayden's words hit a nerve. Fletcher's jaw snapped shut. He lowered his head, shoved his fingers back and forth through his hair, then stared down at his hands. "You ask me what if, Bry? These hands were covered with your blood. I watched it spurt out of you while I felt powerless to stop your slipping away. Have you any idea what that feels like?"

Guilt erupted into his throat, and Brayden forced it back down. "Yes, Fletcher. I believe I do," he whispered, not knowing if he actually said the words aloud or not. The memory hadn't lost any of its sting.

"Oh God, Bry. Forgive me." The moment faded and the intensity returned. "I'm just so worried about Caleb. What if we can't find him now? And if we do what if we're too late? I don't want any more complications."

Brayden was still reeling, and it put him on edge. "What are you getting at? Spit it out. You think Kawley is a complication?" He was concerned that Kawley still had not returned.

"Without him you wouldn't have that hole in your shoulder, now would you? And even if what he says is true, you're asking that we rescue two men instead of one." He shook his head. "Impossible." Fletcher stood tall and heaved a heavy breath. "I'm telling you now. When we find them, wherever we find them, make no mistake if they are together but only one of them can be saved, I won't hesitate. That one will be Caleb. Your manling out there can save his own."

"The 'manling' as you call him is smart and a crack shot. He'll be a help not a hindrance. All I'm asking is that you trust me."

Fletcher opened his mouth to speak when the door flew open with a hail of ice pellets. He turned his back in a huff, rested his arm on the mantle and stared at the fire.

Kawley walked to Fletcher and plopped the bucket by his feet. Water sloshed from the pail and splatted on the floor. She brushed the ice crystals from her shoulders. "Here's your water. I like my coffee strong."

Fletcher scowled at her as she trudged across the room and scrunched into the corner. His anger was so scarcely veiled that Brayden knew he expected Kawley to make the coffee as well. If Brayden had had his second hand available, he would have clapped. Instead he just smiled to himself. *What a performance, Kawley. Damn, what a woman.*

He felt badly that he had reacted so harshly to Kawley's mention of Lavinia when they were by the riverbank. He wasn't pleased that Fletcher had told her anything about Lavinia. He had been savoring their provocative bantering and her question had taken him by surprise with a visceral shock akin to a kick in the gut. He already felt he should wear a scarlet 'M' for murderer. Lavinia now lay cold and still in her grave because of him. He never should have married her. Knowing his discomfiture, in the past years his close circle had ceased to mention Lavinia in his presence but Kawley had no reason to hold back an innocent question. He saw her crestfallen face but could do nothing about it until he could regain his composure. Brayden hoped his change of subject eased her. Once again, and without meaning to, he had hurt another woman. The pages inside the grey journal would be scathed with self-loathing tonight.

———

Kawley had sipped her coffee slowly. She noted that it was Brayden who had handed her a cup, not Fletcher. Fletcher was probably still steaming that the 'manling' had managed to make it back from the river at all, and he was still saddled with him. Little did he know that it was she, herself, who had the last laugh because she had found another bucket not twenty feet from the door as well as an old pump that thankfully still worked. Then she had snuggled with the horses for a while to waste a few minutes. When the sufficient amount of time has passed, she ran back through the hail. She was wary of Fletcher, worried that he might thwart her ability to save Riley.

She sat silent, folded in her corner until both Brayden and Fletcher had finally settled in for the night. The firelight flickered, creating eerie shadows across the walls. She glanced side to side at the two men with her until their loud breathing gave her relative freedom to doze on and off. Terrifying nightmares caused her to wake with a start.

Fletcher lay on his side facing away from her. The first time she wakened, Brayden lay on his back. This time when she woke, he had apparently dragged himself against the wall to a partially upright position. His right hand was inside his shirt gripping his left shoulder, seeming to hold his wounded arm in place. She noted his breathing was not even and deep. Instead it was quick and staccato. He raised one knee while his head rolled slowly from side to side. His brows were furrowed and his mouth in a grimace. He straightened his leg with a thud and moaned softly. It was plain that his shoulder was aching and preventing a comfortable position for sleep. Once again, she was awash with guilt that this man was suffering immeasurably because of her.

Kawley's eye travelled over his sleepy form. There, sticking out near his hip was the grey leather journal. Funny that she had not seen it before, and she wondered how it came to be there. She didn't remember him carrying it when they had stormed the cabin, but their main concern at the time had been Brayden's shoulder. Fletcher had been right when he said the man went nowhere without it. Perhaps he had made an entry while she was outside retrieving the bucket.

Given the chance to study him once again, she could not help the thoughts that washed over her. Even in pain as he was, Brayden remained ridiculously handsome, in fact disarmingly so. No other man had ever intrigued and enticed her the way this one did. In the time they had been together Kawley had come to depend on him, his strength and his intuition. She had never had that in her life and her spirit savored being 'taken care of' for a bit. But it was weakening her confidence in herself and that was something she could not allow. If Fletcher had his way, the 'manling' would be gone as well as Riley's chances of rescue. Despite his reassurances, Kawley worried that in his weakened state, Brayden might not be able to withstand the pressure from Fletcher.

Brayden shifted positions and uttered another muffled groan. As he turned his face, he clenched his teeth and hissed. The pain was clearly getting to him. Kawley wondered if perhaps the fever had spiked again. She silently rose, retrieved the flask from the table and knelt next to him.

"Brayden, I suspect you're awake," she whispered. "I have your flask. It might help to take the edge off."

Apparently, he had dozed. Brayden opened his eyes and blinked several times as if trying to orient himself.

She touched the backs of her fingers to his forehead. His skin was cool. She opened the flask. "Here, take a few sips. It might help ease the fire in your shoulder."

Without a word, he hiked himself up straighter with his right hand and hissed as his left arm shifted forward. He grabbed at his shoulder, muttering under his breath. Kawley leaned into him, held the flask to his lips and he bolted the brew.

"Enough. Enough." She yanked the flask away. "You'll choke on it and have a coughing fit. If you think you hurt now, wait until you see how that would feel."

Leaning on his right hand, Brayden followed the flask and motioned with his left fingers. "Another."

"Slowly, big man." She put the flask to his lips again. "Gently and slowly."

He chuckled and raised an eyebrow. "You're learning fast, little man. That's exactly how a man should treat a woman."

"I'll try and remember that should the situation ever arise." She pushed him gently. "Now lean back and try to sleep."

"Unless I empty the flask, it's hopeless. No matter which position I try, I'm awake every ten minutes."

"How do you expect to ride out tomorrow if you don't sleep?"

"I managed it today, didn't I?"

"Barely. It was obvious you were struggling to stay in the saddle."

"How's your leg?"

"Healing quite well thanks to your concoction. Quit gabbing and drink up. You need rest to heal that shoulder, especially if you suspect something is broken or chipped in there." She handed him the flask. "Here. Put away the rest and perhaps you'll pass out."

Brayden appeared haggard and desperate as he nodded. He reached for the flask but before it was within his grasp he stopped and stared at Kawley with a quizzical expression. He drew back his hand. "Why are you suddenly so anxious for me to sleep soundly?"

"Just trying to be helpful." Kawley lowered her gaze and hoped he wouldn't question her further.

"Look at me. What's going on in that head of yours?" With surprising speed he jerked up straight. "Look at me. I don't like the look I see in your eyes. I've got an eerie feeling you won't be here when I wake." His grimace evidenced the pain the sudden movement cost him, but his wide-eyed expression attested to his concern.

Even as she melted in his gaze, her mind was made up. "I'm leaving."

"Kawley, no!"

"Shhhh." She glanced around at Fletcher. "You'll wake him. Brayden, he's too angry that I'm here. He doesn't understand, and he wants me gone. The only chance I have of finding Riley is if I go alone."

"No!" Brayden muttered. "You're wrong. If Riley is with Caleb, then his best chance is you staying with us. We will find them."

"But Fletcher—"

"Let me worry about Fletcher."

"I heard what he said."

"About what?"

"If they are together but only one can be saved, it would be Caleb. I understand. He doesn't want me here. If I were in his place, I would probably say the same. His words convinced me I have to make my own way."

It felt as though all the air around them was sucked into Brayden's deep breath. His lips were pursed, and his eyes clamped shut. When it appeared he gained control, he whispered, "Kawley, you'll never make it. Don't go. We can help each other."

Kawley slanted her head. "Help each other? Has it escaped your notice it's been entirely one-sided? You kept my leg from infecting and my head from being shot off. For your trouble you've been fire fried, have gaping holes in your shoulder and God only knows what's broken in there. If we hadn't met, you would have been on time to meet Fletcher and the others, might even have caught up to the group by now—"

"And you," Brayden interjected, "would have trailed them and us. You might have even been caught in crossfire. Don't you see we were bound to meet at one time or another?" He hesitated. "Unless whomever shot you once had taken better aim the second time, or worse." He pointed. "That leg might have infected and gone septic." He lifted one eyebrow. "Do you think there are many who would take the time to bury a body without a shovel?"

Despite the truth of his words, she was still unconvinced that staying would be an advantage. She was never one to depend on others because she had always been disappointed. At first Brayden's game of cat and mouse had been amusing and, frankly, lovely but now it was time to be back on her own, depending on herself and making her own decisions.

"Kawley, think about what you're doing."

"I am. I'm thinking you don't even have a plan."

"Do you?"

"I will. It'll come to me along the way."

"Stay with us, Kawley. Do it for your own safety."

Kawley shook her head. "No."

"Then do it for Riley."

"No." She had to maintain her decision. Brayden was so close she could do naught but stare deep into the sea green eyes. She studied his devilishly handsome face, his slightly uneven beard that would soon need another trim, his very kissable lips. He inclined his head. His gaze was warm, beguiling, luring her to him as surely as if his hands reached into her soul and captured her.

"We will find them, I promise. Whether they are at Old Capitol or somewhere else. We won't stop searching until we find them. I swear to God, we will find them. Stay. Please."

Kawley hesitated. "At this moment I almost believe you." No one had ever looked at her that way, and it took her breath away. His eyes were pleading in earnest, clearly because he believed his own words, but she wondered if he had enough belief for the both of them. She lowered her gaze to break the contact, to remain strong in her resolve. Then she heard him shift his position.

"Look at me."

Fiddling with her hands she looked up again. The magnetism of his gaze captured her as tightly as any iron shackles.

"Don't say, no, Kawley. Do this for yourself."

She shook her head. "No." Kawley studied his face a moment longer, trying to memorize every detail to savor during the lonely days ahead. Her gaze lingered on his eyes, one then the other. She willed herself to break away. Her resolve wavered then finally waned. "But I'll do it for you."

Did the man know the power of his eyes? No other man had ever treated her with such gentle kindness. No other man had ever seemed to enjoy sparring with her. No other glance had pierced her heart.

Neither moved a muscle. They could not kiss. They could not hug. They could not even touch. The space between them was inviolate yet in that moment nothing else and no one else seemed to matter. Brayden's gaze was so seductive she wanted to crawl within his arm, feel protected and confident that all would be well.

"What the hell are the two of you muttering about?" Fletcher's raspy voice and abrupt appearance cut through the silence so suddenly that Kawley nearly dropped the flask.

Brayden cleared his throat and coughed. "The pain was keeping me awake, and I was struggling to reach for my flask. Kawley heard me and brought it for me."

"While you, Fletcher, were snoring so loudly you never heard anything." Kawley sincerely hoped that were true.

"Shoulder bleeding again?"

Brayden pulled back his shirt and searched for fresh blood stains. "No, just aching intolerably. I thought my brew might dull the fire."

Fletcher turned with a wave of dismissal. He scratched the back of his head and then the back of his hip as he trudged back to his bedroll. "Get some sleep, you two. I'm leaving at dawn with or without you."

Good night. Kawley mouthed the words. She continued to gaze at Brayden, unwilling to break the contact.

Brayden's eyes travelled from the top of her head to her mouth and back again. *Good night,* he mouthed in return as if he, too, felt the warmth of their prolonged attention.

Kawley reached for the grey leather journal and handed it to Brayden. *Write your thoughts, Brayden. Write them so that one day I might be able to read them and understand.*

Brayden nodded and took the journal as if he understood her silent plea. Kawley rose and walked away.

CHAPTER EIGHT

DENSE CLOUDS DESTROYED ANY CHANCE OF THE MOON LIGHTING THEIR way. The three riders were forced to backtrack several times. Exhaustion was setting in and tempers flared.

"For God's sake, Fletcher. Is your memory that bad? Weren't you just here or did you send Rush and Clive on ahead when you turned back for me?"

"Then why don't you lead on? You've been here before."

"Nearly ten years ago when my father insisted I accompany him to New York. He stopped in the peach orchard by the mission and requested I collect a basket of peaches for my mother."

"The squirrels and the deer are the only ones collecting those peaches these days. The mission has been shuttered tight and deserted for years now. Parts of the roof are missing so I hope it doesn't rain tonight." Fletcher stood in his stirrups. "Damn, I know it was this way."

Brayden's pain was nearly intolerable, and his patience was wearing thin. "If we don't find it soon, we'll have to camp here and join Rush and Clive in the morning."

"We are sitting ducks out here. Anyone could pick us off one by one."

"May I say something?" Kawley asked in a quiet voice.

"No!" Fletcher retorted sharply. "I blame you for our being lost out here in the first place."

Kawley kicked her mare in the sides, and the horse scooted forward.

"As you wish. I guess I'll be meeting Rush and Clive by myself and explaining to them why you and Brayden are out for a midnight stroll."

"Bry, what the hell is the manling talking about now?"

"If you can silence your insults for a moment you might take the time to notice a sliver of light in the grove of trees over there a piece," Kawley berated him. "You did say parts of the mission roof were missing, did you not? I'd take a gamble it's the light of their lantern peeking out. Surely worth a look see rather than sleeping on the cold ground here." She turned Pickles and glanced back. "You coming?"

Even in the dim light, Brayden discerned the redness flooding Fletcher's face as though Kawley's discovery made the other one's blood boil. He nudged Ajax in the sides and trotted after Kawley. Within a few seconds his horse faced both ears backwards assuring Brayden that Fletcher's horse followed them, although he worried that the tension between Kawley and Fletcher was mounting.

As they neared the grove of trees, all that remained of the dilapidated mission came into view. It was difficult to see but it appeared one side of the building had collapsed into the field of weeds. The jagged branches of the old peach trees stretched over the clutter like sinister claws of rot and decay. Brayden was flagging and anxious to be off the horse but knew he had to hide his fatigue from Fletcher and the others. He also dreaded the confrontation which would surely be coming when Rush and Clive saw Kawley coming through the door.

Brayden was concentrating on how he would convince the other three to allow Kawley to continue with them when he saw it—a giant bald cypress—mocking him, nearly blocking the door of the mission, malevolently daring him to enter.

The death tree. The tree concealing the snake. The tree he had had chopped down at Avalon after Lavinia had died. As the three approached the mission the tragedy crashed back in on him. He remembered every word he had scribbled in his journal after they lowered his wife's body into the ground.

"It's been over two years and the memories still shatter me from the inside out. I held her as she slipped away. With surprising strength she pulled her hand from mine. Her eyes opened and closed one last time, but I couldn't miss the accusatory glare in their depths. I whispered my

remorse, but she was beyond my words. The slow hiss of her last breath hung in the air and then I remember the silence. The hush of the room was louder than anything I'd ever heard. I was crushed by the weight of it. Everything about her was the same: the silk ribbon at her temple, the one lock of hair that always fell across her forehead, the locket that hung around her neck. At the same time, everything was different. The dark lashes now hung limp over her lifeless eyes. The smile, erased by my last hasty words, would never again curve her mouth.

A horse whinnied outside, breaking the stillness, as the mantle of my guilt pounded around me. There was no way to undo the misunderstanding. My parting words were impulsive and wounding. Words can hit harder than fists; they cannot be unsaid or unheard. Now those words were the last between us. There would be no forgiveness, no absolution.

The scene crashes again and again through my mind. She spun from me and bolted. Had I followed expeditiously, it would have been my leg, my life. But I hesitated—in a momentary, selfish quandary—and it was Lavinia who startled the snake and been bitten, Lavinia who was lost. Her death was on my head, yet I know I will stay silent. I know I will carry the vile reason to my grave.

I was wrong to have told her. I've been wrong about many things. Sometimes this mantle of guilt tightens around me until I cannot breathe. Prior to the accident, I had never encountered an incident beyond my control. I was confident, sure of myself and what I could do. I dominated everyone and everything. Yet from the moment Lavinia was bitten, doubt has shattered me, has dominated me. From that moment I have been living a life among ruins.

There are just no words for such moments, only a horrific penalty to be extracted. I know in my soul that Fate will be persistent for atonement.

I remember two distinct times that evening when there was a light tap on the door. I ignored both intrusions, trapped in my own prison. When night finally fell, I crumpled on the cold, wooden floor. My entire body shook as never before. I had not the strength nor the will to stop it. Ironic how I remember every detail of that parting and yet the rest is a blur..."

"Bry, you coming?"

The voice shocked him. Brayden realized Kawley and Fletcher had dismounted and were waiting for him to do the same. He slid from Jax's back, careful not to jar his shoulder. "Kawley, follow me."

"Rush, Clive, it's me. Don't shoot." Fletcher yanked the handle and shoved the wooden door with his shoulder. He managed to clear an opening for them to pass. "Lucky we could get in at all. Somebody must have shuttered the doors and windows tight to keep it safe but over time every hinge in the place rusted shut."

Brayden guided Kawley in a wide circle around the tree to rid himself of the frightening images it evoked. He heard Rush yelling at Fletcher as they squeezed through the opening.

"About time you showed up. We were beginning to think you had just left us."

"Nah. I found Bry here shot and bloodied so things took a bit longer than expected."

"Shot? Brayden? Did he ride back with you?"

Fletcher clucked his tongue with obvious disdain. "He's here, and he dragged along a new complication. Bry?"

Ready? Brayden mouthed to Kawley. He watched her draw in a deep breath, jam her hat tighter on her head, square her shoulders and nod. She stomped around the wall with him.

"What is this?" Clive uttered. He leaped from the floor and leered at Kawley. "Who the hell are you?" He slammed his hand against the wall and curled his lip. "Brayden, I thought Rush and I made it clear we don't ride with some waif you found along the way. We sent Trey home remember?"

"Fletcher, you in favor of this?" Rush asked as he shoved himself from the wall.

"Nope!"

"Then why are we even discussing it? Get him out of here or I'm leaving," Clive shouted.

Kawley stood her ground. "I'm here because I believe my brother is being held by the same raiders as your friend, Caleb."

No one spoke. Clive's mouth snapped shut with a loud clap. Rush's eyes narrowed, and he took two steps closer. "Exactly how do you know this…mister?"

"Chatterton, Kawley Chatterton." She shoved her hands in her pockets and glared at the other two. "I trailed them and you. I watched you at the farm. I know about the Yankee dispatch. Best I can figure, they have both of them."

"Fletcher?" Clive demanded.

"Bry brought the little man here." Fletcher shrugged his shoulders. "Obviously, I don't have a say in this."

"Damn it, Brayden. Then he's your responsibility," Rush threatened. He leaned back against the wall muttering, "I don't like it...any of it."

"Me, neither. And I'm warning you, Brayden, if there's any trouble —" He pointed a boney finger at Kawley. "—I'm shoving that one out in front."

"Clive!" Brayden clamored.

Kawley shoved Brayden out of the way and stood tall. "Agreed," she bellowed above the din.

Clive's eyes flashed fire but he trudged away growling, "Ah hell. He's so scrawny, with my luck the damn Yankees will miss him and hit me."

Brayden released a deep breath with the apparent truce, and the five of them settled in for the night. It was only then that he realized neither Rush nor Clive had asked about his shoulder. He chuckled inside. The manling was quite a woman.

———

"Well, well, well. Looky what we have here."

Kawley turned and gasped. Her hand flew to her chest as if her heart were pounding. She was visibly shaking. "Oh my God!"

"Oui, oui, mon cher. Qui attendiez-vous?"

"Certainement pas vous!" Kawley shrieked.

Desperately trying to distract Fletcher and the others from their shock at Kawley speaking French, Brayden bellowed, "Who are you and what do you want?" He slid his hand toward his pistol.

"I wouldn't do that if I were you. Ceisel?" Another man appeared from around the front wall of the mission with guns clearly locked and loaded. The follower seemed to be the henchman though his dusty clothes were shabby in contrast to those of the French spewing intruder.

The lump in Ceisel's cheek on which he continuously gnawed did little to enhance his overall appearance. The flickering light of the lanterns made their appearance all the more eerie.

"There now. Before we get started, why don't the four of you drop all your guns and knives and back up against the wall?"

Fletcher stepped forward instead of back. "Not 'til you—"

Ceisel fired a shot, sending a flurry of wood chips out of the floor, barely missing Fletcher's foot. "You were told back against the wall."

Fletcher, Brayden, Clive and Rush, placed their weapons on the floor and backed up against the wall. Brayden pulled Kawley with him as he moved.

"No, no." The elegantly dressed raider pointed the pistol at Kawley. "That one can come over here." He motioned with the gun for Kawley to separate from Brayden.

Brayden pulled Kawley further back. "Leave him alone. He's just a pup." He wasn't sure if Kawley knew the Frenchman, but plainly his appearance terrified her.

"Over here, now!" When Kawley hesitated he added, "You know I can make you."

"Kawley, stay here." Brayden shoved Kawley behind him. "If you want a hostage, take me."

"You have one arm in a sling. You wish to be missing the other one? Because, monsieur, that's exactly what's going to happen if the little scrawny one doesn't get over here."

"Mister, what the hell is going on?" Fletcher yelled as he stepped forward.

Ceisel cocked the hammer on his rifle. "Listen, big man, you've been told twice now to back up and shut up. Want to risk a third?"

Fletcher backed up. "Bry, what the devil do you know?" he whispered.

The Frenchman extended his hand. "I'll just take that pouch if you please. Kawley, bring it here."

"Bry, if you know something, spit it out now!"

"I'm so sorry. For your own safety, please don't resist," Brayden heard Kawley whisper as she slipped the pouch from around Fletcher's neck. She walked over the planking with small slow steps. "Is this what you want, Philippe?"

Brayden straightened. "How do you know his name?"

The Frenchman snatched the pouch, grabbed Kawley by the arm and threw her to the floor. Her expression clearly implored Brayden not to move. The other one yanked the dispatch from the bag, slipped it into his vest pocket and tossed the pouch aside. "This...and you."

"Dear God, you do know him!" Brayden stammered incredulously.

"I warned you, Bry." Fletcher exploded. "Kawley's a spy or a deserter or something. God damn it. I told you I didn't want him with us. You should have dumped his sorry ass miles ago."

Philippe dug the toe of his boot into Kawley's buttocks. "Sorry ass." He smiled and cocked his head. "But very pleasing."

"You're disgusting," Fletcher spit out.

"Fletcher, stop!" Clive and Rush pleaded. "You're just making things worse."

"Yes, Fletcher, stop," Phillipe retorted. "Your harsh, jarring voice is really starting to grate on me."

Philippe leaned down to Kawley. *"Donc bon de vous retrouver, ma chere."*

Kawley scrunched her face. *"Pitie je ne peux pas dire la meme chose."*

"Speak English, damn it," yelled Fletcher.

"A chaud, n'est-ce pas?" said Philippe as calmly as if they were at a tea gathering, clearly toying with them. He glanced back at Fletcher. "As you wish, monsieur. I told Kawley it was good to finally catch up with her. Sadly, she doesn't return the sentiment. I also told her that if the hotheaded one does not hold his tongue, I will be forced to shoot him."

Apparently, Fletcher was so stunned at the threat that he missed the fact that Philippe kept referring to Kawley as 'she.' Rush clearly caught the change.

"Why does he keep calling Kawley, 'she'?" he whispered to Brayden.

Philippe cupped his hand behind his ear. "I heard that. Allow me to clear up any misunderstandings." He snatched Kawley's cap from her head and thick, burgundy braids fell about her shoulders.

A loud gasp erupted from the trio. To Brayden it was louder than any scream he had ever heard.

"You son of a bitch," Fletcher shot out.

"Monsieur, are you referring to me or your companion who most clearly appears not to be shocked by the revelation? Because I would take your comment rather badly."

The accusatory glare Fletcher cast Brayden was akin to a knife in his belly. He felt quartered and gutted when Fletcher spit at him, "You knew, didn't you?"

"Fletcher, I—"

"You've known the whole time?" he growled loudly. Brayden could tell from his stance that Fletcher most likely would have lunged for his throat if Ceisel had not had a barrel aimed straight at them. "The whole damn time?"

Philippe outstretched his palms. "Gentlemen, gentlemen, this petty arguing is becoming rather tedious and is of no consequence to me. I have to decide what to do with the lot of you." He shrugged his shoulders. "Since your lives hang in the balance, I suggest you keep your silence since I will gladly shoot the next person who speaks." He shoved the barrel of his pistol into Kawley's ear and held another pointed at their heads. "Ceisel, tie each of them securely. If anyone resists, someone will be shot, and it makes no difference to me who that someone might be."

Ceisel bound Rush's hands and feet. Fletcher was the next one yanked around and tied as well as any calf bound for branding. Brayden noted that he would not even make eye contact with him. While it was plain that Ceisel was well practiced in shackling, it took every ounce of self-restraint he possessed not to jump at the Frenchman's throat. Brayden couldn't risk the threat to Kawley's life. His mind was racing in an attempt to figure a plan, but it was too filled with confusion. *Who was this man? How did Kawley know him? Why was he after her? Dear Lord, had he really brought a spy into their midst? Had he brought this hell on them?*

When Ceisel came to Brayden he appeared to take special delight. He ripped the sling from Brayden's left arm and yanked the arm behind him. Brayden choked in pain and fell forward.

Philippe laughed as Ceisel grabbed Brayden around the neck and pulled back upright. "Tie that one especially tight, Ceisel. I have a feeling about him."

Brayden blinked hard and willed himself not to pass out. He could feel something trickling under his shirt and was slowly losing feeling in his arms. He fervently hoped the other three could think of a plan because his strength was fleeting.

As all attention was concentrated on Brayden by Philippe's comment, Clive obviously seized the moment to make a break for it. He jumped up, shoved Ceisel and shots rang out. Clive was thrown by the force of it, his face a portrait of shock, his chest open and bloodied. He dropped to the floor and lay still as blood pooled around him.

"Nooo!" shouted the other three, struggling against their cords. "Clive!"

Ceisel kicked Clive's body as he stood and brushed himself off. "You're quiet now, aren't you?"

Fletcher and Rush both glowered at Brayden. Their heaving chests and expressions of shock and sorrow were laden with accusation.

Brayden stiffened. His mind refused to believe what he had just witnessed. Clive's blood oozed from his body, seeping into the cracks, spreading in random patterns across the floor. When the red flow wet his leg, Brayden saw the stream carried with it a chunk of flesh that moments ago had been part of a living, loyal friend. He gagged, and his eyes watered. Brayden fought back both. Dear God, it was true. Clive was dead.

"He was warned," Philippe stated calmly. "He didn't listen." He pointed the pistol at them one by one. "Who's next? You? You? You? Tell them, Kawley. Tell them I do not make idle threats." When she said nothing, he kicked her again in the buttocks. "Tell them."

Kawley appeared deflated, the fight gone out of her. "Philippe Armagnac fancies himself royalty who commands. Do what he says. It's useless to resist."

"Oh, *ma cher*, you make me out to be a monster."

Kawley's eyes suddenly flashed fire. "A monster? Who but a monster would do this?" She pulled up her sleeve and showed the brand under her left forearm.

"Oh, my God. He branded her."

The barrel of Ceisel's rifle whipped across Fletcher's face. Blood ran down his cheek. "Apparently you don't take orders well, big man. Maybe that little tap on the head will help to remind you."

"Yes, Philippe, you are both monsters. Ceisel for bashing Fletcher and you for your delight in doing this." Kawley yanked down the collar of her shirt to show the stripes from a whip. As her jacket fell open, the small derringer slipped into her hand. She pulled the trigger, but it misfired. The thrust of the Frenchman's kick sent it flying across the floor.

Kawley shot forward and bit him in the thigh. Philippe hollered something in French, grabbed her head by the back of her hair and bent her neck backwards at an odd angle until she released him.

Brayden feared he had broken her neck. In his weakened state, the entire scene was happening rapid fire. What was unfolding before him seemed to be from a grotesque macabre play, a nightmare that could not possibly be real. Yet here it was, with Clive dead in a pool of blood and the three of them trussed like helpless chattel. Ceisel stood guard over them with an expression of sheer relish.

Philippe brought his face down to Kawley's. "Don't ever try that trick again. First of all, *ma cher*, I branded you because you are mine and will always be mine. And those stripes are for reasons just like this. Perhaps I should give you a few more right now?" He threw her away and stood tall. Then a cryptic smile spread across his face that shot shivers through Brayden.

"Tu agis tellement comme in garçon. Permitted-moi de vous aider avec votre deguisement. Il sera plus facile de vous emmener chez vous."

Kawley scooted backwards across the floor. "Don't touch me."

With what evil did he threaten her? Brayden shifted his position, and Ceisel's barrel was immediately in his face. He glanced over at Fletcher's cheek and shifted back. The barrel wound was now just trickling blood. The hit luckily had missed his eye, but it looked painful just the same. Rush hadn't uttered a sound or budged an inch, but his eyes were nearly popped out of his head.

"Oh no, *ma cher*. I don't intend to do it. You will do it while I have the distinct pleasure of watching."

"Do what?" There was a slight quiver in Kawley's voice.

"Why don't you take that little knife out of your pocket? I know you never go anywhere without it. You know the one, *Kiki*...that little Ames with that unusual shield. I knew I had seen it before. Took me a long time to guess what your father must have done for that ambassador to gift you with such a unique trinket."

Brayden remembered the knife but could not remember seeing any seal, foreign or otherwise. Perhaps he was more interested in the name to have noticed anything else. But why would Kawley carry anything with such an adornment?

"Either you retrieve it from your pocket, or I will."

Kawley stretched out her hip and pulled the knife from her pocket.

"I find the hatred I discern in your eyes an intoxicating challenge. You are thinking you would like to plunge that little blade into my chest and twist it, no?"

Brayden imagined that that was the exact thought of all of them. Philippe's manner and voice were evil incarnate.

Philippe picked up one of Kawley's thick, long braids and held the end to his lips. "Yes, this will help you with your boyish disguise. Take your knife and slice right here." He ran his finger along her scalp.

"No!"

"Use your knife or I will use mine." Philippe pulled a long knife from inside his coat. "But I just might slip and slice other things...ears...fingers...necks. Hmm?"

Ceisel chuckled and licked his lips. Brayden wanted to trip him but trussed hands to feet behind him there seemed no point. Even the lantern was out of reach.

"Now, Kiki." He waved his knife at her.

Slowly and deliberately Kawley raised one braid and stared at Brayden. Never breaking eye contact, she severed the braid near the scalp with one swift stroke.

"Tsk, tsk, tsk. That little blade is a might sharper than I remember." He flipped his hand in a wave of dismissal. "It's of no consequence. You may continue. Now the other."

Kawley maintained eye contact with Brayden the whole time as she sliced the other braid through. He could feel the pain emanating from her face.

Philippe snatched the braids from her hand, replaced his knife and held them out like a trophy.

"You're revolting."

He slapped her across the face with the thick ropes of her own hair. "Don't you ever call me names, or I'll use a few of my own. How about traitor?"

"My father was never a traitor. You spread stories that weren't true."

"He and your mother met with some foreign minister on the Lady Elgin. Justice was served when that ship went down. It was my duty to suggest several names of rebels suspected of Liverpool cotton deals."

"You spread lies. They were friends. They had met in London on holiday. You spread lies that cost my family everything."

"Except your father promised me you...remember, cherie?"

Ceisel was so engrossed watching Philippe and Kawley, it gave Brayden a chance to catch Fletcher's eye. At first Fletcher refused to maintain the contact but he plainly realized that working together was the only way to possibly escape. Using the only signals allowed them, Brayden and Fletcher formed an audacious plan that they both knew had little chance of succeeding but they had to try something and soon.

"I will never go anywhere with you. You are nothing but a liar and a fraud."

Philippe harrumphed, stared at the ceiling and scratched his chin. "Oh yes, you will. You see I'm not afraid of you, little one."

Ceisel hooked his rifle under his elbow, grunted and applauded.

"You should be, you dirty Union spy."

Philippe's arm shot out and slapped Kawley in the head. Before her limp body hit the floor, both Fletcher and Brayden slid around, knocking Ceisel to the floor. His body tackled the lantern which broke and sent oil all over, along with the fire. The flames spread everywhere with amazing speed. Covered in oil, Ceisel screamed as the blaze incinerated his clothes and sautéed his skin. The blaze separated Philippe and Kawley as thick smoke filled the mission. Brayden vaguely thought he saw Philippe cover his mouth with his scarf and try several times to grab her where she lay before he turned, ran and slammed the door. But there was no mistaking the death knoll of a bolt being jammed through the handles.

The fire flared out of control, rapidly consuming the dry wood. The smell of burning hair and skin was horrific. Brayden was coughing. Fletcher and Rush were also.

"Kawley," Brayden called out. "Kaw...Kaw...ley," he yelled again, coughing repeatedly. His lungs were burning with the smoke. "Fletcher, if I get close, do you think we—" He coughed and gagged. "—do you think we can untie these?" Fletcher didn't answer. "Rush?" Rush didn't answer either. *Had they passed out; were they on fire?*

Dear God. No door, no windows, no way out. Brayden struggled against his restraints, spinning in useless circles but the tug-of-war with himself merely left him gasping for air. He yanked his arms until he felt the skin ripping from his wrists. Still, Ceisel's knots held.

"Fletcher! Rush!" he screamed again. They were snared and tied like foxes whose wily wits had failed them. Smoke enveloped and suffocated him and oddly, at that moment, he envisioned the roast venison they had savored at their last dinner together. The unbidden image panicked and gagged him. He clamped shut his eyes and desperately dragged in what he was determined would not be his last breaths. Though he knew it to be futile, Brayden yanked the ropes with the terror, brawn and rigor only desperation could muster.

Perhaps it was the blood on his wrists that helped the ropes to slip. The opening was enough to give him hope but unfortunately was not enough to free him. "Damn it," he screeched. His throat was raw, yet he doubled his efforts. "Come on! Let go!"

Suddenly he felt hands behind him, severing the restraints. The hands pushed him.

"I'll slice Fletcher's ties while you drag Rush. Hurry!" Kawley coughed hard and deep. "Hurry! There seems to be more air down low."

His limbs were burning but Brayden slid along on his side with his right arm, dragging Rush who was limp and unresponsive. With limited use of his left arm, the effort was slow and painful. Having little air to breathe required a Herculean effort but death was the only other choice, and a painful choice at that.

Hands reached through the smoke. "Let me help." It was Kawley, pushing him, pulling Rush. "Hurry, hurry."

Rush's limp body abruptly dropped out from in front of him. "Down now, Brayden. Grab the handle and swing down."

Brayden couldn't see anything and groped the air. Kawley's hand grabbed his and slammed it on something metal. Brayden's right hand hung on with the last of his strength, and he plowed through the opening. The swing sent him into a crash landing on his left side, and he cried out before he could smother it.

"I know. I know. I'm sorry for pushing you, Brayden, but—" She coughed repeatedly. "I need your help. This cellar bought us time to find another way out but minutes only."

In the dim light Brayden realized that there was less smoke. They were all beneath the mission. He could make out that one side of the cellar had collapsed. Shards of broken wood littered the floor. The roar above warned of mere moments to find an escape before the air was sucked out by the flames atop them.

"Look, Brayden, roots." Kawley worked at the dirt with a voracious fervor. "It's here. Help me dig."

Fletcher stood and shook himself off, but his grueling cough threw him forward. "What the hell?"

"I pushed you in. Dig, Fletcher. No questions. Dig," Kawley shouted. "Use the jagged wood pieces to tear through this corner."

Droplets of searing oil trickled through the burning floorboards. Brayden worried that they were falling dangerously close to Rush but there was no time to drag him further away. The oil splattered in the dirt floor again and again, as loud as any drumroll, ticking off the seconds of life left to them.

The three of them clawed at the packed dirt, choking with their efforts. They grappled with the roots, scratching and scraping in a unified assault. Finally they saw a twinkling light, the light of the fire above flickering against the trees. The air through the hole was sweeter than anything else Brayden could remember. It held the promise of life. But could they widen it enough for escape before their time ran out?

They attacked the hole but when the opening was wide enough for them to fit through, the fresh breeze fanned the firestorm. They heard a crackling sound, then more crashing. Their sanctuary was crumbling. Billowing smoke swallowed them.

"What's that?" asked Rush who was now up but wobbly.

"Death's calling card," retorted Fletcher. "Let's get the hell out of here."

Kawley pushed through first, then Brayden. Next came Fletcher but as Rush was pushing through, the floor of the mission came crashing down, pinning his legs. He screamed in pain as the other three dug and pulled to free him. Finally they succeeded and dragged him a safe distance from the heat of the inferno. Thankfully the old barn was far enough from the blaze to have saved the horses from certain death.

Brayden held his spinning head and slid to the ground against the trunk of a tree. He grabbed his middle, coughed and gagged. The coughing caused his left side to spasm and send shooting stabs of fire across his chest.

"Damn," said Fletcher as he fell to his hands and knees. "That was too close." He swiped the blood from his forehead and cheek. "Damn thing better stop bleed—" His words were cut off as he collapsed to his side and coughed repeatedly. After several moments he sat up and leaned on his hand over Rush's leg. He whistled. "Doesn't take a wizard to know that leg's broken." Fletcher fell forward, coughing and choking again. "And just as soon as my gut falls back down where it belongs, I'll attempt binding it for you."

Rush didn't answer. He had propped himself on his elbow and quietly emptied his belly in the weeds where he lay.

The fire lit up the dark sky, popping, crackling, sending sparks high into the air. The roof crashed in an ugly monstrous heap, leaving only the broken stone walls as evidence that a structure had ever been there.

———

Brayden must have passed out because the next thing he saw was Fletcher attempting to secure Rush's broken leg. At least his head had settled in one place and the waves of nausea had stopped, but his throat was as raw as his wrists. The fire had died down a bit; most likely there was little left to burn.

"About time you woke up, Bry. I needed your help with this leg, and you were busy napping." Fletcher stared straight at Brayden. "But then again, you've been busy with a lot of other things lately, haven't you?"

Although he knew exactly what the other one meant, he felt the need to explain. "Fletcher, you've been one of my best friends for years—"

"Save it, Bry. That was then," Fletcher shot back. "This is now."

Brayden rose and glanced around. "Where's Kawley?"

"Don't know and don't want to know. She and that prince of Armageddon can go to hell for all I care."

"Fletcher!"

"Don't 'Fletcher' me. Not long ago I had to fire fry your shoulder. Now I have one friend in ashes, one friend in a splint and the lot of us nearly burned to death. The way I see it, all these things have one thing in common...one Kawley Chatterton."

"But she's not to blame for what happened."

"All evidence to the contrary." Fletcher pulled his stock from his neck and wound it around Rush's leg. "I don't know what you knew or when you knew it but when this is all over, unless you can convince me otherwise..." He left the warning floating in the air.

"Fletcher, I knew only that Kawley was a woman, nothing more."

"That alone was enough, Brayden, and I didn't hear you defending her. Maybe deep down you don't believe her either. That imposter cost Clive—" Rush growled and threw back his head, grimacing as Fletcher tightened the splint.

"Rush, Fletcher, I..." Brayden couldn't continue. There were too many pressing questions and there was only one way to resolve them. Outraged that he had been duped gutted him and the shooting pain in his left shoulder threatened to drop him where he stood. He hooked his left hand between the buttons of his coat to form a sling for his arm. "I'm going after her."

"Why? So she can spew more of her honeyed lies? Are you so besotted with her you're willing to send the rest of us, sack and saddle, to an early grave?"

"No! I'm going after her because I want answers, answers that may be the key to rescuing Caleb." Brayden balanced on a knee next to Fletcher and looked him square in the face. "And because I value our friendship more than you know."

Fletcher harrumphed. "You don't even know where she's headed."

"Toward Capitol City, of course. She intends to find her brother."

"You're telling me you still believe that load of nonsense she handed you?"

Brayden was asking himself the same question. "I sure as hell intend to find out."

"You only have one arm, barely enough blood for the strength to sit your saddle, and can't possibly track her at night, Bry."

"Watch me." He stood and backed up. "I'll be back before first light."

CHAPTER NINE

BRAYDEN GALLOPED FULL CHISEL FROM THE CONFLAGRATION. A MYRIAD of emotions flooded him—anger, fear, disappointment, disillusionment. Rush had been right; he had not defended Kawley. Why? Deep down did he not believe her? Surely the other two didn't believe her. But had anyone given her a chance to explain? He had to find her to answer scores of questions. Why had she run? What was she hiding? Why didn't she stay to make sure everyone had survived? Who was this Philippe and what had he to do with any of this? Did she run to meet up with him somewhere else?

The more puzzles that raced through his head, the faster he pushed Ajax to pound the ground. Kawley had a fast horse and a head start. Damn, Fletcher was probably right; his chances of finding her were slim, especially in the dark. Still, he had to try. He had already lost one comrade to a madman. He could not risk losing Fletcher's friendship without knowing the reasons how and why the confrontation with Philippe Armagnac had happened. Was Fletcher also right about the other things? Had Kawley infiltrated their group purposely?

Who was Kawley Chatterton, really? He hated to admit, even to himself, that he truly did not know the answer. Had Kawley been a man would he, himself, have been as inclined to believe such a wild story without demanding some sort of proof? Would he have taken a shot for a stranger? Viewing the sequence of events through Fletcher's eyes, he could not blame Fletcher for thinking him a bit unhinged. Had Kawley bewitched him with her exquisite sapphire eyes? Clive's senseless death slithered under Brayden's mantle of guilt and weighed heavily on his shoulders.

The trail was cold, yet he pushed on, not even knowing why. Still weak from blood loss and exhausted from tunneling under the fire, Brayden was slowly losing hope—hope that he would find Kawley to secure the answers he desperately needed, hope that he could ever repair his friendship with Fletcher, hope that he would have the right words to explain Clive's death to his parents, hope they would find Caleb alive and well, hope…

He reined Ajax to a walk and searched the sky. If the clouds parted, perhaps the moonlight would help to find the way. But which way—the way forward, the way back? Alone, in the weighty silence, events of the last hours caved in on him like a crushing landslide. In his mind's eye he watched Clive lunge at Ceisel, gasped as the rifle fired, saw the blood and flesh spew from Clive's back, felt the thud as his lifeless body plunged to the floor. Brayden's throat tightened and his eyes watered near to weeping at the loss. Were the others right? Had he brought Armageddon to the mission door? Questions battered him over and over until he was drained. At that exact moment even the urgent search for Caleb could not ignite a fire under him.

The wound in his shoulder flared red-hot from the hard ride. The wrist shoved between the buttons of his coat was not supporting the arm. He ripped the stock tie from his neck to fashion a crude sling. Brayden slid the flask from its case and swilled the brew, hoping the burning kick of it would overshadow both torturing plagues—his shoulder and his mind. With a heavy heart he released the reins, allowing Ajax to journey at his own pace, in whatever direction he chose. Brayden had neither the strength nor the desire to make that determination.

One stride became ten; one mile became ten. He dozed off and on amid most of it. He came to full wakefulness with a head-clonking scrape from a low branch. As he wiped his cheek, he stared at the blood on his fingers. Brayden recalled Fletcher doing the same thing as he had scrambled from the fire, releasing his fury, hollering that Kawley was an informant, that Brayden was responsible for Clive's death because he brought 'the spy' and her accomplice into their midst.

No! his mind screamed. *It was not true; it couldn't be!* For his own sanity he had to find Kawley and prove it—one way or the other. Brayden yanked the reins and legged Ajax into frantic gallop.

———

The clouds had separated, giving light to the way forward, and Brayden plunged on. Noting a fork in the road ahead, he dropped the reins, hoping Ajax would be able to fix on Pickle's scent. The equine chose one path over the other without hesitation, without even breaking stride, giving Brayden hope he might be closing in on Kawley's trail. In time he pulled Ajax to a walk to rest both of them. The night sounds all around him, sounds that used to soothe and console, were garbled in a mind full of self-recrimination. He struggled to block out everything and allow his mind a moment of rest in the emptiness. Eyes closed, his muscles flowed forward and back in motion with Ajax's stride, comforting and familiar. Small sounds filtered through—the squeak of the saddle leather, Ajax's breathing from the hard ride, the even cadence of the hoofbeats on the ground. They wandered into the shallow part of the stream and stood. The cold of the water would be good for the horse's legs. After Ajax's breathing had calmed, Brayden allowed him a few sips of the trickling water.

Another sound filtered through. Brayden ignored it, loathe to release a rare moment of peace. The sound was soft but relentless. Ajax heard it, too, swiveling his head in its direction with his ears perked.

The sound stopped, and Brayden continued on his way. Suddenly Ajax stopped dead in his tracks and whirled around nearly unseating Brayden. "All right, boy," he said to his prancing mount. "I heard it again, too. Let's see what it is." Ajax nickered softly. "Shhh, Jax. No sense in letting it know we are coming." Feeling naked without his pistol, Brayden yanked his rifle from its sheath. Step by step they cautiously followed the sound. Brayden ran his hand along the equine's neck to calm him and encourage him to stop his prancing.

As they neared a clearing, the sound suddenly stopped. "I think whatever it is heard us coming, Jax." Brayden urged Ajax three more strides and then he saw her. Kawley sat next to a small fire, hunched over, her back to him.

Brayden sheathed his rifle and dismounted. "Kawley." She remained motionless. Either she had not heard him approach or was deliberately choosing not to acknowledge his presence. He walked closer. "Kawley, look at me." Again, there was no answer. "Kawley, Clive is dead, Rush is badly injured, and Fletcher nearly lost an eye. Fletcher blames you for everything and since you ran from the mission without seeming to care, I can't say he's wrong." He waited. "Kawley, say something!"

The hunched over figure never moved or even acknowledged he had spoken. Brayden's irritation spewed into anger. He stomped toward her and reached to grab her shoulder. "Kawley, I'm in danger of losing a lifelong friend, not to mention the fire fried holes in my shoulder because of you, and I think you at least owe me—"

As he turned her to face him, he couldn't continue. "Oh dear God, woman, what are you doing? What have you done?" It took him a few seconds to fully take in the scene in front of him.

Tears streaked her face, tears from an individual with more strength and resilience than any man he had ever known. Her expression alone shocked and unnerved him—determination to desolation to defeat. He grabbed a knife from her bloody hand.

"No," she whimpered. "Let me finish it."

"Finish what? Your life?" A portion of his original anger returned. "If you intend to kill yourself, I want, I *need* answers before I let you complete what you appear hell bent on finishing."

Kawley exploded with the most woeful laugh, inappropriate and out of place. "That's what you think I'm doing? Something else will take care of my life soon enough. If I wanted to end my life, it certainly wouldn't be with my little blade." She wiped her chin with the back of her hand. "Besides, I don't see a shovel hanging on Jax's saddle."

"I don't see the humor."

"No? Then how about the irony?"

"Irony of what?"

Kawley lifted the bloody leg of her trousers. There was a gash in her leg.

"Your wound broke open again?"

"I wish it were that simple." She touched the skin and winced. "Pickles slipped and threw me to the ground. Unfortunately, I landed on a very angry raccoon."

"You were bitten?"

"I tried to kick it away, but it was relentless. So I jumped into the stream, and it finally released me when it drowned and drifted away. Then I stayed in the water for a long time to clean out the bite."

Brayden examined the wound. "But this is more than puncture wounds."

"I know," Kawley answered in a weak voice. "I cut out as much flesh as I could before passing out."

"You did this?" Brayden's gut lurched at the image of her self-mutilation. He didn't think he could have done it. "But why?"

"When I was a child, I heard that if you quickly cut out the flesh that was bitten, there is a chance the sickness may be cut out as well. For some reason I tucked the information into the back of my mind." She snorted. "Never thought I would ever have need of it." She looked at him with eyes so wide Brayden thought he could touch her soul. "Do you see the irony of it now? In a short time you may have need of a shovel after all."

He ignored her remark but for this first time he spotted the blood dripping from her left arm. The wound alarmed him. "Were you bitten here as well?"

"No." Kawley shook her head. "I just didn't want to face eternity with *his* initials burned into me."

He stood and reached for her. "Let me help you mount up. There must be a doctor around here somewhere."

"Brayden, we both know if the raccoon was sick, there is nothing any doctor can do to change my fate."

"Stop it. You're not going to die!"

Kawley smiled but it appeared a feeble attempt. "Thank you for that."

"For what? I feel so helpless right now." In three strides he reached Ajax and dove into his saddlebag. He returned with bandages, the salve and his flask. "Until someone tells me differently, I'm treating these as I would any other wound. At the very least it will stop the bleeding and ease your pain."

He could feel her staring at him the entire time he poured the alcohol —on her leg, her arm, into her cupped hand—and dressed the wounds. Not once did she cry out or flinch.

"Seems to me, I remember you bandaging a wound once before, when we first met."

Brayden hesitated, remembering the incident, then tied off the bandage as best he could, fumbling with his bad arm. "As I recall, you yelped a bit more that time."

"Let me." Kawley finished tying off her leg wound dressings. "That fire burn was nothing compared to this one." She pointed to the flames.

He sat next to her. "I don't know how you had the courage to do what you did."

Kawley cocked her head to the side. "Did you think about it before you leaped in front of me to shield me from that shot?"

They were both quiet for a long time. Brayden wanted to ask her his barrage of questions but didn't have the heart.

"I can't tell you how sorry I am, Brayden."

"Sorry for what?"

"I've been thinking that if I die from this bite then you suffered that painful shot all for nothing."

"It wasn't for nothing. That leap kept you alive."

"Alive to soon writhe like a savage animal? I've been thinking maybe I was meant to die that day when you intervened. Maybe now the Fates are just putting things to right."

"No, Kiki. Fate doesn't work that way."

Kawley's mouth curved into a cryptic grin. Her full lips beguiled him. "You called me Kiki only once before."

Brayden was intrigued. "When? You forbade me to ever call you by that name."

The grin disappeared. "It was the night you lay bleeding, the night Fletcher and Oscar stitched and cauterized your wound, the night I felt helpless and feared you might die because of me."

Brayden shook his head and stared at the sky. "Thankfully, I have little memory of that night, just bits and pieces of a salacious dream that helped me to push past the pain."

"Will you tell me about your dream? Perhaps it will help me push past my pain as well."

He grunted and raised one eyebrow. "It was a trifle ungentlemanly."

"That's not fair. You've witnessed and, I might add, been party to my most unladylike behavior but I cannot hear about your imagined ungentlemanly behavior?"

"Suffice to say you were in the dream."

Kawley pivoted and didn't look at him. She simply stirred the fire and twirled her hand against the empty gap in her hair that had once been her thick braid. "Was I beautiful...in your dream?"

He gently pulled her back and turned her face to his. Her eyes were cast to the ground. Brayden cupped her chin. "Look at me, Kawley." She resisted. "Kiki...beautiful Kiki, look at me."

Her head came up, but her eyes were welled with tears. "Truly? You dreamed me beautiful?"

"Yes." How he wanted to kiss her but knew he could not. "However—"

"I know. I'm tainted and repulsive to you now that you've seen Philippe's mark on me." Kawley's face fell and she tried to pull away but he kept hold of her.

"—the beauty in my dream cannot compare to the utterly enchanting woman you are now, here with me." He gathered her in his arms and whispered in her ear. "You are such a magnificent mystery to me. Please tell me who Kiki really is. I need to know everything. Fletcher and Rush want me to believe the worst of you, but I can't."

She sat up, hissed and grabbed her leg. In a moment she calmed and let go. "Why can't you believe the worst? What stops you?"

Brayden patted near his left shoulder. "You can be fooled here." He tapped his breastbone. "Not here...not deep inside."

"How do you know that everything I will tell you will be the truth? How do you know, Brayden? What makes you believe me when the others refuse?"

He held her cheek in his hand. "The man known as Kawley Chatterton would lie for protection, would lie to shield a vulnerable secret and yet I would find no blame in that. But Kiki the woman could not look me in the eye and lie—not the woman who had me at knifepoint when we first met, not the woman for whom I freely offered my life, not the woman who had the heart and the fortitude to slice open her own leg and scorch a madman's brand from her arm...no, not that woman. Kiki, I will believe what you tell me, even if it is not what I want to hear."

Kawley's eyes studied his face, from the top of his head to his chin and back to his eyes. "I'm speechless."

"As refreshing as that might have been at another time, clearly that was not my intention now. I need you to speak to me, not stare at me."

"I'm simply overwhelmed." She brought her face close to his and grazed his cheek. "You are a very special man, Brayden Wakefield."

The night sounds, the raging war, the pain all faded away. There was nothing but the two of them, wounded as they both were. Brayden sensed the slender woman wanted to kiss him as desperately as he wanted to kiss her. The moment was sweet, fragile and fleeting.

Kawley spun and stirred the fire again. "I don't know where to begin."

Brayden hiked his back against the large nearby tree. "Anywhere, Kawley, just let the words come."

She scooted next to him and seemed to search for a comfortable position for her leg. "You already know everything there is to know."

"I do not! Are we back there again?"

She patted his thigh. "Shhhh. Do you want to hear this or not?"

Brayden settled himself. "Sorry."

"You already know everything there is to know about the very unladylike Kawley Chatterton." She grasped his hand in hers and placed it between them. "For the first time in my life someone wishes to know, and I wish to tell them, something about Kiki."

She took a deep breath and giggled softly. "I actually found it a bit thrilling to be Kawley, the man. I could do everything Kiki could not."

"For instance?"

"Have an original thought or an opinion and actually give voice to it. I could step outside the strict confines of ladyship and shout from the rooftops if I wanted to. I love books. I love learning and discussing new inventions and theories, but no one listened to Kiki...until Riley came into my life. My father gave me everything money could buy but it was Riley who gave me love." She smiled. "How the two of us managed to grow past childhood is a miracle. Riley would shoot arrows into the air, not caring where they landed. There were a few mishaps that were never to be mentioned again. We would crawl out the highest windows and scramble up the rooftops with everyone screaming for us to come down. The two of us would simply dance a jig up there. I would twirl and curtsy, and he would bow. Riley had such a flair for the dramatic. I used to tell him he was a prince from some foreign land who had been abducted." She growled. "Little did I know then he would live to actually be abducted."

"The raiders?"

Kawley nodded. "I still don't understand what they would possibly want with Riley. Ironically, he was one of the few who spoke out against James Hammond's mudsill speech in fifty-eight, no matter how eloquently it was delivered. But if that was it, why wait until now?" She blew out a long breath. "Nothing makes any sense."

"Will you tell me how Philippe plays a part in all this?"

"Philippe Armagnac. Who knew Satan could be so utterly charming at first. I don't even remember how he wrangled an introduction, but he did. Unfortunately, I had no say in whether a marriage proposal would be arranged. I felt no love for him, but I had no real objection to him either. My mother told me love would come later, and my father expected me to obey his wishes. Thinking back on it now I never really understood Philippe's objection to my time with Riley. In fact Philippe took an immediate dislike to Riley and, I suspect, the feeling was mutual." She slipped her hand from Brayden's and rearranged her leg. She clasped her hands in her lap and sat quietly.

It seemed the connection had been broken. "May I?" Brayden whispered.

"May you what?"

Brayden took her hand in his and intertwined their fingers. "Your words seem to flow more easily when there is a bridge across."

Her hand squeezed his—a movement so slight yet a touch that pierced him in ways and places he had had shuttered for a very long time.

"About a year ago," she continued, "my parents were on holiday to meet friends. How or why they came to board the Lady Elgin that night remains a mystery. Unfortunately, when she sank, they were not among the survivors. Riley and I were in shock. Philippe told us he would handle everything and we, innocently, allowed it. After a bit we decided it was not wise. I was in my father's private study when I found an unopened letter. Thinking it might be important I opened it and could not believe what I started to read. This person strongly advised against a union with Philippe. I scanned further to discover the reason, but Philippe happened to enter the study just then, and I questioned him. He flew into a rage and ripped the letter from my hand, eyed through it in a second, crumbled it and threw it across the room to the grate."

Kawley squeezed his hand even tighter. "I had read stories of fire-breathing dragons rising from the earth but until that moment I had never seen evil emerge from a person's face before—anger, rage, hatred, wickedness and sin. He screamed that I had no right to enter the study or to open the letter. When I screamed back that I had every right, he came at me with his crop. I tried to shield myself, but I was no match for a fully enraged madman. Philippe threw me to the floor and whipped me over and over." Her jaw was clenched, and she bounced their hands on the ground repeatedly as though a whip were in her hand. "I remember screaming but the whip came down again and again. I knew there was no one to intervene. That's the last thought I had."

Brayden used every ounce of self-restraint not to scream what he was thinking. It was Kawley's story and she had to let it out, presumably for the first time. He sat silent and waited for her to continue.

"When I came to, I had no idea where I was. Then I realized I was in one of the quarters. I looked across the room and recognized Moses and Eva. They were whispering, but I could tell Eva was upset. I called to Moses, and he ran to me. He told me he'd heard everything but was too afraid Philippe would shoot him if he interfered. When Philippe ran out, Moses found me bleeding, branded and unconscious. He feared Philippe would kill us both so he carried me away. Eva was worried that no one would believe Moses if they saw my condition, especially if I died. Moses said I had always been too good to him for him not to have risked it." Kawley shook her head and blinked several times. "I'm sure there is more but that is most of what I remember. I told Moses I had to escape but my gown was torn, and I feared returning to the main house. Moses gave me a big grin and told me he figured I should run. He said he had gone back to the house to Riley's room and brought his clothes to disguise me as a man so I could run far, far away."

Kawley jiggled their hands. "You're very quiet over there, big man. You still awake, Brayden?"

"I have no words. Dear God, what you have been through, fighting horrific battles no one else knew about. How did you ever survive?"

"Eva helped dress my wounds, bind me and change clothes. She also dirtied my face a bit. The problem was my hair. Eva braided it and twisted the braids. Moses snugged the hat down and wished me God speed. He handed Pickles to me all saddled and supplied. At that moment if I had had paper and pen, I would have written their freedom papers. I intended to free them all when I returned. Then Moses told me Philippe's last words as he ran out of the house."

"Do you remember what they were?"

"Where's Riley? Find Riley. No one will recognize him after I'm through with him. I want him gone."

"Did you know where Riley was?"

"Not at that point. As I galloped to find him, the 'Kiki' disappeared, hidden deep down inside and scruffy, manly Kawley Chatterton took over. I never found Riley. I tried to return but there seemed to be militia everywhere. I feared Philippe had others searching for me so I ran and never looked back. Later, I heard that Riley had been abducted by raiders and the Confiscation Act had claimed the land with everything on it. I realized I had Pickles, my life, a few dollars in my pocket and the clothes on my back." Kawley shoved her free hand through her short hair. "Now it looks like I have even less—Pickles, ripped and bloody clothes and the days remaining of my life."

He squeezed her hand tightly. "You have much more than that. You have Riley and—" He sat forward and turned toward her. "—and you have me."

"Brayden, I—"

"Shhh. Let me finish. I feel you ready to run again, and I'm asking you not to. The whole time Fletcher was digging in my bloody shoulder, all I could think of was you. Yes, I saved your life, but dreaming of you saved mine."

"I thought you told me you remembered little of that night."

"I didn't lie. The little bit I remembered was you pulling me back. I'm asking you as I did once before. Stay with me. We will find Riley and Caleb, but I need you. Riley needs you—your talents, your resourcefulness." He slid his hand behind her neck and pressed his forehead to hers. "This terrible sickness may not happen, and I want to be there to celebrate with Riley and Caleb at our side. God help me I feel like I've spent my entire existence not knowing anything. Now, for the first time in my life I know exactly what I want."

"And what is that? What is it you want so desperately?"

"You. I want *you*, Kiki."

"Pickles, too?"

Brayden uttered a throaty chuckle. "Pickles, too." He kissed her temple. "Look at me and know I have never whispered these words before. Kiki, I—"

Her fingers shielded his lips. "Shhh. Don't. If you say those words, I will never leave the shelter of your arms. I will never leave you to accomplish what we both know I must." Her voice cracked. "I don't understand any of this. Why is the world crashing around us? Why, when I may have so little time left of my life, is a man so fine wanting me, holding me close?"

"You really need ask?"

"Brayden, I'm hideously scarred."

"I know. You showed us at the mission."

"I wear the brand of another man."

"No," he whispered. "Your courage eradicated and destroyed his claim."

"But I'm scarred more than you know."

He sat back. "Show me, Kiki. Show me the scars."

Without hesitation and without breaking eye contact, Kawley unbuttoned her shirt, pulled her left arm from the sleeve and slowly presented her back.

Brayden touched his fingertips to her pale skin, half expecting her to pull away. When she did not, he kissed every one of the raised marks and blemishes left by Philippe's rage. He shuddered for the pain each one must have caused her.

"Do these still hurt you?"

"Only on the inside."

The bruises on the inside are the ones that fester forever. Brayden knew the feeling. His lips travelled along her neck and under her ear. "You are exquisite, Kiki." A renewed jolt of anger shot through him when his lips left her shoulder to reach the bandage on her arm over the burned brand. He closed his eyes and shoved the anger away. Instead he tenderly placed her arm in her sleeve, wrapped his good arm around her and pulled her back onto his lap with her legs resting to the side. Snuggled against him, Kawley nestled her head in the hollow of his neck, buttoned her shirt and rested her hands in her lap.

Neither of them spoke; neither of them moved. There seemed no need. Brayden closed his eyes, relishing the touch of her soft hair on his cheek. He felt the even rise and fall of her breathing matching his own. The moment was unplanned and unexpected but soothing, warm and welcome, and he suspected Kawley felt the same. He was bombarded by new and uncharted emotions which enveloped him, surprised and delighted him. As his one hand gingerly joined the other, he held sheer joy in the circle of his arms. It was a joy he had never known, and he didn't want to let go of the feeling.

A chorus of night calls intruded on their solitude. "I think we are being summoned because we still have a job to do, Kiki," he whispered against the top of her head. "We have to rejoin the others and find Caleb and Riley."

"I know." Kawley's drawn out whisper expressed she was as loathe as he to surrender their contact.

"We will have to ride out soon if we are to make it there by first light."

"I know that, too, but I worry that Fletcher will not allow me back."

"Let me worry about Fletcher."

"You told me that once before, and it didn't turn out well."

"When Fletcher and Rush hear what you told me, they will understand."

Kawley placed her hands on his. "You have to unlock your fingers if I am to rise."

"Yes, I know." Instead of releasing her, he squeezed her a bit tighter into him. "Before we renew our mission, I'm aching to—"

"Brayden," she broke in, "we mustn't. It's too risky for you."

He sat her forward to face him. "Why madam, such a wicked, scandalous suggestion."

Kawley's face reddened, and she lowered her eyes.

He lifted her chin. "Kiki, before we ride and face God only knows what dangers, I want to seize a moment to *frolic*—" He inclined his head. "—with you."

Her face lit up. "Frolic? Why would you—?"

"Don't you remember? That night...by the river...when you told me someday before you—" He sucked in a short breath. "—you said one day you wanted to simply frolic without a care, without disapproval from anyone?"

She rimmed his jawline with the tips of her fingers. "Yes, that night...by the river. I carelessly said, 'someday before I died.' Little did I know that day would come so soon."

Brayden grasped her hand and kissed her palm, trying to recapture the moment. "I remember that night vividly, a night of such pain I wanted to collapse and wail like a child, but your sweet reverie swept me away. Your dream of frolicking, of wondering where we might have met, how we might have met, cooled the fire and the fever." He chuckled. "At least until the hailstones pelted us."

"You did look mighty silly hopping barefooted over those stones."

With a sudden, mighty effort Brayden rose, pulling Kawley up with him. "Well, Miss Kiki Chatterton, I am not barefooted now." He folded into a deep, sweeping bow. "If your leg can bare it, may I have this dance?"

"Here? Now?"

Brayden nodded. "Yes, Kiki...before the world crashes around us, while you are still whole and healthy, while it is just you and I, come relive that reverie. I want to live the dream that delighted you and saved me at the river. I want to frolic and dance...here...with you."

She sucked in a deep breath. "As lovely as it sounds, and I do thank you for asking, perhaps we really should mount and not waste any more time."

"If Riley were here, knowing what might await you in a short time, do you truly believe he would think this small gift a waste?"

She stared into the distance. "Riley? No. He'd probably say, 'Kiki, the gentleman asked you to dance...so dance'."

"Well then?"

"But my hair—"

He looked around, yanked errant wildflowers still in bloom and slid them behind her ear. "—is beautifully coiffed and adorned with flowers."

Kawley looked down at her clothes. "I have no gown, sir."

He gingerly lifted his arm from the sling, slid his coat from his

146

shoulders and wrapped it around her. "A gown of muted fawn to compliment the sapphire of your eyes." Brayden helped her into the coat, and she held out the skirt of it as she would her gown.

"Now...may I have this dance?"

Her eyes sparkled when she twirled and curtsied. "Of course. I would be honored, sir."

Brayden stood tall and grasped her with his right arm. He bit his lip, then slowly extended his left arm to take her hand. An unbidden yowl escaped him before he could stop it.

"Your shoulder, Brayden. Don't twist it out."

Though the throbbing was raw torture, he refused to release her hand. "It would be more painful to miss truly having you in my arms."

A waltz entered his head. He hummed the melody and whirled the two of them round and round as elegantly as any royal couple.

"Strauss would be honored by the richness in your voice." She twirled and, with her back against his chest, floated in the muddy boots as though they were jewel encrusted slippers to match her gown. He spun her yet again and she came against him, chest to chest, drifting gracefully to the music only the two of them could hear.

"I don't understand how your eyes can remain so playful with what you might be facing."

"Because even though the 'worst of times' may yet come, right now I am basking in what Charles Dickens would call the 'best of times'."

"As well versed in music and literature as you are beautiful, my lady."

"I never want this to end but I'm afraid someone will see us."

Brayden placed his cheek against hers. "But we are alone in the woods."

"Much to the dismay of those plump castigating matrons over there." Kawley inclined her head toward the trees. "See them peeking at us? Their tight-lipped disapproval of our dancing is written all over their faces."

"Ah yes, I believe I see them whispering to one another. You are right. That could be a problem."

"By the end of this dance my reputation will be in ruins just like Melinda Sue." With those words, Kawley missed a step and limped several more.

"Then by all means let us give those pinguescent quidnuncs something to really cackle about." Brayden leaned down, scooped under her buttocks with his right arm and drew her to his waist. "Lock your legs around me," he whispered in her ear as they spun several times.

Kawley released her right hand from his left, locked her fingers around his neck and threw back her head. When they stopped spinning her face was flushed with a smile extending from ear to ear. "I will remember this night, Brayden." She wrapped her arms around him, buried her face in his neck and whispered beneath his ear. "Thank you for your most generous gift."

Without releasing her, Brayden slowly buckled his knees, the two of them coming to sit on his folded legs. The moonlight filtered through the trees and lit her face. "I offered my life for yours once before, and I would gladly offer it again if doing so would stave off this horrific sickness. The fact that we are both powerless to affect the outcome hurts me in places I didn't know I possessed." He kissed her forehead. "Just know I will not leave you."

She stroked her fingertips in the hollow of his neck, let them drift down the front of his shirt and back up. She then raised her eyes to meet his. The playful eyes were now sad and somber. "Not even if... or...when?"

The jolt from her delicate touch shot threw him. A simple gesture, yet he'd never felt anything as intimate in his life. It took a moment to find his voice. "No...not even if, or when, or maybe, or whenever or wherever. You only need to reach out your hand; mine will be always be there."

Kawley closed her eyes, released a deep breath and hugged him. Brayden rocked her while skimming kisses along her neck, under her ear and along her cheek, stopping abruptly before reaching her lips. He gently pulled her arms from his neck. Sickness or not, Brayden knew there would be no stopping himself if the floodgates were opened. He slowed the pounding thunder in his chest and kissed the tip of her nose. "What do you say we mount and ride to find Riley and Caleb?"

Without a word Kawley rose. After they had stomped out the fire, she slipped off the coat and held it open for Brayden. She raised the coat on his shoulders, touched his left palm to her cheek and gently lifted the arm back into the sling. Kawley then pulled the flowers from her hair one by one and arranged them lovingly on the ground.

"Why did you—?"

She put her hand to his lips. "Brayden and Kawley are riding out; Kiki and Strauss have to remain here."

"I don't understand."

"Convincing Fletcher and Rush to allow me back will be difficult enough. If they hear you calling me by my familial name, Fletcher will think you are believing in me with your heart and not your head. I think we both know that would spell disaster."

Brayden picked up one of the wildflowers, walked to Ajax and pulled his journal from the saddlebag. He opened the journal and placed the flower between the pages. Before he closed the book, he looked up at her. "May I?"

Kawley nodded, shoved her left boot into the stirrup and winced as she threw her leg over her liver chestnut equine. She glanced around their camp. "It's comforting to know that a piece of these lovely moments is staying with you. I hope in the future it will bring a smile to your face."

Brayden reined Ajax next to her and squeezed her hand. "To *our* faces, Kiki."

CHAPTER TEN

BRAYDEN RODE INTO THE CLEARING AND DISMOUNTED. FLETCHER WAS still in camp but alone. "Where's Rush?"

"About time you got back. I set his leg as best I could and sent him home. I'm hoping he can spend a few days with Oscar until he's strong enough to travel the rest of the way." With his left eye nearly swollen shut, Fletcher kicked the last of the ashes of the fire and stomped on it with heavy kicks. Brayden sensed it was more a message to him than a fear of fire. "No sense in anyone else getting killed because of the storm you brought on us." He stomped again on the ashes. "Did you at least find the scrawny runt and bring back some answers?"

Kawley appeared from the trees and reined Pickles to a halt. Brayden helped her from the horse, but she stepped back as Fletcher's face darkened to match the black bruise from the slash of Ceisel's rifle.

"Auribus tenet lupum, Bry? Are you mad? You felt compelled to bring a wench as crafty as Peggy Shippen Arnold back into our midst? Haven't those eyes done enough damage? Clive's dead, damn it!"

"I know Clive's dead! I was there, remember? Clive was my friend, too, but Kawley is not a spy nor a traitor, Fletcher."

"Then why did she run after the fire? Tell me that!"

"Do you not remember it was Kawley who *saved* us from the fire."

"Do *you* not remember who brought the firestorm prince down on our heads in the first place?"

"She explained everything last night and I, for one, believe her."

Fletcher threw his face right into Brayden's. "*Et tu, Brute?*"

Kawley stepped forward, her jaw tightly clamped. Brayden knew she was trying hard not to favor her leg. "Fletcher, I'm so sorry about Clive."

He spun and pointed an accusatory finger at her. "I don't want to hear another word from you! *Acta non verba*!!"

"Yes, Fletcher, I'm sure my actions have appeared suspect because I do know Philippe Armagnac—"

"Philippe of Armageddon, you mean. He murdered Clive."

"Ceisel murdered Clive," Brayden shouted.

"That son of a bitch ordered it."

"Fletcher, watch your mouth. There's a woman present."

"Really? Where? All I see is a spy."

Kawley slammed one hand into her other palm. "I am not a spy!"

Fletcher shrugged one shoulder and clucked his tongue. "If you say so."

"But you don't believe me?"

"No, I don't. I know what I saw."

"I realize, considering the tragic death of your friend, apologies would seem shallow and, frankly, worthless. I would feel no differently if our roles were reversed. But Philippe is not my friend, or my lover or whatever else you may think we are. My hatred for him is beyond measure—"

"But he seems to be hot on your trail for reasons I don't know and don't want to know." Fletcher glared at Brayden, patently enraged that Brayden had returned with her. "From what I heard in that mission, where the spy goes, he goes." He hooked a thumb toward Kawley. *Magistra apostolorum Hermagedon* over there apparently gets people killed. *Alea iacta est.*"

"*Nomen Kawley Chatterton.*" Kawley jutted her chin. "My name is Kawley Chatterton, not Mistress of Armageddon. And yes, the die has been cast. I cannot change what has happened. Indeed, Fletcher, I speak Latin and several other languages. Does that surprise you?"

Fletcher cleared his throat, clearly shocked that Kawley had understood his words to Brayden all along. "Prior to your little tête à tête with that madman at the mission, yes, it would have surprised me. At this present moment, however, absolutely nothing about you would surprise me. However, instead of easing my mind as you plainly hoped it would, it convinces me more than ever that you are nothing more than what Peggy Shippen Arnold was…an illusion, a lovely turncoat. You merely nailed the lid on your coffin."

Kawley yanked the cap from her head and plopped on the ground. "That moment may be closer than you think."

"What do you mean?" Fletcher spun and stared at Brayden. "What the hell does he mean?"

Brayden raised an eyebrow. "What does 'she' mean?"

Fletcher threw his arms out to the sides and snorted. "I haven't adjusted yet. I only know that one of you had better explain why you brought 'her' back here before I hightail it out of here and leave the two of you to whatever you've planned because I'm certain I want no part of it."

Brayden knelt on one knee next to Kawley. "Pickles slipped and threw her. That's when it happened."

"What?" Fletcher slapped his forehead. "Where the devil did you get pickles and why, in God's name, do I care?"

"That is Pickles." Brayden pointed to the mare. "She slipped and threw Kawley. When the mare went down, Kawley was thrown into a raccoon. She was bitten in the leg. The critter wouldn't release its jaws, but Kawley's quick thinking saved her because she was able to drown it in the water. Unfortunately, that means now there's…there's—"

"No way to know if it had rabies or not," Fletcher added, his demeanor slightly subdued.

"No," Kawley muttered. "So you see the truth of your words, Fletcher?"

Fletcher didn't answer. He blew out a long-protracted breath, locked his fingers behind his head and paced back and forth. Brayden could not discern whether the trek stemmed from anger, pity, frustration, confusion, suspicion or possibly a combination of all of them.

"Brayden, I told you you should have just let me go. I told you Fletcher would never accept me back," Kawley whispered.

"Yes, Bry. Why didn't you just let her go? I can see from those blood stains on her arm she fought you. Apparently, she took some hard convincing."

"That's enough, Fletcher! Those stains are from—"

"I don't really care what those stains are from. I told you back at the cabin I didn't want any further complications and you just keep adding them one by one." Fletcher raised his hand, clearly demanding silence from Brayden, clearly not finished. "You and I, Clive, Rush and Royce rode out of Avalon with one purpose and one purpose only...to rescue Caleb. Thank heaven Royce took Trey home. Clive is dead. Rush may very well have a pronounced limp for the rest of his life. You have use of only one arm, and I'm constantly swiping blood dripping down my cheek, having nearly lost an eye. We are lagging far behind Caleb's kidnappers, are nowhere near Capitol City and are not even certain Caleb is there. While narrowly escaping certain death by fire, I learn we are apparently being dogged by a madman who lays claim to a woman posing as a man who may or may not have infiltrated our midst for Lord only knows what purpose. I think that sums it up quite clearly, don't you think? We are at war, are we not?"

"Would you rather I'd left her? Possibly to die helpless and alone?"

"Helpless? That one?" Fletcher uttered a mirthless chuckle. He ran his fingers back and forth through his hair and clucked his tongue. "Truthfully? Yes!"

"What? Fletcher, you can't be serious!"

His dark-haired friend fisted his hips and continued pacing. "Maybe. Hell, I don't know." He leered at Kawley. "No, I suppose not. I'm not the sadistic monster her Philippe is."

"He's not *my* Philippe! He's nothing to me but a butcher. Didn't you see what he did to me?" Kawley yanked the stubs of her hair. "What about my hair?"

"Oh yes, I saw. But hair grows back!" Fletcher growled truculently. "And after I escaped the burning jaws of hell, I had time to realize that brand you flaunted could be ink for all I know. Agents have been known to do more than that to keep their furtive activities secret. Philippe Armagnac might certainly have the wealth and influence to have coerced Martin Hildebrandt to produce a perfect brand. And as for the stripes on your back—"

"My God, Fletcher!" Brayden roared. "Stop!"

Kawley jumped up and stomped toward Fletcher. She opened her coat, grabbed Fletcher's hand and shoved it into her chest. "If you want proof then you pull back my shirt and feel the scars for yourself. I have nothing to hide."

Brayden waved his hands. "Absolutely not; I forbid it!"

"Stay out of this, Bry."

His friend stood stone still. With the giant hand captured in hers, Brayden was not entirely certain that Fletcher would resist actually doing what she demanded. The thought shocked and disgusted him. After the night he and Kawley had shared, he couldn't allow it, refused to allow it. Brayden stomped toward them to stop the insanity but Kawley raised her hand to stop him.

"Do it, Fletcher. It's the only way I can prove to you the scars are genuine. Do it!"

The chirping of the birds heralding the new day were louder than Brayden had ever heard them. Tense, prickly moments passed with no one moving. Frozen in his tracks he watched with trepidation as Kawley and Fletcher waged war with one another, a battle fought only with their eyes. The standoff continued. Brayden glanced from one face to the other. Kawley's exquisite sapphire eyes drilled deep into the anger and doubt clearly evident in Fletcher's. It took every bit of self-restraint he possessed not to shout to Fletcher that the scars were real. He had seen them, had touched them, had kissed them. But he realized that in that moment, Fletcher was in no mind to listen and would dismiss him. Fletcher's cheek twitched as he visibly clenched his jaw. A trickle of blood from the gash under his eye flowed down his cheek and dripped off his chin. Still no one moved.

"For the love of God, Fletcher, stop this madness!" Brayden edged closer.

"Brayden, no!" Kawley pulled Fletcher's hand deeper into her chest. "Fletcher needs his fingertips to touch the raised skin before he will accept what Philippe did to me."

A feather fluttered on the breeze in slow relaxed circles, a stark contrast to the palpable hostility penetrating the air around them. Finally, with slow and deliberate movements, Fletcher slipped his hand from hers. "No, there's no need." He stepped back, stared at the ground and rubbed his wrists.

"Would someone care to tell me what just went on here?" Brayden was relieved but suffused with jealousy that Fletcher and Kawley had patently just shared something to which he was not privy. "Well?"

"It's nothing."

"Looked like a lot more than nothing just a few moments ago." Brayden stared at Kawley. "Will someone explain all this?"

"Fletcher saw it in my eyes, and I in his."

"Saw what?"

"The haunting."

"Haunting? You're not making sense."

"The haunted and hateful eyes of someone who has been whipped."

"But that's impossible. Fletcher's never been whipped." Brayden spun around to Fletcher. The other's stance revealed the truth of it. "My God. Someone put the lash to you? When? You never told me."

"That's because I've never spoken of it. Only Caleb knew."

"Caleb...Caleb...once again, it appears that Caleb is the keeper of all of our secrets." He glanced at his friend obliquely. "I knew you had been kept shackled, but I never even suspected you'd been flogged."

"It's something you shove deep down," Kawley added. "But the scars remain...in one form or another."

Whether the scars are visible or not, thought Brayden. *Haunted. Yes, I understand.* He tapped his fingers to his lips. "Is that the reason you forbade any lashings at Seabrook when you returned...why we've had endless discussions of ways to safely free our people after our fathers died?"

Fletcher nodded. "Being held for years in that asylum against my will gave me a unique perspective."

"At least that exhibits one good thing about your character," Kawley muttered.

"Woman, I didn't ask for your opinion."

Kawley waved a seemingly dismissive hand. "Just saying is all." She shuffled to a nearby tree and slid down to the ground. Brayden sensed she was favoring her leg but trying hard to hide it from Fletcher. *What a sorry excuse for rescue riders we are. We don't have a whole person between the lot of us. I only have one good arm, Fletcher has only one good eye, and Kawley has only one good leg.*

"Do you think you can see past your doubts and allow Kawley to ride with us?"

Fletcher looked at him with an expression that Brayden could not discern. "If I said no, Bry, would you leave with her?"

Brayden studied the ground for a moment. He raised his head and looked Fletcher straight in the eye. "Yes."

"You know I need your help to find Caleb, right? Caleb...remember him? Your friend, my friend, the man who saved your life?"

"Yes, and I fully intend to keep that promise."

"How...with...ah...all this?"

"When Russell's dog was bitten, the doctor said they had to watch him for ten days, maybe three weeks to see if it had the sickness. Kawley and I intend use that time to head to Capitol City...scout out the prison. In the meantime I'll be able to...to be there...for Kawley."

"Uh huh." Fletcher nodded with a pensive mien.

The other one's reticence infuriated him. Brayden wanted to blurt out his true feelings. "Fletcher, you don't understand. I don't want to just be there for Kawley, I—"

"You what, Bry?"

With pursed lips, Kawley vehemently shook her head behind Fletcher. Her entreaty steadied him.

"Bry?"

"I..." *I love her.* He wanted to savor the emotion of those words as they floated over his lips, but he knew they would incur Fletcher's wrath and there would be no turning back. "It's called compassion, Fletcher, and I think if Caleb were here, he would do no differently."

Fletcher smacked his lips and scoffed. He stepped back and stared at Brayden, then Kawley, then Brayden again as though digesting everything they had told him. "I sure as hell hope I'm not placing a rope around my neck but on this point I, unfortunately, have to agree with you. The Caleb we know would do no differently. All right, Bry. We'll ride to Capitol City together and pray Caleb is there—"

"Pray Caleb and Riley are there," Kawley interjected.

"Pray they are there, and we are not too late." He held the back of his hand to the wound on his cheek, then pulled it away and glanced down. "Not much. Maybe this thing will stop bleeding after all." He shrugged his shoulders. "Nothing to thread it with in any case." He retrieved his hat from the ground and slapped it against his leg. "Did it die?"

"Did what die?" Brayden asked as he adjusted the makeshift sling holding his arm immobile.

"The dog...Russell's dog that was bitten."

Kawley's wistful expression as she raised her eyes for the answer broke Brayden's heart. He barely managed a nod.

Kawley rose and dusted herself off. "Well, that's it, then. You have the advantages of having me along for maybe the next ten days. Three weeks if I'm lucky."

"Having you along is an advantage? Hah! Hardly."

"She's right, Fletcher. You haven't seen what she can do."

Fletcher kicked a stone with his toe. It sailed into the trees, barely missing a squirrel. "What she can do? Hell, what she's done so far is kill one of us, maim another and nearly fry everyone including herself, I might add. I'm not sure I wish to witness more of what she can do, thank you."

Kawley hooked her thumbs in her lapels and stood rigid. "Mister Stedman, you may not trust me, but I don't trust you, either. In fact, I really don't like you," she piped with perfect northern inflections. Fletcher's jaw dropped, and he looked askance at her. As if by magic her entire appearance softened. She then sashayed over toward him and curtsied, extending her arm with hand bent as if awaiting a kiss. "Why, Mr. Fletcher, sir. How very wonderful to see you. I was so hoping we would meet again." She caressed his cheek with her fingertips. "Darling, *je t'ai manque*! Oh yes, I have missed you," she whispered.

Fletcher backed away, brows furrowed. His eyes squinted with blatant incredulity.

"I've only seen that look on your face once before in my life. We were ten and Caleb split your arrow in two with his own." When Fletcher didn't answer Brayden cuffed him lightly on the shoulder. "Don't you see? Kawley can be whatever we need, a scruffy vagabond, a northern gent, or a cultured lady. We can't slither into the city unnoticed but Kawley can. Fletcher, for God's sake say something."

"Do I want to know how she can possibly do that?"

"Actually it's a—"

Fletcher held up his hand. "Another of your many long stories?"

"Yes, but don't you see what a help she could be?"

"What I see is a chameleon, a lovely chameleon with the ability to charm those around her and then disappear into her surroundings." Fletcher studied Kawley for a full minute, eyeing her from head to toe and then turned to him. "Right now I'm asking myself, Bry...exactly who will she be charming?"

Kawley stomped over to Pickles and checked the girth. "You'll have ten days or so to figure that out. We're wasting time, time Riley and Caleb may not have. I'm leaving. You men coming or not?"

"Exactly how do you plan on sneaking past the sentries?"

"Don't plan on sneaking, Fletcher. Plan on looking them straight in the eye."

"And I suppose they will believe you are a man?"

Kawley turned back, inclined her head and raised an eyebrow. "Fooled you, didn't I?"

Brayden opened his mouth to speak but Fletcher's clenched fists and jaw insinuated he would throttle him if he did.

"All right. Suppose you fool them, too. Why would they allow you to pass?"

Kawley reached into her saddle bag and pulled out the Union pouch. "They always allow a dispatch rider to pass."

"Where did you get that?" the men exclaimed in unison.

"It tripped me as I struggled through the smoke. I remembered Philippe took the contents but threw away the pouch. I thought it might be useful so I stuffed it in my shirt."

"The cipher," Fletcher moaned. "Damn, that's right. Philippe took the cipher, didn't he?"

"What he has are papers not the cipher," answered Brayden.

"Bry, I watched him shove the lot into his jacket."

Brayden nodded. "I did, too. But the papers he has are not accurate. I altered them back at the farmhouse for exactly this reason."

"But we need the original lettering. It might be the only card we have to play."

Brayden grinned. "No, my good man, we have a full deck. We have our chameleon Kawley—" He pulled his journal from his saddlebag. "—and the cipher. I copied everything. Now can we ride?"

"Yes, can we ride now? I'm not your enemy, Fletcher," Kawley added. "I suggest we have a stronger chance of finding them if we work as allies."

"Just so we are clear—" Fletcher pointed at Kawley. "—I'll be watching you."

"So that's the way of it?" Kawley curtsied. With her hands to the sides it gave the impression she held out an imaginary gown; it flaunted her femininity. "That will be lovely, sir. I shall bask in the attention, and I do hope you will savor what you see."

Fletcher made a face. It was the first time since their journey began that the face wore something other than a grimace or a smirk. He shook his head. "Is that how you flaunted your wares to attract Philippe?"

"No, Fletcher," Brayden interjected. "Philippe used his charms to convince Kawley's father to pursue a marriage. Apparently, he thought it would be a suitable match."

Fletcher spun around. "And you agreed to it?"

Kawley cradled her left arm. Brayden hoped the salve was soothing the damage she inflicted upon herself to scorch the madman's mark. "Until that point Philippe was a perfect gentleman. He was introduced to my father—a Marquis, cultured and refined. I'm sure my father thought I would want for nothing and he would pass his wealth to Riley. After my parents died, how was I to know an errant letter could transform him to a sadistic monster?"

"Letter? What letter?"

"May I?" Brayden asked Kawley.

She waved a hand. "Perhaps Fletcher will believe it if it comes from you. His scarcely veiled suspicion of me is etched all over his face."

"Kawley found a letter in her father's desk suggesting that the engagement to Philippe should be broken. The letter begged Kawley's father to reconsider and to sever all ties with the man."

"Why? What reason was in the letter?"

"I don't know," Kawley retorted. "I only skimmed it in haste when Philippe walked in. When I questioned him about it, he became enraged and grabbed the letter from me."

"The letter ignited his brutal frenzy? Was that when he…?"

Kawley reddened. "Yes."

"I think those accusations must obviously have some truth to them," said Brayden. "Otherwise why not just deny them?"

"His reaction certainly does give credence to the charge. However this letter business still has nothing to do with finding Caleb."

"But Fletcher," Brayden muttered, "what if Caleb and Riley are together?" He found Fletcher's lack of interest in the letter irritating but he persisted. "Shouldn't we at least consider the possibility?"

"Do you know who wrote the letter, Kawley, or where it came from?" Fletcher asked with ill-concealed irritation, so subdued it was evident he was merely placating Brayden.

"I saw it was from some foreign place...don't remember where." She glanced up, and her eyes moved from side to side as if attempting to picture the letter in her mind. "I don't remember the entire name, but he was a friend of my father's. I never met him, but I remember Father had mentioned him on several occasions. His first name was Cheston—"

"Cheston?" both men shouted in unison.

"You didn't tell me that last night."

Kawley shrugged her shoulders. "You never asked, and I only had the letter in my hands for a few moments."

Fletcher furrowed his brows and inclined his head. "You're sure the man who wrote the letter was called Cheston?"

"Yes, why? Is that important?"

"It could be very important. Kawley, please think hard," Brayden pleaded. "Was this man's last name 'Jenkins'?"

Kawley thought for a moment and then nodded. "Yes, Jenkins...that was it. Cheston Jenkins. Do you know him?"

Fletcher exhaled sharply and smacked his forehead. "This is starting to make more sense."

"Brayden, what is he talking about? Who is Cheston Jenkins?"

"Caleb's father."

"Not the same Caleb who is possibly being held captive with Riley?"

"One and the same."

"After I escaped and had time to think about it, I considered that letter might have somehow tied Philippe with Riley's kidnapping. You mean you think it might be a motive for Caleb's kidnapping as well? Brayden, I told you I don't believe the letter exists any longer. I think he burned it."

"Nevertheless, that is exactly what it might mean," Fletcher added. "I'm afraid it also means we might not have much time left. Kawley, are you sure you are up to this? I saw you limping. Will your leg hold up until we get to Capitol City?"

"God willing, there and back."

Fletcher gave her a quick nod. "Bry, let me change those dressings before your wound festers and bind that shoulder again for you. It's not much but then you and Kawley can share that roasted rabbit and the hat full of berries. We have hard riding to do."

"You said 'we', Fletcher. May we assume Kawley has put at least some of your suspicions to rest?"

Fletcher clucked his tongue, stared at Kawley up and down for a full minute and then approached. "*Miss* Kawley, when you are ready may I give you a leg up?"

Kawley lowered her head and nodded, almost imperceptibly. Brayden could not discern if she wept.

"What did you do with Bonzen?"

"Bonzen?" Kawley asked.

Fletcher kicked the ashes of the fire. "Clive's horse. I sent him back with Rush. I... ah...also sent along ashes for Clive's parents."

"Did you—"

"Yes, Bry," Fletcher snapped. "Rush and I recited all the scriptures I could remember even if I don't understand how any of this happened." He drew in a heavy breath, held it for a long time, blew it out slowly and scraped his knuckle across the corner of his eye. "It scared me, Bry. I was about to lunge at Ceisel when Clive did. It could have just as easily been my ashes in that tin nestled in Rush's saddle bag. I thought of Kyndee and little Tristan." He shook his head. "So senseless."

Kawley touched Fletcher's shoulder and the other did not pull away. "Fletcher, I am so very sorry about Clive."

Fletcher nodded. "I know. We all are. Clive was a good man...and a good friend." He slapped his gloves into his palm. "Let's mount up and make sure his death was not in vain."

The flaming ache in Brayden's shoulder as he mounted paled in comparison to the heaviness in his chest. Fletcher was right; it could have been any of their ashes in that tin. He watched Kawley canter out in front of them despite the obvious pain in her leg, squarely facing the terror of what was possibly to follow. Philippe may have sliced the crowning glory of her hair but the bold force in her shoulders proclaimed a strength that he suspected Philippe feared. The branding and the whipping struck him as Philippe's sadistic attempts to break and enslave Kawley. Neither had worked. She carried a secret that the heartless one plainly wanted silenced forever. Brayden whispered a fervent prayer that Philippe thought Kawley had died at the mission or, Brayden feared, he would hound her until the day she died. A sudden cold enveloped him. It gripped him so hard he nearly fell from Ajax. Dear God, he had actually formed the ineffable words...*the day she died.*

CHAPTER ELEVEN

HANNA KNOCKED LIGHTLY ON THE DOOR. "BELINDA?"

"Yes, Hanna, what is it?"

Hanna opened the door and slid inside. She closed the door behind her but did not click the latch.

Kawley stood tall and heaved a deep breath as Hanna announced her arrival. She had rehearsed her story in her head over and over. Her chances of finding Riley were slim at best but if she failed to enlist the help of Belinda Dunigan, she feared Riley had no chance at all. Ada had been right to warn her about the woman called Brooke. The grisly matron had approached her, introduced herself and offered assistance. Luckily Kawley had politely refused and walked on. Kawley slipped closer to the door, straining to hear what was being said.

"Yes, Hanna?"

"Belinda, your nephew, Keenan, is here to see you. I only allowed him in because he said he has travelled a long distance to find you. I can attest to that because he is in dire need of a bath, clean clothes and—"

"My nephew, you say?"

"Yes. Your nephew, Keenan."

"Keenan, you say?"

"Yes."

"Well let's have a look at him, shall we?"

The door opened, and Hanna invited Kawley in. "Your aunt will see you now."

Kawley entered the room, slipping past Hanna and her disapproving look of disgust. In that moment, every aspect of her rehearsed story froze inside her head.

The other woman studied Kawley from head to toe for a full minute. "Keenan, how wonderful of you to visit." Belinda Dunigan cast Kawley a wide smile, extended her left arm and grasped Kawley's shoulder. "I must admit that in your frightful state, I might never have recognized you. You have your father's handsome looks, but Hanna was right. You are truly in need of a bath and clean clothes." She nudged Kawley toward the chair. "Sit, sit. You look as if you might collapse at any moment." Belinda seated herself across from Kawley. "It's alright, Hanna. Leave us. My nephew and I have years to talk about."

"As you wish." Hanna gave a terse nod, turned and walked out.

Kawley froze the minute she heard the click of the door latch. *Steady...steady*, she told herself.

"Alright, young man. You insinuated yourself into my home, apparently quite artfully to slip past Hanna. Who are you and what do you want? Looks as if you can't afford a meager meal and haven't eaten in quite some time."

Belinda Dunigan was stunningly beautiful. Her sable hair framed her face and was swept back into a loose knot. Her eyes were the color of honey. If she wore a tiara, she could easily have been royalty. Ada had not prepared Kawley for Belinda's beauty, her surroundings, her home. Kawley had simply assumed Belinda to be a woman of the night. She could not have been more wrong, and it unnerved her. What if Ada had misguided her? What if this was the wrong Belinda Dunigan? Kawley wanted to jump from the chair and sprint out the door but she was out of options. She forced her mind to think of Riley. The image gave her strength, and she sat firm. "I...ah."

"Not the chatty sort, hmmm? I see. Well, allow me to tell you before you say another word, that I have a pistol aimed straight at you and will not hesitate to use it."

For the first time Kawley noticed Belinda's right hand was hidden in the fold of her skirt. Kawley immediately remembered Ada using the same technique. She held out her hands, palms up. "Mrs. Dunigan, I am unarmed and truly mean you no harm."

"That remains to be seen."

"I'm curious why you allowed me to enter. Have you a nephew named, Keenan?"

Belinda Dunigan shook her head. "No. I have neither brothers nor sisters and therefore no nephews. But, like you, I was curious why a young man would use such a ruse to request an audience with me. Judging by the look of you, the dirt and blood on your clothes and the flush of your cheeks, I sense desperation. You are either out of hope or out of time. Somewhere, sometime, someone told you that the widow Dunigan has money and influence. Hence you are here. Hmmm?"

"You are also a woman of uncanny insight, Mrs. Dunigan. You are right on both counts. I am out of hope and may soon be out of time."

"Then let us start at the beginning. What is your name, young man?"

"Keenan Chaddock." The name fell off Kawley's lips with practiced northern ease.

"And you hail from...?"

"Philadelphia."

Belinda nodded slowly and pursed her lips. She stared at Kawley and took a deep breath. "Seems my reputation extends further than I realize. I've never been to Philadelphia. How and where did you come across my name?"

"I swore to keep the identity a secret."

Belinda nodded. "I see. I'll allow that to pass for the moment. What did this person tell you I might be able to do for you?"

"I was told you might have enough influence to discover if my brother is being held prisoner at Old Capitol and, if he is, to help secure his release."

"You want me to help a prisoner escape?"

"Yes. He's innocent of the charges."

"And the charges would be...?"

"It is my belief that he's accused of being a traitor."

Belinda rose and backed to the window, her hand still within the folds of her skirt. "I'm sure you know there is little that money cannot secure. Bribing for a traitor's release falls within that 'little' category. And I would hang a traitor myself before a penny of my money would change hands to free him."

"But he's innocent!" Kawley jumped from the chair, took one step and grabbed at the pain in her leg. She fell to the floor.

"What is wrong with your leg?" Belinda did not move but something in her expression showed genuine concern.

Kawley grasped at the small shred of hope. "I was bitten by a raccoon."

"And you don't know if the raccoon was...?" The older woman left the sentence to float.

"No."

"I see. That's why you said you were out of time?"

"Yes."

"Then I'm truly sorry that you came all this way, Keenan, and that you most likely will not make it back to Philadelphia. I cannot help you." Belinda seated herself at her desk. "Hanna will see you out."

"No, no, please. You don't understand. My brother truly is innocent, and they may hang him." Kawley scrambled from the floor and charged the desk, only to find herself eye to eye with the lethal end of Belinda's pistol.

"I will have no problem pulling the trigger, young man."

"Do you think I care? I'm most likely dead already. You have to help me. You *have* to. Ada said you would—"

Belinda's whole body visibly froze. "What did you say?"

Kawley leaned further over the desk and whispered. "You give yourself away, Mrs. Dunigan. I can see that you recognize the name. A woman called Ada Weston told me to seek you out. She said that you would help me in any way I needed. If this is not true, then tell me now. I will leave and this conversation never took place."

Belinda Dunigan brought her face close to Kawley's. "You know I could have you thrown in that prison and no one would believe a word you say against me?"

Kawley clamped her jaw shut to prevent her lips from spewing her thoughts. Slowly she regained her composure. "I guess I have my answer. I cannot tell you how sorry I am to have risked everything to find you."

The other woman placed her pistol in the drawer and leaned around Kawley. "Hanna?"

At that moment Kawley was awash with the anger and hatred that arrives on the heels of hopelessness. She straightened as Hanna entered the room and waited to be escorted to the street.

"Hanna, my nephew has decided to accept my invitation to stay with us for a few days. Can you please have a room readied and a bath drawn?" She placed her hand on Kawley's shoulder. "Then we'll see about suitable clothes. Right now you look like a wandering vagabond. I intend to speak to your father about this." She shooed Hanna toward the door. "Now, Hanna." Hanna eyed Kawley up and down. "Hanna? Please?"

When the door was latched and locked, Belinda turned and leaned her back against it.

"I was serious about the bath and clothes." She approached Kawley until they were face to face.

Kawley stood her ground. "And then, Mrs. Dunigan?"

"Call me Belinda." She finger-combed a burgundy chunk of Kawley's massacred hair. "And then you are going to tell me your real name, young lady, and we will start from there." She felt Kawley's forehead and nodded. "You are right. The clock is ticking."

———

Kawley took a few moments to sit on the floor next to the bed in the room Hanna had given her. Although she yearned to lay within the inviting comfort of the bed, she felt too dirty. The room was richly decorated and beautifully appointed not unlike the rooms that she had wandered and slept in as a child. Kawley especially liked one giant oil painting. It covered a large portion of the wall, extending nearly ceiling to floor and featured a pretty young woman filling a bowl with milk for several adorable kittens. The colors were muted and soft, filling her with a moment of calm. She closed her eyes, rested her head in her palm and allowed her mind to float back to the days when there was no terror, no fear. The morning drifted into night with tranquil continuity. There had been excitement for books, passion for horses, stirring agitation about sugar and politics. But the days had rolled one into the other unruffled, in complete control of the world and all within it. How silly and inconsequential it all seemed now.

"Fools," she whispered. She blew out a long breath and wondered how everyone, herself included, had existed for so long blinded from the truth in their own lovely, cloistered world. Or possibly was she the only one blinded? Could Philippe have been right? Was her father aboard the Lady Elgin that night to meet that ambassador and had taken her mother as a cover for the trip? Kawley shook her head. It was impossible to imagine her father in foreign dealings, especially if that trip resulted in Riley's kidnapping.

Kawley was ripped from her thoughts by the sound of water sloshing. The sound seemed to be coming from an adjacent dressing room.

Hanna's head popped around the edge of the doorway. "Your bath, sir, will be filled in a few minutes. I would wait a few moments before stepping in as I have made it doubly hot to melt off all the traveling dust."

"That was thoughtful of you, Hanna, as some of it is encrusted on my skin."

"Yes, I saw that. I'll knock when it is ready." Hanna disappeared.

There came a knock on the bedroom door. "Keenan, may I come in?"

Surprised by her fatigue, it took a few tries with her sore leg but Kawley managed to scramble from the floor and answer the door. "Of course. It is your home after all." After having sat on the floor for so long, her leg refused to unlock, and she limped across the room.

Belinda pointed to the chair. "Sit."

"My backside is covered in more than you would care to know."

"I said, sit."

Kawley complied and none too soon. Her leg gave out as she bent to sit, and she plopped into the chair with an awkward ungraceful thud. She stared at the floor and bit her lip, embarrassed. After all, she had been a lady once, a time that now seemed so long ago. She heard Belinda glide across the floor, open a drawer and come to kneel in front of her.

"I'm trusting in Ada's judgement of you so I will wait until you've bathed to extract the truth from you. I don't want the water to cool but there are two things I must do before I send you in there." Belinda produced a pair of scissors and pushed gently. "Lean your head over the armrest. If you are to be my nephew, you have to be a well-groomed one." In a matter of minutes she had clipped the clumps and evened out Kawley's sorely uneven mane. "There."

Belinda stood. "I will have suitable clothes sent up. You certainly can't wear those dirty, bloody—" She reached for Kawley's leg. "Is that where you were bitten?"

Kawley nodded.

The other woman attempted to pull up the trouser leg.

"No!" Kawley pushed Belinda's hand away. "Be careful; you can't touch it. It's too dangerous for you."

Belinda grabbed Kawley's wrist and pulled her arm out. "What's this? Were you bitten here, too?"

"No. That's...that's..."

Belinda yanked up her sleeve. "That's infected is what it is." She slammed her fists on her hips. "Lift the leg and let me see it. I didn't get to this age by being squeamish."

Kawley lifted her pant leg and unwrapped the wound. She hissed when the linen pulled the dried blood and lifted the flesh away from her leg.

Belinda let out a soft whistle and furrowed her brows. "Are you sure it wasn't a mountain lion or something. I've never seen a raccoon tear away that much flesh."

"The raccoon didn't. I did. I once heard that if—"

"If you cut away the flesh very quickly you might stave off the sickness. Yes. I've heard that, too." Belinda smiled and nodded. "No wonder Ada trusted you. I know nothing about you, yet I already know all I need. Anyone with the courage to do this can fight anything." She offered her hand to Kawley to help her rise. "Now you scrub those wounds clean. I'm off to the doctor to have him mix a salve for that infection." She plainly saw Kawley's next question. "Don't worry, I know how to weave a story he will believe." Her eyes lowered to Kawley's chest. "Please tell me you have bound yourself very tightly because, if not, you have the smallest breasts I have ever seen on another woman and that won't help your cause at all with Ben Crawford. He's the commander of that prison you are so interested in. If I'm going to introduce you to him as my *niece* so you can wrangle information from him, those breasts—" She pointed to Kawley's chest. "—had better be voluptuous and perky." Belinda chuckled as if truly enjoying her brashness. "You'll find that I always speak my mind." She pushed Kawley toward the dressing room. "Go. Hop in before the water gets cold. We have a lot to plan, and I expect you have mountains of truth to tell." She turned and headed toward the door.

"Belinda?"

The other one swiveled her head. "Hmm?"

"My real name is Kawley."

Belinda smiled and raised one eyebrow. "I know. Ada told me."

"How did—"

She flicked her hand several times. "Shoo! Bath! Now!" Belinda flew out the door.

Kawley limped to the tub but barely felt the pain. She had something she hadn't tasted in a long time, a very long time—the sweetness of hope.

———

While Kawley was yelping as the steamy water surrounded and penetrated the gaping wound in her leg, Brayden was gasping as Fletcher pulled the bloody cloth stuck fast to the red gruesome lesion in his shoulder.

"Did you have to rip it off? I'm in enough agony without you inflicting more."

"Would you rather I pulled it slowly, Bry? Good Lord, man. You spilled a bucketful of blood. You opened and reopened the wound with your charging around instead of heading back to Oscar's which would have been the sensible thing."

"When have either of us ridden the *sensible* road?"

Fletcher harrumphed. "There's sensible and then there's senseless. Now sit still. This burn has to be changed and kept clean. You could still lose this arm...or worse. I think one tin of ashes headed home is enough."

"No matter. If it were to come to that there's no one back there for you to hand the tin to anyway."

Fletcher dipped the cloth in the clean, warmed water and pressed it to Brayden's wound. "Is that why you're always writing in that grey journal? Someday I'd like to sneak inside the pages of that grey thing. Maybe then I'd understand where you've been these last two years. You can't go back, you know."

Brayden winced at the stinging pressure on his back and shoulder. "Do you think if you say something over and over it will be true?"

"No, but perhaps if you say it out loud instead of to a written page, you can scatter it to the wind. It will be gone, and your mind won't be shackled inside the grey journal." He rose and retrieved a bandage from the saddlebag. Brayden watched his friend's hand rest momentarily on the corner of the grey book.

"Will you ever share that day with me, Bry? Not the mask you show everyone else but the true darkness behind the mask?"

Brayden couldn't bring himself to answer. Fletcher was trespassing on forbidden territory.

"I've seen hell. I've lived it." Fletcher tapped his temple. "That knot of savaged flesh in your shoulder is a mere blister compared to what you've burned in here." He heaved a deep breath, plainly realizing he'd transgressed. "Well let's bandage and bind that wound before something undesirable sticks to it." Fletcher knelt down with bandage and salve in hand.

"I thought you would never touch my salve."

Fletcher shrugged his shoulders and clucked his tongue. "I have nothing else to use and since it doesn't look to be infected, maybe this concoction does have some value."

"It might have stopped the bleeding but unfortunately it hasn't helped the color of your face any. You still look as if you had a disagreement with the wrong end of an agitated mule."

"You mean the wrong end of an agitated Ceisel. At least that bastard got what was coming to him."

"I hope my salve has kept Kawley's wounds from festering."

Fletcher yanked a painfully abrupt tug on the bandage as he twisted it around Brayden's shoulder. "Humph...that one."

"You still don't entirely trust her, do you?"

"Lies pop off her lips as easily as grapes off a vine and just as sweetly. Who does she know in Capitol City and how did she procure these cockades that we're wearing?" Fletcher ripped the cockade from his jacket and tossed it aside. "I hate pretending we're Union. I feel soiled with that rosette on, yet she wore it proudly as she galloped off." Fletcher shook his head. "Something just doesn't feel right here."

"Kawley is coming back to meet us as soon as she connects with some contact in Capitol City."

"Really? How do you know? How do you know she's not in Capitol City right now selling us to the highest bidder and using that money to rescue her *supposed* brother?"

"Truly? I don't know, but I feel in my gut that she's telling the truth."

Fletcher snorted. "That gut of yours is so enamored of Kawley it's probably tied in knots by now. In my opinion you've been thinking a little lower than your gut and it's probably become mighty painful. That is, unless you're a colossal gambler and the two of you did more on your night return than just ride?"

Brayden seized Fletcher by the front of his shirt. "Because of our years of friendship I will forgive you that ugliness just once...just this one time. If you ever sully her name again, when we find Caleb and return home, I want nothing more to do with you."

Fletcher locked his hand around Brayden's and tore it from his shirt. "That's *if* we find Caleb and *if* we live to see home...two uncertainties which had a better chance of success *if* you hadn't brought her into our midst."

Brayden ripped his hand from Fletcher's and glared at him, too angry, too frustrated and too disheartened to be certain of what might spew from his lips.

"I'm sick of waiting." Fletcher shook his finger at Brayden. "If she's not back here soon..."

"What, Fletcher? If she's not back here soon, you'll do what?"

"Damn it! I didn't trust this half-baked scheme from the start." Fletcher turned and stalked away. "Just saying she'd better be back soon."

Brayden searched the skies toward Capitol City. Had Kawley succumbed to the sickness? Had she been captured? Or, God forbid, was Fletcher right and it was all lies? *Kawley, where are you?*

———

Kawley wanted to weep when the water of the bath cooled, and she was forced from the bath with her teeth chattering. She'd almost forgotten the luxurious feel of soap, water and clean skin. When she reached for the robe and stepped from the tub, she could not turn her face away from the hideous sight of her leg in the mirror. Washed and open to the light, she viewed the full extent of what she had done to herself after the fight with the raccoon. She jerked the robe closed and folded herself on the carpet. If she didn't succumb to the sickness, no man would ever want her now. But what difference did it make? She just had to find Riley before the last grain of sand slipped through that dreaded hourglass.

The room around her was warm and inviting. Kawley's eyes were again drawn to the painting of the kittens. How she wanted to hold one of those cuddly soft felines and draw comfort from stroking the silky fur. She rose and limped toward the painting to study its grandeur in full detail. The size alone was overwhelming. Kawley felt as if she were there, in the painting, feeding those kittens herself. As she reached out a hand to touch it, the kitten moved, and Kawley jumped backward. The painting had moved; she knew it did. She shivered as if a creeping insect had crawled up between her shoulder blades. Her heart pounded. She glanced around the room, wildly searching for her discarded clothes. Soiled or not, she wanted to dress and make a run for it. The clothes were nowhere to be found; apparently Hanna had taken them away.

Caught in a city she didn't know, in the home of a woman she didn't know, she was naked, wounded and possibly dying. It was a sobering thought in desperate need of a rapid solution. While Kawley's mind raced, the painting moved again and slid open as easily as a door. Belinda ducked through, her arm draped with clothing. Her sudden appearance did little to calm Kawley's racing fear.

"Did I frighten you?" Belinda hustled across the room and laid the clothes out across the bed. From under her voluminous skirt, she pulled bandages and tins. "There. I think that's everything." She patted all the folds of her dress, most likely checking for leftover items. "Was your bath warm enough? Did I give you enough time? Did you scrub those wounds clean?" She turned, examined herself in the mirror and pinned up a few stands of errant hair. "I've brought a new outfit for 'Keenan'. I also sent several of my dresses to the seamstress to be resized for your meal with Ben Crawford—" Belinda's mouth clapped shut. Clearly, she realized Kawley hadn't spoken a word. "Kawley, we've work to do."

"How did you know my name was Kawley?"

"I told you...from Ada."

"Herself?"

"No, by messenger."

Kawley felt herself shaking. She no longer knew who to trust, if anyone. "What did she say? I want to know exactly what her message said."

Belinda straightened and folded her hands in front of her. "All right, but before the flush in your cheeks turns to a deathly white allow me to remind you that you sought me out not the other way around. Fearing discovery, Ada's message was rather enigmatic. It held only seven words: 'Kawley is coming. Help if you can.' You entered my home posing as my nephew, Keenan. You could have been a trap. It was only when your face came close to mine that I discerned you were more of a niece than a nephew. Still I was wary. If you had not disclosed Ada's name, I would have sent you from the house. Have I set your fears to rest?"

Kawley nodded, then quickly shook her head from side to side and pointed to the painting. "How—"

"Why do I have an opening so small, hidden perfectly behind a painting so that no one would even suspect it was there?"

Kawley nodded again.

"Cat and mouse. Hidden behind the kittens is the mouse hole." Belinda grinned. "And I'm the mouse."

"Hanna?"

Belinda shook her head. "No one here knows about it, not even Hanna."

"But—"

"No more questions until I tend to that leg. I bypassed the doctor because I knew he would ask too many questions. I went straight to Momo, the local midwife. She has all sorts of little jars with leaves and creams and other unidentifiable jelly things. When she knows what you need, she mixes and matches—" Belinda swiveled her hands as if imitating what she saw. "—then she hands you satchels and tins."

Kawley wasn't entirely certain she wished to be lathered with unidentifiable jelly things. She pulled the robe tighter around her leg.

"Before you refuse let me tell you that Hanna once spilled hot oil down her arm. I used Momo's salve, and Hanna does not even have a small scar. When I told her what you had done with the raccoon bite, Momo shook her head. She said that no white woman would have had the courage to cut into herself. I told her you did and that's when she started chanting over the mixtures as if infusing them with powers." Belinda tilted her head and lifted one eyebrow. "While I don't know about its mystical powers, I do believe her ointments will close those wounds."

"Any mystical power it might have would be a welcome bonus given my current situation." Kawley reached for the bandages and the tins.

"Let me do it." Belinda indicated for Kawley to stretch out on the chaise. "I'll listen while you tell me how you met Ada and what desperation drove you to my door in such a haggard and bloodied condition."

———

A short time later, bandaged and dressed in a tailored set of clothes, Kawley viewed herself in the mirror. She was, once again as Ada had called her, a fine-looking little gentleman.

"Tell me more about this Fletcher and Brayden. They both own large estates?"

"Yes. Fletcher hails from the country home, Seabrook, and Brayden owns the lovely manor, Avalon, both in Virginia."

Belinda nodded. "I've heard of both of those, but I've also heard that extensive landowners chase after nothing with such vigor except their human property."

"That's true in most cases but both Fletcher and Brayden have secretly discussed freeing their people. I'm not entirely sure that is not part of the reason for Caleb's abduction."

"And your brother? Why do you think he's been taken?"

"I have absolutely no idea."

"You're certain this Fletcher and Brayden will be waiting where you left them?"

"I believe Brayden will. I'm not too certain about Fletcher. He's not entirely sure I'm not a northern spy. Especially since I'm most likely to blame for the death of his friend."

"You told me you didn't pull that trigger; someone else did." She snapped her finger. "I have an idea how to safely send you to meet them. Can you drive a carriage?"

"I believe so. Why?"

"Because my dear nephew, *Keenan*, is taking me for a picnic, and *Keenan* is charged with choosing the location. We'll bring a large basket of food, and we will have a lovely chat along the way, out of earshot of any gossipers." She leaned closer and whispered. "What you are seeking is hazardous if not impossible. There will be no second chances."

CHAPTER TWELVE

THE RHYTHMIC CADENCE OF HER HORSE'S HOOVES WAS A COMFORTING sound. Kawley remembered the time she and Riley had attempted to teach Pickles to drive. Over and over she let them know, in no uncertain terms, that pulling a cart or a carriage or anything with wheels was beneath her dignity. After many bumps, bruises and scrapes, theirs not the mare's, Pickles declared victory.

Belinda's carriage was as elegant as her home. It was adorned on the sides with shiny brass finishes and a shield crest on the door. When she had ridden in her father's many carriages, Kawley hadn't given it a second thought. She had been the pampered passenger, not the servant driver. When had the world turned upside down? Kawley was ripped from her reverie by the pressure of Belinda's hand on the back of the seat.

"Pull up." As the carriage slowed a man signaled to them and approached. "Why Senator Benson, how very nice to see you." Belinda extended her hand.

The senator took it and nodded deeply. "Mrs. Dunigan, always lovely to see you. Out and about, I see?"

"The day is too lovely to stay cooped in the house. My nephew suggested a picnic."

"Where are you headed?"

"It's a secret, sir," Kawley answered with her perfect northern inflection. She leaned toward the senator. "You know how women love surprises."

"Mr. Lincoln will soon be needing you in uniform, son."

"Not yet, Senator, not yet. Maybe next year," Belinda pleaded.

"I'm hoping the war won't be over before then, sir," Kawley offered.

"Well we'll just have to see what we can do about that, son." He backed away. "You have a good picnic."

"Thank you, sir," Kawley answered. She clucked to the horse, and they started off. They left none too soon because her hands were shaking.

"We had to stop when he waved, or he would have questioned it. Senator Benson is worse than any loose lipped matron when it comes to the private affairs of others. I must say your northern education has served you well when speaking. I do believe even I would have been fooled."

"It has served me well enough, but it couldn't transform me into the son my father wanted."

Kawley felt Belinda's hand pat her shoulder from the back of the carriage. "Who would wish for a son when he had a daughter like you?" Belinda leaned forward. "We're out of sight now. Stop the carriage. I want to sit up there with you."

When the older woman had settled herself, Kawley clucked to the horse and they trotted on. A warmth spread over her that she hadn't felt in a long time. "Senator Benson seemed very friendly."

"That's because I was married to a senator, and a banker before that."

Embarrassed, Kawley turned to her passenger. "But I thought—" She clamped her mouth shut and shook her head. "Doesn't matter what I thought."

"We have a bit of a ride ahead of us. Tell me."

"Ada told me to ask around the city...that you would be easy to find because you were well known." Kawley felt the heat in her cheeks. "I thought...I thought—"

"Ah, I see. You thought that I was a well-*known* woman?"

Instead of being derided for her gaffe as she fully expected to be, Kawley was shocked to hear Belinda's soft giggles.

"Oh my, Ada. Poor choice of words." Belinda dabbed at the corners of her eyes with her handkerchief. "When you've been widowed twice and have possibly more money than is locked in most town treasuries, rumors do swirl around, especially by the spotty skinned matrons. I'm well known yes, but for my charity work at the orphanage and the asylum." She giggled again and sighed as her laughter subsided.

"Please, I hope I haven't offended you."

A grin crinkled the corners of her lips. "I suppose I should be offended but I've lived through enough heartache that sometimes humor is the only remedy left."

"Has Hanna's company helped? When did she come to work for you?"

"Hanna came with my first husband and has been with me through a second husband and the death of two children. Yet I know nothing more about her now than when we first met."

"Truly?"

"She doesn't offer, and I don't ask. It is the same in reverse. I don't offer, and she doesn't ask. We've been together for more than thirty years, and I imagine we will be together until one of us passes on. I'd trust her with my life."

"So when she sees you in the room with your *nephew*, she doesn't wonder?"

Belinda shook her head and smiled. "Hanna knows my predilection for younger men."

"If you trust Hanna with your life then why don't you let her know about the 'mouse hole'?"

"Come now. Don't you know a woman wouldn't be a true woman without at least one secret."

They rode in a comfortable silence. Kawley was surprised with how much she enjoyed the company of this arcane woman who was risking so much.

"Considering the distance between you, how did you ever come to meet Ada?"

"Quite simply put...Ada saved my life. I was returning from a mission when a filthy degenerate grabbed me. In short, he realized I was a woman and apparently decided to rob me in more ways than one. When I fought him he pointed a gun at me. He told me I could lie down or fall down...didn't matter which because he meant to have me either way. Ada came out of nowhere and told him to drop the gun or she would shoot. He didn't listen. He shot me, and Ada shot him."

"You were shot?"

"He had terrible aim and only grazed my shoulder. Unfortunately for him, Ada has perfect aim and shot him through the head. We buried him in the soft marsh and never looked back. Ada and I have been friends ever since."

Kawley was stunned but filled with newfound respect for the two women. Belinda spoke of the harrowing incident as if she were recounting a tea party. She wore her scars well. "Ada seems fragile and frail. I would never have guessed."

"That is why she is excellent at what she does." Belinda sat tall and shifted position on the seat. "We're nearing the spot you described. Where are these two fellas you said would be waiting for you?"

"I'll look for them in the grove of trees over there. I best warn you about Fletcher."

"Warn me?"

Kawley shook her head. "Not warn so much as *prepare* you for Fletcher."

"He sounds challenging."

"When Fletcher speaks, he always sounds as if he's growling and is a bit of a hothead."

"Well, is he?"

"No. Brayden told me that many years ago Fletcher was savagely attacked with a knife. The wounds were grisly. He was badly scarred and left with a raspy voice."

"I imagine such an attack would make me a bit of a hothead, too." Belinda gathered her skirt. "And Brayden? Anything more I need to know about him?"

Kawley lowered her eyes and hoped her cheeks were not as flushed as they felt. She could still feel his hand on her cheek as they parted.

"I think you are fond of this Brayden."

"He shielded me from certain death, suffering a wound that could have killed him."

"But you told me you only met him by accident. Why would he do such a thing?"

Kawley shrugged her shoulders. "I'm not sure but I think Brayden has hidden himself in a dark place for a long time." She raised her face to Belinda. "Until I know whether I have a life to be lived, I can't allow my feelings for him to risk his heart again."

"Seems your little band of deliverance is an interesting mix. From your descriptions, I look forward to meeting these two gentlemen." She looked around. "Perhaps you'd best find them first."

Kawley jumped from the carriage and sprinted into the grove of trees. After searching for an anxious quarter hour, Kawley started for the carriage. Finding Belinda and the carriage missing her mind swirled with reasons, all of which bordered on disaster. She ran back through the grove of trees in a near panic.

"Stand right there and don't move or your next step might be your last."

Kawley halted. "Brayden," she whispered. "Brayden." She ripped the hat from her head as she swiveled.

Brayden continued to hold out the pistol, his face a mask of confusion. "Kawley?"

She ran to him, hugging him hard. "Thank Heaven I found you. I searched and searched. I was afraid you and Fletcher had decided not to wait. I'm sorry I took so long but it took me a while to find Belinda—"

"Kawley—"

"—and then she insisted on suitable clothes and—"

"Kawley—"

"—and then Momo sent her medicine for my leg which she had chanted over—"

"I could have killed you because I did not recognize you in those clothes."

"—and then we had to fool a senator on the way out of town—"

"Kiki, stop. Slow down. I can't follow any of what you're saying." He pulled her away to arm's length. "You're hot and flushed. Any sign of...?"

Kawley shook her head. "Nothing more than could be infection from the wounds. Anyway, that's out of our hands." She stared into Brayden's eyes. "I found someone who may be able to help us. The woman gave me food and these clothes and a carriage to get here." She looked around. "Although I'm not quite certain of where she may have hidden. Where's Fletcher? Please tell me he didn't storm off."

"No, Fletcher is up on the hill, but you are right, he is storming." Brayden turned his head. "Here comes the walking lightning bolt now."

Fletcher stomped closer. "You certainly took your time getting back here. I see you went shopping first."

"Belinda insisted I masquerade as her nephew to sneak us out of town."

"Us? And just who is Belinda? And where is she now?" He scraped his hands through his hair and paced several steps back and forth. "Probably alerting the nearest Yankee to bring three ropes."

"Fletcher, for God's sake let Kawley finish." Brayden turned. "Slowly this time, Kawley. Even I was confused by your last run through."

Kawley took a deep breath and detailed what had happened in the previous hours. When she finished, she stood tall and locked her fingers in her lapels the same way the senator had done. "Belinda is wonderful and influential and if anyone can help us in this city, I believe it is her." She glanced around Fletcher and Brayden. "Have you seen any place that might be advantageous to hide a horse and carriage?"

Brayden pointed behind them. "The only place to fit a horse and carriage would be around behind the large boulder over there."

The three bolted with Kawley leading the way. She sprinted purposely. Fatigue was taking her, and she feared if the others saw her falter, they might forego the best chance they had. As they rounded the corner, Kawley spied Belinda. She was out of the carriage and feeding the horse.

"Good to see you found them. I was feeding Ginger sweet potato pieces so she wouldn't nicker and give us away if other horses came by." Belinda sauntered toward them with her hand extended as if they had all the time in the world. Kawley was bewildered by her demeanor when time was not on their side.

Fletcher stepped forward but did not grasp the proffered hand. "Woman, you are either incredibly brave or oddly insane."

Belinda retracted her hand. "You must be Fletcher—"

"I am. And who might you be?"

"Mrs. Belinda Dunigan." She turned and extended her hand again. A piece of sweet potato fell to the ground. "And you must be Brayden."

Brayden took her fingers to his lips and released her hand. "At your service with my sincere apologies for my friend's rude comments."

"No apologies necessary. Fletcher is very astute for I am both brave and oddly insane at times, namely times such as these."

Fletcher's face reddened. "You had Brayden in your pocket as soon as he spied those sweet potato pieces."

Belinda smiled. "I will do what I can to help the three of you, but I must start by saying I doubt your friends are at the prison."

"What?" said Brayden and Kawley in unison.

Fletcher threw up his hands. "Then what the devil was all the charade meant to do?" He spun. "That's it. I'm heading into Capitol City myself. The rest of you can do whatever you want."

"And with that heavy southern accent you'll be picked up within a block inside the city. How will that help your friends?"

"Curb that temper, Fletcher, and allow Mrs. Dunigan to finish."

Fletcher stopped midstride but did not turn. Instead he fisted his hips and heaved a very audible breath.

Belinda's expression grew deadly serious. "I don't believe your friends to be at the prison because usually I hear about the new inmates within days of their arrival. Since I have heard nothing, I assume either they are not there or they are listed as traitors, placing them under special secret guard."

"I hear what you're saying," offered Brayden. "But your voice indicates to me that you have a plan in mind?"

"Ben Crawford is the head of the prison guard. He and I have shared a meal on occasion. However, I think he would be delighted to share a meal with my lovely niece who, if she is exceedingly charming, might be able to devilishly extract information."

"Would she be willing to do this?"

"I don't know, Brayden. Why don't you ask Kawley yourself if she is willing?"

Fletcher spun around and spewed incredulously, "What? Belinda Dunigan is your aunt?"

Brayden blocked him with a fist to his shoulder. "Fletcher, can you see through the fog of your anger and understand what's so clear to the rest of us?"

Kawley stepped forward. "Yes, Belinda, I'll do it if you think you can fix the damage done to my hair."

"It's settled then." Belinda headed back toward the carriage.

"Mrs. Dunigan?" Brayden called after her.

Belinda turned. "Yes?"

"Our trust in you is risking all our lives, including your own. May I ask why you are helping us?"

"Actually I was wondering why you never asked. It's because I believe in justice. A dear friend told me you are to be trusted. You tell me your friends are innocent of the charges. I don't believe anyone should be held against their will."

"But we are southerners. The ones you help us free might live to fight in this war...to fight against you and yours."

"That's war. In war people die. What we are attempting to do here isn't war, it's what is morally right. There's a difference."

Brayden approached and took Belinda's hands in his. "Thank you for helping but I'm afraid for *her*."

"You should be. Kawley will be waltzing into the lion's den armed with only a smile and sachet."

"But how will Kawley disguise her limp?"

"From what I've seen so far, by sheer force of will."

"Promise me you'll keep her safe...and...I want to be with her if—"

Belinda nodded. "*If* I see any sign of—" Her lips clamped shut. Apparently even she could not utter the unspeakable word. "—I will send for you immediately." She stepped back. "Fletcher, if you can shutter your indignation long enough to listen, I want to direct you to my summer manor. You and Brayden will remain there with less fear of discovery until we find out whether or not your friends are actually being held at the prison. Are you agreeable to this?"

"I am not."

"Fletcher, for God's sake—"

"Stay out of this, Bry."

"I am resolutely against this plan, but it seems I do not have a voice here."

Belinda cocked her head to the side and raised an eyebrow. "Do you want my help or not?"

Fletcher snorted with palpable scorn, and Brayden hustled between them. "Yes, Mrs. Dunigan, and we are grateful for it."

"So be it. There is a basket of food for you in the carriage. Fletcher, come walk with me."

"Fletcher? Now," Brayden growled under his breath. It took several prickly moments for Fletcher to comply.

When the other two had moved to the carriage Brayden gathered Kawley in his arms. "It was kind of Mrs. Dunigan to give us a short moment alone. I was afraid Fletcher would scare her off."

"Not Belinda. The little I know of her will prove Fletcher's match and more. She told me on the trip here that the manor is not really a hunting lodge because her husband abhorred killing animals."

"Then the place should suit Fletcher fine since he feels the same way." Brayden slid his thumb along the line of her jaw. "Are you sure you are up to this? You need your strength to heal."

"I will fight to save Riley and Caleb with my dying breath." Kawley placed her hand on his lapel. "I heard you and Belinda."

"Then you know the danger you'll be facing."

"Your words will give me the strength."

Brayden slipped his arm from his sling and cupped her cheeks with his palms. "I should be facing this commander for information, not you."

"As appealing as that sounds, I think he will be more susceptible to my charms than your fists. Besides I can speak his words and his way."

"I'm in awe of your courage, and I envy this man who will have the pleasure of dining with you." He leaned his forehead into hers. "My Kiki—"

"Time to go," Belinda called. "We have much to plan and little time. If we don't return soon, Senator Benson will suspect a dalliance with someone not really my nephew. Brayden, Fletcher, keep those cockades on your lapels and your mouths shut. Your southern inflections will not improve your situation. Please be on your way soon, before you are found out." Belinda gathered her skirt and picked her way across the pebbles. "Kawley?"

Kawley tore herself away. "Coming." She jammed her hat on her head and wrapped her hand around Brayden's left wrist. "You need to keep this arm tucked in tight or it will never heal." She turned back as she headed to the carriage. Brayden hadn't moved, still staring at her. How she wanted him to complete his ardent words, but she cared for him too much to break his heart in the next weeks. *No*, she thought. Those words could not be spoken until she was sure she would live to love him back. She climbed into the carriage with Belinda, took up the reins and trotted off. As they passed Brayden, who remained rooted to his spot, Kawley thought she saw him kiss the air as they passed. In her mind she whispered a silent prayer to whatever deity might care to listen, that she could remain alive to see him again.

———

Brayden watched the carriage until it disappeared. Kawley's limp was clearly discernible, and he was filled with dread that even hidden under layers of petticoats, the sway and saunter she needed to captivate the head guard might be impossible, if not painful. Was the rosy hue in her face part of her allure and enchantment or the calling card of the dark insidious thief they feared? How could she do battle for Caleb and Riley when she was battling for her own life?

As Kawley's form faded into the horizon Brayden had to resist the urge to gallop after her, to forbid her this folly.

"I know exactly what you're thinking. I feel the same way." Fletcher appeared from nowhere astride Whiz with Ajax in tow. "This plan is doomed to fail, and we should stop that carriage before the manling, turned woman, turned nephew, turned courtier ruins whatever chance we might have." He handed Brayden the reins of his horse. "Mount up. I think we can still catch them."

"Stop it, Fletcher. Kawley *is* the best chance we have." Brayden mounted and turned his horse from the direction the carriage had taken.

"You want me to sit on my hands and do nothing?"

"That's exactly what I intend to do, and you had better do the same."

"Following you I feel like a hostage, a pawn in a deadly serious chess game. It's unsettling."

"Why? Because you know the pawns are expendable?"

"Frankly, yes."

"This *is* a deadly serious chess game and we had better be five or six moves ahead to protect our queen because she's risking her life dining with that guard."

Fletcher clucked his tongue. "She's only risking what little life she may have left."

Brayden grabbed Fletcher by the collar, threw him from the horse and leaped on top of him. They rolled over and over until Brayden had him pinned to the ground. "Unless you want me to black your other eye, you had better cool your temper and shut your mouth." When Fletcher finally stopped struggling, Brayden released him and stood. He sucked his left arm close to his body, doubled over and hissed. Fletcher remained on the ground, his arm resting on a raised knee.

Brayden gingerly placed his arm back into the sling and dusted himself off. "I've listened to enough of your contempt and suspicions of Kawley as I intend to take. She has done nothing but try to help us."

"I think Clive might disagree."

"Are we back there again? Are you blaming Kawley again for the horror Philippe rained on all of us? She had nothing to do with it."

"That mad man was chasing her, not us. We would have been long gone instead of fire fried. Who else should I blame, Bry? You, for bringing her along?"

Brayden grabbed Fletcher's arm and yanked him upright. "You're stepping over a dangerous line here."

Fletcher jerked his arm away. "My God, man. You're besotted with her." He smacked his forehead. "I see it now. That's why you took that shot for her, isn't it? *Isn't it?* You'd die for someone you don't even know?"

Brayden turned and adjusted his horse's girth. "I know all I need to know about her."

Fletcher snatched Brayden's reins. "Well I sure as hell don't. You can't expect me to trust this woman when I know nothing about her. I don't even know how you met Kawley in the first place. As I recall I left you in the woods to check for stragglers and then meet us at the mission. Did you find a damsel in the woods?"

"No. She—" Brayden shook his head. "—*he* got the drop on me with a gun in my back."

"On you?" Fletcher laughed out loud. "On you, Bry? I don't believe it."

The other's unexpected absurd laughter knotted the anger in his gut. Brayden remounted. "I don't see the humor."

Fletcher mounted next to him, and the horses meandered, seemingly without direction from either of their riders.

"We have to go this way, Bry." He gathered the reins. "The manling had the drop on the sharpest shot I know, huh?" He uttered a soft whistle in apparent astonishment.

"You can stop saying it. I was there, remember?" Brayden was appalled that Fletcher suddenly found their dire situation amusing.

"Oh no. It definitely bears repeating. I now see a side of Kawley that makes me hopeful."

"I love her, Fletcher," Brayden muttered before he could stop it.

Fletcher nodded. "I know that now, Bry. And I'm sorry I disappointed you with my mistrust. I've known you all my life. If you could trust her, then I should have, too." He clucked to his horse. "I don't know why I didn't see it sooner but, in my defense, she's been Kawley the man for most of our brief acquaintance."

"I didn't mean to blurt it out—" Brayden hemmed and hawed. "—but there are no maps to follow, nothing to guide you around this or that path to love. It just happened."

"I'm glad you finally shared a part of yourself with me instead of that damnable grey journal. Lord knows I've had to watch what you've been doing to yourself for the last two years." He leaned down and adjusted his stirrup. "We should hurry to this hunting lodge before we lose the daylight."

"Belinda told me her husband stayed there for weeks even though he abhorred hunting. Should be perfect for you."

"She told me her husband loved the solitude there because he enjoyed writing. I thought a scribbling lodge would be perfect for you." He grinned and slapped Brayden in the shoulder. His expression crumpled, clearly aware the reflex gesture was painfully clumsy. "Your shoulder able to last until we find this comfy lodge, or do you need a swigger and new bandages?"

Brayden dug his heels into Ajax's sides. The horse reared and jumped forward. "See if you can manage to keep up."

CHAPTER THIRTEEN

By the time they returned to Belinda's, Kawley was teetering on the brink of exhaustion. Her leg and arm were throbbing, and she walked with a pronounced limp. Despite her best efforts to hide her weakness, it was clear that Belinda understood.

"I think it's time to change the bandages on those wounds. Then you need to drink a cup of Momo's brew. She said you are to drink lots and lots of her brew."

"What is in it?"

"I don't know, and I don't question. When Momo says drink, you drink."

Belinda poured the liquid into a cup and handed it to Kawley. She slammed the cork down into the neck of the bottle.

Kawley sniffed the contents of the cup and wrinkled her nose. "Does it taste as unsavory as it smells?"

"I don't know. I've never had a cup, never had need of it."

With a shaking hand, Kawley pushed the cup away. Belinda handed it back to her. "I'm beginning to think you don't trust me."

"I'm not certain I'm feeling poorly because of my wounds or if things are really not as they seem."

"Such as?"

"This meal with the head of the prison guard taking place with such haste."

"This evening was arranged before you even walked through my door."

"You sending Brayden and Fletcher to your secluded lodge where they might be riding into a trap."

Belinda nodded and shrugged her shoulders. "One word from me to well-placed ears and that would be true."

"And now you ask me to drink a brew that could very well hasten my death, a brew which you just admitted you have never put to your own lips."

"Look at me, Kawley. You know the secret passage from this room to freedom. If you wish it, I will direct you to my lodge where you can meet your friends and be on your way."

"Then tell me why you ask me to swallow this mysteriously concocted potion?"

"It's true Momo's potion is mysterious. However, my reasons are not. I've never had need of her brew because I've never been severely ripped apart—" Belinda raised her eyebrows and lowered her chin. "—by rifles, knives or wild little beasts." She pushed the cup to Kawley's lips. "Drink. It will ease the pain, heal the lesions and, who knows, it may even stave off that which shall not be mentioned."

Kawley sipped the brew. It tasted as vile as what she imagined the witches' brew in Shakespeare's play might have tasted but she said nothing more about it. "I never thanked you."

"For what?"

"For agreeing to risk helping us."

Belinda lathered the salve and leaves and then wound a new bandage around Kawley's leg. "Don't thank me yet. I've done nothing." She washed and redressed the wound on Kawley's arm. "The hard part is yet to come. Moreover, if your brother and the other one are not in this prison, everything will have been for nothing and you and your friends will have lost precious time in finding them." She refilled the cup.

"More?"

"More."

Kawley sipped in silence while Belinda opened boxes and pulled out yards of material. When she held it up Kawley realized it was an exquisite royal blue gown. "Belinda, that will look stunning on you."

"No, it will look striking on you. I chose it specifically to enhance the color of your eyes and these lovely lace gauntlets will hide the gash on your arm. I'm hoping Ben Crawford will find you too enticing to resist your charmingly veiled inquiries." She gathered the dress. "Come, let's try it on you."

"You have thought of everything, but no matter how appealing my face or elegant the dress, my performance is all for naught if you cannot hide this chopped mop of hair."

"Not insurmountable. What color curls would you prefer? Since you are daring to risk your life, I think you should boldly risk a hue other than your beautiful burgundy."

"Although it seems scandalous, it's been too long since I've felt like a woman." In her eagerness to try on the dress, Kawley forgot what lay under her shirt."

"Sweet mercy! Who flogged you like a runaway?"

Kawley spun around, clutching the shirt to her chest. "The one I told you about; the man who I think arranged to send my brother to the prison."

Belinda gently turned her and touched the scars. "Some of these appear barely healed." She shook her head. "May God forgive me for what I am thinking about that man. Why does he despise you with such intensity that he would disfigure you with such cruelty?"

"He fears I will disclose his secret."

Belinda helped Kawley into the undergarments. "I will try to lace you gently but please tell me if it becomes unbearable."

"I will bear anything if it helps my brother." Kawley finally stepped into the gown and turned.

Belinda crossed the room and gathered a swatch of lace from the drawer. "I think a layer of lace carefully draped along the edge of the gown and down your arms will cover his monstrous handiwork." As she slid the delicate patterned gauntlets and tucked the strip of lace into the edge of the gown, she stopped and stared at Kawley. "What is his hideous secret which would warrant such savagery?"

"I have no idea."

"But clearly he thinks you do?"

Kawley nodded. "He must. Why else would he be hunting me?"

"Then your life is in peril. I must remember never to use your real name. There's no way to know who might recognize it."

"I'm hoping he believes I perished in the fire."

The older woman arranged an array of bouncy curls to hide all traces of Kawley's natural hair. The deep mahogany hue enhanced the creamy skin of her cheeks. "You look lovely, *Kinzie.*" She nodded. "Yes, Kinzie. It suits you." Belinda walked to the painting of the kittens. "Remember, you slip out here. Be careful descending the stairs. They are very narrow. The passage will end near the front door." She walked across the room. "I have to hurry to have Hanna help me dress."

"Won't Hanna wonder who I am and how I came to be here?"

Belinda shook her head. "Hanna retires to her room for the evening after she helps me dress."

"Who will serve your meal?"

"Everyone knows I insist on absolute discretion. Ben is coming to dine with me, but I have no doubt the Ben Crawford I know will be delighted by an alluring addition." She turned to leave. "I'll come for you when I am dressed."

———

Kawley heard someone calling her name. She tried to answer but found she could not. The sound came from far away, and she was not at all certain of the voice. She heard it again and again. The heat was unbearable. The river was nearby, and she yearned to dive into the cool water but still she was unable to move. Kawley saw the back of the raccoon. It seemed strong and healthy in its movements. Then the animal turned to face her. Its eyes were glazed, and fluid dripped from its jaws. Its body wobbled as it approached her. A front paw touched her cheek. She screamed and tried to slap it away. "No!" It touched her once more and again she screamed.

"Wake-up. Kawley, wake-up."

The raccoon ran away. Kawley reached to catch it before it disappeared. They had to capture it; they had to know.

"Wake-up!"

Kawley roused with a start. Belinda's face was within inches of her own, her mouth and eyes open wide in unmistakable worry.

"What happened?" she muttered. "I walked in and saw you there, crumpled and still. I thought...well, never mind what I thought."

"I'm not quite sure what happened. One minute I was checking to make sure everything was covered and the next minute you were tapping my face." Kawley touched a handkerchief to both sides of her brow. "I've never fainted before in my life."

Belinda felt Kawley's cheeks. "You're cooler than before. That's good but your part in this evening's meal stops here."

"But I have to dine with Ben Crawford tonight. You know my time may be limited."

"You need to rest. Momo told me the spirits will be fighting within you and her potion helps the evil ones to perish."

"Do you truly believe in her mumbo jumbo of potions and spirits?"

"You mean, am I superstitious?" Belinda looked up and smacked her lips. "Others might view Momo as a recluse of substantial girth, draped in shawls, surrounded by wind chimes. I see an extraordinary woman. She carries within her the vast knowledge of many generations. Time and time again I've seen that skill in her preparations. Momo also gave me a curious gift."

"What was that?"

"She taught me to believe in the power of belief."

"But belief in what?"

"In yourself, your strength, your mind." Belinda offered Kawley her hand to rise. "Let me unlace you to rest until morning. I will do my best to charm Ben for the information you need."

"But what if he refuses to discuss the prison?"

"Then you will enchant him tomorrow."

"But what if he won't accept another invitation?"

Belinda chuckled. "No more buts, little miss. You are staying here, and I'll hear no more about it. Ben Crawford would accept a permanent invitation if I would allow it and why, pray tell, are you giggling?"

Kawley suppressed another titter. "It strikes me silly that when Fletcher first met me, he called me little man. Now I've become little miss." The merriment fled. "I hope I live long enough to one day be me."

The older woman gently took her by the shoulders. "The power of belief, little miss. Believe in it."

A horse whinnied. "Belinda, there's no time to help me undress. Come later when he has left."

As she reached the door, Belinda turned. "Drink and rest."

"I will. You be careful."

———

Within minutes of Belinda's departure, the apprehension Kawley had felt since leaving Brayden and Fletcher descended like a miasmic foreboding fog. She should be dining with Ben Crawford, not Belinda. But could she risk fainting in front of the man?

"Believe," she whispered to her face in the mirror. But how? She felt as weak as a newborn foal and limped so dreadfully she doubted she could fulfill the deception. Kawley reached for Momo's bottle and poured more of the odious brew into the cup. "To you, Momo—" The entire contents of the cup washed down her throat. "—and to Belinda's unwavering belief in your skill." Traces of the brew gagged her as she limped over to the painting of the kittens. Their sweet faces and their fur, splendidly captured in oil, almost invited her to touch and stroke them. The serenity in the scene calmed her. Kawley studied every aspect of the overpowering artwork. Who was this woman with her cryptic smile, happily feeding her kittens? It was as if the woman dared her to uncover a secret. For nearly half an hour she memorized every aspect of the scene, wanting to crawl inside the woman's room, push her aside and feed those kittens herself.

Lost in thought she took several steps backwards to the table. The woman's eyes seemed to invite her to return. Kawley walked back to the painting, suddenly realizing her limp was nearly gone. The pain she'd felt with every step was now a dull ache. Her skin was cooler, her mind calmer and her courage recharged. It was time to do what she came to do. With utmost delicacy, she touched her fingers to the hand in the painting. "Thank you."

Kawley picked up the lamp on the table, reached around the frame and stretched her fingers to find the tiny latch that released the opening. She slipped through and latched the opening shut behind her. Belinda had told her true about the stairs. They were narrow and steep. She held the rail and took them double footed, one step at a time. When she reached the bottom step, Kawley was about to push open the small door but hesitated. Voices! Agitated men's voices! Belinda's was not one of them.

"I know the commander said he was not to be interrupted, but this information can't wait."

"Then you tell him. He's going to be mighty angry."

"He won't be when I tell him the information I beat out of that prisoner."

"What do you think he'll say when he hears two of 'em died."

Kawley sucked in air and quickly covered her mouth so as not to scream. *Riley! Caleb!* No...no...she had to believe it was not them. She *had* to.

"Those two came in so weak and bloodied, they wouldn't have lasted much longer anyway. Besides, there's still four of them left. Come on, let's get this over with."

"Give me a minute to build up my courage. What was it that one confessed?"

"Kept repeating over and over 'It's the BP Moon'. The commander will need that new cipher to know what it means. Odd that a different courier brought in the dispatch this time—some pompous Frenchman. Enough of your dawdling, let's go." Their footsteps waned.

Kawley's heart sank. *Philippe!* Dear God, would she never be free of the man? She had to tell Belinda and warn Brayden and Fletcher. She left the passage and eased through. Only Ben Crawford knew the answers. He was the only way into that prison.

She wandered the rooms, following the sounds. Kawley stopped when she heard Belinda's voice.

"Of course I understand, Ben. If you feel your presence is needed at the prison, then of course you must leave immediately."

Kawley took a deep breath and sashayed around the corner. "Aunt Belinda, I'm very sorry to bother you but may I see you for a moment?"

"Of course, my dear. The commander is just leaving." She took Kawley by the shoulders. "Where are my manners? Ben, I don't believe you've met my niece, Kinzie Dalton."

Ben Crawford's face lit up with a wide smile. "I don't believe I have had the distinct pleasure." He lifted Kawley's hand to his lips. "I'm delighted to meet you." He turned to Belinda. "Miss Belinda, I'm confused. I remember you telling me you had no brothers or sisters."

"Ben, you miss nothing, do you?"

Watching the ease with which Belinda simply laughed and skipped over her mistake, Kawley jumped in to play her part. "Mother was her best friend. I've called her *Aunt* Belinda as long as I can remember. I suppose it does sound childish. My sincere apology for any confusion."

"No apology necessary. Anyone with your loveliness need not apologize for anything, Miss Kinzie."

"Commander, I hardly think we know one another well enough for first names."

Ben Crawford clicked his heels and bowed. "Then it is my turn to apologize."

"I gladly accept your apology, sir."

Belinda rubbed her hands together and folded them in front of her. "Kinzie, can you give me a few minutes? The commander and his men have to take their leave, and I wanted to see them out."

Ben Crawford stood tall. "I'm sure the matter at the prison can wait for a bit."

"Sir, I think you really want to take care of this," offered one of the men.

The commander never took his eyes from Kawley. "The two of you can return to your posts. I will be there directly."

"But sir—"

"Now! That's an order."

"Yes, sir." The two men gave a terse nod, turned and scooted out of the room.

"And now, my dear Belinda, if your invitation still stands let us continue our evening. With your permission may Miss Dalton join us?"

"Of course Kinzie may join us if she wishes but are you certain your authority might not be truly needed at the prison?"

The man waved his hand in obvious dismissal of the idea. "It's most likely some trivial squabble among the new arrivals. Many of them require extra *discipline* to learn the rules." He shook his head. "Shame on me for boring you with such indelicate matters."

Kawley saw her opening. "I find it anything but boring, sir."

"Kinzie, the prison is full of southern rebels, men with whom you need not concern yourself."

"But Aunt Belinda, if these men betrayed our country how will I learn about their reasons if I do not seize the opportunity to speak with someone like the commander—" She faced Ben Crawford and batted her eyelashes. "—someone of authority who is brave enough to walk among these rebels and force them to obey."

"My niece has a very inquisitive mind, Ben. Her father indulged her eagerness."

"I can see that, Belinda, and I find it hard to resist her wide-eyed appreciation of the difficulty in keeping the peace there. God knows, few in Congress value our efforts." He took Kawley and Belinda in each arm. "Staring into your niece's beautiful eyes, I can see why her father had trouble refusing her. Let us all sit down and have our tea, so the very lovely Miss Dalton can have her questions answered."

"Sir, you are too kind." Kawley seated herself, leaning forward in a most provocative manner. Playing her part was easier than she thought. Ben Crawford was not unattractive. His blond curls fell around his collar, but his mustache seemed out of place, as if he grew it to appear older, more authoritative. "I can't imagine the fortitude you possess to face these traitors day after day. Please tell me everything. From the moment they arrive what happens? What goes through your mind? What do you think goes through their minds?"

"While I would happily oblige you, Miss Dalton, much of what happens at the prison is restricted information."

"That's true, Kinzie. Ben has refused my questions many times for the same reason."

Kawley scrunched her face and lowered her head. "Everyone treats me like a spoiled child. How am I ever to learn anything besides embroidery and music?" She faced the commander with entreaty. "Within a few days I return to boring Philadelphia. Who will I tell your secrets to? The old matrons with their disapproving looks? I think they would hardly be interested. The little soldiers in my samplers? I don't think they will be marching against you."

The man put up his hands. "I surrender; I surrender. Belinda, your niece is far too persuasive."

With a self-satisfied face, Kawley settled herself in her chair. "Where do the arrivals come from? Who brings them?"

Ben cleared his throat. "Some are picked up as spies, others are reported traitors, others were accused of smuggling. The latest group were accused of all three crimes. Prisoners are questioned, I admit sometimes severely, to gain their information." He shrugged his shoulders. "Not sure where this last group hailed from. I haven't interrogated them myself yet."

"But you're certain they are guilty?"

"Their guilt is beyond question. Highly placed individuals have sworn to it."

"But you will still question them?"

"I want to know what is inside the grey."

Kawley tilted her head to entice her victim to continue talking. "Inside the grey? Whatever do you mean, sir?"

"I want to know what is inside the grey chest. What drives them to defy their country with such intensity? What is inside the head under the grey hat? If I understand what is inside the grey, I could use it against them."

"If what's inside the grey could provide information the Union needs, your own position might improve handily."

"Your father was right, Miss Dalton. You do have a quick mind."

Kawley jumped from the chair and stood. "May I visit the prison and meet them?"

Belinda stepped in. "Absolutely not. It's far too dangerous."

"And strictly against the rules."

"But you are the head there." Kawley could feel his palpable indecision. She pushed her advantage. "Surely a man as important as you makes those rules or at least can bend them." Her finger brushed her cheekbone. "I just want to see them." She extended her hand. "I just want to touch a true traitorous spy."

"Kinzie! Remember yourself," Belinda exclaimed. As Ben's face turned, she winked.

"Sir, I've never met a real southerner. I've heard they are rebellious as their stallions, wild, unruly, refusing to obey. I've heard that is what emboldens them to challenge and resist the laws of their country. Oh I too, sir, want to know what is inside the grey rebel. I beg you not to refuse me."

"Miss Dalton, I—"

Kawley played her winning card. She placed her hand on his. "Kinzie please, sir."

Ben Crawford nodded. "Miss Dalton, Miss *Kinzie*, I will see about making it happen."

"Tomorrow?" Kawley paced a bit. "I can move about them as a missionary come to give them comfort." She surged ahead. "They might even disclose information useful for your cause."

"Any man who would see you as a missionary," Ben countered, "does not deserve to call himself a man." His smile widened. "Wear something to compliment your lovely eyes." He drew a deep breath. "Shame though—"

"What is a shame?"

"That your veil will deny the prisoners the joy of drinking in your resplendent features."

Thinking of Philippe and the chance they might meet, Kawley was grateful for the suggestion. "Whatever you think best." She clasped her hands together. "Does that mean I can visit the prison? Tomorrow?"

"Well..."

"Save yourself, Ben. Acquiesce."

The man nodded. "Tomorrow. However..."

"Yes?"

"I will want something of you in return."

"It would be my pleasure."

"I'm hoping so."

"Ben!" Belinda exclaimed.

Kawley raised her hand. "Now then, Aunt Belinda, it's only fair."

"Kinzie!"

"What is it you wish, sir?"

"Since Belinda has yet to succumb to my charms, perhaps I can persuade you."

Kawley titled her head. "I'm listening."

"Would you please honor me with a piece on that beautiful instrument over there?"

It was an obvious test to see if she were the cultured young lady she purported to be. Apparently, Ben Crawford was not as gullible as she first anticipated. From where Belinda stood behind the man, Kawley intuited apprehension in her face.

"Why sir, I would be most happy to play for you." Kawley watched Belinda nod almost imperceptibly and smile.

Ben took Kawley's hand and led her to the piano. She settled herself and lifted the lid from the keys. The backs of her fingers slid along the ivories. Ben Crawford's eyes gleamed in clear appreciation. She touched the keys to make them sing. The music resounded from the strings.

"*Pachelbel's Canon*, one of my favorites," the man uttered. He listened for several minutes, stood tall and tipped his head. "Until tomorrow, Miss Kinzie. Please continue playing. Belinda, will you see me out?"

Her heart pounded, and her fingers flew over the keys until she heard the door click. The music overrode her fear. She wanted to continue playing until the horrific nightmare was over. Her hands were shaking but still she performed her part.

Belinda finally returned. "You were marvelous."

Kawley heard her but was driven to continue.

"He's gone. You can stop now."

Kawley felt as if cotton bolls were stuffed in her ears. She felt herself falling but was helpless to stop it. She saw twinkling stars. The room dimmed, then darkness, then nothing.

CHAPTER FOURTEEN

BRAYDEN FINISHED WRITING AND CLOSED THE GREY JOURNAL. HE slipped it into his pocket. Belinda had been right. The manor was very conducive to writing, decorated with warm mahogany furnishings and thick oriental rugs. "Fletcher, stop pacing. We only left them hours ago. I'm certain Belinda Dunigan will not appreciate a path worn through her fine carpet. Pacing will not bring Kawley or her news through that door any sooner."

"Then you had best put me to work changing those dressings on your shoulder. I'm sure Miss Belinda would be more upset by red blood stains on her fine carpet than my footprints."

With sling, coat and shirt off, Brayden gritted his teeth against Fletcher's ministrations. "Not so tight. It's a bandage not a tourniquet. I need to have a trickle of blood running through the arm if I am to have any strength to use it." He slowly flexed his shoulder several times before redressing and securing his arm in the sling. He strode to the drop leaf table and picked up a goblet. "Now sit down and avail yourself of the late senator's excellent brandy."

Fletcher grunted. "I'm sure the late senator's brandy did wonders for his writing...and yours, of course. But sipping brandy will do little for my agitation."

"You're pacing again."

"What if this is an elaborate trap? This Belinda escorts Kawley into Capitol City to meet the head guard at the prison. How does Kawley think she can talk him into giving up any information? I'll grant you she can speak like a northerner but she's sick and has a pronounced limp. What if that wretched fever has already taken her?" Clearly, he saw Brayden's face fall. He hustled across the room. "I'm sorry, Bry. That was unwarranted."

"Not entirely unwarranted. The same thought has been worrying me since they rode away." He handed a snifter to Fletcher. "Here. Drink it. Might as well. We haven't tasted anything as fine in many a day and are not apt to any time soon. Your wife will give me a severe tongue lashing when she sees how much flesh you've lost since last she saw you. Hopefully your face will heal by then, too."

"I'll tell her you punched me fighting over a Yankee's bottle of fine brandy."

The two of them chuckled but the uneasiness was nearly tangible. Brayden refilled both their crystal vessels. As he placed the shaped bottle on the ornately carved sideboard, he turned, and they clinked their brandy in a toast. The fineness of the crystal with the quality brandy offered a rich sound, reminding Brayden of happier times. The far off look on Fletcher's face seemed to indicate he, too, was remembering many similar occasions.

"Fletcher, do you think we will ever be back there at Avalon with Kyndee, Caleb and Sage retelling the events of this journey?"

"If the God I pray to will allow it. But those guileless days will have disappeared. Our naïveté in believing we could remain cloistered from the war have brought us to this place. I would never forgive myself if Caleb paid the price for my impudence." He strode to the window and stared into the darkness, swirling the brandy in his hand. "He was the best of all of us."

"*Is*, Fletcher," Brayden scolded. "Caleb *is* the best of all of us."

"That he is."

"My friend, I've never seen you so unsure."

"I've never been this unsure. I stand here swilling brandy while Caleb could be anywhere—in prison or hanging from a tree somewhere. The only thing standing between us and those bastard northerners is Kawley and she, herself, could very well be in need of rescue at this moment and we would not know it. I'm helpless with indecision, and I hate it."

"It's been worrying me, too, but at the moment there's nothing more for us to do. Give Kawley a chance to at least discover if Caleb is at the prison. If he's not there we have to hightail it out of here, retrace our steps and pick up his trail."

Fletcher's entire body stiffened. He swung the snifter to the table. Droplets of brandy sloshed to the wooden floor. "Douse those lamps. There's movement in the trees. Damn it! If this was a trap, we're sitting ducks." He threw his back against the wall beside the window. Scooting along the wall, he reached for his rifle and cocked it.

Brayden doused all the lamps, ran to another window and did the same in readiness. "Fletcher, I know you abhor killing anything that breathes but, in this instance for both our sakes, aim for the heart." He surreptitiously glanced out the window. "I don't see anything. Are you sure there's something out there?"

"Something or someone is out there, all right. Now it's just a game of cat and mouse and, damn it, we're the mice." He crouched under the window and looked out. "Oh, dear God!"

"I see them now. They're heading to the stable! If they chase away the horses, they'll have us on foot. Then they can cut us down at their leisure."

"Come on. We have to beat them there. So help me God if they touch so much as a strand on Whiz's mane, I'll cut them down with my bare hands."

As the two of them slithered out a side door, Brayden slapped Fletcher's shoulder. "So you wouldn't aim for the heart to protect me, but you'll murder anyone for Whiz?"

"That horse saved me in more ways than one. I owe him my life."

The two men scuttled through the brush and dodged back and forth to evade detection. They paused momentarily to discern how far the intruders had come. Brayden elbowed Fletcher and pointed toward a grove of trees. He swirled a raised finger, indicating he intended to circle around behind them. Fletcher nodded.

Brayden crouched down and silently covered a sufficient distance for the two of them to surround whoever was headed for the stable. Something in the back of his mind wondered why the stranger had been careless about discovery but he dismissed the thought. Gambling now could mean their lives. He sprinted behind the stranger and jammed the barrel of his rifle in the center of the blue coat.

"Don't move. Raise your hands nice and slow. Whether you live or die is completely up to you."

With hands raised, the prisoner stood stone still. "In truth whether I live or die is up to a higher power than you and the hardiness of a wild raccoon."

Brayden was afraid to believe what he heard. "Kawley?"

The prisoner spun around and ripped the hat from her head. "No long braids to unfurl this time. Something tells me we met this way once before."

"Dear God, woman, I could have killed you." With the gun safely placed on the ground, he reached for her and pulled her close with his good arm.

"Brayden, I—"

"Shh, shh, shh. Give me a minute to stop shaking. Torture though it is not to kiss you, I just want to feel you in my arms again, to feel the silken skin of your cheek against mine. Whatever you have to say won't change in the next minute. Please tell me you are all right, that there has been no sign of fever. Talk to me, dear heart."

"Philippe is here," she whispered into his ear.

Without releasing his hold around her, Brayden pulled back, as if dipped in the cold ocean, and stared into those blue eyes wide with discernible fear. "Here where?"

"He's in Capitol City. I heard two guards talking and—"

"You were already at the prison?"

"No, I was hiding in the stairs—"

Brayden held up his hand. "Wait, not another word. Fletcher needs to hear this."

"Belinda said—"

"Belinda? Did she ride here with you?"

"She was ahead of me, over there."

"Is she dressed as you are?"

Kawley nodded. "She accompanied me because she feared I would not be able to follow her shortcut in the dark."

"God help us if Fletcher spots the blue coat first. He's been an explosive powder keg since we've been here. Let's hope he hasn't tackled her to the ground before we find them."

"Or worse. Hurry. Hurry."

The two of them sprinted through Belinda's last known path. When they reached the stable, they dared a guarded peek through the edge of the window and spotted Belinda and Fletcher plopped on a pile of hay. Belinda, seemingly unscathed, held Brayden's saddle flask in her hand.

It was Fletcher who spoke first as they entered. "About time you two appeared."

Belinda lifted the flask in apparent tribute. "Your brew is quite delicious, Brayden, and quite appropriate after I was so rudely set upon in the woods. Kawley, you look like you could use a bit of it."

Kawley reached for the flask. "I could indeed." She had nearly put the flask to her lips when she stopped and pulled it away. "No, I mustn't, not yet."

Brayden cupped his hand, poured the libation into his palm and held it to her lips. "Drink now." He tipped the flask into his palm two more times.

"Did the brew give you the strength to talk? Brayden and Fletcher have to know everything you discovered tonight."

"You found out about Caleb?" Brayden uttered.

Fletcher pressured her further. "Is he at the prison? Is he alive?"

Belinda stood between them. "Stop badgering her. Kawley played her part tonight and played it well. We have little time before starting back, and Kawley has much to tell you."

"Well then, spit it out," Fletcher bellowed. "Did you find Caleb or not?"

Kawley shook her head. "No, but—"

"That's it," Fletcher roared as he jumped from the hay pile. "I'm going myself."

"You can't," Brayden countered.

"And who's about to stop me, Bry? You?"

"Someone named Philippe," Belinda offered.

Fletcher spun around. "Philippe? Philippe Armagnac? The butcher who killed Clive?"

"Do you know any other pompous Frenchman in possession of a Union dispatch?" Kawley asked. "Because that's how the guards described him. That's why you cannot go. Philippe would recognize you immediately."

"What else did you hear?" Brayden prompted.

Kawley slipped an errant strand of hair behind her ear with her fingers and sucked in a deep breath. "Apparently there were six recent prisoners."

"What do you mean 'were'?"

"The guard said that two of them were so bloodied and weak that they..." Her voice faded away.

Brayden leaned forward. "That they what?" When Kawley didn't respond, he asked again. "Two of them were so bloodied that they what?"

"That they subsequently died," she blurted out.

Her words hit like fists to his gut. Bile threatened to gag him, but he forced it back down and swallowed hard. Fletcher's anguished expression showed he, too, was fighting for control.

Kawley threw her face in her hands. "I have to believe it was not Riley and Caleb. I have to believe it."

Belinda apparently realized that Kawley was fading because she stepped forward. "Ben Crawford has agreed to allow Kawley into the prison to see the prisoners."

Brayden was hopeful. "Well at least that's one step in the right direction."

"There's more," Belinda added.

"The guard said they beat one of the prisoners until he gave up what they think might be a vital piece of information. He said Ben Crawford would need the dispatch that Philippe brought in to decipher the message."

"Bry, get the cipher. Kawley, what was the message?"

"The prisoner kept repeating, 'It's the BP moon'."

Brayden retrieved the grey journal from his pocket and leafed through it. With his finger checking every line carefully he asked, "Say it again."

"It's the BP moon," Kawley repeated.

"Well, have you figured it out? Do you know what it means?" Fletcher ripped the grey journal from Brayden's hands. "Here let me see it." As if counting numbers with his fingers, he went through every letter, every word. "My God. The message reads they are planning to attack the BP arsenal at two in the morning. Hey, Bry, did you hear what I said? It's perfect. We could use the explosion as a diversion to sneak inside the prison."

Brayden's mind was spinning with the possibilities. He'd heard those sounds before, somewhere, sometime. Suddenly, the answer seemed so obvious, he was hesitant to speak it.

Fletcher slammed the grey journal into his other palm. "Bry, answer me."

Brayden snatched the book from the other's hand and shoved it back into his pocket. "No one is attacking anything. I believe I know what the message means."

"What in God's name are you talking about, Bry. It's right there in the cipher."

Brayden took Kawley by the hands. "Repeat the message over and over, only this time say it quickly."

"It's the BP moon...it's the BP moon...it's thee bippy moon...itsy bippy moon...itsy bippy moo."

"Am I so tired I'm delirious or do you hear it, too? Are you thinking what I'm thinking? Do you hear it?"

"Hear what?" Fletcher's voice was shrill; he was clearly irritated. "All I hear is a bunch of gibberish made understandable by a cipher."

"Remember the rhyme you told me about on the trail, those lines you crooned, the rhyme Riley taught you when you broke your arm? Kawley, I think he's repeating it to strengthen himself while throwing the guards off the track at the same time. It's brilliant."

"Whatever made you think of that little ditty?" Kawley's eyes opened wide. "Yes, I hear it now and, if it is the rhyme, then that means —" She threw herself into Brayden's embrace. "—it means that Riley is alive."

"And possibly, if they are together, Caleb is alive, too."

"What the devil are the two of you jabbering about? I think you're both delirious. Bry, we have to deal with facts in front of us, not some imaginary nursery rhyme. The cipher was clear on every point. I say we leave Kawley out of this. You and I are going to finish what we started."

Belinda shook her head. "Impossible. Even with an explosion the soldiers would never leave the prison unguarded. Think it through.

You don't know *if* your friends are there, or where *there* even is. You would have to blast your way in, find two prisoners who may or may not be chained together and then blast your way out, dragging your friends with you." She shook her head and blew out a long breath. "Fletcher, you are thinking with your heart and while it may be sincere it isn't sapient. You strike me as strong and determined. You may even be able to shoot a fly off your horse's ear. But this plan of yours makes me fear there will be four bodies bagged and buried instead of two. I told Kawley there are only two ways to escape from there...with a pardon or in a package." Belinda's eyes darted back and forth.

"I assume no pardon will be forthcoming?"

"Brayden, are you thinking what I'm thinking?" Kawley asked.

"Oh no! I have a sneaking suspicion of what's in your three heads, and the answer is a resounding no!" Fletcher spewed. "First, you want me to believe in some child's nursery rhyme, then to risk Caleb's life on some aberrant plan."

"I'm risking my brother's life as well. But I know he would rather die trying to escape than to languish within those walls and wait for death to be yanked around his neck." She turned to Belinda. "Do you think Momo could help us? Would she be willing to help us?"

"Momo?" Brayden and Fletcher both questioned.

"You mentioned that name once before, but you never really explained who she is," Brayden noted.

"Momo is—" Kawley stopped and glanced toward Belinda.

"—an extraordinary woman who has the knowledge of past generations to heal—" Belinda cocked her head. "—or harm those she cares to treat."

Fletcher smacked his forehead and paced. His eyes seemed to roll back in his head. "Bry, are you listening to any of this? Nursery rhymes. Witch doctors. It's insane."

"And only those who were half mad themselves would dare to risk it," she added.

With blood trickling down the side of his face from his smack, Fletcher shoved his hands in his pockets, pursed his lips and stared at them. "You had damned well better be right about that rhyme, Bry, or so help me—"

"Then you're willing to chance this with us?" Brayden asked with trepidation.

"I was kidnapped and spent six years locked away in an asylum. I would say that qualifies me as the most 'half mad' person among us."

"Kawley, there's much to do and little time."

Brayden turned. "Fletcher and I will get saddled."

"Only Kawley and I ride out. You and Fletcher are safe here until I send word."

"Just when did *we* turn into the two of you?" Fletcher uttered.

Belinda mounted with amazing ease. "Because the two of us can move about town without being stopped." She circled her index finger. "*We* cannot. This plan demands speed and precision, or your friends will surely die."

"Bry and I twiddle our thumbs here and wait for your word? That's our contribution to this insane plan? I don't like it!" He spun on his heel and stomped toward the lodge. "Not any of it!"

"This insanity is going to need a streak of Divine Intervention," Brayden mumbled as Fletcher stormed off. "He once told me that's what kept him alive in that asylum. While we wait, I'll remind him of it and maybe, just maybe, that Intervention will help us bring Caleb and Riley out alive."

"Say your goodbyes, you two. Kawley, we have to ride out."

Brayden watched Kawley meander toward Pickles as if reluctant to leave. "I should be the one plunging headlong into the lion's den, not Kawley."

"Would that you could," Belinda replied softly. "This is a lot to place on those small shoulders." She leaned down closer. "Brayden, be honest with me. How sure are you of that rhyme?"

"If the BP arsenal explodes in a few hours, you'll know the answer."

"If it does explode, should I still send Kawley to the prison with Ben Crawford? Would there be much point?"

"Do you really think you could stop her?"

Belinda shook her head. "Short of gagging and bagging her, probably not."

"Kawley needs to go. She needs to be certain...for all our sakes. Besides, if the explosion does take place, there will be need for reprisals. A few hanging southerners would go a long way toward calming a blood thirsty crowd." He smacked his lips. "And who knows? Maybe Riley is there; maybe he did recite that rhyme. Maybe it's just a haphazard coincidence that the rhyme and the arsenal have letters with the same sounds."

"A coincidence of such monumental proportion?" She smiled. "But then again, in the midst of this war, what would have been the chance that a northern senator's wife would be conversing in the dark woods with a landowner from Virginia?" Belinda nodded. "Let's play the odds."

"You are a remarkable woman, Miss Belinda."

"Thank you for the compliment, sir, but the truly extraordinary woman is the one over there retrieving her horse. She is very fine and very rare." Belinda gathered her reins and backed her horse. "I'll give the two of you a moment."

Kawley winked as she approached. "I didn't know you favored older women."

"What are you talking about?"

"You and Belinda had quite a tête-à-tête. She does have beautiful hair and eyes."

"I prefer burgundy and blue."

Kawley's face grew serious. "Will you do something for me if I asked you?"

"Anything."

"If..."

Her voiced faltered but Brayden knew what she meant.

"Find Riley for me. Tell him I came after him. Keep him safe because he'll have no one."

"Only if you stop talking as if you're not coming back." He caressed her cheek with his palm. "Promise me?"

She touched the backs of her fingers along his temple. "Brayden, I don't know if I'm destined to see the end of all this, but I want you to know you've given me a whole life of wonderful in the time we've shared. That's more than most people can say in a lifetime."

With his chest pounding, he bit his lip. "Kawley, I—"

She put her fingers to his lips. "Shhh. Give me a leg up and send me off with a full heart."

Belinda rode up next to them. "Ready?"

Brayden extended his hand to her. "However this ends, Miss Belinda, I want to thank you for your part and your efforts on our behalf. Perhaps, when this violent conflict between our two sides ends, we might share a visit? As friends?"

"I would like that very much, Brayden."

"Would our hotheaded friend in there be included? Whether it seems so or not, his heart's in the right place."

She chuckled. "I know. Yes, Fletcher included and, God willing, the two comrades for whom you have all risked your lives. They must be two very special people."

Kawley hesitated a few moments before she turned Pickles to gallop after Belinda. She tilted her head slightly, and her eyes widened. It felt as if she were branding the sight of him into her memory. The horse reared. In that moment, as she locked eyes with him, Kawley had seemed wearied and frail. Then Pickles spun and leaped into the darkness.

Brayden chided himself. Why didn't he stop her? He shouldn't have let her go. Kawley was already fighting her own feral demon. The rescue was too much to have asked of her. He should have been the one to risk it. Brayden shivered.

As the two horses disappeared, he stood rooted to the spot. He was loath to leave the last place he drank in the sight of her, not knowing if she would live to ever embrace him again.

———

The return ride was sheer torture for Kawley. Her leg throbbed and her arm ached. Yet, as she turned away from Brayden and galloped after Belinda, her heart was full—full of joy for the time they shared, full of sorrow for the time stolen by a feral accident, full of apprehension for the risks ahead, yet full of resolve, searching for the strength to keep pushing through the pain and exhaustion. She prayed to last for two more days. Things should be resolved by then, one way or another.

The winds had increased, and the air was wet with mist. As moisture dripped from her chin, she swept it away with the back of her sleeve. Brayden had been about to stop her. She could read it in his face. She had stopped him from uttering the words when everything in her wanted to cry,

Yes, yes, yes! I'll stay. You and Fletcher go. I don't have the strength or the courage. But she knew, as Belinda did, that their going would most certainly result in their deaths. She was the logical choice. Through Ben Crawford she could waltz into the prison without raising suspicion. Through Belinda she could obtain the potions needed to pull off this audacious scheme. Through a feral accident she had nothing left to lose; she was a walking dead woman. Yes, though she was fading, she was the logical choice. But did she have the finesse to pull off the charade—the speech, the saunter, the shroud of Philippe? Could she remember her lines, continue to play the part with the sickness waiting to rage through her at any moment?

Kawley placed both reins in one hand to swipe the corner of her eye with her left arm. The sleeve pulled on the wound where she had gouged out Philippe's brand. She yelped. The pain threw her onto Pickles' shoulder just as the horse tripped. The struggle to stay in the saddle wrenched her leg, and she yelped again as she gripped tighter.

Belinda obviously realized the danger because she galloped closer, seized Pickles' rein and yanked the horse to a halt. "We can walk for a few minutes to give both of you time to rest. The cut-off is just up the road a piece."

"What cut-off?" Kawley was glad of the short respite. "We came through no cut-off on the way out."

"The one that takes me to Momo, and you to town. That is what you want, isn't it?"

Wracked by indecision, Kawley hesitated before answering. Her brash words to Brayden and Fletcher now demanded a commitment. Could she knowingly poison Riley in the scant hope of saving him? Fletcher understood the precariousness of the scheme. His response was patently obvious. Did Brayden? Would Caleb willingly take the risk? They were already in peril. Was this plan a quicksand of catastrophe? What if she destroyed two lives instead of saving them? Was it worth the gamble?

"You know, Kawley, this is their only way out of there. If they are held in the belly of that hellhole, *you* are their only chance." Belinda took a deep breath as if choosing her words carefully. "I don't know these two, but if they are anything like the three of you, I think they'd hazard any way out."

Kawley squared her shoulders and gathered her reins. "Ask Momo to choose her elixir wisely and tell her—" Her voice cracked. "—tell her...tell her thank you."

———

A light scraping sound intruded on Kawley's dark thoughts as she sat curled in the chair by the window. Shadows from the flickering lamp danced across the walls but, instead of soothing, they created an eerie pervading melancholia. More annoyed than frightened, she turned her head to identify the sound. She heard the sound again and realized it was a light tapping at the door.

"Yes?" Kawley questioned through the closed door.

"It's Belinda. Are you still awake?"

Kawley quickly opened the door. "What's wrong? Did you hear something?"

"No, I just couldn't sleep."

"You couldn't either? I've been sitting in that chair just staring out the window." Kawley turned and limped back to the chair. She crossed her arms and scrunched her shoulder and back muscles as tightly as she could. Without thinking, she rocked slowly forward and back. The motion soothed the threatening fear.

"I was disappointed to see the light under the door. You should be resting. Tomorrow will tax the very best in you."

"When I close my eyes all I see are Riley and Caleb cold, still and dead by my hand. It's not a picture to lull me to sleep." Kawley raised her eyes. "Do you truly trust Momo? Does she understand we are trying to free them, not put them out of their misery? Tell me, Belinda, what did she give to you? What is it and how does it work?"

"I was planning to tell you in the morning because I hoped you were sleeping. Momo gave me two tiny vials, no larger than pearls."

Kawley sat straight in the brightly colored chintz covered chair. "Show me."

Belinda arranged herself in the matching chair opposite Kawley. She reached into her pocket and produced an ornate handkerchief. She opened it slowly as if afraid to lose its precious contents. A heavenly scent filled the area, stemming from an array of dried leaves and flowers.

"I'm confused. Momo gave you a sachet? How in the world will that help what we are trying to do?"

Carefully balancing the bottom of the handkerchief in one hand, Belinda pulled a horn comb from her hair and used it to search the handkerchief until she discovered the prize. She pointed to what looked like two large peas and smiled. "Don't touch."

"Why not? They look as if they should be boiled with carrots."

"Momo told me they are coated with something."

"But what...and why? She's making no sense. Fletcher was right. This whole plan is insane." Kawley jumped up in exasperation but quickly grabbed her leg.

"Does the leg still hurt you that badly?"

"Only when I move too quickly and jar it."

"Then perhaps you'd best sit still and allow me to finish."

Kawley dragged herself back to the chair and sat. "You've been so kind. Please forgive me."

"I didn't ask questions because Momo told me it was necessary to the masquerade to convince the guards. Your friends need to rub the tiny pods across their chests and then swallow them."

"Did she tell you what was in the pods?"

"Momo spoke of so many plants, I'm not really sure. She smiled as she handed the handkerchief to me. She said, 'There is a legend that the gloves on the little pads of the foxes would hide your friends in their den under the poison flowers'."

"But what does all that mean?"

Belinda shrugged shoulders. "I think she was hinting at what was in the pods. I hope it means your friends will be hidden from the guards under the guise of poison until you can drag them safely away."

"God willing."

"My dear, Fletcher was fiercely against your plan, but you and Brayden seemed sure about a rhyme. Since this is such a tremendous gamble, would you tell me the rhyme and the story behind it?"

Kawley searched the ceiling, trying to remember all the lines to the long-ago beloved rhyme that Riley composed in his head. "Itsy, Bippy and Moo. They are friends like me and you. They are bugs and slugs with lots of hugs. Itsy, Bippy and Moo." She closed her eyes. Except for the one time on their journey that she had reeled off the rhyme to Brayden, it had been years since she had recited all the lines. Just repeating those cherished words brought peace to her heart. "Riley made up that rhyme when I broke my arm to keep me from the pain. Brayden and I think Riley must have been uttering those words to distract himself from his own pain now."

"If he and their friend, Caleb, are there."

"Dear God, I want them to be there yet, on the other hand, I don't. I want them to be anywhere else," Kawley whispered as she rose and stared out the nearby window.

"Tomorrow will come soon enough. Do you think you can rest a bit now? Remember you have your own battle to fight and this whole attempt hinges on you. Let me pour more of Momo's tea. Relieving your pain might help you to sleep."

Kawley turned to the other woman just as a deafening roar crashed through the window. She was thrust to the floor covered in shards of glass. She shielded her face and curled, crouched and angled away as best she could as a second blast shattered more of the windows. Afraid to move in any direction lest more sharp wedges be blown toward her, she remained motionless on the floor.

"Are you all right? Stay low. Come with me. Crawl away from the windows." Belinda was on her hands and knees, dragging Kawley away from the glass that continued to fall from the broken windows. "Were you hit? Are you bleeding anywhere?"

Kawley was so stunned from the force of the blast that she was having trouble breathing much less form an answer. She rolled to her side and placed her palm on her chest, trying to force breath to come.

"Are you in pain? Dear God, Kawley, answer me."

She nodded and held up her hand in the hope that Belinda would allow her a moment to reassemble her scattered thoughts and stop the intense ringing in her ears.

"Yes, you're in pain or yes, you are all right?"

"All...right," Kawley managed to punch out. "I think." She closed her eyes and rejoiced with ability to suck in a deep breath. "You?"

"I'm fine. I was further from the windows." She rocked back. "Can you sit up?"

"I doubt I can move, let alone sit up." She slowly raised herself to her elbow. "If I find who shot that cannonball boom, I intend to—" Kawley snapped her jaw shut. "Belinda?"

"I don't think it was cannon fire, not an explosion of that magnitude. Look at the time." The other one was staring across the room with an expression of horror.

Kawley followed where the Belinda's stare led. The clock across the room confirmed the time. "No! Oh dear God, no! It can't be. But that means..." She couldn't even give voice to the obvious. "That means the cipher was right, and we were wrong. Riley and Caleb aren't there." Her eyes welled with tears, and her chest pounded from more than the blast.

Belinda grabbed her by the shoulders. "You don't know that."

"Then where could they be?" Kawley scrambled to rise. "Let me go. I have to ride to Brayden. We have to retrace our tracks and find where we lost them. Oh God. Oh God. This is all my fault! If only I hadn't—"

"Kawley, stop it!"

"But there's no point to check the prisoners; Riley and Caleb aren't—"

"Stop ranting and start thinking, Kawley."

"About what? It's over. I've failed."

Belinda settled herself on the floor in front of Kawley. "Look at me."

Kawley laid her head in her clasped hands and shook her head from side to side. She wondered how she would summon the courage to tell Brayden and Fletcher that all their sacrifice had come to nothing.

Belinda grabbed her wrists with a grip that was nearly painful. "Look at me! We don't know anything yet. Only that the arsenal was blown."

"Yes, the arsenal was blown exactly when Fletcher said it would be. Do you honestly believe now that the rhyme could be true?"

"Honestly, I don't."

"Then what is left? I have to ride out, hope Brayden and Fletcher don't hang me, and find another way to pick up the trail."

"Yes, you do."

She struggled to retrieve her hands. "Then let me go."

"Not before you visit the prison."

"But why? Even you think they are not there."

The other woman took a long-protracted breath. "Since I do not mince words, I will tell you straight out. You don't know if or how much time you have before that raccoon wreaks his havoc on you." She shook Kawley's wrists. "Don't look away. You know I'm right. Right now the bravest, kindest and most helpful thing you can do for your friends is let Brayden and Fletcher know for certain that those two prisoners are not the ones you seek. Even a shred of doubt could cost them dearly. Fletcher and Brayden cannot enter the prison. Only you can do that."

"But—"

Belinda shook her head. "No buts, Kawley. Tomorrow you will go with Ben Crawford to that prison, and you will play your part to the bitter end. You will be the woman I have come to believe you are." She rose and pulled Kawley up with her. "You rest over there while I attempt to do something with these drapes. It's a dangerous game we are playing, and the explosion has changed all the rules."

Kawley limped across the room and fairly plopped into the chair. Weakness had settled on her, and the mantle she carried seemed more than she could bear. Apparently, Belinda believed in her. Why could she no longer believe in herself? "Why are you helping me?"

The other woman raised an eyebrow. "I've wondered the same in my quiet moments. I've come to believe it's because I envy you."

"Envy me? I might only have days to live."

"True but I can see you've experienced something I have never had nor will have."

"I'm penniless, came dressed in rags with possibly a horrific demon lurking inside me. What could you possibly want that I have?"

"Your freedom. It's what drives you and sustains you. As a senator's wife, I have a role to play. I am bound by rules I cannot change. You, by comparison, you did not submit to that madman, Philippe. You have torn through the countryside answering to no one. You obviously can handle Fletcher, and you've bedazzled Brayden. That is quite a feat for a penniless, rag ridden woman." She smiled. "And as for that horrific demon possibly lurking inside...well...you and your knife did your best. That's now in more powerful hands than yours."

"Is that why you ride your secret missions?"

Belinda cocked her head to one side. "Perhaps."

"I'm afraid, Belinda." She licked her lips to collect her thoughts. "Not of dying, but of failing, failing to find Riley and Caleb. I've never known such fear."

Belinda sat in the chair facing Kawley. "The only failure would be not to try." She seemed to want her words to linger as her eyes widened and a cryptic smile emerged. "The new day will break soon. How about we plan with something a mite stronger than tea? I'm feeling a bit shaken by tonight's excitement."

Suddenly feeling stronger than she had in days, Kawley nodded, straightened her back and sat taller in the chair. She had never thought of her life in those terms and somehow it pleased her. Belinda was right. She had to go. Brayden and Fletcher needed to know; she had to know. Kawley accepted the goblet from Belinda with a renewed sense of purpose, of courage.

"Let's conjure up a new plan, shall we?"

CHAPTER FIFTEEN

KAWLEY HEARD THE HOOFBEATS OF BEN CRAWFORD'S MOUNT. BELINDA had helped her to dress and ready herself for the hardest performance of her life. She glanced in the mirror but barely recognized the woman looking back at her. Tilting her head side to side she decided that perhaps the different appearance was in her favor with Philippe lurking about in the city.

The cup on the table held more of Momo's brew, and she sipped it as she waited for Belinda's summons. Hopefully, the brew would keep her pain at bay to prevent her from limping or crying out if Ben happened to take her left arm. There was so much to remember and so little time...for them and for her.

Belinda called for her in a soft, quiet voice. However, as Kawley descended the stairs, Belinda's eyes belied the subdued sound. "My dear, Ben has been apologizing that he cannot allow you to visit the prison. He had to rescind his promise."

Kawley's heart sank. "But why, sir?"

"Belinda told me several of her windows were shattered last night. That was because the rebs attacked and exploded the BP arsenal."

"That was the explosion we heard?" Kawley feigned. "How dreadfully awful. I do hope no one was injured."

"Truth be told, several men were seriously hurt, and one was killed. The city is on guard and I fear for your safety in this turbulence."

Kawley brandished her most fetching smile. "But what would I have to fear with an important man like you by my side?"

"I told you, Ben, that my niece would not take no for an answer. She is determined to go with you or, I fear, even without you." Belinda lightly brushed her fingers under Kawley's chin. "And which one of your guards would say no to this face?"

"But I didn't even bring the carriage," Ben Crawford stammered.

"You may use mine," Belinda countered. "Ginger will take you there and back safely if you are easy on the bit."

"But it looks as though it might rain," he continued toward Kawley, "and you are too sweet. You might melt."

Kawley clucked her tongue and shook her head. "You are too kind, sir, but I won't melt." Her strength was rapidly dwindling. *I might collapse at your feet,* she thought, *but I surely won't melt.* "I refuse to leave town without standing face to face with a real, live dirty rebel."

"You'd best hold that sachet close because dirty they are."

"And you'd best face it, Ben, and give in. My niece is going to collect on your promise either with you or without you. Personally, I would prefer it be with you."

Ben held up his hands in apparent surrender. "I can't fight both of you. A brief inspection, and I'll have you home here. I want both of you behind locked doors with so many calling for retribution."

———

Kawley gripped the seat with her fingers. The bouncing of the carriage wheels on the street was aching her leg. If they didn't arrive soon, she might be limping as badly as any prisoner within those walls. She gripped Momo's precious sachet in her other hand and held it to her lips. She silently kissed the delicate embroidery surrounding its contents. The carriage bumped something in their way and the carriage lurched. Pain shot through her, and she had to resist the urge to bite down.

"Tell me, Miss Kinzie. Why do you have this fervid desire to touch a 'real live dirty rebel' as you called them?"

His question took her by surprise, and her mind dashed for an answer. "I've heard they are different from us. They are heartless and shoot pell-mell."

Ben clucked to the horse and snapped the reins. "The attack on the arsenal was obviously well planned and anything but pell-mell." He sucked in a deep breath. "No, Miss Kinzie, I think it's more than that. Come now. You and Belinda preyed on me and finagled this visit. I think you owe me the true reason."

Kawley was happy for the rumble of thunder while she scrambled for an answer. Ada and her son, Micah, came to mind. "A dirty rebel shot my dog."

"That's it? All this effort for an animal?"

She sat tall and jutted her chin at him. "How can you be so unfeeling? I'll have you know that my dog was quite dear to me and very talented."

Ben Crawford's face crinkled into a wide grin. "Oh? How so?"

He had thrown down the gauntlet, and she was caught. Kawley stalled for time. "Laugh if you will, but he was unusual, and that rebel shot him for it."

"Do tell."

"I would ask him, 'Pepi, would you rather be a southerner or a dead dog?' Pepi would drop to the ground and stick his feet in the air." She huffed. "A man passing by yelled that he could make it happen for real. He pulled out a pistol and shot Pepi dead." She squinted her eyes. "With every word he said I knew he was a southerner. I was so angry I ran after him and pelted him with every rock I could find but then he climbed on a nearby horse and galloped away."

"They are an ungodly sort. I hope one day to get inside that grey mind." He snapped the reins again. "Step lively there, Ginger. Today purports to be the day of Pepi's revenge."

———

The carriage rattled along the cobblestones of First Street. Kawley pulled her wrap tighter around her as the wind from the threatening storm had put a chill in the air. Perhaps it was her growing fear. The sky was darkening as was her mood. They had all been right; this plan was lunacy. But the curtain had been raised on this performance, and she now had to play her part.

Kawley gripped the sachet in her hand to give her courage. "The rain threatens to shorten our afternoon. Will we be there soon?"

Ben Crawford pointed down the street. "We are nearly there. That brick building up ahead."

Her eyes followed where he indicated. The building had bars on the windows which overlooked the street. She had expected a building housing prisoners to be separate from the city but it definitely was not. On the remote chance that Riley and Caleb were inside those walls, Kawley despaired of being able to scurry them out with any secrecy. She scoured the area. While there were a few passersby, the streets were littered with men shouldering rifles. "Are there always so many guards around the town?"

"There are extra patrols because of the explosion last night. I have every available man on lookout to prevent another attack. That insidious explosion took us all by surprise. The senators are scratching their heads wondering how our informants could have missed it."

Kawley inwardly smiled. Perhaps, she thought, if you had had the correct cipher you could have seen it coming. The small victory strengthened her.

As they approached the building, an armed guard ran to the carriage. "Commander, we have been waiting for you. The Marquis is in your office demanding to speak with you."

"He did not have an appointment, and I am busy. Tell him he will have to wait."

"But, sir, he says that his business is of utmost importance."

"I gave you an order."

The guard turned and started away, shaking his head. "Monsieur Armanac was most insistent."

"Did you say Armanac? Philippe Armanac?" Ben questioned loudly. The guard stopped, turned and nodded, clearly relieved.

Kawley shuddered and sucked in a loud breath before she could stop herself. Realizing her mistake, she shook her head and fluttered her hand.

"Are you all right?" Ben asked her.

"Bee," she muttered, moving around in feigned avoidance. "There was a bee."

He waved his hands to shoo it away. "I think it's gone now." Looking contrite, Ben locked the reins and rubbed his thighs. "My sincere apologies but I think I have to meet with this man for a few moments." Ben came around the carriage and helped Kawley to the ground. "May I leave you under the protection of the guard while I see to this important matter?"

"Please, sir, you and the Marquis take all the time you need secluded behind the doors of your office. He need never know I am here."

Ben Crawford ushered her inside. "Sergeant Hamlin, do not allow this lovely lady out of your sight. You are to remain here on the first floor where she will be safe. However, if any of the prisoners dare to reach out to her, shoot them." He strode down the hall and disappeared into a room.

Kawley was thankful she heard the latch click as the door closed behind him. She lowered the veil of her bonnet. Guise or not she feared Philippe would surely recognize her. "Shall we, Sergeant?"

"Shall we what, miss?"

"Your commander offered to allow me to see the prison from the other side of these walls. Since he is otherwise occupied, I'm certain he would have confidence in your ability to protect me." She started toward the stairs. "Since he said I would be safe on the first floor, that would mean the prisoners are up here?"

"Ah, Miss? The Commander said we were to remain here."

Kawley was already halfway up the stairs. "He said you. I don't recall hearing my name." The rain had begun to pelt the roof as she scurried to the second floor.

Knowing she had little time, she slid across the floor opening doors. The rooms were dank and dingy with a smell of unwashed bodies. She didn't want to think of what vermin might well be under her feet. There were men on numerous cots. Their whiskered faces scrunched with expressions of incredulity at seeing a woman wandering the halls. Some whistled softly. Others muttered crude remarks. While she knew in her head that it was unlikely Riley and Caleb were imprisoned here, she still had hoped for a miracle. Now she knew for certain and was forced to deal with the crisis at hand—escaping the prison out of sight of Philippe Armanac.

"Miss? Ah, ma'am, where are you?" Kawley heard the young guard's hurried footsteps.

Kawley turned to answer him when she spied one last small door. She had to duck her head while she stepped over the threshold. The room had only one small window but the light from the hallway showed there on the floor two bodies lay crouched, their knees pulled to their chest in pain or cold. Their clothes were filthy and torn. Their feet were tied with rags. One body didn't move; one turned his face. Even bloodied and bruised, she knew that face. Dear God, she knew that beloved face. She bit her fist to keep from screaming. How she wanted to run to him, but her mind screamed for her to hurry. The guard would find her in seconds. Kawley lifted her veil and put her finger to her lips lest Riley cry out in recognition. She pointed to the other body. "Caleb?" Riley nodded, eyes wide with disbelief yet clearly understanding their precarious situation. She held up the sachet. "Look inside," she called to him softly. "For both of you."

The guard appeared in the doorway as an explosive clap of thunder boomed overhead. The crackling flash that lit up the windows in the hallway showed the guard with abject fear on his face. Kawley knew she had to cover her tracks.

"You disgusting rebels," she screamed under another round of thunder cannonade. "You killed my dog. I hope you rot. I hope they hang you." She threw the sachet at Riley. He caught it and ducked away.

"Please, miss. We have to go back down. Please. If I'm found out I'll get a week in the guard house for sure if not worse," he whined. He tugged at Kawley's arm and, as much as she wanted to slap his face in anger, she meekly obliged.

As they descended the stairs and walked through the hallway, Kawley stiffened when she saw Ben Crawford and Philippe. She quickly yanked the veil over her face and flattened herself against the wall while the other two walked to the front door. From the corner of her eye she watched the men shake hands. Thankfully they did not glance in her direction. Philippe opened his umbrella and ran out. Kawley was so relieved she nearly fainted, recovering merely seconds before Ben Crawford reached her.

"My apologies again. Are you ready now?" The windows shook with an explosive racket.

Kawley covered her ears. "This thunder has given me a terrible ache in my head. May we please return to Aunt Belinda's instead? You were right, sir. This visit was ill-advised." She turned to the young guard. "Thank you for protecting me. You were most kind." The scarcely veiled lift to his face assured her the trek through the upper floor was a secret he would take to his grave.

"Are you certain?" Ben waved off the guard. "Leave us." When the other man left Ben lifted Kawley's veil, an action which made her shudder with discomfiture. "A short time ago you were most insistent on avenging your Pepi's death," he whispered and leaned his arm to the wall, blocking her escape. "You nearly demanded to see and touch those rebel bodies, did you not?"

She was cornered and caught like a rabbit in a trap. Kawley's mind scrambled for an answer to outfox the fox himself.

"Yes, sir, I did. However, lucky for me, I have your strength and wisdom to save me. I see now Aunt Belinda's confidence in you as a chaperone is well deserved." In one swift motion she ducked under his arm and scooted from the wall. As he clucked his tongue and turned, she linked her arm in his as if nothing were amiss. "I'll leave it to your cunning to see me safely home to Aunt Belinda's without being singed by a fiery blaze from the sky."

Perhaps it was her bold reply or perhaps some long forgotten gentleman portion in Ben Crawford emerged. Kawley didn't care the reason but she breathed easier when the man ran a finger around his collar and harrumphed. "I best get Ginger home safely also or your Aunt Belinda will skin me alive. She seems to be quite partial to that mare."

———

Kawley could barely wait for Ben Crawford to be out of earshot. She and Belinda sat in their chairs appearing as though they had a lazy afternoon stretching in front of them. Glancing out of the window, she could see Ben galloping down the street, sloshing water in all directions.

She turned and recounted the prison meeting with hands flailing and exaggerated body movements—the intrigue, the fear of meeting Philippe, as well as Ben's outrageous behavior.

"Belinda, do you believe it? I found them!" She hugged herself and spun until she was dizzy. She hobbled to the other woman and hugged her tightly. "It's a true miracle but I found them."

"I knew even before the words were out of your mouth."

Kawley pulled back. "But how could you possibly have known?"

Belinda smiled. "Your entire demeanor when you arrived told me you had found them, and they were alive."

"We have to let Brayden and Fletcher know. I can't wait to give them the news. "I—""

"They can't know yet." Belinda shook her head. "Not just yet. Both of them will bustle into town and be shot as conspirators the moment they open their mouths."

"Yes, yes you're right. I didn't think it through." The initial joy faded and desperation suffused her. Kawley shuffled a few steps and leaned against the arm of the chair. "Riley and Caleb are alive, but I fear just barely. Riley raised himself to one elbow, but Caleb never moved. Even though the afternoon light was dim, I could see that they were bruised and broken. It took every ounce of willpower I possessed not to cry out and run to them." She rubbed one hand against the other. "And thin, Belinda. They were both skeletal."

"Do you believe Riley recognized you?"

"Oh yes, I'm certain of it."

"And you're certain that Riley has the sachet?"

"I saw him roll on it to keep it hidden."

"And he knows what they must do with the beans...and soon?"

"Yes. I placed a tiny paper inside with drawings they could easily understand."

Belinda nodded thoughtfully as she paced. "Good...that's good."

Kawley was gripped by a crushing fear. "Belinda, what do you know and what are you not telling me?" She took Belinda's arm and turned her. "Look at me. What missive has put that expression on your face?"

Belinda's eyes darted back and forth, and she mumbled as if distracted by her own thoughts. "If Riley and Caleb follow Momo's direction, everything will be resolved before it can take place." She nodded repeatedly and shrugged her shoulders. "Yes, it might not even be them. Oh God, there's just no way to know and there's no stopping it."

"What, Belinda? You're scaring me more than I already am. There's no way of stopping what?"

"While you were at the prison, one of the guards stopped here looking for Ben Crawford. I winked and cajoled and pressured him into telling me."

"Lord, give me patience! Pressured him into telling you what?"

Belinda took Kawley by the shoulders. "The town is hungry for reprisals for the BP explosion. Your Philippe has fingered two southerners held at the prison as the spies who organized the attack. To appease the town they plan to hang them the day after tomorrow. That must have been why he was at the prison today."

Kawley fell back into the chair. "Oh, dear God, no!"

"The guard never mentioned the names of the two prisoners. Maybe it's not them. Maybe—"

"It must be Riley and Caleb. That's why they were held apart from the other prisoners. If Philippe has any hand in it—" She shook her head in disbelief. "—it's the perfect way to rid himself of Riley."

"Why does this Philippe despise Riley with such a vengeance?"

"I have no idea...and poor Caleb." She leaned her head back and covered her eyes with her palms. "Riley and Caleb are going to die. I'm going to die. This entire journey has been a waste...a complete waste!"

The woman grabbed Kawley's wrists and pulled her forward. Belinda was kneeling on the floor in front of the chair. "Stop it! That's your fear talking, your exhaustion, not you. You've carried the entire load thus far. It's no wonder you're talking this way."

Kawley tried to pull away but Belinda's grip tightened. "I don't deserve your confidence."

"You deserve it more than anyone I know. Listen to me. When this plan succeeds, and it will, the five of you will be on your way back to Virginia with no one searching for you. It's going to happen, Kawley, long before they tie any rope to a gallows."

"A least four will be headed back."

"Five, Kawley. Five. Let me hear you say it. Say it!"

"Five."

"We have to be ready. Now since Ben thinks that you, as my niece, will have returned to your home north, we need to transform you back into the bravest gentleman I know. First though, since you seem to be limping more, let's redress those wounds."

"Belinda, you keep saying this plan will work. You did your part. Momo did hers, and I did mine. What happens now? How will we know if Riley and Caleb understand, rub and swallow?" Kawley could not stop blurting out the myriad of questions swirling in her mind. "What does Momo's potion do to them? What if no one finds them until it's too late?" She pushed the heels of her hands into her eyes. "Dear Lord, I just poisoned two men and here I sit waiting to see what happens?"

Belinda pulled Kawley's hands away from her face. "Yes, Kawley. Here we sit and wait. You knew this plan was an insane bluff, but it was the only one we had to play. The bets are down. Now we wait to see who calls." She rose and gathered clean linen and salve. "This may be the last time your wounds will be dressed in a while so you'd best do a thorough job." She lifted the decanter and chuckled softly. "I'd suggest we dress them *inside* as well as out." She skillfully unhooked and unlaced all the trappings of Kawley's ladylike appearance. After rewrapping her arm and leg, Kawley dressed and again took on the veneer of a gentleman.

"I realize that Fletcher referred to you as 'little man' in the most sarcastic manner possible, but I think it rather suits the whole look." Her crooked smile seemed a valiant attempt to ease the tension in the air.

Kawley glanced at the clock. Her mind was in shambles. Had it been minutes or hours since her return? She was not sure of anything anymore. Could the insidious death sentence have started to affect her mind? She scraped her fingertips across her forehead. No fever yet, but this blasted waiting was intolerable. "Belinda, did you ask Momo how long we had to wait for her potions to work?"

"I was in such a hurry to return to you that, regrettably, I never thought to ask." She placed her hand on Kawley's shoulder. "I'll go to her now if it would ease your mind."

"Yes, please, would you? At least then we would know." A clap of thunder boomed overhead. Her hand flew to her mouth. "Oh, Belinda, forgive me. I don't know what I'm saying. I'm so sorry. I can't believe I would even utter such a selfish request. I'm so sorry. You have been a wonder through all of this mess. Forgive me?"

"There's nothing to forgive. Had you asked, I would have gone to her."

"But why? Why have you risked so much? Nothing of this plan and, for that matter, none of us mean anything to you."

The other woman held out her hands. "Because, be it north or south, I value life, not death. And the three of you have come to mean more to me than you know: Fletcher with his hotheadedness, Brayden with his open heart and outpouring of love and you, the feisty manling as well as the most courageous woman I have ever met. I will truly miss the lot of you. Sadly, after you leave, all of us will have to deny any knowledge of what has happened here. Our very lives may depend on it."

"I will be overjoyed never to mention any of this again." Kawley withdrew her hands and paced the room. "But right now we're here, and they are behind those accursed walls. How will we know anything?"

"Because Hanna is sitting across from the doctor's office. If he leaves and heads in the direction of the prison, she will tell me immediately."

"But why would Hanna do such a thing? Wouldn't she be suspicious of your motives?"

"I told you, Hanna asks no questions of me and I ask no questions of her."

"And if the doctor heads toward the prison, then what?"

"*Ad libitum.*"

"Oh no... you can't possibly mean...we improvise? No plan? That's the plan?"

"Kawley, our plan dissolved the moment the Marquis fingered Riley and Caleb as the conspirators for the BP attack. From this moment on we have to simply outsmart them."

"Agreed." She paced again but spun within a few steps. "But how?"

"Do you think my midnight runs are scripted plans? Most times it is hour by hour, sometimes minute by minute. We will simply seize what fate provides and use it to our best advantage." Belinda tilted her head. "The rest is up to a power greater than all of us."

Kawley closed the space between them. "If I weren't so afraid of the danger, I would kiss you. You are such an amazing woman, Belinda. I wish I had met you in another time and another place. In these few days you've been more family to me than my own."

A loud clap of thunder boomed over their heads, followed by a hearty thump below them. Kawley turned her head to identify the sound and the thumping continued. "Sounds as if someone is banging on a door."

"I know. But thumping of that sort is never good news." She shot out the door, then turned. "Stay out of sight unless I call for you."

As soon as Belinda headed for the stairs, Kawley slipped behind the painting, tiptoed down the passageway and peeked through the slit.

"Yes? Who is it?" Belinda asked through the door. Thunder boomed again.

"It's Ben Crawford. Please, I need to speak with you."

"I'm not really up to receiving guests at the moment, Ben. Can you come tomorrow?"

Kawley was appalled. Why would Belinda send him away? Weren't they waiting for whatever information Ben Crawford might provide?

"Please, I must speak with you," Ben repeated. "Please see me, if only for a moment."

Belinda opened the door. Ben Crawford slipped in and ripped the wet hat from his head.

"Please tell me what was so urgent that it could not have waited until tomorrow?"

"Would you know of two able-bodied men from the asylum who might come quickly to be of assistance at the prison?"

"What's this about, Ben? You have an abundance of men at the prison who jump at your every command. Why do you need two simpleminded men?"

"I am trying to avoid a panic."

"I'm listening."

"Two prisoners are dying."

"And you've come to warn me because my niece was at the prison today?" Her hand flew to her mouth. "Dear God, she wasn't anywhere near them, was she?"

Ben shook his head. "No, no. She never left the first floor. I came for a different reason. I need two gravediggers as soon as possible."

"Assign two officers or two of the other prisoners. Why have you come to me?"

"Because anyone in contact with these prisoners might contract the sickness and also die."

"Is that what the doctor told you?"

"You are the only one who knows about this. I need those two out of the prison before it spreads to the other officers and prisoners. It could start an epidemic. I thought—"

"You thought two men from the asylum would not be missed because they are expendable?"

"But this is an emergency. I've seen it before. If this turns out to be what I think it is, there's no telling how many could die. These two prisoners were isolated in a separate room. I need them out of there."

"No."

Ben Crawford was plainly outraged, plainly used to being obeyed. "No?"

Kawley was dumbfounded. This was the perfect solution to their problem, and Belinda was refusing. It took every ounce of restraint she possessed not to jump from her hiding place.

"I will not knowingly endanger two simpletons to satisfy your supercilious measure of the value of life. Who is worthy and who is not?"

"What if I paid them?"

Belinda threw out her hands. "To die?"

Ben sucked in a deep breath. "To accept the risk?"

"How much?"

Ben dug into his pocket and held out a bag of coins. "It's all the gold coins I had with me."

Belinda snorted. "To come to my door that well prepared tells me you must be desperate."

"Then you will do it? You will send two men...and quickly? Everything left in that room will have to be burned as soon as they are gone."

"Yes. I'll help you. I know of two mutes. Then there will be no one to tell tales. I'll have them bring their own shovels so they can snatch your bodies and bury them elsewhere. That should solve your problem."

Ben's relief was palpable. He licked his lips, blew out a patently relieved breath and shoved the hat back on his head. "Thank you. I truly believe you have saved many lives tonight."

As he turned to leave, Belinda said, "One more thing, Ben. After tonight, don't ever darken this door again. I don't want to know you anymore. Perhaps I never did."

"I don't understand."

"In the nights ahead you'll have plenty of time to figure it out."

Ben harrumphed and yelled over his shoulder. "Just have those men there soon."

Belinda locked the door, spun around and yanked up her skirt. "I know you were listening. I need to change. The curtain for act II is about to rise."

"Then we'd best reach Fletcher and Brayden...and fast. I'll saddle the horses."

———

"Why did we agree to this plan? I hate this plan." Brayden threw up his hands. "Why didn't you talk me out of it? You're supposed to be the clear thinking one. Why did you—" He growled loudly. "—why did you let me send her off with no more assurance than a child's nursery rhyme? Dear God, what was I thinking?"

"Bry, we don't even know if Caleb and Riley are there. They've sent no word."

A barrage of thunder roared overhead. "Exactly. Kawley is sick, maybe—" His mouth snapped shut because he could not even voice the word. "—and I cast her to the wolves of that prison with only her wits and an insane idea to guide her. We should have heard something, anything, by now...at least something other than that blast in the middle of the night." He stomped his foot. "The cipher was right, and the rhyme was wrong so why hasn't Kawley come back?"

"You're right," Fletcher mumbled.

"Which part?"

"All of it. We should have heard something by now, the cipher, the rhyme, the fact that we let her go at all. All of it."

Brayden wadded a linen napkin and threw it at Fetcher. "Don't you do that. Don't you dare do that."

Fletcher didn't even look up from his chair while he swirled his brandy. "Do what?"

"You said I was right. In all the years I've known you, you've never said that."

"And you never will again, but this one time you're right."

"No...you saying I'm right means you've given up." Brayden stomped over to him and kicked his toe into Fletchers foot. "Fight with me, damn it. Tell me I was wrong to have allowed her to go alone. Tell me Kawley will survive. Tell me we will think up a new plan to bring everyone home safely. Lie to me if you must, only don't tell me you've given up." The thunder crashed overhead as though adding punch to his words. "Fletcher, you said we were in this until the end."

Fletcher lifted his arm and swept it out in front of him. "And here we are."

"Damn it! You may have given up, but I have not. With you or without you, Fletcher, I'm saddling up and heading into town."

"Well, thank the good Lord because I'm too wet and weary to do it."

Brayden spun around. Kawley and Belinda stood dripping in the doorway.

"Kiki, oh thank God you are all right," Brayden gasped as he shot across the room and clutched her. He reached a hand to Belinda. "Thank you for bringing her back safely."

Fletcher jumped from his perch. "You didn't find them, did you? After that loud blast last night at the predicted time, I knew we were hunting our tails on a wild-goose chase."

"Don't mollify your opinion, Fletcher. Kawley and Belinda are strong enough to hear the truth."

"The question is whether the two of you are strong enough to live with the truth," Belinda uttered as she snatched the bottle of brandy from the sideboard. She held up the bottle as she crossed the room toward the door. "We have flasks to be filled."

As Belinda disappeared, Brayden pulled Kawley from him. "What is she talking about? Did you find Caleb and Riley?"

She watched Fletcher shoot out from behind Brayden. "Were they alive?"

"Yes and no."

"What the devil does that mean?" the two men shouted at once.

She pulled on Brayden's arm. "There's no time to explain."

Fletcher blocked Kawley's path with a menacing stance. "You'd better explain and right now."

Kawley shoved past him and headed out. "I'm leaving," she blasted as she spun around. "And if you two want to see your friend alive again, you'd best saddle up and ride." As she turned back and passed through the doorway, she hesitated for a millisecond to collect her thoughts, her strength and her willpower.

"Did she just order us to follow?" Fletcher grunted.

"I suspect if we want the details, we'd best do as she says."

CHAPTER SIXTEEN

BELINDA AND KAWLEY HAD RECOUNTED THE NIGHT'S EVENTS AND THE parts that he and Fletcher were to play if Caleb and Riley could be saved. The decrepit wagon they were given to use bumped and swayed and jolted every bone in Brayden's body. Even his muscles were screaming from the abuse of the trip in the drenching, dark night. Whatever animal fat or oil had been used in an attempt to waterproof the clothes Belinda insisted they don was foul smelling. It also did little to protect their skin from the rain. Fletcher had been oddly quiet ever since they left the asylum. He clucked to the horses as they cantered along on their journey.

Brayden ripped open his shirt. "These clothes reek."

"That's because they were probably taken from a dead body and saved for just such a purpose. One can never tell when it might be necessary to pose as a mute simpleton."

"What a disgusting thought." He tore off his hat, raised his face to the rain and allowed to water to run down his cheeks. "I do hope there's no vermin residue."

"Do you still have Belinda's note to the prison guard? Remember we're mutes so without that note, vermin residue will be the least of our problems."

"You do know this plan is insane?"

"Ah, hell." Fletcher wiped his chin with the back of his hand. "This entire journey has been sheer madness."

"And only a pack of deranged fools would possibly attempt it."

Fletcher elbowed him in the ribs. "Then stop complaining. You're appropriately dressed. Most likely the worse we smell the more people will leave us alone. Now start practicing being mute."

"How do I practice being mute?"

"Bry?"

"Yeah?"

"Shut up."

———

The prison loomed in the distance ahead of them. Several sentries had stared at them but, oddly enough, had allowed them to pass without incident. Brayden held Belinda's note to Ben Crawford clenched in his fist. The closer they rolled to the prison, the more Brayden realized that note was their only route to rolling out with none the wiser. Their four lives were neatly folded in that little pouch. They drove the wagon to the front gate. As expected because of the BP explosion, the sentry raised his weapon at them.

"What's your business here, boy? State it or keep moving on."

Brayden raised his hand with the note clutched inside and waved it. Being mute certainly did pose a problem.

"Don't you be waving no pistol at me, boy. State your business or I'll shoot."

The small pouch looked nothing like a pistol. The trigger-happy sentry was more of a simpleton than the two of them. Fletcher elbowed him in the ribs and motioned for him to climb down and hand the note to the guard. Brayden followed directions and submissively relinquished the note. The guard read it and directed another one to inspect the wagon for anything hidden. The other man waved them on.

"Open the gate," shouted the menacing one.

Brayden stood his ground with his hand extended.

"What do you want, dummy?"

Even though he wanted to crash his fist into the guard's haughty face, Brayden lowered his eyes and pointed to the note in the other one's hand.

"You'll get it when you clear them two bodies out of here. They're stinking up the place. But then again, maybe it's the two of you. Now follow me."

Fletcher snapped the reins on the horses' rumps to urge them forward. Brayden walked alongside, thankful he didn't cluck to the horses out of sheer habit. Mute. Remember mute. He bit the inside of his cheek to keep his mouth shut.

The guard stopped and indicated with the tip of his weapon where they should enter. "In through here. Up the stairs, second door on the right. Take everything with them, bedding, blankets. I want nothing left with their stench on it."

Resisting the urge to fly up the stairs to Caleb, Brayden and Fletcher played their parts and trudged toward their duty. The guard had been right; the stench was foul. Two bodies lay on mats and did indeed look dead. Knowing there was little time, Brayden silently prayed as he smoothed the hair away from one face. Caleb! *Dear God, Caleb, please be alive.* Not certain if the guard had followed them, he surreptitiously felt Caleb's neck. Was life beating there? He couldn't tell. He glanced at Fletcher who was doing the same with Riley. Fletcher slyly shrugged his shoulders. They slung the two prisoners over their shoulders and carefully carried them down to the wagon.

"Drag out what's left of their trash. My orders were to make sure it was all buried with them."

Brayden was quite content to follow the guard's last order. The mats would certainly soften Caleb's and Riley's wagon ride while they made their escape. As he lumbered toward the wagon with the mats in his feigned submissive posture the guard cracked a whip across his left shoulder. Pain shot through his whole left side like a high poker, and he nearly cried out as he stumbled.

"Quit plodding along like some old mule. The plot is in the back of the yard. Get 'em dug and get 'em planted before I'm soaked through."

Still reeling from the whip, Brayden knew exactly who he wanted to plant but he merely nodded and trudged forward as the wagon followed. His mind was spinning. How were he and Fletcher to bury Caleb and Riley with the guard watching? The two would surely suffocate before they could pull them out. If they killed the guard and buried him, someone would certainly notice.

The rain pelted them as they dug in the soft ground. Fletcher looked at him and Brayden could not discern whether it was raindrops or tears that streamed down his friend's face. They were failing, and there was not a damn thing either one of them could do to stop it.

Just then another man came running. He and the young trigger-happy guard walked off and had a discussion out of earshot.

Their guard stomped his foot. "Are you sure? This goes against procedure."

The other man nodded and kept whispering.

"Then why the hell wasn't I told this before I stood out here in the soaking rain?" He shoved the other one, turned and stalked over to Brayden and Fletcher. "Orders are you are to bury these bodies off prison property. Get 'em out of here. Now!"

Wanting no evidence of their existence, Brayden again stood his ground and extended his hand.

"I'm not shaking the hand of no idiot. Get the hell out of here!" He slapped away the proffered hand.

Brayden tapped his right fingers into his left palm. He hoped the idiot with the weapon would understand.

"Oh, that's right. The dummy wants his note back. Well, come and get it." The guard took the note from his pocket and ground it into the mud under his boot. "Now pick it up and get out. If the wagon isn't through the gate by the time I count to ten, I'll bury the lot of you."

Fletcher slapped the reins against the horses a second after Brayden grabbed the note and jumped aboard. They sloshed through the gate into the night, both too afraid to whoop and holler until they were safely away.

Within a few miles the rain had become a drizzle. When Fletcher pulled the horses from their breakneck gallop, neither man spoke as they hopped off the seat.

Fletcher was noticeably shaking as he jumped into the back of the wagon. "Are they alive? Please God, let them be alive. I wanted to kill that trigger-happy little bastard. The way he treated Caleb like a dead animal was disgusting."

"One swipe with that shovel, and I would have dropped the son of a bitch right in the hole. That image is what kept me going."

Fletcher checked Caleb and leaned back. "Thank God. Riley?"

"I heard a beat." Brayden looked down to see if his palms were bleeding because he had dug in his nails so hard.

They walked the horses and wagon down to the lake where Belinda had directed them. They gingerly placed Caleb and Riley in the soft moss, unhitched the horses, swamped the mats, and scuttled the wagon into the lake. When they returned, Riley had begun to stir. As Brayden touched him, he thrashed and twisted to get away.

"It's all right, Riley. You're safe. Be still. We're here to help you," Brayden whispered but Riley had lost consciousness again. He glanced up at Fletcher. "Caleb?"

"Nothing yet but we have to get them out of here and back to Belinda's fast. Caleb seems the lighter of the two of them. With your bad arm you take Caleb, and Riley will ride with me. Think your shoulder can handle it, Bry?"

"To get out of this God forsaken place, my shoulder will handle anything."

———

The ride to Belinda's seemed to take forever. They were nearly discovered and had to backtrack to evade detection. With no saddles to stabilize them, Caleb nearly slipped off twice and Brayden's strength was ebbing fast. While grateful they had mounts at all, the animal under him had high withers and a short choppy gait, a gait that felt like a hammer hitting each and every bone in his back. Nevertheless, had Brayden noticed any sign of life in Caleb's limp body, he would have gladly ridden the gelding through the gates of hell. Why was Caleb not shivering as he, himself, was? They could not lose Caleb now, not when they were so close to heading home.

Brayden pushed on behind Fletcher until they were at Belinda's. When Fletcher jumped down to open the stable door, Brayden was stunned that Riley stumbled alongside of him, wobbly but definitely conscious. Hope surged through him as he urged the horse inside, hauled Caleb to his shoulder and carried him through the dim light to where Riley was stretched out.

"Riley?" he asked.

The man lying next to Caleb nodded, rolled to his side and wretched.

He locked his arms across his belly. "Kiki," he croaked. "Where's Kiki?" His voice was barely above a whisper. "Kiki."

"She's safe. You and Caleb are safe, too."

Fletcher lit the lamp and hung it on a specific hook that Belinda had directed. "Riley, I'm sure she is watching for our signal and will be here soon. Rest for a bit." He grabbed a few dry saddle blankets and covered Riley, then stepped around to Brayden. "Any sign Caleb is coming out of it?"

Brayden covered Caleb. "He started shivering when I laid him down. That must be a good sign, no?"

"Means he's alive, at least."

"Sage might not recognize him. Looks like they beat up on him pretty good."

"They did," Riley added behind them. He was leaning on one elbow, rubbing his eyes with his free hand. "I think someone had it in for us, but him most of all. It was as if they thought he had some information they wanted. I think they beat on me just for the hell of it. Then they accused us of being spies, and I guess you know what they do to spies." Riley's teeth chattered. "Who are you and where are we?"

"We're friends, Riley, and you're in a safe place. Save your strength," Brayden assured him. He felt Caleb's forehead, but he could not discern whether it felt feverish because his own hands were freezing cold. We have to get him into some dry clothes."

"I'm certain Belinda and Kawley will be here with supplies as soon as they can. I lit the signal a while ago."

"The idea of warm clothes and a stiff drink is sounding mighty good to me right about now."

Fletcher tapped Caleb's cheek a few times. "Come on now, Caleb. No more snoozing. Time to wake up." When Fletcher raised his face, his wide-eyed expression sent daggers of dread down Brayden's back.

"What's wrong?"

"He's not shivering anymore."

Brayden shoved Fletcher out of the way and knelt next to Caleb. He laid his ear against his friend's chest. "He's alive but I think we're losing him."

Belinda and Kawley burst through the door. Their arms were full of clothing, boots and blankets. Kawley dropped everything and ran. "Riley!"

Belinda stopped her, and they struggled. "Kawley, no, unless you don't cry."

"Let me go, Belinda. Let go of me. It's Riley!"

"Remember your wounds and what you might be facing."

Kawley stopped scrambling to free herself, clearly realizing Belinda's reasoning. "Yes, of course you're right. I'll be careful." She dashed to Riley, and he reached for her. "Riley, I'm so happy I've found you but before we touch there is something you have to know."

"Kiki, your hair. What happened to your hair?"

"It's a long story..."

Their voices were drowned out when Belinda knelt next to Brayden. "What's wrong with Caleb? Why isn't he awake?"

"I don't know! I don't know! Fletcher, bring those blankets; wrap his head with that towel. We have to get him warm. Hurry, hurry."

When Caleb was snuggly wrapped, Brayden glanced up at Fletcher who shook his head and shrugged his shoulders in apparent paralyzed exasperation. Riley, Kawley and Belinda sat helplessly to the side.

"Belinda, did your Momo give you any sort of antidote in case her potion went awry?"

"I'm sorry, Brayden, but no, there's nothing. Don't you remember? That was the risk you all took when you agreed to the ruse."

"It was the only way to pull them out of there, Brayden," Kawley whispered.

Fletcher shoved his fingers threw his hair. "Why did I ever let you talk me into it?"

"Stop it, all of you! There's no undoing what we've done to him." He looked down at the man who had once saved his life. Brayden had held another in his arms while life slipped away, and raw fear gripped his heart with an icy hand. He leaned close to Caleb. "We've ridden so hard to find you. Granted we poisoned you to sneak you out from under those guards, but it was only to keep you from having your neck stretched. I'm certain you'll find a way to return the favor when we are all home again. Please open your eyes." Brayden was glad his back was turned from the others because he was fighting back the tears that threatened to spill over his cheeks. He remembered another time they had been at death's door, but the roles had been reversed. Brayden used his friend's own words. "Don't you dare die on me, Caleb. Do you hear me? Don't you dare. Swim, Caleb. That's right, keep swimming."

"Swim? Bry, have you lost your mind?"

"Fletcher, hush. I think I know what he's trying to do," Kawley interjected.

"I can't do this alone, Caleb. I need your help. Swim, Caleb, swim! We're not dying today...not today. Come on, Caleb, move those hands. I know you're struggling...I am, too. Move those hands!"

Caleb remained still.

Something else came to mind. "You have to keep trying, Caleb...for your child. That's right. You're going to be a father. Now swim!"

Nothing.

Brayden rocked back on his heels. A low unbidden, deflated cry escaped him when Fletcher knelt next to him and squeezed his shoulder. Neither of them spoke. The only sound was the rustling straw as the other three crept closer. For what seemed an eternity, the five touched shoulders as if in silent prayer.

"To have come this far, Bry. We found him, snuck him out of the prison, brought him safely here only to have him—"

"Don't say it, Fletcher. Don't you dare utter that word," Brayden shot back. As his throat constricted, he rubbed his palm over his forehead. "Dear God, first Clive, now Caleb, soon..." Brayden sucked in a quick breath, pulled his hands away and glanced at Kawley. She was staring at Riley with an expression of sheer joy. He clamped shut his eyes and lowered his head. *Please, please don't take Kawley, Lord. I beg you, don't take Kawley, too,* he repeated in his mind over and over in a fervent litany.

"Brayden, what is that?" Kawley asked.

Her words jolted him. "What is what?" he grunted, immediately regretting the force with which he uttered it. He was in no mood for guessing games.

"That lump under the blanket." She pointed. "Look. There it goes again."

"Bry, what the devil is that?"

"Fletcher, help me." Brayden reached under the blanket until he felt Caleb's hand. "Swim, Caleb, swim." Caleb's fingers seemed to tap his own with a faint touch. The tap was so weak, he was afraid he had imagined it. "Swim, Caleb. Show me you are swimming." There was no mistaking the tap. Brayden squeezed Caleb's hand and sat back.

"Anything, Bry?"

Brayden wiped the corners of his eyes with the back of his hand. A wide grin spread across his face, and he nodded. "Caleb is swimming back home!"

———

It took nearly two hours for Caleb to come fully awake. He insisted that he could ride as well as any of them, but Brayden held off their departure for yet another hour. As anxious as they were to be gone, they knew that Caleb and Riley were in no condition to tear through the countryside evading detection.

They used the time to change clothes, eat, drink and fill in each side with information. Unfortunately, Caleb and Riley were as much in the dark as he and Fletcher were. There had been no specific charges brought against the two and certainly no formal trial.

"So, Caleb, you have no idea why your father might have written to Kawley's father or what might have been the reason for the letter?" Brayden asked.

Caleb shook his head. "I didn't even know they knew one another. I've never heard the name mentioned."

"Do you know of any dealings your father had overseas that the northerners might have deemed traitorous?"

"My father was always in Europe handling one deal or another. There were months my mother considered herself a widow because she was always alone. You know that better than anyone, Fletcher."

Belinda smacked her lips. "Quite a mystery but, as an outsider, it seems as though one or more people went to a vast amount of effort to make the two of you disappear...and for good." She held out a platter. "Eat up, gentlemen. You two are so thin you are disappearing as we speak."

Caleb took another piece of chicken. "Thank you for your kindness, Miss Belinda. I can't remember anything tasting this delicious."

Riley nodded. "It even looks as delicious as it tastes."

"They kept us tied and blindfolded along the way," said Caleb.

"And we were lucky if they fed us a disgusting gruel every other day," Riley added.

"With our hands tied, they would put the bowl on the ground by our faces, and we had to suck it out of the bowl. It was disgusting. Then they'd laugh and call us pigs."

"If we said a word or made a sound, we'd feel their boots—"

"—and they took ours—"

Riley nodded. "We'd feel their boots in places not seemly to mention in the presence of ladies."

"Then we'd heave up the gruel and go hungry for days."

Kawley gasped and covered her mouth as if she, herself, would heave her meal. Then she shook her head and waved her hands. "Stop. Please stop. I can't listen to anymore."

Brayden urged her back toward him as he cradled her where they sat. She laid the back of her head onto his shoulder, and he encircled her waist with his arms. He kissed the top of her head. Several days had passed since Kawley was bitten. There had been no infection and no visual signs, and he was hopeful. "They are here, and they are safe."

Fletcher wiped his lips and his fingers. "And we will be heading home as soon as we pack up—"

"—and fill the flasks," Brayden added with a smile as they rose. "Because we have much to celebrate."

Belinda stood, rustled in the large pouch beside her and held up a bottle of fine brandy. "Here is my contribution to your celebration."

Brayden took her hand. "My dear Miss Belinda, you yourself are the greatest contribution to our celebration because without you there would be nothing to celebrate. We owe you a debt that can never be repaid."

She handed him the bottle. "Oh piffle." Belinda reddened. "I learned that not all southerners have horns."

Caleb came up and kissed Belinda's right cheek as Riley kissed her left. "We owe you our lives, and we will always be grateful."

Riley fussed with his hat and pointed to Caleb. "What he said, and thank you kindly." He and Caleb busied themselves with the horses.

"I won't kiss you because...well you know why...but I truly want to," Kawley said. "You've been more of a mother to me in this short time than my mother ever was, and I do love you for it—" She gestured around. "—for all of this and for what you did to help save Riley and Caleb."

"Thank you right back for giving me a unique perspective, as Ben Crawford put it, 'inside the grey'." Belinda blew her a kiss as Fletcher approached. "Safe home, Kawley. I will pray that things continue to go well for you."

Brayden watched as Fletcher took her hands in his. "Belinda Dunigan, I am at a loss for words."

"I don't think that has ever happened before." Brayden glanced skyward. "Be careful, everyone. I think lightning is about to strike us down."

Fletcher waved off the comment. "I actually thought about what I would say to you if this plan succeeded."

"I think he also thought about what he'd say if it didn't."

"Bry, will you allow me a moment?"

Belinda giggled. "Fletcher, don't mind my saying this but under all your fiery temper beats a very soft heart."

Fletcher's face reddened. "And don't mind my saying this—under all that northern fuss and feather, you would have made one heck of a southerner." He turned and walked to his horse.

Belinda smiled. "I'll take that as a compliment."

"Of the highest caliber," Brayden said as he approached her.

She handed Brayden a small pouch. "These are gold coins Ben Crawford gave me for the two mute gravediggers."

"I can't take these."

"Take them. You have no idea what you might face on the way home."

He clicked his heels and tipped his hat. "Ma'am."

As he turned, Belinda touched his shoulder. "Be good to her, Brayden. She loves you so."

"You can count on it."

The five of them led their horses outside and mounted. Belinda shoved the door closed. She fisted her hips, stared at each of them for a minute and gave a quick nod. "You are one sad, motley looking bunch but that should play to your advantage. Head west through the woods until you come to a fork. Take the left fork. That will lead you to the river. Riding through the river will hide any tracks in case anyone is on your trail." She smiled. "It's been an honor to have met you. I will pray for your safe journey home." Her hand brushed Kawley's knee as Pickles passed her, and Brayden was sure there were tears in Belinda's eyes.

"Belinda is a remarkable woman," Brayden said to Kawley after they had ridden a few miles. "She risked her life for us, and I'm trying to figure out exactly why."

"That same question has been pestering me all along," Fletcher added.

"She told you at the beginning. To her it's not north or south, black or white. It's about life, death and the justice that divides them."

Brayden scratched his cheek. "But she didn't know us or owe us so why did she help us?"

"Instead of questioning *why* she did, be thankful for *what* she did."

"But—"

Kawley raised her palm. "All right, you two. I will break a confidence for the first time in my life. In our private moments together Belinda shared with me that she first agreed to help me because not too long ago a southerner saved her life. She further agreed to help Caleb and Riley because the two of you lacked something."

"Obviously our friend, Caleb," Fletcher retorted.

"Belinda knew of your vast wealth and grand estates. She, of all people, understood the power they wielded, but she most respected what you *didn't* have."

"What we lacked?" Brayden and Fletcher asked in unison.

"Conceit."

Kawley pointed up ahead. "There's the fork."

"That's it? You're explaining a puzzle with a riddle?"

"Brayden, you have a long ride home and many miles to sort it out. Belinda said to head to the left. Riley and I are heading to the right."

"What?" Brayden ground Ajax to a halt. "What do you mean? We have a better chance of making it if we stay together."

Fletcher rode up close to them. "Bry, what is going on?"

"I'm not sure but I intend to find out." He jumped down, handed the reins to Fletcher and lifted Kawley from her horse as gently as he could without hauling her from the saddle. He carried her a distance and set her feet on the ground. "What's this about?"

"Brayden, I have Riley now to see me through to the end. I don't have to make a mess of your life with the end of my own. Everyday has more hope. Yes, that's true but tomorrow could quickly be the end...or the day after that. Fletcher told me you've already buried one wife. I care for you too much to put you through what could be my hideous, vicious end. I release you from your promise."

Fletcher was wrong to have told Kawley about Lavinia. Brayden cast the thought aside. "You care for me? Is that all you think this is? A promise? A gesture? Pity?" He took her by the shoulders and stared deep into her cobalt eyes. Again he was lost in the allure of her exquisite features. The last days filled with disaster and dilemma had filled his mind and clouded his eyes to her charm. "Kawley...Kiki, my words were not a promise." He leaned closer. "They were...and still are an avowal of my undying devotion."

"Yes, that's right. You are undying, and I'm dying. What greater love can I show you than to spare you that pain?"

"Because that pain will not be spared. If it happens, it will be *shared*...by all of us," whispered Fletcher who had come up behind them. "Bry's little cohort manling has put us all to shame with persistence, courage and sheer grit."

"Come with me, Kiki. I want you with me forever...however long forever turns out to be."

Kawley took a step and grimaced. Brayden caught her. "You've worried over everyone but yourself." He carried her back to her horse and helped her mount. "We're going home...all of us."

———

Watching Kawley as she rode ahead of him was breaking his heart. Fletcher was right about her courage and her grit. Even now she was favoring her arm and her leg, yet she had played her perilous role with Ben Crawford as if nothing were wrong. Without her wit and cunning, Caleb and Riley would have been hanged as conspirators. He and Fletcher would have been helpless to have prevented it. Even wounded as she was, Kawley never stopped until she found them.

Brayden's mind was swirling. He was riddled with guilt. Lavinia had died because of his callousness. Now Kawley could be facing the same because of his mistrust. She fled because of him and that flight set in motion her fateful encounter with the raccoon. He had been helpless to save Lavinia and now he was helpless to save Kawley if the sinister, malicious villain lurked within her wounds.

As if sensing his thoughts Kawley slowed her horse's pace until she was next to him. The other three continued on, plainly giving the two of them more privacy. Pickles and Ajax walked side by side, their long strides still managing to keep the rest in sight.

Kawley glanced sideways at Brayden. She heaved a heavy sigh. "You're not a poker player, are you?"

Brayden snorted and furrowed his brow. "Why do you ask?"

"You can't bluff. Your expression betrays you."

"Do tell."

"Your thoughts are written all over your face."

"I'm thinking of nothing but your beauty."

Kawley flicked her hand. "Liar. You should be joyful. You are returning home with Caleb. But I watched your face when I limped. You're blaming yourself for my fall on the raccoon. You're thinking I fled because you had doubts about me. You're right. I did. But the fall was an accident."

"But my mistrust put you at that river."

"Pickles tripped. It was not your fault."

Brayden's throat closed up, and he couldn't continue. Remorse sucked him down like quicksand.

"Fletcher told me you blame yourself for your wife's death. Is that why you bury yourself in your grey journal? And now you worry that you may have killed me, too?"

"He doesn't know the truth. No one does."

"I was told your wife died of snakebite. Unless you wrapped it around her, how could there be an evil truth?" She dropped one rein, reached out and touched his arm. "Brayden, please...tell me."

Brayden clenched his teeth to hold it back, but the floodgates opened. "Lavinia darted from me just as you did. You fell on the raccoon; she stepped on the snake."

Kawley was silent as through digesting what he had shared. "Will you tell me why Lavinia ran from you that day?" she whispered.

247

In his mind he could see her running, could still hear the screams. Brayden closed his eyes and shook his head.

"Please."

He forced himself to look at Kawley. "God forgive me, I had just told her that our marriage was...that I never said I loved her because I didn't know what real love was."

He rubbed his forehead. "She asked, and I couldn't lie to her. Dear God, if I had known she would flee I would have kept silent."

"Guilt cheats you out of everything but crippling loneliness. You have to forgive yourself, Brayden. The snakebite was an unforeseeable accident."

He drew in a deep breath and held it to slow his thundering heart. The cadence of Jax's hooves reached sixteen before he finally released it. "I didn't know what true love was until..." His voiced failed him.

"Until?"

Brayden wanted to memorize the dreamy quality of her face. "Until I met you."

Her eyes studied him for several minutes as though knowing it was the first time he had spoken the ugly truth aloud. "Thank you for letting me in."

Her simple quiet words touched him as intimately as a kiss. Every word, every gesture she made warmed him, surprised him at the depth of his love for her. He prayed she would not be sacrificed as punishment for his past shameful, selfish deed. He clucked to the horses and the two of them trotted up to join the others.

CHAPTER SEVENTEEN

HOURS LATER THE FIVE OF THEM REACHED THE RIVER. BRAYDEN WAS wearied and drained. He worried that Kawley, Caleb and Riley were failing but reluctant to show it. "Why don't we hold up here for the night and get an early start in the morning? I am bone-tired and could use a few hours out of this saddle."

It appeared that Fletcher picked up on the hint. "I've been waiting miles for one of you to suggest it."

"I'm not falling out of the saddle yet but if you insist," Caleb answered.

Kawley's eyes were closed, and she was leaning to the side.

Brayden leaped from Ajax and shot to her side. "Let me help you down," he whispered. "You've carried the load long enough. It's my turn to carry you." He set her down against the trunk of a tree. "Close your eyes and rest here while we make camp."

She scooted gingerly against the tree.

"Kiki, is it your leg? Is it worse?" He reached for her wound. "Let me check it."

She waved him away. "No, no, it's not my leg. I'm just tired."

Brayden lifted her chin with a gentle nudge. "Truly?"

"Truly." She waved him away. "Help Fletcher with the horses but remember to give Pickles extra line."

"I'll remember." He stroked her cheek before he rose and joined the others nearby.

"I don't know how to thank you, Fletcher," said Caleb. "And you, too, Brayden. You both risked so much to find us."

"We surely wouldn't have lasted much longer," Riley added.

"It was..." Caleb covered his face and his shoulders shook.

Riley jumped in. "They hated us something awful, more than any other prisoners. Some of the others were treated almost kindly. Some even had ladies visit."

Caleb regained his composure. "Riley and I couldn't understand why we were kept separated from the others. We were too weak to have offered any resistance, yet they starved and beat us."

"I don't why or how but, through it all, Caleb never gave up hope."

"Kawley never gave up on finding you, Riley," said Brayden. He bit his lip as he watched Kawley tuck her arm to her midsection and rub her leg. "Kawley?"

She scooted over to join them as though trying to allay his fears. "I couldn't have done it without Brayden and Fletcher."

"And we wouldn't have succeeded without you, Kawley," Fletcher piped in.

"I'll drink to that," said Brayden. He jumped up and pulled his flask from the saddle.

Kawley's face lit up as she appeared bolstered by the praise. She grinned, grabbed the flask and opened it. "Ladies first." She poured a puddle into her palm and slurped.

"At any other time, I would be appalled, little sister, but considering what we have all just survived, I say to drink up and pass it around."

They were all aware of the fragility of the moment but as the flask was lifted again and again, Brayden savored their success, their camaraderie and the welcome moments of peace. The last time the flask was passed to Caleb, he turned it upside down and sniggered, "One more please, barkeeper." His expression suddenly changed. He chucked the flask to Brayden, slapped his hand to his mouth and headed to the woods.

Brayden blew a soft whistle. "Fletcher, I think we'd best save your flask for tomorrow."

"Brandy never did sit well with Caleb."

Riley shook his head. "The brandy didn't sit well with his sorely walloped belly."

The welcomed moment of peace quickly fled as the four of them ruminated on what Riley and Caleb had endured. At the same moment Brayden somehow sensed all was not right when he saw Caleb emerge from the trees with a wide-eyed expression on his face and his hands up by his shoulders.

"Well, looky what we have here. I must be a soothsayer because I'm looking at five people risen from the dead." The shadow's voice cackled through the trees. "It's a miracle!"

The sound of that hateful voice jabbed Brayden in the gut. It felt as though all the air had suddenly been sucked out of the clearing. The audible gasp from Fletcher and Kawley proved they felt the same.

Mounted behind Caleb rode Philippe Armanac. He poked Caleb in the back with his rifle. "Get over there with the others." Philippe wore a sadistic smile on his face. He urged his mount to circle the group. "When I heard from that stupid Ben Crawford about the two prisoners dying of some dreaded disease, I thought it was a stroke of luck. But when he told me he'd had them taken away so as not to infect the other prisoners, I grew suspicious. Two mutes?" He howled an ugly laugh. "How convenient." He reined his horse back and forth in a stalking pace, his weapon aimed at them the entire time. "Crawford doesn't suspect a thing, but he let it slip about some woman named Belinda who found the mutes." Philippe harrumphed. "Being of a suspicious nature, I think I'll have to pay this woman a call to tidy up all loose ends."

Kawley sucked in a quick breath. "Belinda!"

Philippe raised his eyebrows and nodded. "Why thank you, Kawley. You just confirmed what I have suspected all along."

"Leave her alone!" shouted Brayden.

"Or you'll what? Kill me?" He brandished the rifle at Brayden. "I think not. But speaking of killing, I intend to relish what I started. The world already thinks you are dead. You three in a fire, and you other two by deadly sickness. I'll just toss your bodies in the river, and the fish will do the rest. It's genius because you five were long ago deceased."

Fletcher crept forward. Philippe fired a shot, whizzing Fletcher's hat from his head. "Back up, big man. Don't ruin my amusement because my next shot won't miss."

Fletcher gingerly fingered the side of his head and pulled his hand away as though checking for blood. "Before you kill us, may we at least know the reason you hate us with such a vengeance?"

Philippe snickered. "*May* we, is it? Ah, the hotheaded one speaks a bit softer now. I see Ceisel's slash to your head has improved your manners."

"It's improved nothing. Just think if we're about to die, we should at least know the reason why," Brayden spouted.

"You mean other than the fact that you are traitorous, southern trash?" The Frenchman snorted. "That fact alone is sufficient reason to stretch all your necks from the nearest tree."

"And other than that fact? Speak oh, mighty one." Brayden swooped into a sarcastic bow, hoping to stall for time, time to form a plan.

Philippe paced his mount back and forth with slow steps, a clear attempt to terrorize his prey. His odd little smile fairly dripped with overt arrogance. He halted the horse in front of Brayden.

"Why, you ask? Because it simply pleases me to do so."

"Sneer all you want," Brayden scoffed at him. "I'm not afraid of you."

The intruder leaned forward and dismissed the taunt with blatant malevolence. "You should be."

"You can't take all five of us," Fletcher shouted.

Philippe dropped his reins on the horse's neck and pulled a revolver from his pocket. "How you do underestimate me, sir." He kicked his horse toward Riley. "I think I'll start with this one."

"No, Philippe, wait," Kawley begged. She slowly approached him. "You once said you wanted to marry me."

"Kawley, stop. Don't do it," Brayden screamed.

"Philippe, if you let my friends go, I will marry you. I will do anything you ask until the day I die."

Brayden couldn't believe what he was hearing. Kawley was sacrificing herself, and there was not a damn thing he could do about it. Filled with rage, he started toward Philippe.

Philippe cocked the hammer of the revolver. "Get back, all of you." He fired at Brayden's feet in his game of cat and mouse.

Brayden halted. He would be of no help if he were shot. "Kawley, no!"

Kawley stepped closer. "If you still want me, Philippe, I will go with you now and be faithful to you—" She glanced at Brayden and back at Philippe. "—until the day I die."

Philippe eyed her from the top of her head to the tips of her toes and back again. "Look at you," he scorned her. "You're not worth the trade."

Brayden lunged. Philippe fired, and Brayden fell.

Philippe's horse reared. Philippe grabbed for the reins to secure his seat but ended up pulling the screaming animal off balance. Twelve hundred pounds of struggling animal fell backwards on him. Blood spurted from his mouth, his neck cocked at an odd angle. The horse righted himself but kicked out in anger, plowing a one-two punch of hooves into Philippe's midsection. The body was thrown face down into the river. The horse snorted and shook off.

Brayden sat up, and the others ran to him. "I'm all right. I think it just grazed me." He winced and grabbed his shoulder. Something rustled in the trees. "Fletcher, there's someone else out there."

Fletcher snatched up Philippe's revolver and took off into the woods.

"Are you sure it's just a graze wound?" asked Caleb.

"This is the second time Brayden has taken a shot for me." Kawley pulled the hair from her face. "Unfortunately, I think he knows the difference."

"And I would appreciate it if this does not become a habit." Brayden tore off part of his shirttail and waded it under his coat. "There's something very familiar about this."

"Look what I found." Fletcher emerged from the trees holding the revolver to the back of a black man.

"Moses!" Kawley shouted and jumped up.

"Fletcher, put down that gun. It's Moses," Riley roared.

Brayden remembered Kawley's story of how Moses had saved her after Philippe's vicious rage. He quickly whispered the same to Fletcher.

"Moses, what are you doing here?"

"Miss Kawley, I'm so sorry," Moses replied. "I couldn't let him hurt you again."

"Kawley, there's someone else over there." Brayden pointed back behind them.

Riley came forward with a woman. "I found Eva."

"Moses, you're running north?" Kawley asked quietly.

"Do you know you and your wife could be whipped...or worse if you are caught?" Fletcher blurted out. "You two could be shot on sight. What were you thinking?"

Riley put up his hands, clearly to stop all the questions. "Moses, what did you mean you couldn't let Philippe hurt Kawley?"

Brayden slipped a slingshot that peeked from the back of Eva's pouch. He held it up for the others to see. "I think this might explain things." He ran his hand over the flank of Philippe's mount. There was a distinct slice in the flesh. "This is why the horse reared."

"Dear God, Moses. The man died," Riley gasped.

"I didn't mean for him to die. I jus' wanted to spook his horse to give you all a chance to take him. I didn't know the horse would fall on him."

"Nevertheless, killing a white man means hanging for sure."

"Not if no one knows about it." Kawley turned. "Brayden, Fletcher, please. You wouldn't turn him in, would you? He saved our lives."

Brayden rubbed his shoulder. He knew immediately what his answer would be. He would refuse Kawley nothing, even if it be illegal. Besides, she was right. Moses had saved their lives. But could he convince Fletcher? No one spoke. The tension in the air was palpable.

Fletcher turned his face toward the river. Brayden followed the stare and intuited that his friend was reliving the horrors inflicted on all of them by the man whose lifeless body floated downstream with the current. The water lapped around the rocks on the bank. Its comforting sound conflicted with the rigidity visible in Fletcher's stance.

"Good God, man, think," Brayden pleaded. "Did you not mean what you said at Seabrook?"

His childhood friend kicked dirt over the puddle of Philippe's blood left on the ground. "I don't see a killing here," he finally said and kicked more mud on the pile. "Nothing more than an accident. His horse spooked and fell on him in the river. The horse struggled to right himself, saddle slipped off and the horse bolted. These kinds of tragedies happen."

Riley slapped Fletcher's back and grabbed his shoulder. "Yes, they do, my friend. Indeed, they do."

Fletcher smacked his lips and smirked. "And such a grievous loss at that."

"But somehow these two still have to hightail it north. If only I had paper," Kawley whined.

Brayden pulled the grey journal from his saddle bag. He carefully ripped a page and handed it with pencil to Kawley. "Would be best if both you and Riley signed their papers."

Fletcher pulled the saddle from Philippe's horse. He rifled through it for supplies, shredded the end of the girth on a jagged rock and threw the leather bundle in the river. "Just as I said, the girth snapped, and the saddle slipped off. Downright calamity." He handed the reins and supplies to Moses. "No sense inviting questions about the fancy saddle and luckily he's not been branded. The horse is a sturdy mount. He should take you far and fast. Good luck."

Riley helped Eva to mount, and Moses hopped aboard. "It's the best we can do for you."

"Not quite. We can do one thing more." Brayden shoved his hand into his pocket and pulled out the bag of coins that Belinda had given him. He handed the pouch to Moses. "These will help you build your new life."

"Thank you kindly, suh." Moses' voice cracked, and it took him a moment to continue. "God bless you, Miss Kawley, and you, Mist' Riley. We'll never forget you." Moses clucked to the horse, and they walked into the dark.

Brayden stood on the edge of the river. Philippe's body had already floated further downriver. How ironic that Philippe would now be the fish bait he had intended them to be. His evil was the one loose end that had worried Brayden constantly. Where or when might Philippe show up? He sensed Kawley's presence behind him even before she spoke.

"At least this time we didn't need a shovel."

He slipped his good arm around her shoulders, inwardly vowing to never let go again. "Thank God this nightmare is finally over."

"Philippe's part in it anyway."

"Kiki, I—"

"Brayden, I'm trying to be hopeful. Truly, I am." She laid her head against him.

He kissed her soft hair. "You're here. You're safe from Philippe, and we're together." He squeezed her. "And at this moment, with you snuggly tucked against me, it's enough."

"Belinda would be happy we gave Ben's money to Moses."

"Yes, I think she would."

"I'm glad now Belinda is also safe. We owe her so much."

Brayden heard rustling in the trees and tried to push Kawley behind him, but she broke free.

"Moses? What's wrong? You have to be on your way. There's no time to lose."

"I know, Miss Kawley, but I forgot to give this to you. I wrastled it from the ashes the night that Mist' Philippe beat on you. I figured if it was enough to get that man so riled, it must be mighty important. I hoped you'd be back for it." He handed her a crumpled, singed letter. Then he turned and trotted off.

"What's that?" Brayden asked.

Kawley tried to unravel the smudged, puckered and scorched pages. "If Moses is telling the truth, it's what's left of the letter Philippe threw into the grate. Brayden, my hands are shaking. You open it."

"Can you still read anything, Bry?"

"Some of the words are still there."

"Now I'm shaking," Caleb piped in. "On the ride, Fletcher related your frantic journey to Riley and me. He told me about the correspondence from my father. May I see it? I remember that his scribbling was often hard to decider even under the best of circumstances." He turned the pages over and over. "There'll be no reading it in this light."

"Lighting a fire would be too dangerous."

"Even a small one, Brayden?" Kawley queried. "We could all hover around it to shield the light, then snuff it out as soon as Caleb takes a look at the pages."

"I think it's worth the risk, Bry. Those crumpled pages might give us answers."

"Or give us nothing but a passel of trouble by bringing God knows what or whom out of those woods. It should be light soon."

"Brayden, please. I almost died because of the words on those pages. Please, I have to know."

"If it would change your mind, Bry, I agree with Kawley."

Her eyes pleaded. Her expression begged. His heart melted. "All right. Everyone gather close."

The fire took forever to start. Brayden wondered if it was some sort of sign from above that they should wait until first light. Finally with a bit of luck, a shredded page from Brayden's journal and a bit of brandy, the twigs offered a small flare, and they all blew gently to encourage the flame. Caleb leaned in close.

"Careful of that letter, Caleb."

"As careful as I can be and still see to read it, Brayden." He squinted and shifted the angle of the pages side to side. "That's my father's signature all right... 'discovered a lie...halt all plans...Philippe Armanac'..." Caleb brought his face closer to the paper, shuddered and sucked in a quick breath. He looked up at the others.

"For God's sake, Caleb, what does it say?" Fletcher demanded.

"As best I can read his smudged handwriting, it says that Philippe Armanac is a fraud. He is not the rightful marquis."

"No wonder your father warned that Kawley not marry him." Brayden clasped Kawley's hand.

Caleb read more, whispering to himself as he scanned the pages. He stared at Riley. "Philippe had every reason to want you dead."

"Me? Why? I barely spoke to the man."

"Because you, Riley, are the rightful Marquis d'Armanac."

"What?" the others shouted at once.

"That's impossible," Kawley muttered. "Riley was raised in some orphanage."

"I ran away and survived however I could until Kawley's father found me dying in a field."

"Apparently this Philippe fellow would have preferred you had died in that field," Caleb stated. "My father writes he found out that Philippe was the illegitimate son who usurped the title and arranged for Riley, the true son, to be kidnapped and shipped overseas. Philippe obviously hoped Riley would never be seen or heard from again, especially since Riley was unaware of his heritage."

Kawley ran to Riley, reached to hug him, then pulled back. "I knew it, Riley. I knew it! Now you can travel there to claim your inheritance and your rightful place. I'm so happy for you."

Brayden whistled. "The man was truly evil incarnate." He snapped his fingers and pointed at Kawley. "That must be the reason he wrangled an invitation to be introduced to you...to get to Riley." He hesitated. "But when he saw how beautiful you are, he had to ask for your hand."

"I think he wanted more than my hand."

Fletcher kicked at the growing flame. "I'm stunned. I'm standing here at a total loss for words."

"Again, Fletcher?" Brayden asked. "That's twice now. You're going back to Kyndee a changed man."

"Bry, I think this journey has profoundly changed us all...and in some very unexpected ways."

"Caleb is going home a father, and Riley is going home a marquis. I'd say both of those were very unexpected," added Brayden.

Riley held out his hand to Caleb. "But our returning at all was the most unexpected." Caleb pulled Riley into a hug and pounded his back. "Amen to that."

"Can you decipher anything more, Caleb, before we douse the fire?" Kawley asked.

Caleb spanned the pages again. "Not much is still readable. Just a few words of what are probably my father's overseas cotton dealings."

Brayden stomped out the fire. "With the war and the blockades, even a mention of overseas dealings would certainly be reason enough for that Prince of Armageddon, as Fletcher called him, to want you captured, too, and win laudation for himself."

"Had Moses not snatched that letter from the ashes, no one ever would have known the truth." Kawley turned to Riley. "Moses gave you a whole new life."

"I know," Riley replied. "I can't believe all of this." He strolled to the edge of the river, shoved his hands in his pockets and glanced skyward, as though attempting to understand what had just happened and the whole new journey ahead of him.

Brayden walked up behind Kawley, placed his hands on her shoulders and whispered in her ear. "You did the same for Moses."

She laid her head back into the curve of his neck. "I hope they escape to freedom."

"Moses helped you, to help us, to help Riley and Caleb escape to freedom. I cannot believe the God I pray to would do any less for him." Brayden nodded. "They'll make it." He turned her to face him. Her beautiful eyes, normally so wide were half closed. She had not even a hint of a smile for him, and her shoulders slumped. "Kiki, you are exhausted. You need to rest."

"But—"

"No buts. Riley is over there with his head in the clouds. From what I can hear, Fletcher and Caleb are busy mapping out our route for tomorrow. You've been strong for so long—"

"—And I have to stay strong in case—"

"Shh...shh...shh. Yes, you have to go on being strong but right now, it's time for you to rest." He took her hand and led her, limping, to a nearby tree. He sat and tugged at her. "Lay your head on my leg and close your eyes."

Kawley gingerly lowered herself and snuggled, curled up leaning on his right side and laid her head against his shoulder. "Is this all right? I fear I've done enough damage to your left side."

He wrapped his arm around her. "Shhh. Rest."

"Brayden?"

"Hmmm?"

"Will you write about me in your grey journal?"

"If it would please you."

"What would my story be? Tell me."

He took a deep breath. "Once upon a time—"

She elbowed his side. "That's how fairy tales begin."

"No, that's how love stories begin."

"I think I'll like this story." She cuddled closer against him.

By the time Brayden had whispered two sentences, Kawley's head slipped slightly forward. Her breathing became slow and deep. He was glad she had finally drifted off. Brayden knew he, himself, could never have pushed through the pain without sleep as she had.

"Yes, Kiki," he whispered to her sleeping form. "I will write our story. The words will show how our story began with a kiss and soon, God willing, will start a new chapter for a lifetime with another kiss."

CHAPTER EIGHTEEN

DUSK HAD FALLEN ON THE MOONLESS NIGHT WHEN THE WEARY bedraggled group reached the borders of Seabrook. Brayden was the first to see the outline of the statue that welcomed all to Fletcher's magnificent country home. It was a life-sized wooden horse carved to resemble Whiz, the gelding Fletcher rescued and rode home after a ten-year absence, the mount that carried him home once again tonight.

"Fletcher, I have never been so happy to see your wooden horse as I am now—" Brayden grunted and shifted positions in his saddle. "—and not a moment too soon."

"Must admit my backside is feeling mighty flat," Caleb added. "Riley?"

"I think mine is blistered."

Fletcher dropped his reins and stirrups and stretched his arms high in the arm. "Whiz knows his way home." He reached over and slapped Brayden in the right shoulder. "Going to be quite a reunion, Bry." His face widened into an enormous smile. "God, it's good to be home."

Brayden glanced at Kawley. Her face was unreadable. He wondered if she was thinking about the home where she and Riley were raised that now was lost to them. Seabrook felt as much home to him as did his own but watching Kawley peruse what might be her new surroundings, Brayden worried that she felt lost and alone. Thinking about it he realized Riley seemed excited at the prospect of a newly acquired title and lands, but Kawley appeared weighted down by a mantle of doubts.

He offered her his hand. She clasped it and even offered a weak smile, but the smile did not reach her eyes.

The stately mansion loomed large in the distance. The closer they came, the more numerous dim lights flickered through several windows. A stunning thought occurred to him. The last time he was here at Seabrook, he had no idea Kawley even existed. Now, after what seemed an eternity since he had cantered down this very lane, Brayden could not fathom an existence without her. Kawley continued to drink the brew and treat her wounds with the compounds Momo had carefully prepared for her but nothing could stave off the demon affliction. If only they could have known if the little beast were rabid or not. Tomorrow he intended to consult with the finest doctors he could summon.

Their walk became a trot. In their excitement of the arrival, their trot kicked into a canter and gained momentum into a gallop. They whizzed along the tree-lined lane into the wide circle that graced the massive wooden door.

Apparently, Fletcher could not contain himself. "Kyndee!" he shouted. "Kyndee, we are home! Sage, we found him." He leaped from his horse and bounded up the stairs in time to nearly collide with his wife and son. Kyndee cried out his name and openly wept as they embraced.

Sage pushed past them with her arms outstretched to Caleb. "I don't believe it." Caleb practically fell into her arms from his mount. "You're really here. I can't believe you're really here."

Brayden dismounted slowly and turned to the other two. Kawley and Riley had not yet dismounted but sat quietly watching the scene before them. Riley was smiling, plainly charmed by the unabashed display of affection. By contrast Kawley sat stoic, seemingly unmoved by the sheer joy of the reunion.

Kyndee and Sage broke free of their embraces and ran to him. "Oh Brayden, we're forgetting you." They hugged and kissed him. "Thank you, Brayden. Thank you, thank you!"

Sage turned and lifted her face to Kawley. "And who is this young man you've brought home?"

Brayden lifted Kawley from Pickles' back and gently set her feet on the ground. "This young man—"

Fletcher rushed over. "May I?" he asked Brayden. He slipped the hat

261

from Kawley's head. "This little manling is one of the bravest little women with whom I have ever had the pleasure to ride. Everyone, this is Kawley Chatterton without whom this reunion would never have happened."

"And over there," Caleb added, "is her brother, Riley, who kept me alive until these three—" He waved his hand in a broad gesture. "—could hatch an audacious plan to swoop in and snatch us from the jaws of most certain demise."

"Everyone, please come inside," cried Kyndee. She shifted her son to her other hip and wiped her cheeks with her hand. "I don't even know how to begin to thank you. You are all so thin. Dear Lord, you must be starving. Fletcher, your eye is a terrible color and Brayden, you have bloodstains all over you. I'm not certain who rescued whom." Tears streamed down her face. "Oh, I'm so sorry; I'm rambling. Please, let's come inside. We have much to celebrate."

Fletcher grabbed his son and kissed his cheek, clutching the child to him. Arm in arm, he and Kyndee walked into the house.

Sage grasped Caleb's arm. She waved her other hand in and out like a mother hen collecting her chicks. "Kawley, don't hang back with those two. When you are up to it, I want to hear every minute detail of how a woman saved the day."

Kawley hung back with a distressed expression, clearly begging Brayden to rescue her. "Sage, I...um..."

"I'll make sure Kawley finds her way inside," Brayden offered.

"Alrighty." Sage offered her arm to Riley. "I don't mind having a man on each arm." The three of them marched inside.

"I know meeting all of them at once is a bit overwhelming."

"Just a bit." Kawley bit her lip. "I want to accept their gratitude but do we have to tell them about...you know...about the raccoon right away? They won't want me around especially with a child nearby. I'll feel like a pariah."

"Kiki, we don't even know if the wretched beast was sick when it bit you. Any wild animal would bite if you fell on it."

Riley appeared in the doorway with arms flailing. "Kawley, Brayden, put one foot in front of the other and join the festivities. Fletcher is already pouring for the toast. We can't start without you." At that moment his bruises were barely visible under the tousled hair, the bright eyes and wide grin. "Come on…everyone's waiting." He spun around and hustled into the house.

"He seems to have stepped into his new life with alacrity. Even with this war, I expect he'll find a way overseas to step into his rightful place," Kawley said. "It's the way it should be, but I will miss him."

Brayden hugged her. "Then I will have to make sure your every moment is filled with joy."

"All right, you two. We are waiting," Fletcher's voice boomed.

Brayden rested his lips against the top of Kawley's hair and whispered, "Ready?"

There was no answer. Kawley wavered, and her body shook.

"Kawley, are you all right?"

"Brayden, I—" She collapsed in his arms.

"Fletcher, Riley, help me!" Brayden screamed. He scooped Kawley into his arms and nearly collided with the other two as they came running.

"What the devil happened, Bry?"

"I don't know. We were about to join you when she took a step and just toppled over."

"Dear God, you don't think it's—"

"No!" Brayden bustled past him.

Sage met them as Brayden headed for the sofa. She placed her hand on Kawley's forehead. "She's burning up."

Kyndee hiked up her skirt. "Not down here, Brayden. Carry her upstairs. Follow me. Fletcher send for Doc Gordon."

The grand staircase seemed to go on forever but he followed Kyndee and gently laid Kawley on the bed. Inwardly he was praying this was not the start of the dreaded symptoms from which there was no return.

"I'll go down and wait for the doctor and collect whatever he might need." Kyndee turned in the doorway and stared at Kawley for a moment. Then she quietly latched the door.

Brayden unbuttoned the top buttons on Kawley's shirt and opened the collar. He stopped and dragged his fingers through his hair. "This can't be happening; it can't be!"

"I can ready her for bed, Brayden." Sage's voice shocked him because he hadn't realized she had followed him into the room. "It wouldn't be seemly for you to do it."

"Sage, there's—"

"Something you need to tell me?"

"Something you need to know first."

"Is that what Fletcher meant downstairs?"

Brayden nodded but his eyes never left Kawley's face. "It's a long story."

"The doctor won't be here for a bit, and I want to understand why Fletcher seemed so concerned." She pulled a chair next to the bed.

"Kawley was bitten by a raccoon."

Sage never uttered a sound, merely put her hand to her lips. She looked at Kawley and then back at Brayden. Then her eyes softened, her expression rife with tenderness. "Perhaps you'd best start at the beginning."

———

Brayden finished relating the horrific details just as the doctor opened the door. Fletcher followed closely on his heels.

He touched Kawley's ankle. "Fletcher told me what happened. Is this the leg that was bitten?"

Brayden nodded. "She had to drown the beast to make him release her. The river water washed the wound, but she cut out the bite and the flesh around it."

The doctor lifted the trouser leg to expose the wound. "But this leg was burned, badly burned."

"I think she cauterized it with her knife. I'm not sure."

"This poor soul cauterized her own leg?" The doctor whistled softly. "She is one brave woman because she did exactly what any doctor would have had to do had they been there." He straightened. "You know there is nothing more I can do?"

"That's it, Galen? For God's sake you're a doctor. There's nothing more you can do?"

"I'm sorry, Fletcher. It's now a waiting game until symptoms appear or not."

The doctor took his bag and headed for the door. "Just keep her as quiet as you can. Send word if anything changes."

"Galen! Galen come back here!" Fletcher fled after him. "I'm having him wire other doctors in the area. There has to be something more to be done."

"I'm sorry, Brayden. I can see how much you care for her." Sage looked over the wound. "We should redress this and the one on her arm as well. Considering what she's been through, I'm amazed that Kawley managed to stave off any festering."

"Considering what Momo did for Caleb and Riley, Kawley heeded her warning and used the powders exactly as she advised."

"May I see what she gave her?"

Brayden smacked his forehead. "Sage, that's right. I've been so worried about Kawley I forgot that you have a vast knowledge of herbal remedies. Caleb told me you once saved his mother's life. Sage, can you...?"

"No, Brayden. Doc Gordon was right...not if the animal was sick."

His heart was crumbling. Brayden leaned closer to Kawley and slid the backs of his fingers along her cheek. Her long eyelashes fluttered, then lay quiet atop her cheeks. He felt Sage's hand on his shoulder.

"Pour yourself a brandy while I take care of Kawley. Tell everyone we will call them if anything changes."

"Sage, I can't ask this of you."

"Kawley risked her life to bring my husband home to me. Helping her now is a pittance by comparison." She pushed him toward the door. "Leave. Kawley needs me now."

"You're a good friend, Sage."

"The woman lying there is the best friend of all. I pray I will have the opportunity to know her."

Brayden descended the stairs as Fletcher came through the front door. "Is the doctor sending wires?"

Fletcher nodded. "Any change?"

"No. Sage is dressing her for bed." Brayden shoved his hands in his pockets and paced the room until his knees ached. How long had it been since he had left her? It felt like an eternity.

"You look like hell. Let me pour you a brandy."

Brayden huffed. "That's what Sage said." He glanced up the stairs. "Do you think she's ready yet? Can I go back up? What's taking so long?"

Fletcher slapped a glass into his hand. "Drink. Now. That's an order."

"Where are the others?"

"In bed amid protests."

"I can't lose her, Fletcher," Brayden muttered before he threw his head back and guzzled the brandy. It burned a slow path to his belly. He grimaced, slammed the glass on the ornate baluster gracing the volute and stared up the stairs.

His lifelong friend squeezed his shoulder. "If the power of our combined love counts for anything, you won't."

Sage appeared at the top of the steps. "You may come back now, Brayden."

He bounded up the stairs two at a time. "Did she wake?"

"She mumbled and cried out when I changed her leg bandage but she's quiet now. Kyndee brought clothes for her. I need a moment to check on Caleb, then I'll be back."

"No, Sage, stay with Caleb. That's where you should be tonight."

"Caleb knows we owe Kawley our happiness. I'll be back."

As he approached her bed, Brayden wondered how Kawley could be so beautiful while fighting for her life. Sage had brushed her hair and sponged the smudges from her face. Brayden leaned into her and kissed her forehead. She was cooler now. Kawley's eyes opened halfway, and his heart skipped a beat.

"You gave me quite a scare, Kiki."

Kawley licked her lips and swallowed. "Brayden?" Her voice was just above a whisper.

"Yes, dear heart."

"You never...never finished reading my...my story in your grey journal." Her fingers touched his hand with a featherlight touch.

"I wrote that you are the radiant rose streaking across the eastern sky of my mornings, that my life began the moment two silky burgundy braids tumbled from under your cap, that you are the sun warming the cold, dark places within me—" Brayden's voice cracked, and he bit the inside of his cheek to compose himself. "Kawley, your story isn't finished. Please don't leave me. Please fight."

"But what if—" Her voice faltered as though there was little left of her. "—what if this is a fight...a fight we can't win?" Her eyes closed.

"Kawley, stay with me!" His hand shook her cheek. "Kiki?"

"She's just sleeping, Brayden," Sage offered behind him. "I made her more of Momo's tea."

How had he not even heard the door open? He dragged in a deep breath to ease his pounding chest.

"Now that Kawley is wrapped and abed, will you allow me to tend to whatever is under your shirt?"

Brayden waved her off. "I'm fine; I'm fine."

"I'm not as learned as Doc Gordon, but I do know that blood does not gush out spontaneously." She touched his shoulder. "May I?"

The coat slipped off his shoulders. Looking down at himself, he realized his shirt was covered in dried blood. He pulled his arm from the sleeve.

"Brayden, your shoulder! You were sorely wounded. And this one on the side looks fresh. How did you ever carry Kawley up those stairs?"

"Truly? I never even noticed."

Sage unwrapped the bindings. "You were burned! Were you bitten as well? You never mentioned any of this."

"As I said, it was a long, arduous journey. I took a shot for Kawley. She and Fletcher seared it with a hot knife to stop the bleeding."

"And the fresh one?"

He uttered a quick, mirthless chortle. "I took another shot for Kawley but was more fortunate this time."

"Seems Kawley was the fortunate one. I'll use Momo's preparation on these, and then I'll bind it again. I'm certain Fletcher will have a clean shirt for you."

"Do you know what Momo gave Kawley?"

"I recognized many of the herbs but not all. I see now why Kawley's wounds are healing nicely. Your Momo gave her clusters to cleanse and purify as well as alleviate pain."

When Sage was finished, Brayden threw his shirt in the corner and slid back into his coat to cover himself. He gently stroked Kawley's forehead. He wanted to weep to release the ache in his heart, but no tears came. He swallowed hard. "Sage, if...if the damnable scourge wins, would enough of Momo's herbs..." He couldn't even give voice to the words, still he had to ask.

Sage's head tilted sideways with her lips clamped tight. Her face crumbled into an overt portrait of compassion. Plainly she understood his meaning. She studied Kawley's still form for a full minute as though pondering the dual edges of mercy. Sage turned to him. "Yes." Her single hushed word was like a searing knife ripping through him. She pushed a blanket into his arms. "You must rest, Brayden. I'll check on both of you later."

———

Despite his best efforts to keep his eyes open, Brayden drifted in and out, but his slumber was anything but restful. A whole new set of nightmares waited to torment him. He relived the night he found Kawley at the river, saw the pain in her eyes as she recounted the raccoon doggedly refusing to release her leg. His imagination flashed image after image of her in the river drowning the accursed animal, then slicing and singeing her flesh.

He awoke to the sound of his own guttural eruption from deep inside. "Nooo!" A light tap on the door startled him. It took a full moment to steady his breathing, compose himself and cross the room. There stood a disheveled Riley.

"I know Fletcher said you would get me if there were any changes, but I had to see for myself. May I come in?"

Brayden stepped back. Riley crossed to the bed in four long strides and studied his sister. "Do you think it's painful for her?"

"Right now I'm not sure of anything, Riley." Brayden scuffed the floor with his foot and plopped into the chair.

Riley sat next to the bed and took Kawley's hand in both of his. "She's an exceptional woman. She never resented her parents taking me into their home. Kawley accepted me as a brother from the moment her father dragged me kicking and screaming through the door." He was silent for a moment. "Do you truly love her, Brayden?"

"More than I thought possible."

"Then you have to believe the way she did." Riley tucked Kawley's hand under the cover. "She believed I was a titled child. I was. She believed she would find me. She did. She believed she could fool Ben Crawford that she wasn't lame. She did. She believed the three of you could rescue Caleb and me from that hell hole. You did. Now Kawley needs your help to believe the raccoon was not sick. Can you do that? It's possible, you know?"

"Of course, I know it's possible." Brayden shoved his fingers through his hair. "It's also possible Lincoln will offer his sword in surrender." He jumped up, locked his hands on the top of his head and squeezed with both arms, hoping his pacing and the pressure would obliterate the swirling grisly images. "I keep thinking over and over the raccoon might have just been startled, enraged and in pain." He threw out his palms in adjuration. "My God, don't you think I'm grasping at the possibility with both hands, remote as it may be?"

"Then believe in her belief, Brayden." Riley headed toward the door and rested his hand on Brayden's shoulder. He leaned closer, presumably to prevent even the possibility of being overheard. "Kawley needs your strength now...strength to live...or strength to die. Allow her to believe that what lies ahead for her...in this world...or the next...is joy."

"How do I do that?" Brayden asked the other's retreating figure.

Riley turned in the open doorway. "If you truly love her, you will find the way."

———

The night that portended a celebration of jubilance, turned instead into days and nights of vigilance. Watching over Kawley, sponging her forehead and the back of her neck, begging her to open her eyes was rapidly draining Brayden. Several times her fist opened and closed, and her eyes moved beneath her lids, though just as he opened his mouth to call for help, she slipped away again. The doctor visited, shook his head and scurried out. Fletcher brought him fresh clothes, and Sage carried in trays of biscuits, meats and tea. Both of them offered to sit with Kawley while he rested. Riley even tried chastising him for his insistence that he be alone with her. Brayden shooed them away within minutes. He could not bear to be away from her. He kept holding her limp hand and praying for the moment she might finally hold his firmly in return. Brayden kicked off his boots, and donned another clean shirt, fearing his shoulder's blood stains might scare Kawley should she waken.

"Kiki, I don't know how to reach you." Riley's parting words, the night Kawley fell ill, spun in Brayden's head, mocking him. He dragged himself to the window and peered out at the streaks of rose in the eastern sky. Never in his life had he experienced the excruciating pain that enveloped him. He hitched a hip unto the sill, crossed his arms and pressed his head into the window frame, reliving day after day of their turbulent journey together. How could things have spiraled out of their control? His eyes lingered on Kawley's still form. She had survived it all, everything their outrageous campaign had demanded of her. Never once did she complain or back away as though she always knew they would succeed.

Brayden slid across the floor to her. He eased himself next to Kawley until they were face to face. The backs of his fingers stroked her forehead and through her hair. "I want to run barefooted through hailstones with you. I want to camp out in a barn, dazzled by the look of you nestled in straw, wrapped in my coat." A smile crinkled his face as he remembered both incidents. "I want to dance in the moonlight feeling your legs wrapped around me." Two fingers caressed the hollow in her throat. "I believe it, dear heart." Kawley never responded, however this time Brayden would not be deterred. His mind searched for the words of her rhyme, but he could only remember the first line and strove to make up the rest.

"Itsy, Bippy and Moo...belief is hard, 'tis true...the raccoon is dead because you drowned his head...this rhyme saved your brother, now you." He slid his hand around the back of her neck and caressed her cheek with his thumb. "Itsy, Bippy and Moo...belief is hard 'tis true...the raccoon is dead because you drowned his head...this rhyme saved your brother, now you." He whispered the little ditty over and over, even as his eyelids grew heavy, and he closed them for a moment's rest.

———

"Your beard is sorely in need of a trim, sir, but it seems I've misplaced my knife."

Brayden was afraid to believe he had heard her voice. Her skin was cool and her eyes bright as she tugged at his beard. Fighting back a turbulent rush of emotion, he wrapped his hand around hers. "Good morning."

"I should be saying that to you. I've watched you slumber for some time now." She furrowed her brows. "What happened to me?"

"You collapsed, and we thought—"

Kawley pulled her hand away and put her fingers to his lips. "Don't say it. Don't spoil this moment." She smiled. "Imagine my bewilderment when I woke in strange nightclothes, in a strange bed, in a strange room yet there you were sleeping by my side with your arm wrapped around me." Her fingertips brushed his temple, his cheek and trailed along the side of his neck. "In the dawn light, I wanted to touch you to be certain you were real, but I feared you might wake if you were."

"Yet you didn't hesitate to tug my beard."

She hooked several strands. "These stragglers bothered me before, and they do now. You look frightful." Her smile disappeared. Kawley dragged her hand across her own chopped hair and harrumphed as though she likely fared no better.

He hiked himself to his elbow and trailed his fingers through her hair along the same path her hand had taken. "Having you awaken, watching your blue eyes peek at me in amusement, hearing the feistiness return to your voice—" Brayden turned his head and swallowed. When he looked back to her innocent gaze it took all his strength not to wrap himself around her. "Kiki, will you—"

There was a soft knock on the door a moment before it opened, and Sage bustled through with a tray. "Brayden, I thought you might need...oh my...good heavens...I'm so sorry. Please forgive me." Sage whirled around and headed out.

"Sage, wait. Come back. Kawley is awake."

The other woman stopped in the doorway. "Yes. Yes, I see that."

Reluctant to leave Kawley's side, Brayden sat up and rested his arm on his raised knee. "Sage, it's all right. Just as you entered, I was asking Kawley to marry me, and I believe she would have said yes." He turned back to Kawley. "You would have said yes, wouldn't you?"

Sage turned back, placed the tray on the table and gathered the silver from the night before. "I'll leave the two of you and send word to Doc

Gordon. I'm certain he'll be out to check on Kawley. I expect boots and a coat might be in order by then, sir."

Brayden was convinced he spied a wide grin on Sage's face just before she spun and left the room. Her rapidly retreating footsteps assured him the word would quickly spread. He stretched next to Kawley. "I fear we've shocked the poor woman, but my dear friend gave you time to think. So, I will ask you once again. Kiki, will you marry me?"

"Did you ask Riley for permission?"

"Dear heart, we've literally been through fire and hailstones together and without us, there would be no Riley."

Kawley giggled. "I know. I just wanted to hear you say it."

"So you're implying I must ask you a third time? You'd best say yes before our indiscretion is the scandal of the county."

She bit her bottom lip and tilted her head.

"Is that a yes, ask again or yes, I'll marry you?"

Kawley tugged his beard. "Will you find my knife and allow me to snip these stragglers?"

"Will you answer my question?"

"Will you bring a biscuit for me? I'm starving."

In one swift motion, Brayden wrapped the blanket around Kawley and scooped her from the bed. "Lord, give me patience!"

"Brayden, put me down."

"Yes, Brayden, put her down," Fletcher added as the door swung open. Riley followed. Sage, Caleb and Kyndee trailed behind.

"Does no one knock anymore?" Brayden growled.

"Why would I knock? This is my home."

"Then I shall just take Kawley back to Avalon."

The five others surrounded the two of them. There were smiles and grins all around.

"No one is leaving until we finish the celebration we started as well as give thanks for Kawley's recovery," Fletcher ordered.

Riley nudged closer with his arms crossed. "And Sage informs me there are whispers of future festivities about which I was not consulted."

"Seems my life is an open book," Brayden countered.

Fletcher gasped. "That grey journal of yours is hardly an open book."

"Since apparently all of you know the question I have repeatedly asked this lovely lady, I will ask her one last time."

"Get down on one knee."

"Kyndee!" the others admonished.

"Miss Chatterton, with one knee bent as deeply as I dare, before my shoulder gives out, and I drop you in front of my dearest friends, will you…be my wife?"

Kawley buried her face in his neck and hugged him tightly. He felt her nod.

Brayden leaned into her. "She said, yes," he whispered. The anxiety and exhaustion finally took its toll. He stumbled two steps back but landed his hip on the arm of the chair. It was the happiest moment he could remember.

CHAPTER NINETEEN

"I must say, Miss Kawley, you look much better than the first time I was here." Galen Gordon wiped his hands on the linen towel and set it aside. "Both your leg and arm are healing well. There's no more fever, and Sage tells me you've shown no other symptoms. These are all good signs and every day that continues is a reason to hope. Your brother told me there were several sick men at the prison the day you visited. There is a good possibility your collapse might have had absolutely nothing to do with the bite." He packed his instruments in his bag. "I understand Brayden is anxious to bring you to Avalon."

"Yes." Kawley buttoned the sleeve of her dress. "Fletcher and Kyndee have been most gracious, allowing me to recover here, and Sage has checked in on me."

"I know. Sage has sent word of you every day."

Kawley straightened her skirt. Both Sage and Kyndee had offered their dresses since she had arrived at Seabrook with nothing but her ripped and bloodied 'manling' clothes, and the blockades had diminished the supply of silks and materials. Everyone was excited about the upcoming nuptials, something joyous to counteract the winds of war. The Confederacy boasted their victories would lead to a swift end to the conflict, yet Brayden related that members of the county had still lost loved ones. He said fortunately Royce and Trey had returned unscathed, but Rush had trudged home in severe pain from his broken leg and the agony of bearing ashes to grieving parents. Clive's family had been devastated. Although she had been forbidden to leave her bed, Riley told her the service was heart-wrenching, especially knowing Clive had died so he and Caleb might live.

"Miss Kawley? Miss Kawley have you heard a word I've said?"

"Hmm?" Kawley glanced up to Doctor Gordon's stern face. "I'm sorry, Doctor. I'm still trying to make sense of all that has happened."

"All things in good time."

"Do you truly think I have more time?"

Galen Gordon cleared his throat. "Like I said, Miss Kawley, all things in good time. I will tell Brayden you are strong enough to travel to Avalon, but you must continue to rest." He grabbed his bag and headed for the door. "I will check on you at Avalon when I make my rounds."

Kawley closed the door and scanned the room. She was traveling to someone's else's home, in someone else's dress, to join someone else's life. Was she also on borrowed time? Was she having second thoughts about marrying Brayden? No, not that. It was the way it was happening. She was coming to Brayden a waif, a penniless orphan without even her own clothes on her back. She had never really imagined a picture of her wedding, but she knew it wasn't this. Kyndee's shawl was hanging on the back of the chair. Swinging it around her shoulders, Kawley left the room.

The pride of Seabrook was its grand staircase. As she descended, she stopped to savor the view from the window. The home of her youth had been grand, but nothing compared to Seabrook. Kawley wondered if Avalon would be as striking and stately. She continued down the stairs and wandered along the side to admire the intricate carvings that graced each stair edge. A shadow caught her eye in the far room where the door was ajar.

"My advice would be to wait, Brayden. Rushing into a marriage could be deadly for you."

"Galen, you haven't even heard back from the doctors in New York and Philadelphia."

"The war has delayed many things including my medical supplies. But Brayden, I have to vehemently caution against this. Have you thought of the restrictions? You're a man with needs, for God's sake."

"You think I don't know that? Besides, it wouldn't be forever."

"Maybe not forever but you couldn't and shouldn't be a proper husband to her for possibly a damn long time. Your very life depends on it. Nothing is absolute with this terrible scourge...two weeks, two months. There's no way to know. The longer you wait, the surer and safer you'll be."

"I'm not listening to any more of this."

The door flung opened and the wide-eyed expression on Brayden's face meant he realized she had heard their cruel words. He came to her with outstretched arms.

Kawley stepped back out of reach. "It's all right, Brayden. I understand."

Brayden shook his head. "No! No, you don't understand."

Galen Gordon approached from behind them. "My advice to the two of you—"

"You've said enough, Galen," Brayden shot out. "Thank you for coming. I expect you'll send word if you hear anything from New York or Philadelphia."

When Doctor Gordon left, Brayden drew Kawley into his arms. "Kiki, do you love me?"

His embrace felt strong and warm, his words sweet. "Brayden, I have nothing to offer you, and we both know it."

He smoothed her hair with his hand. "I'm not letting you push me away. You say you have nothing to offer but you are wrong. You have you...and that's more than enough for me."

"But the doctor is right. Until we know for sure you can't...I mean we can't—" Kawley turned her head away as the heat rushed through her face.

Brayden nudged her back with a knuckle under her chin. "Do you really think that's all I want from you...that's all you are to me?"

"But you can have anyone."

"I don't want anyone. Don't you love me at all, Kiki?"

Kawley gazed into his eyes, trying to reveal everything that was in her heart. "Yes, very much. I've loved you since the night I watched you dance on tiptoe through the hail stones." She could hear the laughter bubbling in his chest.

"Those little stones of ice were so cold and bristly." The laughter ceased. His eyes bored into hers as he palmed her cheek. "Dear heart, you are a gift. No matter how long we have to wait, no matter how much cherished time the good Lord grants us, I would rather lie chastely in marriage with you than ever touch anyone else."

Kawley snuggled within the solace and peace of his embrace. How she wanted to wrap her arms around his neck and kiss his lips for those beautiful words. She could hear his heart pounding or was it her own? "I think the wait will be hard on both of us," she whispered into his ear.

Fletcher rounded the corner. "If the two of you can step away from one another for a moment, I've been informed we have a visitor asking for Kawley."

"For me? But I am a stranger here."

"Nevertheless, you are wanted at the carriage."

———

As they approached the door, Kawley grasped Brayden's hand. Her fingers tightened around his when she stiffened her back and took a deep breath. It was the first time she was suffused with fear. What if they were searching for Philippe? Or worse, they had found his body and followed her here. A myriad of 'what ifs' swirled in her head, none of them good.

Brayden clutched her hand. "Don't be afraid."

"I'm not afraid." She squeezed back. "I just wish I had my knife."

"The woman of mettle returns, just the way we met. But now you don't need your knife," he whispered. "You have me."

The matched pair of black horses stomped their feet. From the top of the steps two women were visible in the carriage. Both wore veils, and Kawley dreaded who might be out of view. She was screaming deep down but bit her bottom lip to keep the sound inside.

Kawley touched the side of the carriage door. "Yes? Who's there?"

The woman closest to the door lifted her veil. "Since I was not formally invited to the wedding—"

The hard held scream burst its way to her lips as nothing more than a shocked whisper. "Belinda!"

"I wasn't certain I would be welcome."

Kawley jumped on tiptoe and reached inside the carriage. "Brayden, it's Belinda and Hanna! I can't believe it. How? When did you—" She shook her head. "—it doesn't matter."

"Does your exuberance mean we may stay?"

Her heart sank. "Belinda, it's not my place to say. Seabrook is not my home."

"No, but it is mine," said Fletcher who suddenly appeared behind them. "Miss Belinda, we are honored to have the two of you here."

"Honored, Fletcher? To have two northerners?"

"Honored, Miss Belinda, Miss Hanna," offered Brayden. "Here, as well as Avalon, there are no northerners or southerners, only friends."

———

Kawley kept pinching herself to be sure it was not a dream. She pulled back the curtain and peered out. Avalon's charm and whimsy provided a backdrop only Brayden could have scripted. A light tap on the door broke her reverie. "Come in."

Belinda scurried inside. "May I act as your mother for the day?"

"I cannot believe your generosity, Belinda. This beautiful wedding gown and an entire trousseau. Just having you here would have been enough."

"You are the daughter I never had, Kawley. The blockades are preventing necessities from arriving, let alone goods and luxuries. I wanted you to have the silks and laces you deserve."

"I just hope you didn't bring all these beautiful dresses for nothing. The doctor counseled us to wait."

The older woman lifted the voluminous silk with scalloped lace creation over Kawley's head and worked the numerous tiny buttons. She slid on the pearl embellished gauntlets to hide the scarred arm. "No, I'm glad you didn't wait. Every day is a promise of another tomorrow, a promise that wretched little animal was merely angry, not sick."

"I must confess I'm nervous about afterwards, Belinda."

"Brayden told me everything that happened on your journey back to Seabrook. Kawley, you survived not one but three horrific confrontations with the Prince of Darkness imposter. Without you to love, Brayden would never have stopped the fiend, Philippe, from shooting Riley. For that matter, without you there would be no Riley to claim his title. There would be no Caleb. They hanged two prisoners the very next day. Without you, Moses and Eva might never have been free. You were horribly wounded, and yet you believed and forged on. You now are afraid of being alone with a man who twice knocked on heaven's gates to save you?"

Kawley sauntered across the room, swaying to and fro, momentarily savoring the beauty of the gown. She swiveled, and the short train spun and bunched behind her. The tall mirror reflected the embroidered elegance of her raiment. "You've given me so much."

"Nonsense. What I've given you here are easily attainable goods had the war not come. But the war did intervene, and you've given me that which all my money cannot buy—the pride in a daughter which I thought I would never have and, though I may not agree with it, an understanding into the motivation behind the grey array. What Brayden and Fletcher did for Moses, how they are planning to help their own, leaves me proud to call them friends." The clock in the hall chimed the hour. "Sage and Kyndee fluffed your hair beautifully. I'm loath to mask its glorious color with tulle." Belinda stepped back. "Yes, it's perfect."

Brayden stood at the fireplace, shifting from foot to foot. He heard the clock in the hall and pulled on each cuff. The knot in his throat would not move even though he swallowed repeatedly.

"Heaven's sake, Bry. You've faced the wrong end of a barrel with less trepidation. I do believe you're moonstruck."

He opened his mouth to utter a stern retort just as Kawley appeared on Riley's arm. Amid the silk, lace and pearls, all he imagined was a mass of burgundy tresses surrounding sapphire eyes and a determined woman dwarfed in his coat, sitting on a bed of straw in a darkened barn. After the ceremony, after the toasting and the well-wishing, it was that determined woman Brayden carried through the door of the bedroom in the wee hours of the morning and slid onto the bed.

"Nervous?"

Kawley's face reddened. "I'm ashamed to let you know there was a moment during the ceremony when I dreamed of dashing past the happy faces and galloping Pickles across the field, gown and all."

"Gown and all, you say?" Brayden laughed out loud.

"Shhh, they'll hear you. What will everyone think?"

He poured two goblets from the decanter on the mahogany dresser and handed one to her as he sat alongside. "It's the same brew from my flask." He gulped the blend, savoring the memories it evoked. "I don't care a lick what everyone thinks. But you have my humblest apologies. I was laughing because, given the slightest prod from you, I would have happily grabbed your hand, bolted through the door and ridden off with you—" He raised an eyebrow. "—yes, gown and all."

Kawley giggled and sipped her drink. She swirled the crystal and set it in her lap.

"I seem to remember you swigging my mixture with more gusto on the trail."

She held the lace of her gown out to the side. "It wouldn't be proper. I am in a silk gown, after all." Kawley saluted him with the glass and bolted the brew. When their quiet laughter eased, she sighed and fingered the edge of the goblet. "How I wish I had known what you were thinking, you and I running hand in hand out the door. We would have set their tongues wagging but what a wedding night that would have been."

"What do you mean? We've already had our wedding night."

Her goblet hit the side table with a whack. She stood and faced him with her fists snuggly tucked into the waist of her gown. "Mr. Wakefield, sir, how dare you sully my reputation with such a bold lie."

Brayden pulled her to him. "Mrs. Wakefield, your honor is intact. But had I wanted to ravish you that night in the barn—"

Her hand flew to her mouth, and her eyes grew wider. Clearly Kawley remembered.

"—I had ample opportunities."

Kawley kicked off her shoes and jutted her chin. "And why didn't you?"

"Because you were too fine, too determined—" He tilted his head. "—too difficult to be sure—" He stroked her cheek. "—and too vulnerable."

She undid the dressings, opened the collar of his shirt and caressed the hollow of his neck with her fingers. "Well, if we have already had our wedding night, what does this night purport to be?"

His finger tapped the end of her nose. "Anything we want it to be."

"Belinda told me you and Fletcher offered to see her and Hanna safely out of harm's way."

Brayden chuckled. "As expected, she flatly refused. She told me in no uncertain terms that a certain Mary Todd, herself, would come to their rescue if she failed to return."

"Mary Todd? Mary Todd *Lincoln*?"

He nodded. "One more mystery to add to the paradox known as Belinda Dunigan."

"Belinda and Hanna risked coming here to present me with an exquisite trousseau."

He reached to the bottom of the bed, snagged a beautifully wrapped package and handed it to her. "I have another wedding present for you."

She gestured around the room. "This magnificent house, a splendid wedding, my handsome husband, what more could I possibly want or need?"

"Open it."

The ribbon slid through her fingers and the top came off. "Oh Brayden, thank you. Where did you find it?"

"After you mentioned you yearned for your knife, Riley and I combed the area where you collapsed at Seabrook. I'm sorry, it looks as though one of the horses' hooves scratched it."

Kawley held it to her chest as she lifted the paper to see what else was in the box. "But these are—"

"The clothes and boots you wore as you boldly rode to find and meet Belinda. I had them sewn, washed, pressed and polished."

Her face fell. "So I have something to wear when you send me packing?"

Brayden came to her. "No, never! You're not getting away from me that easily. I had them done because I fell in love with the sassy, captivating woman who wore those clothes."

She hugged him. "I'll try to be a good and proper wife to you, Brayden."

He pulled her arms away and clasped his hands around hers. "Forgive me. Once again, I've done or said the wrong thing. I don't want you to be a good and proper wife. I want you to be you, the feisty woman who survived the evil of Armageddon, the woman who had me at gunpoint, the woman with the courage to slice her own flesh hoping to remain alive, who brazenly marched into a Yankee prison pretending to be one of their own. I love that you quote Shakespeare and senator speeches, that you challenge my ideas, that you have a thought in your head besides fuss and furbelows. I love you, Kiki, not all the trappings but you."

Kawley didn't speak. She lowered her head, and Brayden feared in his zeal he had offended her without meaning to and without cause. He gently shook their joined hands, urging her to look at him. Finally she raised her eyes to his.

"If you love me as you say, will you do something for me?"

He nodded but with misgivings as to her intent.

"I know you and Fletcher have been summoned to the war and are leaving within the week." She tossed her head and smacked her lips, clearly forestalling any attempt for him to speak. "I wormed the information from Sage when she and Kyndee were so sad. Brayden, I don't want us to spend our first night apart with me in this bed and you on that chair. I don't want possibly to die without feeling my husband's skin against my own. I see the love in Kyndee's eyes, in Sage's eyes. I need you beside me. I want that love to hold on to and savor until you return and truly celebrate our marriage."

"I want that closeness more than you know." Brayden hugged her. "Dear God, I want you."

"We can just hold one another."

"Sweetheart, I don't know if I have the strength not to…"

She stepped backwards, urging him to the bed. "I do…for the both of us." Kawley turned her back and pointed to all the buttons. "Help me?"

With her salacious invitation, his reservation and resistance fled. At first, he struggled with the tiny pearls. "So many buttons. It could take the rest of the night to have you out of this gown."

Kawley chuckled. "Knowing our situation, perhaps Belinda planned the problem to save us from ourselves."

"Remind me to thank her one day," Brayden muttered. Each button brought him closer to touching her, loving her and his heart thundered with anticipation. Finally the sides parted, and his hand slid the puffed sleeves and gauntlets down her arms. The bandage on her arm was a grim reminder of what his wife had endured but also a testament to her resolve. The top edges of the horrific stripes inflicted by Philippe were visible even in the candlelight, shocking him, nearly stopping him.

She must have sensed his reluctance. "Are my scars so repugnant?"

He kissed the raised bands one by one. "Never, Love. I will have grisly scars of my own."

"I know. God help me I caused them."

He kissed her shoulder. "Shhh. If I had it to do over, I would do no differently."

She stepped out of the gown, out of the petticoats and the hoop. She turned and stood close. His eyes savored her lithe frame until they lingered on the bandage encircling her leg. It was a stark reminder of what they still faced.

Her fingers deftly undid the buttons of his shirt, yanked it from his trousers and nudged it from his shoulders. The bandages covering his wounds had been bound tight. Her cheek brushed the hair of his chest. "Momo advised no kissing." Kawley pulled back and lifted his hand until his fingers touched the ribbon of her chemise. Her eyes met his. "I want to lie in my husband's arms tonight."

Brayden turned down the bed. He slowly drew out the ends on Kawley's ribbon. The thin chemise and undergarments fell from her slim form. In that moment he could hardly draw breath, doubted his strength to fulfill what she asked of him. With one tender tug he drew her into a tight embrace, worried he might endanger them both with a deep searing kiss. When he had regained a modest composure, he scooped her into his arms and onto the bed. With practiced ease he turned his back, shed his boots and trousers and joined her beneath the covers.

A moan escaped him as he touched full length against his new bride. "You are so beautiful." Her skin was warm and silky soft. None other had been such a gift. He raised himself slightly and kissed her neck, along her shoulder and lingered on her breast. Another moan spilled over his lips before he could stop it.

"Does your shoulder still hurt you that much?" Kawley whispered as she ran her fingers along the dressing encasing his chest and arm.

He cupped her chin. "No, you do, my sweet. I am hurting everywhere for want of you." The fluttering pulse in her neck bewitched him. Her fingertips gliding along his back and thigh, her uneven breathing urged him on, told him his spirited, spunky wife was as anxious as he for the waiting to be ended. He gathered her into his arms and rocked her gently to slow down his racing blood.

"You are as tender as I dreamed you would be," Kawley purred into his ear. "Rugged and strong yet able to touch and kiss with the gentleness of a feather. After Philippe, I feared how men acted behind a closed door." She trailed her fingers down the hollow of his back. "How ironic that it was his very cruelty which brought me to you."

Brayden raised above her. "I shudder to think what would have happened if Caleb's father had not penned that letter to your father. You would have been bound to that madman and his depravity forever. God only knows what malevolence he would have heaped on Riley to keep his deception hidden. I don't doubt shortly after you were securely his, Philippe would have secretly arranged for Riley to meet with a tragic accident."

"His depravity was his undoing and ultimately created our joy." She touched his temple. "I love you, Brayden."

Her tousled burgundy hair, those cerulean eyes, her soft porcelain skin and her unique raspy voice murmuring her love drove the turmoil within him to erupt like a volcano. He showered her face with kisses, behind her ear, the hollow of her neck, traveling between her breasts, daring to wander lower until she urged him back to her. His hips pressed against hers while his lips adored her breasts. Galen Gordon's dire warning sprinted to the back of his mind as he thrust against her.

"Brayden, we can't risk it, not yet. You heard the doctor," Kawley muttered on a ragged breath.

"I don't care anymore. It's been long enough," he managed to sputter.

"You've risked your life twice for me. You may not survive a third time."

His world was spinning. "Kiki, I'd rather die with you than live on without you." All that mattered in that moment was the two of them and his need to love her.

She wiggled under him. "Brayden, think. You're not Shakespeare's cat with nine lives, especially going off to the war."

War!

The word hammered him as if he had fallen into an icy pond. With a harsh growl he pushed to a sitting position and rested his arm on his knee. "I'm sorry, Kiki." He couldn't utter another word until his breathing slowed. "I... I..." He dragged his fingers through his hair. "It won't happen again. I promise I'll stay on the chair until I leave."

Kawley sat up behind him and hugged him tightly. "I want it as much as you but not this way, not until I can be lost in the feel of you everywhere." She caressed the back of his neck and between his shoulders with her cheek.

Brayden attempted to cover his raging need. "I'm sorry I've spoiled our night."

She edged around to face him. "Nothing is spoiled. I don't care that we aren't—" Kawley glanced at the ceiling. "How did Dalisco Moore write it, '...lying exhausted in an enraptured haze?'" She gathered herself in the bed linen, trotted to the window and pulled back the drapes. "We still have an hour until daylight, and the moon shows a haze over the fields." Running back, Kawley forced him to stand, opened her cover, pressed her body to his and wrapped the two of them. "Maybe the doctor warns it is too soon to share our love in here, but we can share our other love out there."

The feel of her warm skin was making his heart pound all over again. "But out there would be cold and prickly."

She squirmed against him. "Not on horseback." She gazed up at him with the broadest flashing smile he had ever seen gracing her face. "Ride with me, Brayden. Let's take Pickles and Ajax and spend the first dawn of our marriage watching the haze over the hills of Avalon dissipate in the sun's morning array."

Brayden could barely contain the rumbling in his chest, but he was reluctant to let go of the enchanting, fascinating siren who had him captured in her grasp. He lifted one eyebrow. "Last one dressed saddles the horses?"

Kawley stomped her foot. "That's not fair. I have nothing in this room to wear but my gown."

He winked at his bride. "Not so, madam."

Kawley's eyes lit up, and she ran for the box. She ripped off the top and tossed the wrappings to the floor. "You'd best be stepping into your own trousers, sir, because I have no intention of saddling your unruly beast."

As he watched her shoot toward the door ahead of him, Brayden somehow knew in his heart the raccoon had never been sick, and Kawley would survive. He whispered his gratitude to whatever god might listen and yanked on his clothes and boots. His eye spotted the grey journal on the desk. He picked it up and rippled its pages under his thumb. The journal had been his confessor and his solace. Its pages counterfeited a Yankee dispatch. Its pages freed his heart to love. Its pages freed Moses to live. His hand tapped the grey cover before closing the journal in the drawer. Brayden turned to see Kawley leaning against the doorframe.

"The new chapter is our own." Her arm beckoned. "Gallop with me to the top of the hill. There, saddle to saddle, hand in hand we will watch the veil of haze rise for our new day."

———

Don't miss out on your next favorite book!
Join the Satin Romance mailing list
www.satinromance.com/mail.html

ABOUT THE AUTHOR

Raised in the suburbs of Philadelphia, her family moved to a remote rural farmhouse with an in-ground spring and a twenty-two person party line telephone. Wandering through fields of corn, hanging in the branches of an apple orchard, milking cows, churning butter, driving tractors, haying fields, and shattering nineteen out of twenty clay pigeons with a .410 shotgun provided the fodder for the imagination and numerous scenarios that enrich the scenes of her stories.

Following an education at an East coast boarding school, Ms. Groover graduated with a B.A. in psychology and English and secured her M.S. from the University of Pennsylvania, all of which help her reside in the heads of her characters. With drawers full of stories, both finished and 'cooking' she has been writing as long as she can remember. She has been published in numerous papers and periodicals, grounding her in the real world, while researching and wandering through the nineteenth century to create the complex individuals who inhabit the worlds of her romances.

As a third generation equestrian, Ms. Groover rides, trains and hunts her three beloved horses. The personalities and antics of her equines are woven into the storylines. These querulous, four-legged rapscallions offer a unique flavor as they wring emotions from the characters and readers alike.

At home, Ms. Groover shares her life with her husband and a

menagerie of animals. Dividing her time between the stable and the studio, she spends her days doing what she loves best—writing and riding!

www.Bobbiscorner.com

facebook.com/Bobbis-Corner-1619350924975873